The great monolith looked like a living form as it moved. Two great legs, thicker than massive tree trunks, supported it and carried it cumbersomely forward. Two arms, human-like in shape but tipped with wicked talons of crooked stone, swung at its sides.

The form of Zaltec disdained the broken causeways that still connected the island to shore. Instead, the huge stone form waded into Lake Zaltec, striding easily through the thick mud. The water came only to the monstrous form's knees.

Then it emerged onto the lake's south shore, its heavy footfalls crunching into the ground. It passed the smoldering remains of Mount Zatal without a sideways glance. Instead, the glowering eyes, gray orbs of granite in a stark, stone face, remained fixed upon the desert, in answer to some distant and unknown compulsion.

And Zaltec marched on, until a watcher on the rim of the valley could have seen only a huge, monolithic form, moving into the remote wastes of the desert, like a towering, sheer-sloped mountain.

A mountain that walked . . .

FANTASY ADVENTURE

# FEATHERED DRAGON

## by Douglas Niles

**Cover Art**
**FRED FIELDS**

**TSR, Inc.**
**PRODUCTS OF YOUR IMAGINATION™**

# FEATHERED DRAGON

Distributed to the book trade in the United States by Random House, Inc., and in Canada by Random House of Canada, Ltd.

Distributed to the book trade in the United Kingdom by Random Century Group and TSR Ltd.

Distributed to the toy and hobby trade by regional distributors.

FORGOTTEN REALMS is a registered trademark owned by TSR, Inc.

PRODUCTS OF YOUR IMAGINATION and the TSR logo are trademarks owned by TSR, Inc.

First Printing, April, 1991
Printed in the United States of America
Library of Congress Catalog Card Number: 90-71498

9 8 7 6 5 4 3 2 1

ISBN: 1-56076-045-1

TSR, Inc.
P.O. Box 756
Lake Geneva, WI 53147
U.S.A.

TSR Ltd.
120 Church End, Cherry Hinton
Cambridge CB1 3LB
United Kingdom

For Don and Ann,
with a warm welcome to Angela

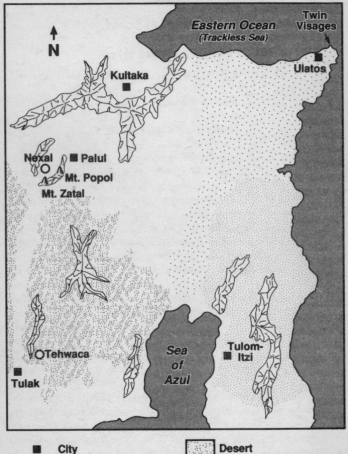

# MAZTICA
## After the Night of Wailing

**N**

Eastern Ocean
(Trackless Sea)

Twin Visages

Kultaka

Ulatos

Nexal
Palul
Mt. Popol
Mt. Zatal

Sea of Azul

Tehwaca

Tulom-Itzi

Tulak

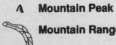

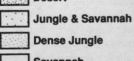

■ City

○ Ruin

Λ Mountain Peak

Mountain Range

Desert

Jungle & Savannah

Dense Jungle

Savannah

# Prologue

From the chronicles of Coton:

### THE TALE OF TEWAHCA

*At the time immediately preceding the great God War, when Qotal and his sisters battled Zaltec and his brothers for mastery of the True World, the gods commanded their worshipers to build them a temple greater than any other in the world, in a place from which the gods could rule their lands in sublime solitude.*

*The gods selected a wasteland, a dry valley in the heart of the deepest desert, and here they commanded the people to come. The humans obeyed their immortal lords, and the gods gave them food to eat and water to drink, that they would not perish. And they gave to the people their commands, and again the people obeyed.*

*The humans built the grandest pyramid of all in the center of the place called Tewahca, the City of the Gods. For decades they toiled, carving a wonder from the wasteland, raising their children, living and dying in this place selected by Zaltec and Qotal.*

*The structure towered skyward, as big as a mountain. The temple building, a massive stone rectangle atop the highest platform, loomed huge enough to house the gods themselves. The greatest of artisans came from all over Maztica to work their pluma and hishna magic upon the pyramid, to paint it with brilliant colors and bright mosaics.*

*Around the pyramid, a city sprang to life. Humans built streets and plazas, wide courtyards and lush gardens. They built for themselves houses and palaces, struggling to make* the structures worthy of the blessed locale. Yet all these constructions served as mere adornments to the true center of Tewahca, the pyramid of the gods.

Finally the Pyramid of Tewahca was completed. The gods commanded the humans to go, and the waters dried away. The food that grew here withered and died, leaving once more the barren waste of sand and stone. The great city stood like a firm, dry husk in the center of nothing.

The humans had no way to live here now, so they fled to more fertile lands.

And the war between the gods began.

# ❧ 1 ❧

# WINDS ACROSS THE
# TRUE WORLD

A great gulf of ether separates the planes, the dwelling places of gods and mortals. Billowing outward, murky and obscure, the ethereal mist settles and seethes like a vast, cosmic cloud bank. It fills the space between the flesh-bound worlds and the higher planes of the immortals, a place of emptiness, a void.

It lay thus, eternal and unchanging, through eons of mortal lives. Occasional travelers passed through the ether, aided by magic or godlike power, yet such journeys left no trace of their passage. Always the ether settled back, washing smoothly over any spoor.

Even when the gods of the many planes grew restless, when epic destinies clashed in convulsions of good and evil, did the ether ebb and flow in its timeless tide. It held no track, showed no clue.

Now color flashed in the ether, bright green trailed by red and orange and yellow. An iridescent glow, like the blue of a shallow coral sea, surged and as quickly faded again into the massive fog of ephemeral essence.

For a while—ages, perhaps, or mere minutes—all remained gray and featureless. Then the colors flamed again, and now a form appeared within the mists of the ethereal plane. No basis for comparison existed here, yet the shape seemed unspeakably massive, worldlike in breadth and inexorable in momentum.

A pair of great wings, huge enough to embrace the sun, spread to either side of the form. Each swept the mist with blazing hues, leaving a wake of color in the ether like streaks of a rainbow. The body between the wings appeared, serpentine and massive, ringed by brilliance.

The form vanished into the mists again, reaching places where the ether washed against the worlds. Only the eternal mist remained, still seething, still swirling. Then, abruptly, the shape broke free and dazzled in the full glow of the sun. It circled the great star, searching for the world it sought, and settled toward that troubled, turbulent globe.

As it descended, its passage cast a broad shadow across the Realms.

\* \* \* \* \*

"Water here, too!" Luskag scratched his bald, sunburned pate. The desert dwarf felt a great puzzlement, tinged with a little alarm. True, extra water in the sun-baked wastes of the House of Tezca could not possibly be bad. Or could it?

"More strangeness, like the beasts rumored to control Nexal," muttered Tatak, his equally sunburned companion. Like Luskag, Tatak wore a smooth leather loincloth, with a band of snakeskin about his scalp. In the younger dwarf's case, this served to restrain his long, shaggy growth of hair. Both dwarves concealed mouths and chins behind bristling, waist-length beards.

The pair stood beside a long pool of clear water in a twisting, rocky vale, where two days previously had lain a dust-filled depression in the desert. Craggy bluffs, their red stone faces glowing like fire in the hot daylight, towered overhead. Ripe, green shoots sprouted from the stony ground around the precious moisture. If the pattern observed throughout much of the House of Tezca was repeated, within weeks this former wasteland would produce an abundance of life-giving mayz.

"And the humans? How do they proceed?" inquired Tatak, knowing his chieftain had ordered spies to observe the great exodus from the wasteland that had once been fabulous Nexal.

"Southward, as before," grunted Luskag. "They cross the House of Tezca like locusts, descending on these newly created water holes, scourging them of food, and then starting south again."

"As if the gods had placed the food for them . . ." mused young Tatak.

Luskag huffed, uncertain and annoyed. He, the chief of Sunhome, had known an unchanging world for more than a century of life in the desert. He and his folk coped with that harsh environment, and if they did not master it, neither did the land master them. They found what water they needed from the plump sand mother, the cactus that grew to serve their needs. Food remained scarce, yet the desert dwarves needed little to survive.

Now, when confronted with a multitude of changes, Luskag could not dispel a sense of unease that closed in around him, disturbing him like a shadow on this bright, sunny day.

Indeed, as if to echo his thoughts, a great flicker of darkness passed over the land. The dwarf ducked reflexively, as if a monstrous hawk passed overhead, but when he looked upward the great dome of azure loomed empty above him.

"Did you see that?" Luskag inquired.

"What?"

Not answering, the chief of the desert dwarves studied the sky for some clue as to the origin of the shadow. "We must beware," he said, his voice a low rumble. "And prepare."

"Our craftswomen work hard on the *pluma*stone," offered Tatak, though of course his chieftain knew this fact very well. "Already they have built many sharp arrows."

"Indeed. Another group, ten sturdy dwarves, left just this morning on the journey to the City of the Gods. In ten days, they will return with yet more of the gods-blessed obsidian."

"How is it, Chieftain," asked Tatak, scowling in confusion, "that the gods can allow the desert to claim a place like that? A pyramid such as stands there shows the work of many faithful followers, does it not?"

Luskag grunted. "Our lot is not to question the acts of the gods. Perhaps they placed the City of the Gods in the desert so that only we could find it—only we could master the *pluma*stone." The chief chuckled wryly. "Though perhaps the gods will now show us why we need such weapons."

They both knew that it had been luck, more than any recognizable destiny, that had allowed Luskag to discover the shiny, super-hard obsidian. The stone seemed to exist only in the ridges around the City of the Gods, the sand-swept ruin that stood in the heart of the bleak desert. From the stone's icy smooth surface, the stoneworkers of the desert dwarves had begun to form weapons far stronger than any they had known in Maztica; indeed, the blades were reminiscent of the steel edges dating back to the dwarves' origins, before the time of the Rockfire.

"They say that the arrowheads are hard enough to shatter boulders," observed Tatak.

"Yes, and they have begun to fashion the heads of axes from this stone as well." Indeed, Luskag himself carried one of the weapons, its obsidian edge rendered keen and reputedly unbreakable by the feathermagic of skilled dwarves. "Perhaps spears will follow, but still, our numbers are small."

Luskag felt, rather than heard, a presence behind him. The ground shook with the weight of a heavy footfall, and the desert dwarf spun, swiftly pulling his stone axe from his belt. He noticed Tatak's face blanch, but the young dwarf sprang to his chief's side without hesitation.

The creature looming behind Luskag almost sent him reeling backward in astonishment and dismay. Huge and vaguely manlike, it towered eight or nine feet in the air. Broad sinews rippled across its torso and limbs as it raised a club the size of a small tree. He dimly noted the blood-red brand, like the diamond-shaped head of a viper, on the thing's chest.

But it was the face that drew Luskag's attention, for he stared into the most horrifying visage he had ever seen. Tiny bloodshot eyes gleamed at him while a broad mouth, flecked with drool, gaped open to display sharp, finger-length tusks. Something within his nature rose in deep loathing at the sight of the monster, and Luskag's body tensed in primitive hatred.

"Watch out for the club!" cried the chieftain, seeing Tatak charge forward.

The young desert dwarf carried merely a stone knife, yet he thrust the weapon at the beast's sagging belly. With surprising quickness, the monster stepped back, at the same time hammering its club toward the charging dwarf. The stout limb met Tatak's skull with brutal force, crushing bone and brain in the same instant.

Luskag snarled his rage, flinging himself into battle with all the primordial hatred this creature aroused in him. He had never seen such a beast, yet the thing's mere appearance drove him into a killing frenzy.

Luskag's stone axe, encircled by the tiny tufts of *pluma*, sought the monster's bulging gut. Before it lifted its club again, the keen obsidian edge scored a deep gash across the creature's flesh.

The sun-browned dwarf shouted his joy savagely, a harsh bark of vengeance as he saw the monster's blood. A killing rage upon him, Luskag crouched, watching for the beast's return blow.

With a bellow that shook the valley, the creature swung wildly at the desert dwarf. Luskag easily twisted away from the blow, and this time he chopped hard into its knee. The monster's cry held tones of fear now, and Luskag attacked again, and again. His fury burned through his body, becoming a murderous rage that sent him after this grotesque aberration with brutal determination. Even without the slaying of Tatak, he would have had difficulty restraining his hatred.

As it was, the need for vengeance left no room for any thoughts of mercy.

The beast cowered backward, stumbling away from the furious slashes of the gleaming stone blade. Suddenly it dropped its club and turned to flee, lumbering frantically up the loose stones toward the rim of the valley.

One sharp chop into the creature's thigh tore its hamstring. With a panicked bellow, the beast flopped to the earth, writhing pathetically. Luskag's next blow, to the creature's brutish neck, silenced it for good.

Gradually the battle frenzy disappeared from Luskag's eyes, and he felt a great tiredness press upon his shoulders.

Sadly the chieftain turned back to Tatak's body. He remembered the shadow across the sky and looked upward again, but only the clear blue sky arced above him, mocking in its pristine clarity.

Luskag gently lifted the body of his companion and turned his steps toward Sunhome.

\* \* \* \* \*

The man and the woman rested, enjoying the quiet peace of their rocky niche. From here, atop the red-ribbed, twisting ridge, they looked westward across a brown and sandy expanse of desert. They savored these moments alone together, for they were young lovers, and of late times such as this had become increasingly rare.

They faced the pristine wild lands, away from the bitter trail and the thousands of footsore, weary humans camped behind them to the east. Now, finally, after weeks of flight, the great smoldering mass of Mount Zatal lay out of sight, below the northern horizon. Throughout their long trek, the volcano's towering summit had loomed above the mass of terrified Mazticans, a scarred and jagged reminder of the night of violence that had driven them from their city and left wondrous Nexal a wretched, smoking ruin.

The Night of Wailing, it had come to be known, and an apt name it was.

"How long must we flee?" Erixitl asked wistfully. The evening's chill began to settle in, gently urging them back to a place where they did not want to go. She was a woman of striking beauty, with long black hair cascading across her shoulders and flowing down her back. She wore a bright cloak, smooth and soft, with a lushly feathered surface of brilliant colors that seemed to shimmer in the pale light.

At her throat, she wore a jade amulet, surrounded by the silky plumes of emerald feathers. The wispy tendrils seemed to float in the breeze with a life of their own, and the rich green of the amulet's stone heart reflected a sense of verdant vitality.

"We can survive a long time, as long as we keep finding

food," countered Halloran, avoiding a direct answer. "I know that it's no future, no life for us . . . for . ." His voice trailed off as she took his hand. In contrast to the woman, the man was tall, with pale though ruddy skin, and a smooth brown beard.

At his side, in a plain leather scabbard, he wore a long, straight sword. The weapon's keen steel blade gleamed in the narrow gap where, near the hilt, it lay exposed to the air. He also wore a breastplate of steel, once shiny but now stained from the rigors of the trail. His heavy leather boots showed the scuffs of a long, rugged march.

Only at his hands did a sense of cleanliness linger, a brightness that the lowering dusk seemed to accentuate. A thin, colorful strap of beaded leather encircled each of his wrists, tiny tufts of plumage puffing from them, blossoming in the twilight.

"What other kind of life can there be now?" Erix sighed. "Perhaps this is the beginning of the end of the world."

"No!" Hal sat upright. "The desert is only a pathway for us, not our life! As long as the food and water hold out, we can keep moving. Somewhere we'll find a place where we're safe, where we can build a home! Your people have built cities before; they can do it again! They—we—can do it again, with your leadership, your guidance!"

"Why does it have to be me?" Erix demanded, then grew suddenly tired as she answered herself. "Because I wear a cloak made from one feather? Because the people—the *priests*—claim that I am the chosen one of Qotal?"

"I've never claimed to understand the workings of gods," Hal responded quietly. "But you are trusted by the people, and they need you! Even the men from the legion, my own countrymen, look to you.

"If a prophecy of the return of the Feathered Dragon is the thing that brings us all to you, don't question it!" he continued. "Use that belief to try and bring us together!"

"Yes," Erix sighed, "I know. All of the signs have been fulfilled. First the couatl returns to Maztica, only to die on the Night of Wailing. Then his cloak is discovered—the Cloak-of-One-Plume—and I happen to be wearing it. Finally we have the Summer Ice."

"The ice was the only thing that allowed us to escape Nexal," Halloran reminded her, "and the last sign that was supposed to predict his return."

"But he comes too late, if he comes at all!" she snapped harshly. "Where is he now? And why could he not come when Nexal could still have been saved, before all the killing and war?"

"Perhaps nothing could save Nexal," Hal suggested. Though the city had been magnificent, he couldn't forget the files of captives that had been claimed daily by the priests of Zaltec, their hearts offered to their bloodthirsty god. The whole image was one of vast and sinister darkness, an evil that could not long remain upon the world.

"Remember, your cloak saved our lives on the Night of Wailing."

"That it did," Erixitl admitted. She leaned against her husband. "And for all the terror and fear we've experienced since then, I would not want to relinquish one minute of the time we've had together."

"There will be many more," Hal promised, and he made the vow deep in his heart.

He took her in his arms and held her against the chill of the night that now surrounded them. She melded to him, and for a time, they knew of no one, of nothing beyond themselves.

And for that too-brief time, they had all that they needed.

\* \* \* \* \*

Smoke drifted upward from the mound of shattered stone that once had been the Great Pyramid of Nexal. The surrounding space of the sacred plaza, now torn, buckled, and cracked, stretched like a hellish wasteland of steaming ruin.

Still, the site remained sacred, for here had been buried, centuries earlier, the sacred talisman of the Nexalan tribe. It lay in the ruins now below the torn surface of the plaza and the shattered pyramid, yet not lacking in potency.

This talisman was a pillar of sandstone, discovered by a devout cleric of Zaltec many centuries earlier. Legend claimed that this pillar had come to life, speaking as Zaltec to the cleric, commanding him to lead his people on an epic pilgrimage. It had been borne by the wandering tribe of the Nexal until they had come to this valley and claimed this island as their home.

Before they erected the first pyramid to their hungry god, they had buried the pillar in the earth below the temple site. As succeeding generations had expanded the tribe's influence, they had also added layer upon layer to the simple pyramid. At last the structure had become the Great Pyramid of Nexal, even as its people became masters of the True World. And always, at the base of the towering pyramid, the sandstone pillar formed its solid foundation. It symbolized the deep and abiding power of the god, much as the looming volcano overhead had come to represent his fiery and explosive hunger.

Months had passed since the eruption of the great volcano, Zatal, yet still the waters in the valley seethed with heat, and gouts of foul gas exploded upward with unpredictable violence.

The island that had once sheltered the humans and their great city of Nexal now suffered the anger of the gods. Great cracks scored the land, filled with black water or bubbling, steaming muck. The fabulous wealth of its gold had sunk into darkness, buried beneath stone and dirt and flesh, while its art, its *pluma* feathermagic, its brilliant mosaics and magnificent architecture, all vanished in the violence of the destruction.

Around the shore, the other towns and cities of the valley lay wracked and abandoned. Once fertile fields had been flooded by the ancient clear waters of the lakes and now stood as vast swamps, steaming and fetid, or even poisoned by the foul spume from the still-smoldering mountain.

Dark creatures moved about here, shadowy beasts of tusk and fang, leering hatefully through the murk at the world that had cursed them to their fate. All humans who had not fled had long since perished by the tusk and claw of the city's current masters.

The greatest of these monsters dwelled in the ruins of the pyramid itself. Hoxitl, once high priest of Bloody Zaltec, now became his master's ultimate tool. His grotesque body towering to a height of twenty feet, Hoxitl's face bore no resemblance to its formerly human nature.

Instead, a great protruding muzzle snapped savagely, revealing row upon row of sharp, wickedly curving fangs. His arms and legs, long and sinewy, ended in hooked talons, while a long tail, tipped with venomous barbs, lashed behind him. A thick mane surrounded his head, a mane of blood-caked, thick fur that bristled when he vented his rage. And now Hoxitl knew naught but rage.

Often did the beast curse his master—Zaltec, god of war— who had condemned him to this fate. Yet at the same time and despite his most venomous curses, Zaltec ruled him yet. On those rare occasions when a human was found hiding among the rubble of Nexal, the captive was always dragged, shrieking in terror, to Hoxitl. Leering over the pathetic victim, Hoxitl would tear out his heart and then cower, offering the gory sacrifice upward in craven obeisance to his ruling god. Always Hoxitl prayed for the guidance of Zaltec, for the beast could form no ideas of his own.

One of these victims, an old man who accepted his faith with the stoicism of a true believer, finally seemed to provoke a response. Hoxitl tossed the heart into the maw of the shattered statue that had once represented the god Zaltec. As he did so, he felt a rumbling, centered deep within the earth, far below his feet.

The cleric-beast moaned in terror, remembering the wrack visited upon him during the Night of Wailing. All around him, the craven creatures of his cult howled in fright and cowered in any niche they could find, fearing the further wrath of their master.

A great shaking and crashing shook the ruins of the temple, and Hoxitl prudently backed away as large boulders rumbled from the pile. A form rose from the wreckage, stonelike of visage and mountainous in size, driving back the rubble as it slowly emerged from the ground.

At last it stood like a monolith, high over the head of even the towering Hoxitl. Around him his creatures cringed, begging for mercy, but the cleric-beast stepped boldly forward and knelt before the form.

For the stone pillar before him, he knew, was none other than Zaltec himself, the god of war. For long centuries, he had lain at the center of the pyramid, buried beneath the layers of construction added by successive Revered Counselors of Nexal. But now, unconstrained by the city and the faiths above, he emerged as a mighty colossus, and he made his will known to Hoxitl.

And Hoxitl knew that Zaltec still favored him. Despite his misshapen form, despite the wracking of his people and his world, Hoxitl howled his gratitude.

"My Master! You speak to me! I am your slave!"

An image jolted Hoxitl to his full height, an image of blood and death and fire.

"War!" Hoxitl gloated. "Master, I shall make war in your honor! I shall lay waste to all who do not hail your name!"

"My creatures!" He summoned his followers to him with a vibrant command. Despite their fear of the colossus, they heard Hoxitl and they obeyed. "We go forth to make war in the holy name of Zaltec!"

He howled and cursed his creatures, ordering them into ranks and legions. Cuffing and battering the ogres, he sent them to do the same to the orcs. He took his fleet, savage trolls and formed companies of death-dealing hate.

The great mass assembled in the ruined center of Nexal. Black and green trolls stood sentinel around the army, their dark, sunken eyes peering suspiciously. They raised great sinewy limbs, clasping their talons at the sky. Some of them carried clubs, or crude stone *macas*, while others held tattered shields or bore some torn relic of human garb. Others stood naked. But all of them came.

The brute ogres clubbed and whipped the masses of orcs, and the smaller creatures scurried to obey their monstrous leaders. The orcs gathered in companies with spears and bows and clubs, the weapons they had borne as warriors of the Viperhand.

And the whole rank formed a snakelike column behind their master. Hoxitl raised his voice and stood to his full height so that he towered over even the trolls. He led them across the ruined causeway, past the festering mire of the smoking lakes, and then took them southward, toward the desert beyond Mount Zatal.

They would find the humans who had fled their city. They would find them, and Bloody Zaltec would feast once more.

\* \* \* \* \*

The eagle entered a billowing mass of cloud, diving lazily. The bird's vast wings caught each gentle updraft, speeding its flight and holding its altitude at the same time. For long minutes, the black and white form slid easily through the encloaking vapor, finally bursting free into the sunny expanse of the southern sky.

Never had Poshtli flown this far south before. The eagle's body relished the freedom granted by his total mastery of the skies, as hawks, vultures, and lesser eagles—and all other eagles were lesser eagles—dove away from the great bird's flight.

Yet within that powerful, plumed body, a man's mind wondered at the changes in the land below. Poshtli saw the new greenery, oases of water surrounded by mayz and berries, where once the brown sands of the House of Tezca ruled supreme.

The sands still existed—indeed, they dominated the landscape—but the precious islands of vitality dotted the True World to the far northern and southern horizons like a series of cosmic footsteps leading away from the devastation that had once been mighty Nexal.

With a human sob, Poshtli remembered his grand city, now reduced to ashes, rubble, and mud. The volcano, Zatal, had finally ceased its convulsions more than a month after its initial eruption. By then, little remained of the once beautiful, vibrantly fertile valley except the wasteland.

And the creatures! Hideous monsters, born in the cataclysmic forces when the god of war claimed his faithful and made them in his image. Humans branded by the Viperhand, marked as Zaltec's servants, became beasts the like of which the eagle had never seen before and man's mind could not have imagined. Never before had these monsters roamed the True World, though Poshtli's friend Halloran had told him of their existence in other parts of the Realms.

Now they laid claim to all of Nexal. Even more frightening, Poshtli's aerial observations had showed him that these monsters had formed legions, and now they began to march.

The eagle had soared over the muddy encampments of refugees, many scores of thousands of humans fleeing Nexal, following the verdant islands southward into the desert. The monsters pursued, and the humans fled. Each oasis, with its surrounding food, fed the people for several days, but then, its bounty exhausted, compelled the population to flee farther to the south, away from the press of bestial fangs and talons.

Poshtli observed the struggle from his position of sublime detachment, for he no longer belonged to that earthbound world. Yet he could not totally remove himself, for too long had he been a noble leader of the Nexala.

So now he flew to the south, to see where the path of fertility drew his people. Always his eyes, far keener than any man's, searched the horizon before him.

And finally he reached the end of his trail.

It appeared as a small mound on the horizon, growing swiftly as the eagle soared closer. It did not lie along the path of greenery, but rather some distance to the east. Soon he recognized it for the shape it was, though how it had come to the desert he could not explain. Higher and higher it towered, seeming to rear upward as he closed.

The structure rose from a flat expanse of barren sand, but around this area the eagle saw other ruins: a low building, partially covered with sand, revealing a few dark, half-obstructed doors and a courtyard consisting of many rows of parallel columns. A smaller pyramid stood nearby, mostly eroded, and he saw square outlines that showed where other structures had stood.

Over it all loomed the towering pyramid, clean and bright and pristine in its regal beauty. As he neared it, Poshtli saw that it was greater than any other such thing in the land, easily reaching twice as high as the now-ruined Great Pyramid in Nexal had stood.

Finally he circled the bright, steep-sided pyramid. Many terraces scored its sides, and steep stairways, of many hundreds of steps, ascended each of the four sides. Bright mosaics marked all of its faces, in colors more brilliant than any he had ever seen before. Sharply outlined, freshly colored, it showed no sign of ruin nor abandonment.

He swooped closer, past the dark, gaping door to the temple consecrated to whichever god the pyramid glorified. Atop the structure itself, the building stood windswept and empty.

It seemed he had found the greatest pyramid in the land, yet it was a temple that still awaited its god.

\* \* \* \* \*

The Night of Wailing was viewed by the inhabitants of the True World as a monstrous calamity, a disaster visited upon them by vengeful gods. Those humans who had been corrupted by the storm of arcane power—the members of the Cult of the Viperhand, now in the form of orcs, ogres, and trolls—cursed and reviled their fate. Those who had survived the violence of that portentous night and had not suffered such a transformation fled in terror, thinking of little more than safety.

How different was the perspective of that night when viewed from the realms of the gods themselves!

Zaltec had grown tremendously, and the power of the convulsion had allowed him to insert his physical presence into the prime plane. This presence manifested itself in the stone statue that now towered over ruined Nexal. His most faithful followers, those who had taken the vow of the Viperhand, he had bound to him forever by transforming their very bodies into creatures of death and war.

Qotal, the Feathered Dragon, was a powerful deity who had been driven from Maztica by the growth of his brother Zaltec's power. Serene and aloof, he remained distant from the world of humans, worshiped by some few of them, forgotten or ignored by most. But the Night of Wailing had created a crack in the barrier formed by Zaltec's faithful. Now Qotal moved toward the world, and people terrified by the specter of Zaltec's destruction cried and pleaded for his return.

Helm, the god of the legionnaires, had been all but driven from Maztica by the brute power of his foe. Though he had worshipers in Maztica among the legionnaires who survived, no cleric of that vigilant god remained to guide them. So they blundered blindly, while Helm's power retreated across the sea, to the palaces and temples along the Sword Coast, at the heart of his faith. But the god viewed his withdrawal as a minor setback; someday soon, borne by the hearts and will of his followers, he would return.

Yet a fourth deity, a dark goddess of venomous evil, poured her power into the convulsion. She was Lolth, and her vengeance exploded first toward her servants, the drow elves.

But she did not slay the elves. Instead, she perverted their clean forms into beasts of chaos and corruption and allowed them to live and to suffer. Her vengeance would not end there — she would set her creatures, her driders, free upon the world, where they would wreak further havoc.

To do so, they would need tools. This need brought Lolth's power once again to the world as she sought the proper materials to make tools for her driders. She probed the dark spaces, the smoldering caverns beneath the surface of the earth, in search of her goal.

Far from Nexal she found that which she needed, in the forms of insects—thousands of small, red ants. Her power entered the nest where the creatures huddled, dismayed by the chaos stirring the world above. The might of Lolth surrounded them and took them in her smoky grip.

The nest area expanded, growing quickly from a small den into a vast subterranean cavern. Rock melted away and dirt flowed like water, until a huge cavern gaped in the earth.

The ants, however, in their thousands, took no notice of the change. For they had grown along with the nest. They stared at each other, their multifaceted eyes glittering in the dim light. They huddled and twitched, all unknowing.

But now, each was more than six feet long.

From the chronicles of Coton:

*Now the Waning is past, and I commence the tale of the Reawakening.*

*I depart Nexal on the Night of Wailing, as do so many others—all, in fact, who would live and remain human. But the force of the convulsion tears me from my people. While the mass of the Nexala flee southward, my own path compels me to the north and east.*

*My vow of silence, symbol of my pledge as patriarch of Qotal, entraps me, prevents me from speaking with those I see. At the same time, my white robe protects me. Now that Zaltec has shown himself, through the wracking of the True World, as the monster that he truly is, the worship of Qotal, the Plumed Father, flowers among the people again.*

*It is beyond the city where I receive the first sign of the Plumed Father's blessing, in the form of a black, snorting beast.*

*This is not a beast of the Viperhand, transformed by the gods' vengeance on this night of horror. Instead, it is a beast of the strangers, come with them to Maztica and now escaped and panicked. A beast such as the strangers call "horse."*

*This one comes to me, in supplication it seems, and allows me to mount it. Thus borne, I ride, far faster than human feet could carry, toward the east.*

# ❧ 2 ❧

# THE FERTILE DESERT

"We'd better get back to the camp. It's dark already." Erixitl slowly rose to her feet as Hal followed. They had only to turn, to look down the other side of the ridge, to see the scene they had escaped for these few precious moments.

The vast, straggling camp lay like a muddy blotch on the land, barely visible in the light of its thousand campfires. Still, that mud was a sign of good fortune—the blessings of gods, or of providential nature. A year earlier, there could have been no mud, for there would have been no water.

Now water was reasonably plentiful in the desert, and the humans who churned its neighborhood to mud lived where they would have died. The nature of the life, it must be said, gave these miserable folk little thought of thanksgiving.

Halloran and Erix did not know how many people fled in this great procession, moving gradually southward, away from ruined Nexal and the beasts that now claimed the city as their home. Like a swarm of locusts, the humans scoured each water hole, quickly baring the surrounding fields of mayz and berries. No single location provided a long rest; in a matter of days, the great march southward would commence again, for this was the only way the people could eat.

For now, this new water hole promised a brief respite. Even in the darkness, women moved through the fields, gathering mayz, while children splashed around the fringes of the once-blue pool, washing away the dust and weariness from the long day of marching. The water occupied the center of a shallow, bowl-shaped valley. The desert stretched for miles beyond the rim of the vale, an expanse of brown, windswept dunes and even harsher patches of rocky plain.

Within the bowl, a miraculous transformation had shown

itself. Green fields of sweet, waving mayz formed a belt around the valley, below the crest of the hill but some ways above the water. Around the water's edge grew a lush circle of wild rice, while plump berries sprang from bushes that ringed the marshy fringe.

The spaces in the valley that had not grown food, or where such food had already been harvested, now served as living space for the population of a massive city. Nexalans, the citizens of vanished Nexal, formed most of this group, but a small fraction of the humans showed different origins. The latter were bushy of face and wore breastplates and carried weapons of steel. The Mazticans, of course, carried obsidian-edged clubs, called *macas*, as well as arrows and spears and knives of stone, and they wore armor of padded cotton.

Now these folk lived in uneasy truce, bonded by a mutual fear of the greater, and common, enemy lurking in the nightmare of Nexal. The truce did not approach camaraderie, but it was eased by the fact that the spokesmen for the deep religious schisms between these two diverse peoples were no longer with them.

Indeed, the fleeing Mazticans had even abandoned their practices of human sacrifice. The priests of Zaltec, universally transformed into trolls on the Night of Wailing, no longer hounded them for victims. The devastation, commencing at the height of a sacrificial orgy, had caused many to question doctrine they had always accepted at face value. Who were they to question the hunger of the gods?

But now, in the face of the potential starvation of their children, the hunger of the gods did not seem so tragic a thing to the people of Maztica.

Erixitl and Halloran slowly descended from the ridgetop, through a fringe of the camp in a clean-plucked field that had yesterday grown lush with mayz.

"Sister! Sister of the Plume!" A voice called out, and more of them joined in as several women recognized Erixitl. They quickly gathered around her, eagerly thrusting their children forward so that Erix could touch them. Gently she brushed her hands across their tousled, black-haired heads.

"And see? See her cloak," said a round-faced mother, look-ing at Erixitl's garment with an expression approaching rap-ture. "The sign! Soon Qotal will be here, and then all will be well again!"

Abruptly Erix's throat tightened and she turned away, led by Halloran farther into the camp.

A small stand of stunted cedars, a rare grove in the House of Tezca, proved that this vale had once retained some mini-mal moisture, enough to grow these hardy desert trees. Now the grove, newly green and lush from the suddenly in-creased water supply, sheltered a group of people from the growing night. Here gathered those who led the procession and protected it.

A fractious group, formed by disaster and held together by necessity, they nevertheless strived for cooperation, for they knew this was the only way they would survive. Their numbers included Eagle and Jaguar Warriors, priests of Qo-tal, Azul, and Calor, and even several steel-helmed officers of the Golden Legion.

As Erixitl approached, her cloak puffed outward from her shoulders and colors seemed to rise in the silky plume. Like an aura, bright hues surrounded the woman, and all the others in the group stood back a small distance from her. The blessing of Qotal lay upon her, and it was to Erixitl of Palul that the people turned for leadership, hope, and comfort.

She looked at them now, despairing. What did she know about leading people? Why did they look to her? Because, she knew, of the cloak she wore—the brilliant, scintillating Cloak-of-One-Plume that signified the blessing of Qotal, the Plumed Serpent. Erixitl silently cursed the blessing of that god, for this was her feeling now toward all gods. What kind of deities could wrack their people with a cataclysm like the Night of Wailing?

"Greetings, Gultec," she said quietly to a dark, smooth-chinned warrior wearing the spotted tunic of a Jaguar Knight. Gultec was the warrior who had told them of food in the desert on the morning after the destruction of Nexal, thus insuring their survival.

He, together with Halloran, formed Erixitl's strength and her shield on this hellish journey. Gultec had come to represent to her the same kind of friendship, she realized with a twinge of pain, as had the Eagle Knight, Lord Poshtli. He had aided Halloran and her on their desperate attempt to avert the catastrophe.

Now, as she despaired of leading these people, her heart ached for Poshtli! The great lord and warrior had been a true friend to her and Halloran, and he had been with them atop the volcano at its moment of eruption. Though her cloak had protected her husband and herself, there had been no immortal shield for Poshtli. Rationally, as Halloran had tenderly tried to convince her, there could be no hope that Poshtli had survived. Yet still somehow, in her heart, she believed that he had to be alive.

White-robed priests of Qotal who had escaped the chaos in Nexal stood anxiously behind the pair, eager to counsel Erix. The Plumed Serpent would now return, for all the prophecies had been fulfilled, and they now preached a newly vitalized faith. The preaching was done by the younger priests, those who had not yet taken their vows of silence. But only the younger priests had escaped Qotal. The patriarch, Coton, was assumed to have perished in the chaos.

A warrior sprinted toward them from his guard post at the edge of the camp. He reached the group among the cedars and threw himself flat upon the sand before Erixitl.

"My lady, the foreigners return!"

Moments later, a trio of horses appeared behind him, cantering through the encampment. One, the leader, dismounted, while the other two held back some distance from the proud figure of Erixitl.

"What have you learned, General?" she asked, as the black-bearded rider bowed before her.

"The monsters move out from Nexal," Cordell reported. "My scouts have observed long columns of orcs, commanded by ogres and flanked by trolls, moving into the desert. They come southward, following our trail."

The commander spoke in the common tongue of the

Realms, but Halloran smoothly translated his speech into Nexalan. A rumble of concern rippled through the gathering until Erixitl raised her hand.

"How far away?" she asked.

"Still four or five days," replied the captain-general. "But they march swiftly. Their columns extend to the east and west, barring our flight in those directions."

"Stand and fight them here, then!" growled Totoq, a grizzled Jaguar Knight. A chorus of assenting voices joined him.

"Wait." Gultec, also dressed in the spotted skin of a veteran Jaguar Knight, lifted his hand. Though not a man of the Nexala, his steadiness on the long flight had earned him the respect of the others.

"What is it? Have we not waited too much already?" demanded Kilti, a young Eagle Warrior.

"Gultec counsels wisdom," Halloran added. "We have already exhausted most of the food here. True, we could establish a strong defense with a four-day delay, but what will we eat before and after the battle?"

"We must move south," Erix stated with finality.

"It is the will of Qotal," added Caknol, one of the white-robed priests of the Plumed God.

Erixitl, still surrounded by the glowing cloak, surprised them all by whirling on the priest.

"The will of Qotal?" she spat. "Why should we take note of his will now, after his complete abandonment of us, his people? He sent his signs—the couatl, who died bravely in the battle with the Ancient Ones, and the Cloak-of-One-Plume, which covers my shoulders, but for what purpose? And even the Summer Ice, which enabled us to flee Nexal at the moment of the city's destruction, has but prolonged our misery!"

"But his mercy—" the cleric stammered, surprised by the woman's anger.

"His *mercy!*" Erixitl practically sneered the words. "What kind of mercy is this?" She gestured to the ragged collection of humanity around them, angrily turning her back on the priest.

Then, with no warning, she collapsed onto the ground.

\* \* \* \* \*

Lava seethed in great seas, surging against rocky shores with hellish force, crashing upward to coat scorched boulders with fresh layers of molten stone. Cavern roofs pressed overhead, rocked by convulsions, reflecting back the infernal heat. Massive chunks of rock broke from the ceilings of vast caverns, tumbling into the flaming, blood-red liquid and shattering convulsively from the pressure and the heat and the violence.

Everywhere this world lay wracked by flame and fire, yet overhung by leaden darkness as well, for it was a world beneath the earth, where the torturous wracking of the underdark emerged as mere tremors on the surface.

It was a world without life, without sun or water or sky. The only illumination came from the crackling, seething lava, hissing upward with crimson explosions of flame. Each burst of violence consumed precious oxygen, and the air in the huge caves hung heavy and thick with poisonous vapors and choking smoke.

It was through this world that a file of repulsive, spider-like beasts made its way. Led by the one of purest white, these, the several dozen corrupted monsters of the spider goddess Lolth, passed slowly and carefully along the seething shores, in search of escape from the wrath of their angry god.

The driders were beasts of hideous aspect and foul, unnatural desires. Each walked upon eight spider legs, covered with coarse fur and bristling with venomous spines. Their bodies, bloated and distended like the abdomens of spiders, swung beneath the legs.

Only their torsos and heads showed signs of their former existence. Sleek black skin covered wretched faces that had once been proud and handsome. Long dextrous fingers held black-bladed swords or long, dark bows.

But these features, formerly noble if cruel, were now scarred by flame and distorted by corruption. Great patches of skin had burned from them, and their pale eyes no longer held the gleam of power. Instead, they stared in terror at the hellfires around them, wildly, desperately seeking escape. Even the one who led them, the one that was pale white where all the others were dark, thought of nothing other than refuge.

Escape! For now, release from this nightmare mattered more than anything. The vengeance of Lolth had scarred and terrified them, and they scuttled, as mortal creatures will, in search of refuge against the further wrath of their god. They could not know that Lolth was finished with her vengeance and now looked toward further, evil employment of her servants.

Yet the nature of the driders was too hateful, too vile, to long remain content with an existence of flight. Here again the pale one showed her leadership, for she looked upward and shook a scarred, raw fist at the fires looming overhead. She cursed the name of her god, of all the gods, and hatred grew in her like a poisonous flame.

Ultimately her thoughts, and soon those of her kin as well, began to turn toward vengeance.

\* \* \* \* \*

Small-mouthed caves ringed the base of the narrow box canyon. Above these dwellings, others—structures of adobe, with round doors and tiny, latticed windows—extended across the face of the yellow, wind-bitten cliff face itself. The latter perched precariously, reachable only by ladders and forming an easily defensible barrier against attack from below.

Yet never in its three centuries of existence had Sunhome known attackers. Indeed, the desert dwarf village suffered no threats other than the implacable sun and parched air that provided security even as they challenged its residents to survive.

But now Luskag wondered if it were indeed impregnable. He stood at the mouth of the canyon, greeting the headmen and chiefs of other desert dwarf communities as they arrived at Sunhome for the conference, and he no longer thought of his village as an island immune to the storms of war.

"It's a long trek you call us to," grunted one named Pullog, whose village lay far to the south, at the fringe of the House of Tezca. As Sunhome was the northernmost of the dwarven settlements, Pullog's trek had indeed been arduous.

"But no less important for that," answered Luskag. "I am glad your journey passed safely, my cousin. Come, sup with us, and then the council will begin."

The other chiefs, a full score in all, had already arrived. They gathered in Luskag's cave, served by his daughters and warmed by the light of a mesquite fire. They talked idly during a meal of snake meat, cactus, and water, but the conversation revealed that all of them had observed the changes that had come over the desert during the past summer and the current autumn. Finally they concluded the repast, and Pullog, always impatient, turned to Luskag.

"Now, cousin, tell us why your children come to our villages, out of breath and wild-eyed, to compel us to leave our wives and make the journey to Sunhome? Is it to tell us that there is water in the desert? Or food?"

Luskag chuckled wryly, but then his expression turned grim. In answer, he reached beneath a blanket and tossed forth a large white object. The skull of the ogre rolled forward to rest before Pullog, its eyeless sockets gaping upward at the southern chief.

"What in the name of the gods is *that?*" demanded Pullog, blanching beneath his sunburned skin.

"A sign," Luskag answered. "To show that there are more changes in Maztica than a newly fertile desert." Briefly he told the tale of the ogre's size and ferocity. "As I fought with it, a killing frenzy consumed me. The abominable creature awakened some deep and abiding hatred within me." Luskag shuddered at the memory of that uncontrollable rage, and the other dwarves looked from the monstrous skull to the small, sturdy dwarf, with something resembling awe.

"Now I have sent my sons northward," he explained. "They have learned that Nexal is full of such beasts—or, to be more accurate, *was* full of such beasts. Now they have formed armies and marched into the desert."

He told them of the humans, a hundred thousand or more of them, fleeing southward, making their way from one water hole to the next, fleeing the monstrous legions.

"It is clear that our world faces a serious challenge," observed Traj, chief of the village nearest Sunhome. "Can we not fall back to our villages and wait for the threat to pass?"

"This is why I have called the council," replied Luskag. "It is true that since the Rockfire sundered the underdark, separating us from the known world, we have dwelled in peaceful isolation. We have known no enemies, and the land has given us what we need to live."

"Aye," grunted several chiefs, for the history of their people was only a few centuries old, and most had heard the tale from older dwarves who had actually experienced the great war with the drow that had led to the Rockfire. Though that schism, terrifying in its magnitude and violence, had forever separated the desert dwarves from their kin in other parts of the Realms, it had also eliminated their most hated enemies, the drow. Through the centuries, the people of Luskag's tribe had come to accept, if not praise, this exchange.

"And good years we have had, too," observed Harl, the most venerable of the chiefs. Though his hair and beard were snow-white, the grizzled dwarf still marched proudly at the head of his tribesmen.

"So they should remain," Pullog added, "lest we act foolishly and, in our rashness, ruin that which is our blessing. Rashness, such as the idea that we can make war on such monsters! Far better to remain in our villages, secure and hidden, until the scourge passes."

"Would the years pass in peace, so be it." Luskag spoke forcefully, and all the dwarves looked to him. "But it will not be so."

He paused, mildly relieved that none argued with his point. In a moment, he continued. "You all know of the City of the Gods—greater, even, than splendid Nexal. Now it is too dry even to support a family of desert dwarves, yet still it lies in the desert and continues to taunt us with its mysteries and wonders."

"Aye," Traj assented readily. "Oft I have journeyed to its rim, only to sit and gaze in wonder on the pyramid that rises from the desert, lifeless."

"The gods have given us a blessing, even in that desolate place." Luskag reached behind himself to pull forth a heavy lump of sandstone. With a grunt, he dropped it to the stone floor before him. Then he slowly removed his axe, so that the others could clearly see its gleaming stone blade, shiny black and as smooth as a mirror. Tufts of red, yellow, and green feathers encircled the haft just below the head.

"I have discovered obsidian in the city of the gods—great blocks of stone that we can craft into weapons." He raised the axe and brought it down sharply on the block of sandstone. The rock burst apart, showering the dwarves with shards.

The blade, however, stuck clean and unshattered into a newly made crack across the floor.

"It seems that now our time of sanctuary draws to a close. The desert dwarves are once again drawn into the conflicts of the world, and we must be prepared to face this threat together."

"Do not be hasty," countered Pullog. "True, your demonstration of weaponry is impressive. Perhaps, armed thus, we could field a strong force. But how do we face this threat?"

"It is for that reason that I have called you here," answered Luskag. "I ask, nay beg, that you all accompany me in the morning.

"I propose that we climb the great mountain and seek the wisdom of the Sunstone."

\* \* \* \* \*

"Don't try to get up. Just rest." Halloran tried to keep his voice level, but his concern for his wife emerged as taut fear. Erixitl lay on the soft ground beneath a canopy of cedars. The others, out of respect and worry, gave them space to be alone. Around them, dawn had given way to full and already scorching daylight

"I'm all right," she replied, smiling gently. She reached for him, her fingers feeling cold and weak to Hal.

He clenched her hand as his eyes instinctively dropped to her belly. A slight swelling, unnoticeable to any but him, remained the only outward sign of the life that developed there. When he looked back to her face, his fear for that life as well as hers tightened his voice even further.

"We'll stay here for a few days. Then, when we leave, you'll ride a horse. Nothing but harm can come from these long marches, and I will not let that happen!"

Erixitl sighed, squeezing her husband's hand, for this was an old argument. "I'll be fine. You can't expect me to ride, when old men and women, even little children, all walk on their own feet."

Among the throng of refugees were some fifteen horses, all that were left of the forty brought to Maztica by the Golden Legion. The others had almost certainly perished in battle or in the convulsions of the Night of Wailing. If a few had escaped to freedom, which was possible, they were of no use to them now.

"But . . ." Hal groped for new reasons. "You're too important—to everyone! The people look to you for leadership, for comfort!"

"Why?" Erix's tone became sharp. "Because I wear the Cloak-of-One-Plume?" She sat up abruptly and gestured toward the colorful mantle hanging from a tree branch beside her. "I'll gladly give it to anyone who wants it!"

Halloran sat back, deeply disturbed. He wanted to offer comfort, but Erixitl's tension held him at bay. Finally she relaxed slightly, turning back to him. He could see that she was thinking about something else.

"I hope my father's all right," she said softly. "I'm afraid for him, though. Palul is so close to Nexal, and he's so helpless. If the creatures of the Viperhand come there, he wouldn't have a chance!"

Halloran thought of the blind featherworker, Lotil. His wife's father had seemed to be a very wise man, very keen in his understanding of the world despite his lack of sight. He worked the magic of feathers—*pluma*—and his gifts were with them now, in the amulet that Erix wore and in his own wristbands, jokingly termed Erixitl's "dowry" by the old man.

The powers of Erixitl's amulet had offered them protection against a variety of threats. Conversely, the bands that he wore had increased the strength of his arms to that of ten men when Hal's energies focused on battle. Surely a man with such potent skills could save himself from the chaos sweeping the land. At least, so Hal hoped.

Erix turned back to Hal, her expression once again peaceful. "Can you send for Poshtli? I'd like to talk to him."

Hal's heart twisted in pain, a hurt that showed clearly in his face, and his wife's expression grew concerned. "What is it?" she asked. "Has something happened?"

"Don't you remember?" he asked softly. "The volcano . . . the Night of Wailing? Poshtli was with us when the explosion occurred, but he didn't have the protection of your cloak. He's . . . gone." The man couldn't force himself to say that the noble warrior was dead.

"But he's not gone," Erixitl countered, still strangely calm. "I remember all that—how could I forget?—but Poshtli did not die there. He's nearby . . . he comes to us!" She smiled gently, as if Hal were the one having flights of fancy. Even against the beauty of her face, Halloran nearly wept to see how pale she was, how distant was the look in her eyes.

A shadow flickered off to the side, and Hal looked up to see Xatli, a priest of Qotal, approaching.

Like the others of his order, Xatli prided himself on personal cleanliness, but now his once-white robe was tattered and stained from the rigors of the flight. His cheeks, plump and rosy two months earlier, now formed sagging jowls on either side of his face. The eldest of the priests among the refugees, he had become the unofficial spokesman for his sect, which had become once again the dominant faith of the people.

Ironically he had been about to take the vow of silence that was the highest badge of honor known to his order when the disaster that the Nexalans called the Night of Wailing had disrupted his plans. Now he employed his skills as an eloquent speaker often, to raise the spirits of the refugees during their long marches through the desert.

"Can I do anything to help?" the cleric inquired hesitantly. "The blessings of the Plumed One have given me some small measure of healing."

"No. No thank you," Erixitl said, tensing.

"If not for you, think of the other life that grows within you," said the priest quietly, kneeling beside her.

Erix looked at him in surprise as Xatli smiled gently and continued. "The god who has chosen you has placed a heavy burden upon you. This I understand. But he would not have chosen you if you were not strong enough to bear the load."

He placed a hand on her shoulder, and she did not try to evade his touch. For a second, she felt a brief warmth, and a renewed sense of energy filled her. And then she couldn't help but pull away.

Xatli rose and bowed to Halloran. He turned once again toward Erixitl before he departed. "Know this, Chosen Sister. Our god is not unmerciful."

Hal feared for a moment that Erix would erupt in anger, for such had often been her response to talk of the Plumed Serpent. But instead she turned to him and nestled in the shelter of his embrace.

The moment was broken by a call from a nearby warrior. Worriedly Hal saw Erix start to climb to her feet. Knowing the futility of ordering her to rest, he helped her up.

"What is it?" she asked as several warriors, their tall emerald plumes swaying above their painted faces, trotted closer.

"We don't know what it means, sister," one announced, "but a great eagle has landed in the midst of the people. It stands and stares at us, as if in challenge."

"An eagle?" Erix's voice sang, once again vibrant. She hurried ahead of Hal, pulling away from his supporting arm until he had to trot to keep up with her.

The crowd of men, women, and children parted for Erixtl and Hal and soon they saw the bird, resting upon a large rock in the center of a vast and growing circle of humanity.

The eagle stood nearly as tall as a man. Its feathers, clean and smooth, etched its form in pristine black and white. From its vantage point on the rock, the bird's glittering yellow eyes looked down on the assemblage. Proud and noble of bearing, the eagle turned its head this way and that, until finally those keen eyes came to rest upon Erixitl.

For a moment, the great creature shimmered before them, as if the bright sunlight reflected from a rippled surface of water. Then the image grew larger, manlike.

The Mazticans around them gasped, many falling to the ground and pressing their faces in the earth. Others fell back, staring in awe as the shape of the bird changed.

"By Helm!" growled a burly legionnaire in the crowd, awestruck.

The shape of the bird remained visible, like a shade in the background, but overlaying it stood the image of a tall, brown-skinned man.

"Poshtli!" Erixitl whispered, scarcely daring to breathe the word aloud.

The noble stood tall and silent. A cloak of black and white feathers, faint but visible, swung from his shoulders. Gold plugs ornamented his lip, his nose, and his ears. The great beaked helmet of an Eagle Knight he carried under his arm, so that his long black hair flowed freely in the breeze. His other hand he raised, pointing southward and holding it there for several beats, then suddenly wheeling and pointing to the east before he lowered his hand.

For a long time, the image of the warrior stared at Erixitl, while the watchers remained breathless. Finally he bowed, a deep and honorable genuflection conferred to one of great power. A sudden gust of wind whirled a funnel of blowing sand through the crowd, and for a moment the image was obscured. When the wind and sand passed, there remained only the great eagle, still staring at Erixitl with those sharp black eyes.

Then the eagle raised its huge wings, driving powerful strokes toward the ground. With serene grace, the bird rose from the rock and glided over the heads of the assembled humanity. Slowly climbing, it soared in a vast circle around them before turning toward the southern horizon. The bird remained visible for many minutes, steadily climbing, always flying south.

"Lord Poshtli did not die in the volcano," Erix announced confidently as the Mazticans around them looked at her in wonder. The noble Eagle Warrior of Nexal, nephew of the city's late ruler, had been widely respected through his life and widely mourned after the Night of Wailing.

"Now he comes to us, with hope and promise," she continued. Though she spoke softly, everyone heard. "This is not an idle preaching of blind faith. This was a clear omen that stood here before us. We must follow him now—follow him to the south, and to our future."

\* \* \* \* \*

From the chronicles of Coton:

*Borne by the steed of the strangers, I ride toward the destiny of my own world.*

*The presence of the One Plumed God is nearby, imminent. I can feel his breath on my shoulders, propelling me. All the signs of the prophecy have been met; the pathway for his return lies open.*

*Yet I sense that a new obstacle has arisen from the chaos of the Night of Wailing. The acts of the bloody clerics and the fury of the Viperhand Cult have combined to bring a great presence into the world—a presence no longer content to be worshiped and fed from afar.*

*He is Zaltec, god of night and war, and he is here.*

*I sense his power in the darkness all around me. I see it in the vile corruption that has claimed his followers. What power it must be, to take tens of thousands of humans and pervert them into the beastlike forms we now see! He looms more mighty, more dangerous than ever, for now his legions of followers are not restrained by even the thin veneer of humanity.*

*Qotal is our hope, our only hope. Yet, witnessing the com-*

ing of Zaltec, I see that Qotal cannot enter this world un-aided. He will require the help of humans, of people who will open the path for him and guard it until he has re-turned to the True World. Then his power will meet Zaltec's, and the two gods—the two brothers—will wage war for the mastery of the land.

So now I ride, and I care not where the horse takes me. I will be one of those humans who opens that path and guards it; I will leave it to my destiny to guide me to the place.

# ❧ 3 ❧

# CONVERGING PATHS

The tortuous trail twisted across the sunbaked face of the mountain, climbing ever higher, forcing the monsters of the Viperhand to narrow their column to a single file for the ascent. The barren ridge above them marked the far southern extremity of the Valley of Nexal. Behind the beasts, to the north, the ruins of Nexal lay like a dark stain among the murky pools of the valley's four lakes.

Thousands of snarling, misshapen humanoids formed Hoxitl's army, now a column several miles long confined to the trail over the steep pass.

Other bands of monsters, smaller but just as fierce, had followed Hoxitl's orders to spread through the lands and villages around the city, scouring it for human prisoners and destroying any remaining evidence of its original inhabitants.

But this trail held the greatest number, the beasts that marched with Hoxitl at their head. Along the valley floor, they had marched in a shapeless mass, flowing across smooth ground like water sweeps across a beach. Here, however, the narrow path forced them to alter the form of their advance.

Hoxitl, the will of Zaltec burning in his breast, lumbered forward at the head of the column. He lunged up the ridge, pausing only for a few seconds at the jagged, windy crest. The trail behind him, crowded now with the troops of his army, clung precariously to the steep slide of the ridge. Any misstep could tumble one helplessly toward the sharp rocks below. Nevertheless, the monsters hastened to follow their master toward the desert.

Inevitably conflict arose among the chaotic mass. Near the top of the ridge, two brute-faced ogres jostled and pushed, eager to be first through the narrow pass. The file came to a stop behind them as they pounded each other with hamlike fists. Finally they closed in savage, snapping combat, each tearing chunks from the other's skin with sharp rips of their savage tusks.

For several seconds, the beasts teetered on the brink of the sheer drop, growling and snarling. Orcs, in a long column behind the huge ogres, cringed backward, away from the larger brutes' crushing blows.

Then a rumble of panic spread through the ranks as a huge presence loomed before them. Hoxitl, disturbed by the delay, reared upward, lashing out with his tail and striking several orcs from the cliffside.

The cleric beast shrieked his rage, pushing his way roughly through the column until he reached the battling ogres. The two monsters, suddenly distracted by the shadowy form looming over them, gaped stupidly upward.

"Fools! Imbeciles!" Hoxitl's shrieks of rage terrified them, yet, perversely, rooted their feet to the trail.

With one savage blow, he sent an ogre tumbling off the cliff, the beast's dying scream shattered by the jagged rocks below.

"This is the fate of the weak and the foolish among you! Let all pay heed!" he howled. "Save your warfare for the enemies—humans who still escape our vengeance!"

In the next instant, his paw, tipped by wicked talons, reached forward. The claws sliced into the other ogre's belly, tearing the creature's flesh and bowels in a spray of gore.

With a grunt of astonishment, the beast looked down as its insides gushed out onto the stony trail. Hoxitl's other paw lashed forward, tearing into the creature's neck and ripping the heavy skull away from the dying beast's body. Contemptuously he kicked the gory corpse off the edge, where it tumbled like a bundle of wet rags onto the jagged spines of rock below.

A flush of excitement tingled the cleric-beast's body as the scent of blood reached his nostrils. He felt the presence of the god of war—Zaltec was *near!* Eagerly Hoxitl turned his thoughts to the trail and the victims ahead.

"Advance!" howled the maned beast. Mindless of the blood spattering his feet, Hoxitl started through the pass.

Behind him, his grumbling file of monsters started to follow.

\* \* \* \* \*

Through the long subterranean night, the driders crept onward, gradually leaving the flaming seas of lava behind. No path upward greeted them, but this was satisfactory to the corrupted creatures of the drow. As dark elves, they had shunned the sun; now, as driders, they had little desire to walk the surface.

Yet only on the surface, sensed Darien, could they begin to wreak their vengeance. The queen of the driders now, she led her creatures eastward, thirsting for the blood of her enemies, desperately craving the chance to attack. Her albino skin, which had allowed her to conceal her drow nature among the humans, now set her apart from the black driders. Yet the fire that drove her to lead them came from within, blazing in hatred and power, giving her the strength to master her kin.

Her bitterness and hatred encompassed all the world and beyond, even including the dark form of Lolth, goddess of the drow. Yet, though she hated all things, she feared Lolth. Lolth had wounded her too profoundly, taking her lithe, female body and corrupting it into this malformed monstrosity, this hideous *creature!* And because of this, she feared Lolth.

She knew that the time for vengeance must wait for now until the driders recovered their strength. Allies—an army of them— would be necessary before the humans could be made to suffer the full wrath of the spider-beasts. She could not know that Lolth herself propelled her toward these allies.

Darien led her followers to the east, far from the volcanic reaches below central Maztica. Through great schisms in the limestone subsurface of the world they crept, finally reaching the jungled stretches of Payit. Always they traveled underground. Here great pools of water blocked their passage, but they plunged ahead, swimming for hours.

Once a channel of brine rose around them, and here she turned southward, for she knew that they approached the sea. Ever onward they pressed, until the dank, impenetrable recesses of the Far Payit jungle lurked above them. Now she was guided by a deep, primordial memory, a lingering awareness of a presence that the driders could employ for their own ends. Here, she sensed, they would find the tools of their vengeance, awaiting only her masterful command.

Darien did not sense the hand of Lolth in her discovery. She did not know that, once again, she had become a tool of that hateful goddess. Instead, she only knew that she herself burned with hatred, and perhaps now she discovered the means to act upon that malevolence.

They came upon the nest in a great, moss-draped cavern, far below the steaming jungles. All around her were the eggs, and the dormant forms of the giant ants. Thousands of them, her army, cowered here and awaited her command.

A myriad of dark antennae flicked upward as the driders entered through a narrow, connecting cavern. The soldiers rose to meet her, but Darien raised a hand and twisted it before her, employing the magic that had so empowered her as a drow. It did no less for the drider.

The soldiers, antennae quivering with tension, stood aside as the pale, spider-shaped woman-thing crept past. The red ants stiffened and jerked with conflicting compulsions, but the might of the drider held them at bay. Holding her torso erect, Darien at last confronted the queen.

The great insect, her belly bloated with eggs, sensed her doom in that moment. Glittering, multifaceted eyes faced the drider as Darien again raised a hand.

This time she barked a harsh command, and power flew from her lips, wrapping the queen in a hazy glow of blue sparks. For long moments, that arcane might surged, and the great form before her twisted in unspeakable agony. The segments of the queen's body bent and creaked, spilling eggs and ichor throughout the nest, until at last the magic tore her to pieces.

The great ants looked impassively at their queen's gory remains. Again antennae twitched along huge, dark columns of soldiers. Hundreds and hundreds of the creatures, each nearly as large as the driders themselves, observed the killing and saw the spidery creature that now claimed them. Darien raised a hand, and they obediently followed her forward and upward.

She had found her army, and now the driders' vengeance could begin.

\* \* \* \* \*

Erixitl looked at Halloran. She said nothing, but the joy radiating from her face was a great tonic for him. All around them the camp of the Mazticans was breaking up as the refugees once again started their southward trek.

He looked upward, at the soaring eagle, and shook his head in wonder at the miracle that had apparently befallen him.

"You told me all along Poshtli was alive," Hal admitted. "I shouldn't have doubted your faith."

"My faith." Erix smiled wryly. "My faith in Poshtli was one thing; why can't I find the same faith in Qotal?" She looked at the bright cloak that swung from her shoulders, touching it with her long brown fingers. "Perhaps there is a lesson for me in the return of our friend. Perhaps if I showed the same belief in the god who has chosen me . . ." She did not conclude the thought.

"*Something* must have brought him out of that mountain alive," Hal observed. "What's more likely than the power of Qotal?"

She looked at him seriously. "You're right, you know. I have to find the hope and the strength to keep searching. Poshtli could be the sign that brings me to that point. After all these days of running and fleeing, maybe there is a goal for us and for our child."

"The eagle will show us the way," said Hal, going to Erix and taking her hands. "But after all this is done, we'll go where we please. We won't run from anything, and we won't chase anything—just go and live where we want to."

She leaned against him and pulled his body close to hers. The slight roundness of her belly was a firm bond between them. "Where should we go, then?" she asked. "Where do you want to go?"

Hal was silent for a moment. "Someday I'd like to go back to the Sword Coast—with you. Would like to see my world?"

"I . . . don't know," she replied honestly. "It frightens me, the thought of going so far away. So much frightens me now!" He could hear her voice tighten and could feel the tension in her body.

He held her for a while, not speaking, and they stood together among the departing folk. His arms wrapped and protected her, and in the warmth of his embrace, once again she grew strong.

\* \* \* \* \*

Thousands of miles away, eastward across the Trackless Sea, the sun warmed a long coastline. Many nations thrived here, trading and building and warring among themselves. These lands, places with names such as Calimshan, Amn, Waterdeep, Tethyr, Moonshae, and the rest, had developed a certain smugness over the centuries.

Were they not the highest centers of culture and learning—indeed, of civilization itself—to be found among the Realms? True, the recent advances of nomadic horsemen, raging from the great central steppe, might give this smugness a short jolt. And of course the great oriental nations of Kara-Tur offered certain amenities not to be found here on the Sword Coast. . . .

But still, the center of everything that mattered couldn't be declared to be elsewhere, at least not by any rational individual.

The serene merchant princes of the Council of Amn considered themselves to be very rational indeed. Masters of all within their borders and influential over important matters without, the six anonymous men and women who ruled the mighty southern kingdom expected obedience and performance from those in their service.

Amn, a nation of traders, shippers, buyers, and sellers, controlled its empire not by the might of its swords nor the range of its catapults, but by the power of its gold. Governed by the six princes, all of whom kept their identities carefully concealed, Amnite trade extended across all the known Realms and worked its way toward unknown reaches as well.

These princes had invested a great deal into the expedition of Captain-General Cordell and his Golden Legion. More than a year had passed since the departure of that legion on its quest for gold over the western seas, and as yet no profits had found their way to the princely coffers.

Now the princes, each meticulously masked and robed, met in private session to discuss the disappearance of Cordell and—more significantly—the potential loss of their investment. The domed council chamber was darkened as usual, a further aid to the masquerade.

At last the golden doors opened softly and a courtier entered.

"Don Vaez is here," said the silken-dressed attendent.

"At last," rasped one of the princes from beneath his—or, perhaps, her—dark mask. "Send him in."

In moments, a tall figure passed through the door, removing his broad-brimmed hat with its ostrich-feather plume in a sweeping bow. The man stood erect again, a thin smile playing about his lips. He was smooth-shaven, with long blond, almost white locks that fell about his shoulders.

"Ah, Don Vaez, you may do us a great service," murmured another of the princes.

"As always, I exist to serve," offered Vaez, with another courtly bow.

"Indeed." The prince's sexless voice dripped with irony. "You know, of course, of the Golden Legion's expedition to the west?"

"Naturally. A great promise lay upon it. I trust there has not been . . . trouble?"

"For long months, we received steady messages through the Temple of Helm here in Amn. The Bishou, chief cleric of the mission, provided good reports. It seems that our expectations of gold were met, even exceeded, in this land Cordell had claimed for us."

Don Vaez's eyes gleamed, but he remained silent.

"Several months ago, however, these messages abruptly ceased," offered another prince, in a higher but still subtly masked voice. "We have reason to expect the worst."

"That explains many things," replied the adventurer. None of the merchants made any response, so Don Vaez continued. "Two dozen carracks gathering in Murann, companies of harquebus, crossbow, and horse. Even some of the veterans of Cordell's legion, those that did not sail with him to the west. The rumors that Amn has decided it needs an army. . . ."

One of the princes raised a cautious hand. "We do not need an army, not *here*. But quite possibly such a force will be required in order to see a proper and deserved return on our investment."

"Do you suspect that Cordell has betrayed you?" inquired Don Vaez sympathetically. He now knew why he had been summoned to appear before the council. He knew, and he was well pleased.

"We do not know. Perhaps he ran into greater difficulties than he anticipated; he took but five hundred men. Now we will send nearly three times that number on his trail. We know, through the temple, what course he sailed, even where he made landfall."

The air seemed to grow heavy in the room for the space of a brief pause. Don Vaez waited.

"We want you to lead the expedition after him," a prince finally offered. "We send you after our gold, and to learn Cordell's fate. If he lives, you are to bring him back—in chains, if necessary."

Another of the princes raised a golden bell, shaking it slightly to elicit a musical tinkling. In moments, the golden doors opened to reveal the courtier who had admitted Don Vaez.

"Summon Pryat Devane," ordered the prince curtly.

In a few moments, the cleric entered, bowing first to the

princes and then to Don Vaez. The adventurer studied the short pryat. The clean-shaven priest wore a close-fitting cap of steel and a loose robe of fine silk. His hands were cloaked in the silver gauntlets of Helm.

"Pryat Devane was Bishou Domincus's closest aide," explained the prince.

"You're the one who maintained contact with Domincus?" asked Don Vaez.

"Indeed, my lord. Every few weeks, through the conduit of our faith, the Bishou informed me of the progress of the mission. They made good progress for a time. They penetrated to the heart of the continent, to a city that was overflowing with gold. Then . . . silence."

"That's a mystery we'll soon solve," the captain said heartily. "You'll be making the journey with me, I presume?"

"With my lord's pleasure," explained the pryat, with another bow.

"Of course!"

"I am sure you will find the pyrat a useful addition to your expedition," remarked one of the princes. "We have provided him with a small gift, that he may aid you more effectively—a flying carpet."

Don Vaez nodded to the cleric and then bowed, more deeply than ever, to the council. Indeed, he could think of many uses for a cleric that could fly. As he turned from the masked princes, a sly smile toyed with his lips. The task pleased him—pleased him greatly—for Cordell had long eclipsed the Don's own reputation as a loyal mercenary.

And to use Cordell's own men against him! The irony did not escape Don Vaez. The Council of Six had granted him the opportunity of a lifetime! When he finished with it, he determined that his name would hold a high place in the annals of the Sword Coast.

\* \* \* \* \*

Cordell shifted uncomfortably in his saddle. He had always been a hard campaigner, but never had he pushed himself as hard as in the last months, since the escape from

Nexal. Now there was no part of his body that did not ache, throb, or cry out from fatigue, hunger, or thirst.

He looked across the vast encampment. His own legionnaires, the hundred and fifty that still survived, spread in a ring around him, working at polishing and sharpening weapons, oiling tattered boots, or sewing plates of armor together where the desert heat had rotted worn straps.

Six of the men, led by young Captain Grimes, rode patrol in the desert. They needed more scouts, but only fifteen horses remained to the legion—fifteen horses in all the True World—and the unfortunate steeds all were near total exhaustion.

So were the men, for that matter, he realized. Now his legionnaires, the remnants of his once valiant force, fled alongside their former enemies, the Nexala. The greater enemy of the monstrous horde menaced both groups equally. He realized with bitter irony that the gold of Nexal had also been lost. There was no longer any reason to make war with the Mazticans.

One bright spot in the months of flight and disaster had been the loyalty of the Maztican warriors from the nation of Kultaka. When he had first entered that nation on his march inland, Kultaka had resisted his legion furiously. Following Cordell's victory, however, the young Kultakan chief, Tokol, had become his most staunch ally. Now some six thousand Kultakan warriors marched alongside the Nexalans and the legionnaires. The ancient rivalry—hatred, in reality—between Kultaka and Nexal had been temporarily subordinated to the pressing need to escape the monstrous horde that threatened them all.

Nearby Cordell saw Captain Daggrande, the doughty dwarven captain of the crossbow, talking with a small cluster of Maztican archers. Daggrande was one of three dozen dwarves to live through the Night of Wailing. Unlike most of his comrades, Daggrande had learned to speak the Nexalan tongue.

For a moment, the general's mind drifted as he thought of other men—Captain Garrant, Bishou Domincus, many faithful soldiers—who had met their ends in the dying city. He thought of the mountainous trove of gold there, now buried beneath tons of rubble and guarded by tusked and taloned beasts. Once the loss of that gold had seemed the end of the world to him. Now it seemed but one more thread in the doom that still threatened him and his men.

Still, there remained the gold buried within the walls of Helmsport. This, the trove he had claimed from the conquest of Ulatos, had been left behind when the legion marched to Nexal. All of the men who knew the exact location of the treasure had accompanied him to Nexal; among the small garrison left at the port were none who knew where the gold was buried.

The general dismounted and walked over to Daggrande as the dwarven veteran looked up from his discussion of weaponry. Cordell winced inwardly at the look of guarded suspicion in his old comrade's eyes. Even Daggrande loses faith in me!

"How can you speak that Helm-cursed tongue?" the commander asked, joking.

Daggrande ignored the humorous intent. "It only makes sense, since it seems as though we might have to spend the rest of our lives here."

"Nonsense! We've got good men left. As soon as we get out of this desert, I see no reason why we won't be able to reach the coast and make ourselves some ships."

Daggrande grunted, and Cordell sensed blame in the sound. His own conscience growled at him daily. If only I had been satisfied with the gold we had already gained! Why did I march on Nexal? Now an expedition that had, at one point, owned a tenfold profit was reduced to struggling for escape for the fortunate survivors.

"We're leaving today," Daggrande said. He gestured across the camp, and Cordell saw that many of the Mazticans had already begun to trudge wearily from the valley, heading southward in search of more food and water.

"So I heard. I don't know why, though. There's still enough provisions here for a few days."

"We march to follow a bird. That's what these warriors tell me, anyway," Daggrande added. "It seems some eagle came to camp, and Halloran's woman decided we all should follow it south." His tone as he spoke of "Halloran's woman" remained carefully neutral.

Cordell turned away, suddenly irritated with the dwarf. Daggrande started to pack up his weapons, preparing to march.

Among the warriors, Cordell saw Chical, proud chief of the Eagle Knights. Chical wore his cloak of black and white feathers and his wooden helmet with its curved-beak visor extending over his rugged face. The man had been a stalwart enemy, leading the attacks against Cordell's legion during the struggle to escape Nexal, but then quickly realizing the greater threat when the world had come to pieces around them all.

Now Chical had become the accepted war chief of all the Nexalans, though there had never been any formal acknowledgment of such status. Cordell had found him to be a proud, brave warrior who understood perhaps better than any of his people that his world was never again going to be the same.

He looked across the valley, spotting Erixitl easily by the brightness of her cloak. She stood beside the trail as a wide column of Mazticans marched past. Beside her, tiny in the distance, he recognized Halloran.

How had that man reached inside these people the way he had? How, indeed, had Daggrande been able to understand and converse with them? The general felt a sharp jolt of envy for these soldiers, both of his legion but now his no longer. They might even be able to make a home here.

To Cordell, Maztica remained a great, faceless void. But where once it had been a space beckoning to adventure, promising reward, now it was a nightmare, threatening extinction, promising only constant flight and terror.

His reverie of self-pity suddenly broke as he sensed someone approaching behind him and saw the pudgy figure of Kardann, the Assessor of Amn, hurrying toward him. Appointed by the council of the merchant princes, the accountant had been an annoyance and a bother throughout the expedition. Now the mere sight of him aroused Cordell's ire. Why did the useless assessor live when so many good men had perished?

"Hello, general," gasped the red-faced accountant, mopping his brow.

"Yes?" inquired Cordell coldly.

"I've been thinking," began Kardann, speaking carefully. He crossed his arms over his chest and met the commander's gaze. "Perhaps we can go back to Nexal. That gold can't be too hard to find. And with this group as an army, we could surely drive those monsters away from there!"

"We?" Cordell asked angrily. He well knew that Kardann's taste for battle grew in direct proportion to the distance between the accountant and the prospective combat. "I've had enough of your mad schemes, Kardann!" he snapped. "Look around you. Do these people look like an army? Even the warriors can think of nothing more than protecting their families!"

Kardann's eyes glowered, but finally he turned and stalked away from the Captain-General. Cordell watched him go, feeling his own frustration rise again. Pushed by the circumstances of their surroundings, he saw no prospect other than flight. Yet this fact burned painfully inside of him. He didn't like to yield to destiny.

Instead, Cordell liked to sweep fate before him.

\* \* \* \* \*

From the chronicles of Coton:

*In flight before the ranks of chaos.*

*The horse carries me like the wind across the face of the True World, but always the places I pass are realms of darkness, destruction, and despair. We fly along the road to Cordotl and pass the smoking ruins of that town.*

*Here the monsters of the Viperhand have erected a great edifice atop the pyramid, like a great skull image of Zaltec. They seek to raise their bloodthirsty god to new heights, but they do not understand that it was he who cast them down among the beasts. The folk of Cordotl are gone, either fled or given to the fanged jaws of the war god in sacrifice.*

*Now past ruined fields of mayz, the great flat valley between Cordotl and Palul that has been trampled into mud. Palul, too, lies in ruins, though again the pyramid has been raised to new heights and crowned with its grotesque image.*

*Here the horse carries me up the face of the ridge, crossing back and forth along a winding trail. We see none of the beasts of the Viperhand here, for they have been summoned back to Nexal by Hoxitl.*

*Finally the horse crests the ridge, and we pause before a small cottage. It is a place of holiness, I sense, and strong pluma.*

*The man who comes to the door to greet me is old; he is also blind.*

# ❧ 4 ❧

# WARNINGS IN THE SUN

The vast circle of gleaming silver lay quiet, still dark under the fringe of morning shadow, deep within the mountain's central crater. The chiefs of the desert dwarves sat patiently atop the rim of the volcano, opposite the rising sun. Soon the miracle of the Sunstone would begin.

Luskag felt Pullog shift uneasily beside him, and the chief of Sunhome smiled to himself. The ritual of the Sunstone held risks to the faint of spirit, and Pullog had never before experienced the revelations of the gods through the great silver lake. Doubtless he had heard tales of men driven mad, of dwarves blinded by the searing truth of their visions.

Still, Luskag felt certain his fellow chief—in fact, all the chiefs of his clan, gathered here at his request—would face the Sunstone steadfastly. He wouldn't have brought them to the mountaintop if it were otherwise. And Luskag understood that only if all the dwarves experienced the same revelation would cooperative action be possible.

The sun crept higher, and soon its rays washed over the western shore of the silver disk. As the minutes passed, the area of brightness grew. The bright metal gleamed with a transcendent purity, perfectly smooth. As large as a huge courtyard, the metal showed no trace of wrinkle or dip.

Then slowly the surface of the lake moved, like liquid. With serene grace, the lake began to spin, as if a giant vortex compelled its slow, majestic wheel. The shimmering glow increased as the sun rose.

The vortex gathered momentum as the sun spread across its surface, until finally the rays seemed to focus in the very center. There every color became one in a magnified, mirrored display of the sun's power.

A beam of hot light lanced into the desert dwarves atop the rim of the crater. For a long time, the squatting figures remained immobile, transfixed by brilliance.

Luskag stared into the white glow. For a time, he saw nothing, but then a creeping darkness came into view in the very center of the glow. Slowly it expanded, reaching outward with smoky tendrils that grew like the limbs of a spider stretching out from a black, venomous body.

Now Luskag stared at the expanding cloud, and he felt glimmerings of deep fear seize his soul. For the first time, he felt the true, awe-inspiring might of the Sunstone, and his fear quickly blossomed into stark terror.

The smoky limbs became solid tentacles, grasping upward, threatening to seize him and drag him down into darkness. Never before had the images of the Sunstone been so tangible, so ultimately terrifying. The dark tendrils twisted into a circle, and suddenly they framed a place in the vision—a place that he knew.

The City of the Gods! He saw the great pyramid rising from the sands, impossibly beautiful. Around it sprawled the other ruins, rows and rows of columns, massive portals with no buildings, and tall mounds of sand that betokened mysterious shapes beneath.

Like smoky limbs of pure, unadulterated devastation, the tentacles wrapped around the ruins in a doleful embrace. Luskag's chest tightened in pain as he saw the blackness creep toward the pyramid, slowing masking its piercing beauty. At the center of that bright swirl of color, Luskag saw a brilliant flower of light, a blossom so heartbreakingly beautiful that it cried out for his protection.

And shelter it required, for now the encircling tendrils of darkness threatened to smother it, forever blotting its beauty from the face of the earth.

Luskag did not see a nearby chieftain, overcome by terror, leap to his feet and try to turn away. None of the desert dwarves heard him cry out in despair. Even had they watched, they would not have seen the tentacles wrap his body in an iron-hard grip, for there was no thing of substance in the air.

But they were nonetheless real in the mind. The unfortunate chieftain, his face wracked by horror, toppled inward, rolling and scraping down the steep inner surface of the crater. He did not stop until he reached the great silver lake.

Still unseen by the others, his body struck the liquid metal and instantly disappeared. No ripples spread outward from the scene of his vanishing.

Luskag remained transfixed. He saw the darkness more clearly now, as a black blanket of doom that seeped into the House of Tezca and spread across his desert home like an all-consuming plague. Finally the last gleaming brightness from the City of the Gods darkened and then vanished.

He stared into a vast, limitless expanse of blackness.

Finally the vision broke as the sun climbed higher into the morning sky. The chiefs awakened from the thrall of the gods, frightened and dismayed. They did not talk of their vision, yet by looking into each other's eyes, they knew that they had shared a common experience. Even the absence of one of their number went, for the time being, unremarked. They had all come perilously close to such a fate.

Yet now, at least, they knew what they had to do.

\* \* \* \* \*

Halloran watched Erix carefully as they walked. He was relieved to see that her gait was steady, her spirits high. Indeed, she paid heed to little else than the great eagle that soared lazily before and high above them.

"Remember," he finally offered, "you can ride if you start to get tired."

"Really, I'm fine. The walking feels good." She smiled patiently at him. Her humor remained even as Xatli caught up with them. The priest puffed slightly, mopping his brow.

"This sun is enough to broil me!" he groaned. "But I guess that's why they call it a desert."

Erixitl laughed, then looked upward, making sure that the great eagle remained in view. Poshtli wheeled majestically, just to the south.

"His return is a miracle, don't you think?" inquired Xatli.

"A miracle, perhaps. A just reward for his courage. Is it the magic of *pluma?*" she queried in turn.

"Or the blessing of Qotal. Can you not admit, sister, that his goodness could have brought Poshtli back to us?"

For once, Erixitl seemed to ponder his question. "Perhaps. I know that it is the most joyous news I can imagine."

"It is a sign to you of the Plumed One's pleasure," observed the cleric quietly.

"How do you know that?" asked Erix in good-humored skepticism.

Xatli shrugged, grinning. "I don't. But it could be, couldn't it?"

Erixitl looked at him curiously, without replying, so the puffing priest continued. "I only mean to suggest that you need not fight the will of the god. You are his chosen daughter; that much we all know. He spared your life on the Night of Wailing, and you have led your people away from the horrors behind us. He has a great purpose in mind for you, Erixitl of Palul!"

She turned back to the trail before her, her expression serious. "I *have* fought against that will—that purpose." Once again she looked at the great eagle, wheeling lazily above. Her joy at Poshtli's return remained, and she admitted to herself that his presence seemed miraculous.

"I shall try to accept his wishes, to do as he wills," she finally promised, almost inaudibly.

\*     \*     \*     \*     \*

Jhatli hurried toward the rise in the undulating desert terrain, panic urging him forward. How could he lose a thousand people? He asked himself the question angrily, but then his body weakened with relief as he reached the crest and looked into the shallow, windswept vale beyond.

Quickly the youth tensed again, mindful that he would let no one know that he had been lost. Already the hours of fright faded, and he began to look upon his daylong trek as a sort of grand exploration.

That, in fact, is how he had gotten separated from the

column of refugees in the first place. In the valley before him trudged a small part of the survivors of Nexal, trailing the vast mass by several days. These included some of the weaker and injured folk, many of whom had already perished on the trek through the desert.

They followed the wide valley on the well-trodden trail blazed by the main body. For most of its length, that pathway wound through parched desert valleys, surrounded by bleak, rocky heights or vast expanses of rolling dunes. But every so often—two to three days' march apart—the trail descended into a deeper valley, and here water had somehow burst from the ground. In these valleys, the procession remained for a few days, resting and preparing for the next march before the food was totally exhausted. Thus the straggling groups such as Jhatli's still found sustenance as they moved along after the rest.

Jhatli and several other youths approaching the age of warriorhood served as the scouts and runners for the band. In this constant, wearing routine he had begun to find solace from the nightmare he had left behind in Nexal. The images of his mother, swallowed by the steaming crack opening in the ground, or his older brother, torn asunder by a monstrous green beast even as he bought time for Jhatli to flee, still lived in his mind. He had not seen his father die, but Jhatli knew he could never have escaped the crumbled house alive.

These visions remained with Jhatli throughout each long night, and so he filled the hours of light with hard work and complete vigilance. At dawn of this day, the young man had taken up his bow and obsidian-tipped arrows and his flint dagger, setting out to explore a shallow canyon that seemed to parallel the course of the valley.

But the canyon had deepened and diverged in course from the valley followed by the rest of the group. Finally forced to scale a rough, cactus-studded cliff, Jhatli had hurried in order to rejoin his family by sunset.

Or at least, what remained of his family. He had fled with his father's brother and the man's two surviving wives. In a wide, straggling column a mile long, the folk of that family and a hundred others marched steadily southward, along the trail of the Nexala. Weary, but determined not to let his exhaustion show, Jhatli strutted toward the distant group.

Then he froze, suddenly alarmed. He hadn't noticed the clouds of dust roiling along the opposite side of the vale. Now, however, he saw creatures—*huge* creatures!— trundling from the rocks. Vaguely manlike in shape, they loomed over the humans before them. Hundreds of others followed these monstrous forms, merely human-sized but just as beastlike of aspect.

Even at this distance, he could tell that they were armed and that they were attacking! Wave by wave, the creatures burst from concealment. Jhatli heard snarls and howls, mingled with the terrified screams of women and children.

"No!" Jhatli howled his anger and sprinted forward, watching the people reel backward from the surprise attack.

The initial slaughter quickly gave way to full massacre as the mostly defenseless Mazticans tried to flee, but quickly fell to the talons of the attackers. The few warriors and armed youths leaped bravely to the defense, but the superior numbers of the foe and crushing strength of the attack soon doomed them to a man.

Gasping and sobbing, Jhatli slowed his pace. He realized that he was too late to fight, for already the killing was complete.

"Monsters!" he cried, shaking a fist. Several of the beasts, a few hundred paces away, looked up and growled.

"I will avenge my people! You will all be slain!" Furiously he nocked an arrow to his bow and let fly, though the missile carried barely half the distance. Now, he saw with grim satisfaction, several of the smaller man-beasts started toward him. The creatures' pig eyes were narrow in their bestial faces, above beastlike muzzles that gaped to display long, curved teeth. Yet their hands and arms were manlike and clutched the *macas* and shields of Maztican warriors.

Jhatli nocked another arrow, drew back his bow, and waited, using the first shot as his range mark. Squinting, he released the missile and watched it soar true toward its target. It struck the beast in the chest with a solid thunk, and the creature cried out as the force of the shot knocked it to the earth.

But the thing snarled and climbed back to its feet while its companions broke into a trot. More of the beasts looked up from the gory trophies around them.

Jhatli sensed the futility of further combat and quickly turned away. He paced himself slightly faster than the lumbering beasts pursuing him, and as he had expected, they soon broke off the chase.

The young man jogged southward as night fell across the House of Tezca. He felt a dull pain for the deaths he had witnessed this day. But too much of his recent life had been spent in sorrow and mourning. Now, Jhatli decided, it was time to think of revenge.

\* \* \* \* \*

A dense thicket of jungle growth masked the mouth of the cave, indistinguishable on the outside from the rest of the bramble-covered slope. From within, however, the verdancy merely proved that the surface world lay beyond.

Darien, leading the column, paused and listened. The white drider sensed the sunlight before her, and her old sense of revulsion returned. But she was a dark elf no longer, and the light of day was not a thing that could master her.

"*Incendrius!*" she cried, pointing a pale finger at the obstructing foliage. The power of fiery magic blasted the lush barrier, and the leaves and branches crackled into smoke. Without a pause, she pressed forward, creeping for the first time in months into the surface world.

Behind her followed the rest of the driders, their black longbows held ready. The spider-beasts walked with mechanical, insectlike motions of their eight legs. Their weapons, however, they wielded with the familiar fluid movements of drow veterans.

Following the driders came the army of giant ants. The red insects lurched awkwardly but quickly from the cavern. Antennae tested the air before them while their huge, blank eyes looked about the jungle. The creatures of Lolth emerged from the darkness into a world that lay vulnerable and unsuspecting before them. Immediately the ants began to eat, and as the file emerged from the cave, a steadily expanding area of devastation grew around the entrance.

The ants turned to trees, bushes, even grass, tearing and chewing, reducing all to a wasteland. They pulled the bark from the trees, killing centuries-old forest giants in a matter of moments. Hard, knife-edged mandibles ripped and splintered the wood of the forest, while more and more of the monstrous insects poured from the cave.

Darien and the other driders began to move, compelling the ants to follow their new masters. Still more of the creatures emerged from the cave, expanding into a column twenty paces wide, steadily growing in length, pressing through the jungle.

And everywhere the ants destroyed.

*　*　*　*　*

"Do you know where he's leading us? Or why he comes in the body of an eagle?" Halloran wondered aloud about the majestic bird wheeling gracefully above them.

"No . . . of course not." Erixitl, too, followed Poshtli with her eyes. "I saw something in his eyes, though, when he perched on that rock. A message, or a plea of some kind. It seemed to promise hope."

"We could use a little of that," Hal agreed.

They looked backward from the low rise where they rested, along with a hundred others who had collapsed to the ground in exhaustion. The file of refugees filled the valley behind them, stretching to the dusty horizon in the north. Before them, the column continued unbroken to another rise, perhaps a mile away. A further elevation, even higher, beckoned beyond the next ridge.

"How is your strength, today, sister?" The voice, behind them, signified the approach of Xatli.

Erixitl looked at the priest, a wan smile across her dust-

and sweat-streaked face. "I'll make it the rest of the afternoon, but I think I'll sleep well tonight."

The priest chuckled and lowered himself to the ground beside the couple. "You will have earned your sleep, for certain," he agreed. "May Qotal see that you are untroubled by dreams of ill."

Erix looked upward, quickly spotting the eagle as Poshtli soared over the winding trail that led steadily, endlessly southward. "Once I would have argued with you, you know," she told the priest. "But now I can only hope that the blessings of Qotal are real, that he *will* return to us."

She sighed, then asked no one in particular, "Without that hope, what do we have?" She met the eyes of an old woman who walked slowly along the trail, clutching the arm of a young man. The woman smiled, and then the steady march carried her away. But her face was replaced by others—a pair of young children holding hands; a man carrying a child; a husband and wife. All of them looked at Erix, and each sought some measure of comfort and hope from her face. She tried desperately to communicate her own sense of hope.

"Faith can only lighten your burdens," declared the priest. "The signs have been fulfilled; his return is imminent! Accept his help, and you will gain his everlasting strength!"

"But it must be soon!" the woman said, sitting up and staring into the priest's dark eyes. Slowly Xatli nodded. He understood.

"My friends!" A voice pulled their attention toward the front of the column and they saw the broad-shouldered form of Gultec approach. The Jaguar Knight wore his tunic of spotted jaguar skin, with the helmet that framed his face through the open jaws.

"Gultec!" Erix cried, brightening immediately. The lanky Jaguar Knight crossed the ground in long strides, coming back toward them beside the file of Nexalans who marched steadily southward. In moments, he reached them and squatted, resting easily on his haunches. "What did you find?" she asked, seeing the look of promise in the warrior's thin smile.

"Water. A day and a half away. A large lake, with marshes—and even fish!" The warrior's eyes flashed as he conveyed the news. "To the southwest . . . this trail leads directly there."

"That's splendid!" Erixitl looked skyward. The great eagle wheeled overhead, as if patiently waiting for them.

"Perhaps we can remain there for a while," said Halloran. "Let everyone rest and restore their strength."

"Yes," said Erixitl absently as she cast another look skyward. Hal knew that she would only be content to rest as long as the eagle did not urge them on.

There was also the matter of her father. When the two of them had journeyed to Nexal before the Night of Wailing, he had seemed safe in his house, high on the ridge above the town of Palul. Now, with chaos spreading across the land, the blind old man's life could not help but be endangered. Erix spoke of him only rarely, but Halloran knew that Lotil was much on her mind. He, too, worried and wondered about the old man. Yet he accepted the fact that they could not go to him—not with the horde of the Viperhand looming between them.

With the growing life of their child, the man knew that his wife needed a quiet, secure place to live, to go through her pregnancy and to make a home. Yet for now they could have none of that, and this knowledge tore deeply at his soul.

"I hope that we may have that time," Gultec added, "but I fear it will not be so. I myself may have to leave you."

"Leave us? Why?" Erixitl looked at the Jaguar Knight with genuine fondness.

"I owe a debt to one who is my master in all ways, in a place very far from here. He granted me freedom to journey to Nexal, to witness the shape of the threat looming over the world. But always I await his summons to return, and when he calls I must obey."

"Have you been called?" asked Halloran.

"No, but I sense . . . *things* in the air around me, in the earth beneath my feet. Terrors stalk the land—terrors beyond those we know and already fear. It is this, I am certain, that will call me back to Tulom-Itzi."

Erixitl nodded, meeting the warrior's gaze as her own eyes misted. "We cannot long escape the needs of . . . fate," she said.

"Or gods." Gultec smiled, raising his eyes but still speaking to Erix. "Perhaps we can use whatever help is offered."

Erix sighed. Abruptly she turned away from the priest, from all the Mazticans, and started away from the procession. Halloran stepped after her.

He took her hand, silently accompanying her as they walked slowly over the brushy, rock-strewn ground. He sensed her need to get away from the silent, shuffling mass of people. He tried, by his presence, to comfort and shelter her.

Finally Erixitl sat on a boulder. She was not out of breath, but lines of strain showed around her eyes and mouth. Halloran sat beside her.

"They all need so much," she said finally. "And all we can offer them is *hope!* When will something *happen?* How long do we have to wait?"

"We're alive, we're healthy," Halloran said. "The important thing is to stay that way. The rest will take care of itself." It has to! he added silently.

While the people of Maztica marched past, she leaned against him and he held her for a while. Then Halloran saw a horseman galloping toward them. At the sound of hoof-beats, Erix stiffened and stood up.

"Hello, milady . . . Halloran," grunted the rider, Captain Grimes, as he dismounted. "We've got some bad news."

"What is it?" asked Erixitl.

"A young lad just caught up with the rear scouts. Seems he was with a group bringing up the rear. They were attacked, massacred almost to the last man, woman, and child! He gave some details. Sounds to me like it was orcs and ogres."

"How far back?" asked Hal.

"Don't know. He said it happened this morning, so not more than a few miles."

"It's more than that to the next water," Erix reminded them.

"There's another question," said Hal, suddenly looking skyward. "Gultec said that the water lay to the southwest, right?"

"Yes," Erix said, also looking upward. And as she did, she understood Halloran's concern.

The eagle had veered away from their path, now soaring with greater speed. His path lay eastward.

\* \* \* \* \*

Zochimaloc arose early on a mist-shrouded morning, passing from his small house through his garden. Soon he reached the broad, grassy street leading to the observatory.

The air lay dense across the jungles of Far Payit. The great buildings of Tulom-Itzi stood like sentinels against the fog, but the bright mosaics, fountains, and *pluma* bedecking the structures merged into a pale sameness, diffused by the creeping mists.

The old man tried to shake off a feeling of dull menace, but he could not. Resolutely he turned toward the dome-roofed observatory. There, so many times before, he had found the answers to his questions in the stars.

The city in the jungle was silent at this early hour, as it was silent for all the day and night. The great buildings emerged from the mist and melted away again, monuments to the hundred thousand or more who had once built Tulom-Itzi and mastered the surrounding lands.

But most of them were gone now, and the vast city sheltered a population perhaps a tenth as large as it once held.

Now, as always, Zochimaloc found the emptiness of his city strangely soothing, as if he lived in a library or museum dedicated to the study of people, not among the people themselves.

Yet no longer could he deny that fact, for he knew that the gap between Tulom-Itzi and the world around it would soon close violently. The feeling had risen within him for years, and it was the reason he had brought the Jaguar Knight Gultec here, to train the men of his city for war. This Gultec had done, though Tulom-Itzi was no nation of warriors.

Gultec was gone now, and Zochimaloc sensed the importance of his student's mission. Soon, however, it would be necessary to call him home.

The old Maztican finally entered the observatory. The building, with its domed roof of carefully cut stone, stood in the center of Tulom-Itzi, a place of sacred peace and wisdom. Now Zochimaloc went to the center of the round chamber and looked at the apertures in the roof. The stars lined up with those openings at precise moments, he knew.

But today it was not the stars he sought. Zochimaloc needed deeper, more practical knowledge, and so he produced a small bit of plumage from his belt. He kindled a small fire in the floor, and then dropped the tufts of feathers in a ring about the bright blaze.

The feathers caught the light and dazzled with colors. On the encircling wall of the building, the feathershadows appeared as black pictures, marching around the observatory, around Tulom-Itzi.

They marched as a file of giant ants.

For a long time, Zochimaloc touched the earth beneath his body. He touched it, and he sensed its distress. Waves of pain radiated outward from the ground. He sensed a scourge upon the land, and it was a threat that he now understood to be near.

Hours later, though still well before dawn, the moon rose. The sliver in the east cast its pale beam through a slit in the building's ceiling, and soon the moonlight washed over Zochimaloc.

He sat, immobile, until the moonlight faded. Even then he waited, until finally the cool blue of dawn lightened the eastern sky. Then his eyes closed and his lips moved.

"Gultec, we need you," he whispered.

\* \* \* \* \*

Hoxitl thrilled to the extent of the slaughter, howling gloriously as his minions grunted across the battlefield, ripping and tearing the corpses until the victims no longer resembled humans.

"Let that be their lesson," chortled the great beast that had once been patriarch of Zaltec. "They will be even less human than us! And the might of Zaltec will prevail!"

For a long night, the beastly army remained on the bloody field. More and more of the monsters joined them, for the attacking group had only been a small advance guard. It pleased Hoxitl to see how effectively they had slain a group of the enemy that had outnumbered them substantially.

Of course, most of the humans had been helpless, but that mattered not to the maned figure. Indeed, he identified the fact as his greatest advantage: His forces could travel quickly and strike hard, unencumbered by noncombatants. The refugees, on the other hand, moved slowly and tried to protect the great majority of their number, the ill, the sick, the aged, a majority that could offer no aid in battle.

Dimly Hoxitl remembered the great sacrifices with which he had celebrated victories as a priest. What a waste, he realized now, to capture and hold captives for ritual execution when it was so much more gratifying and appropriate to slay them on the field.

The idea settled into the beastly, but still shrewd, mind of the monster. Hoxitl began to see some of the reasons that the armies of Maztica had suffered so horribly in combat with the foriegn invaders. The strangers had no such compulsion to take their opponents alive.

"Feast, my children! Feast and exult!" he howled in the language that had become his own. The orcs and ogres and trolls understood their master, for they, too, spoke in the bastardized tongue that had come to them during the Night of Wailing.

"Feast and give thanks to Zaltec for his mercy!" cried the priest-monster, startling the vast assemblage of gore-soaked humanoids.

"Yes, you hear me true—thanks to Zaltec!" Hoxitl's voice rumbled through the shallow valley as he surprised even himself with the power he felt thrumming through him at the name of his god. He thought of the great stone monolith, the statue back in Nexal that had come to embody all the might and terror of this bloodthirsty god.

"We will wage war in your name across the width and breadth of the True World!" gloated the beast, tearing a heart from the cold corpse of an old man and holding it upward.

And Zaltec heard, and rumbled his pleasure.

\* \* \* \* \*

From the chronicles of Coton:

*In the nearness of Qotal, now the True World knows its hope.*

*I sit with the blind featherworker, Lotil, and we hear the beasts snuffling outside the house. The horse of the legionnaire remains in the building with us, while the monsters of the Viperhand prowl without.*

*They plunder each home on the ridge above Palul, smashing and burning and looting. Great cries of glee explode from monstrous maws when a golden treasure or piece of salted meat is discovered.*

*I fear not so much for myself, but for the old man. The blessing of the Plumed One surrounds me, and if his pleasure brings me to my end amid this sea of chaos, so be it. The plumaworker, however, must be spared this fate. He is needed for something greater. What this is, I cannot know, but I shall stay with him and try to help him fulfill his destiny.*

*For some reason, they pass the house of Lotil, these panting monsters, and do not enter. And so we wait out the scourge, alone and helpless, yet somehow alive.*

*Again I sense the imminence of the One Plumed God.*

# 5

# A GOD ALIVE

Seabirds wheeled above the great white sails, cawing and diving at the foaming wake. Don Vaez left Murann at the head of a proud fleet of twenty-five heavy carracks and more than fifteen hundred armed men, all of them thirsting for gold.

The young captain, his silver-blond locks flowing freely in the wind, stood in the bow of the lead ship. Scribes, sorcerers, and clerics had briefed him well on Cordell's voyage, and though he sailed toward a land of mystery, he at least knew that land lay before him.

"And by Helm, it will be mine!"

Like many men of action, Don Vaez had little use for gods, except as they could help him in his endeavors. As such, he had casually adopted Helm as his patron deity, for a god of eternal vigilance is of obvious worth to a soldier.

Don Vaez struck a determined pose, well aware that his men watched him. A great believer in leadership by appearance, he constantly took pains to see that his troops saw him in the best possible light. To this end, he had no less than four wardrobe trunks stored in his cabin, so that he could insure a fashionable and well-groomed presence at all times.

The captain allowed himself to reminisce as the sea wind tugged at his hair. He had followed a long and convoluted road to reach this point, but now every audacious step of that dangerous path would be made worthwhile.

The fleet progressed steadily, under the guidance of a veteran navigator named Rodolfo. Indeed, the man had been hailed as one of the most fearless sailors on the Trackless Sea. Years before, he had served Cordell when the captain-general had needed a fleet. Since then, the navigator had returned to land, though he had been willing enough to accept the fee offered by the princes to induce him to join this expedition.

"A fresh wind moves us. We make good time," remarked Rodolfo, coming to join Don Vaez at the rail. The commander nodded disinterestedly, content to leave such details to his navigator. With a thin grimace, Rodolfo stalked away, but Don Vaez was still lost in his own thoughts.

He chuckled wryly as he thought of his earliest training, at the Academy of Stealth in Calimshan. What a terrible thief he had made! Why sneak through the night to snatch something surreptitiously, he had wondered, when he could walk up to the owner, bash him over the head with his sword, and take it in broad daylight?

The masters of the academy had reached the same conclusion, and Don Vaez and Calimshan had parted ways—for the most part amicably, since the masters had not taken a thorough inventory until their ex-student was a good distance away. Aided by the disguises of a guileless servant girl, he had escaped from the city and journeyed north along the coast. The girl, he assumed, had paid for her complicity with her life, though he had never bothered to find out for sure.

Following these experiences, Don Vaez had served in one of the mercenary companies aiding Amn in its two-decade war against the pirates of the Sword Coast. After the unfortunate and mysterious demise of the company captain—no one had ever been able to identify the archer that had slain him from behind while he led his troops into battle—Don Vaez had risen to command the company. In this capacity, he had first attracted the attention of the merchant princes.

And in the same capacity, he had been forced to compete with the soldiering of Captain-General Cordell and his Golden Legion. When Cordell had won the ultimate victory against the scimitar-waving horde of the pirate lord, Akbet-Khrul, Don Vaez's rival had been assured the place of highest honor before the Council of Amn.

For the suddenly unemployed Don Vaez, there had been a

lady—a very wealthy, albeit very married, lady. Yet somehow her favor had carried him to the council again, now that Cordell had apparently disappeared and, the don hoped, betrayed his employers. Don Vaez had even wondered if the lady might be one of the merchant princes herself, though of course that fact would remain secret.

Nevertheless, her influence must have been significant, for he had been selected to command this glorious endeavor.

The merchant princes of Amn had given him a great force and a strong charter. Somewhere out there, he felt, his old rival Cordell was still alive. The gods would not, could not be cruel enough to deprive Don Vaez of the confrontation he so rightly deserved.

"You know that he lives out there, do you not?" The question came from Pryat Devane. The cleric, wearing a close-fitting cloth cap and a woolen cape, joined him at the rail of the ship.

"Cordell?" Don Vaez turned to the cleric, surprised at the man's accurate guess. He smiled thinly. "Yes, I believe that we will . . . encounter him."

"Good!" The pryat spoke sharply. "His reckless behavior has no doubt cost my mentor his life!"

"Bishou Domincus? You feel that he has been slain?"

"I'm certain of it," announced the cleric. "But he will be avenged!"

"Indeed," agreed the captain, turning back to the sea. It seemed that he had an ally, a spiritual brother, in this dour priest of Helm. And, remembering the flying carpet the princes had told him about, he felt that Pryat Devane could prove to be a very useful ally indeed.

In his mind, Don Vaez pictured the encounter with the defeated Cordell. The man would beg for mercy, and Don Vaez would make him wriggle and plead for his life. Of course, all the while he knew he would grant that life, for his moment of true triumph would not arrive until he returned with Cordell to Amn and marched the traitorous mercenary through the streets of Murann in chains.

Or in a cage, perhaps. Suddenly Don Vaez had an inspiration! He would take the gold of this new world—some of the gold, anyway—and he would have a cage made. The cage would be mounted on gilded wheels, and within it would ride the grand prisoner of his expedition.

Yes, thought Don Vaez. That would be a fitting return home for the leader of the Golden Legion. With this idea, and a thin smile on his too-handsome lips, Don Vaez went to his cabin belowdecks to sleep.

And, of course, to dream.

*　*　*　*　*

"How many were there? Did you have a chance to count?" asked Halloran.

The youth, Jhatli, looked at him suspiciously. Intelligence gleamed in the lad's eyes, but so too did anger and hatred. I can't blame him for that, Hal thought.

Along with Daggrande and Gultec, Hal tried to coax description from the youth. Erixitl slept nearby, exhausted finally by the day's march. Somewhere overhead, Hal knew, the eagle waited for them. In the morning, they would need to face a difficult decision: head for water, or follow the path of this great bird of prey.

For now, they sat around a small campfire, using some of their precious firewood to light this council. Some of the Maztican scouts had told them Jhatli's tale, and his heart broke for the pain the young man had suffered. At the same time, anything he could tell them about the nature and tactics of the pursuing horde could prove very useful.

"Not as many as my band . . . less than a thousand. They burst from the rocks as we passed, attacking by surprise. I don't know of anyone else who escaped," Jhatli said after a brief pause. "I got away only because I was just returning from my hunt. I was separated from the main group, but I could see them."

His dark eyes flashed. "We could return and kill them, with your warriors and their silver weapons! They can all be killed!"

"No," Hal sighed, with a shake of his head. "By now they've

certainly grown in number. You saw just a small portion of the mob that pursues us."

The youth's eyes darkened and his body tensed. Then he settled back, though his voice carried a hint of a sneer. "Very well, but I will kill many of them when I get the chance!"

"A warrior, eh?" said Daggrande, the dwarf's voice uncharacteristically gentle.

"Yes . . . one who is not afraid to seek a battle!"

"Careful, young man," Gultec growled, his face grim between the fanged jaws of his jaguar-skull helmet. Jhatli's eyes widened, then fell to the ground.

"I—I'm sorry," the young man sighed, his breath ragged.

"I know the fury that compels you to battle," Halloran told Jhatli, "but that rage must be tempered by wisdom, or it will only destroy you."

The youth looked at him, anger still flashing in his black eyes. But then he lowered his gaze back to the fire, a weakness suddenly collapsing his posture.

"Come on, lad." The dwarf, speaking his awkward Nexalan, clapped Jhatli on the shoulder. "Let's go find something for you to eat."

Gultec and Halloran sat in silence for a time, the desert growing dark around them. Finally the Jaguar Knight spoke. "It galls me, this constant flight from an enemy we cannot see."

"And me," Halloran agreed. "Yet what choice do we have—to stand and die, along with all these people, before a horde of unnatural beasthood?"

"How long must we fly?" Gultec persisted. "Is it right to move farther into the desert? Could not the gods have laid for us a cruel trap, and we will reach the end of this chain of food and water only to starve and perish of thirst?"

"This new valley you found . . . it sounds as though there is food there, enough to last a long time," Halloran observed.

"Indeed there is, and enough land to cultivate. If the water remains, a city could be built there that would rival Nexal."

"Provided we're not driven away like a herd of goats," Hal said bitterly.

"I do not know what 'goats' are," Gultec said, "but I share

your feeling." The warrior paused a moment before raising a question that had obviously occupied his mind for some time.

"You and your people have used powers in the battles against us—sorcery, you call this. Is there not some sorcery that could defend us against the Viperhand?"

Halloran shook his head in resignation. "Sorcery is a skill known only to a few. Among the legion, there was the wizard Darien, the albino elf. She had great powers of wizardry, but she used them in the service of the drow. She died—she must have—when the top of the volcano exploded."

"She was the only one?" asked the Eagle Knight.

"The cleric, Domincus, had powers of clerical sorcery He perished on the altar of Zaltec. Otherwise, there are a few men among the legion who practiced low levels of magic—not many, and their skills are not very great." Halloran chuckled.

"I am one of them, as a matter of fact. I once studied as an apprentice to a great sorcerer, and I still know a few spells. An enchantment of light, for example, or a magic arrow. I can increase the size of an object with an enlargement spell."

Gultec looked at him in amazement, but could see that Halloran spoke the truth. They both remembered the great fireballs or the blasts of killing frost or the poisonous smoke with which Darien had made her presence known. "As you can see," Hal concluded, "there is little I could do to change the course of a battle."

For a while longer the men lapsed into silence. Then Halloran looked back toward the sky.

"There's the matter of Poshtli," he ventured. "He flew east late today, over land we know is dry desert. How can we take all these people on such a path, simply because of a *bird*, despite what he used to be?" Halloran understood that the folk of the Realms he came from would never have made such a choice; about Mazticans, he was not so sure.

"Perhaps he does not mean for all of the people to follow him," mused Gultec. "Just those who can make a difference."

Halloran looked at the Jaguar Knight in surprise. He had never considered that possibility, but the notion seemed to make a lot of sense. Before he could reply, a shape materialized from the darkness, and they saw the priest, Xatli, approach.

"May I join you?" asked the cleric of Qotal.

"Please sit with us," Hal replied as Gultec nodded.

Xatli looked toward Erix, her cloak dimly visible even in the darkness. "It is good she sleeps. Her burdens weigh heavily upon her, and slumber is the greatest healer of all."

"It seems that she only knows peace when she is asleep now," Hal agreed softly.

"I have heard that a lush valley awaits us," ventured the cleric after a short while.

"Gultec has seen it. There's food and water aplenty."

"Yes," the Jaguar Knight said, nodding. "The first of our people will reach it late tomorrow; by the morning after, everyone should be there."

"A good place to camp," Xatli said, squatting on the ground. "A thing to look forward to."

"A good place to camp, perhaps," agreed the warrior. "But a bad place for war."

"You know," the cleric announced, sitting upright again and fixing his two companions with his gaze, "there is a place in this desert that was made for war."

"What do you mean?" asked Hal.

"It is called Tewahca, the City of the Gods. I have never seen it, but the tale of its making is known to all priests. It was the scene of Qotal's last victory over his brother Zaltec."

"Zaltec, Qotal . . . brothers?" Hal was genuinely surprised. "I didn't know this."

"Brothers indeed, though very different from each other. The one desired only killing and blood; the other could not bear to hurt a living soul."

"That must have been a liability if he had to fight a war," Hal observed dryly, and Xatli chuckled.

"To the point," the priest continued. "The gods commanded the humans of the world to build them a great edifice for this war, a pyramid greater than any in the True

World. They made the desert fertile so that the people could build this place.

"Of course, the details are as old as legend, but all the tales point to a place somewhere here, in the House of Tezca. No man has seen it, certainly not in a dozen lifetimes or more. Perhaps the desert has swallowed it.

"But I am certain Tewahca is out there somewhere, long abandoned by man. Could not the gods again desire a confrontation there? And the tales of the desert made fertile . . . is this not what sustains us, what sustains all these thousands now?"

"Do you think we are being led to Tewahca?" Gultec asked, his tone telling Hal that the tale of the great ceremonial center was familiar to him.

"I doubt it," said Xatli. "The gods created a wasteland around the place to keep humans away. It seems unlikely they would desire to bring us back in great numbers.

"Still, the building of such a place makes one think that it could be done again," mused Xatli. "It gives me faith that the Nexala will again have a home."

Hal nodded, for a moment almost relaxing in the vision of the cleric's hopes for the future. In the next second, he remembered Jhatli and the cruel and violent presence that loomed close in the desert night.

The beasts of the Viperhand remained a great cudgel hanging over them, prepared to smash any hopes into a hundred thousand bleeding shards.

\* \* \* \* \*

Steam hissed from wide cracks in the ground, forming a dense fog, a funeral shroud for the valley of Nexal. Now the beasts had departed, and except for the rats that picked their way through the ruins, the rubble on the flat island lay still and lifeless.

From the center of the dead city, the pillar of stone towered like a great monolith, a hundred feet tall. Only by the most careful inspection could one make out the details of arms and legs, the snarling, tooth-filled maw, that caused this rock to be regarded as the image of Zaltec.

But its strength did not lie in its visual power, but rather within the essence of the pillar itself. Hundreds of years ago, this same rock—at that time, not much larger than a man—had been discovered by a faithful cleric of a primitive, warlike tribe. The pillar had spoken to the cleric, commanding him to lead his tribe on a great pilgrimage through desert and mountain, until they came at last to the great valley with its cool, clear lakes.

Others dwelled here already, in cities around the shores of the lakes. The newcomers chose for their own rude village a low, marshy island. Still bearing the pillar that had come to symbolize their god, the people placed the stone monolith at the site of their first small pyramid.

Centuries passed. The village grew to a town, and the people formed shrewd alliances. Layer upon layer was added to the pyramid, and the town became a city. The people of the crude tribe practiced diplomacy and war, and at last came to be masters of the beautiful valley. Never did they forget that they owed their success to Zaltec, god of war.

Now that god claimed his reward, and the people who had praised him fled in terror across the fertile desert. The pillar grew, bursting out of its confines, looming far above the rubble strewn around it.

Then, in the dead city, even the rats fell still. A tremor rippled through the earth. Mount Zatal, lost in the gray fog above the valley, rumbled.

And the statue began to move.

\* \* \* \* \*

The swath of death cut through the jungle like a cosmic scythe, leaving behind torn tree trunks, shredded brush, and the skeletons of any creatures foolish enough to stand before the inevitable advance of the ants. Whole meadows became festering swamps of brown mud, while great tracks of forest were reduced to bare, twisted trunks and a decaying wasteland of rot and waste.

The track followed an apparently random route, twisting

and turning at whim, fording the occasional streams of the Payit jungle or easily cresting the steep limestone ridges that sometimes jutted from the land. It followed a northerly course, then twisted east and south, even turning around and crossing itself as it again swung to the north.

The track may have seemed random, but it was not.

In fact, the giant ants followed the commands of an intelligence every bit as keen as it was evil. Darien used the march to gain absolute control over the ants, directing them to follow her commands. She narrowed the column to a file of five or six ants abreast when she wished it to move quickly, for she found that she could turn it more easily this way and avoid obstacles such as marshes or thick brambles. When she desired a wide swath of destruction, she broadened the column; though it moved more slowly, with a hundred or more ants marching at its head, it left nothing living through its broad path.

Each of the ants was a mindless monster in its own right: bigger than a huge jaguar, with a mechanical intensity that knew neither fear nor dismay, each ant marched and attacked and devoured wherever and whatever its mistress commanded.

All the while Darien's mind seethed with hatred. She grimaced at the pictures in her mind of humankind, its miserable failings and faithlessness. She spat her venom upward at the thought of the arrogant gods, wreaking havoc among the mortals at no risk to themselves.

And she drove her ants, the thousands of massive insects that spewed from the bowels of the earth, ready to obey her every command. Finally she felt ready to begin her revenge.

This region of Payit, though sparsely populated, hosted several small villages. It was toward one of these that, at last, she marched her ant army. Soon she reached the fringe of jungle around her goal, and she looked across several small fields of mayz toward a cluster of thatch huts.

*Wait, my soldiers.*

Her command, silently compelling, reached all of her subjects. The leading ants held at the edge of the jungle while their brethren marched up to join them from behind. Gradually the marching file expanded into a broad front of twitching antennae and slowly flexing mandibles. Black and hulking, the ants trembled with energy, yet remained in place. As more and more of the army reached them, Darien smiled thinly.

*Forward—kill!*

Now the rank of massive insects broke from the jungle, sweeping through the fields of mayz. Great jaws snatched the grain from its stalks, devouring ears, leaves, and all. Jerking forward with steady momentum, the ants quickly scuttled toward the village.

First to see the horrifying attackers were several women who were gathering corn when the nightmare horde suddenly burst around them. They screamed only for a second, dragged down even before they could turn to run.

Their screams brought men running from the huts, and they met the ants at the fringe of the village. The powerful forelegs of the soldiers knocked their weapons aside and cracked the bones of these warriors. Then the insects' mandibles seized them with bone-crushing force.

The first rank of the ants ripped through the line of spearmen, whose missiles merely bounced off the hard insectoid carapaces. They tore and crushed, ripping limbs away and leaving bleeding, helpless victims still alive to face the hunger of the second rank.

Screams rang through the air, sending flocks of noisy parrots and macaws squawking from the trees. All the villagers not caught in the first wave of disaster turned to flee. The ants scuttled awkwardly after these morsels and quickly overtook most of them. The smallest humans, the ants snatched up and carried back to their new queen. The larger ones, they cut down where they caught them, tearing them to pieces so that each ant could carry a portion.

With the swiftness, if not the grace, of deer, they raced among the buildings and through the small village square. Without pause, the ants overran the tiny cluster of huts, probing inside each building, emotionlessly gobbling those too infirm or young to flee. Soon they started on the thatch itself, tearing and ripping until the buildings fell in ruins.

The center of the village sheltered a small pyramid, topped by a typical Maztican temple. The ants swarmed up all sides of the structure, brushing aside the few warriors who stood in their path. At the top, the village priest stood in the temple door, brandishing his stone dagger. An ant sliced his arm off at the elbow before he could strike a blow. Another seized his foot and dragged him, screaming, down the pyramid steps, while still more ants plunged into the temple building itself, tearing at the wooden walls with their steel-hard mandibles. Soon the entire building collapsed, crashing around the stone altar in a heap of rubble.

Somewhere within, a brazier must have contained hot coals, for shortly after the collapse, a wisp of smoke erupted from the wreckage. In moments, orange flames licked upward, and soon the ruined temple crackled into a hot blaze. Sparks, wafted by the gentle wind, floated tantalizingly over the dying village. Some of these nestled among the heaps of torn thatch, and soon the ruined huts began to burn.

In a few minutes, there was little sign of any human habitation here, save for the squat stone pyramid amid the glowing piles of crackling ashes and coals.

At the edge of the clearing, the driders watched the destruction with grim satisfaction.

"You have found us our army," hissed one of Darien's driders, a sleek male with a powerful longbow. He, like the rest of her kin, had looked quietly on while the ants attacked.

"My soldiers kill very well," agreed Darien.

Lolth, too, was well pleased by the carnage, though of course her driders could not know it.

*　*　*　*　*

From the chronicles of Coton:

*In the embrace of the Plumed One, may we live to see another day.*

*The door to Lotil's hut crashes inward, and a great beast stands there, slavering. It is monstrously tall, green of skin,* and possessed of long, wicked claws upon its fingers. The crimson brand of the Viperhand throbs on its chest. Its black, sunken eyes focus on the featherworker and me as we cower in the corner.

But then the presence of Qotal becomes manifest.

Lotil's loom, decked with feathers and cloth, stands in the corner. As the beast advances, the partial tapestry tears free from the loom. It floats toward us, then hangs motionless in the air, between the monster and our terrified selves.

The creature stands dumbfounded, but no more so than I. For upon this uncompleted scrap of tapestry appears an image of a place, an image rendered so clear, so unmistakable, that it would seem to be the place itself.

The beast stumbles backward in confusion. Finally, silently, it departs from the house. I stare, transfixed by the image before me.

Then the blind featherworker beside me, who cannot see the sun in the noonday sky, speaks.

"It is the Pyramid of Tewahca," he says, and I agree.

# ❦ 6 ❦

# MARCHES AND AMBUSH

Luskag felt a strange mixture of sadness and pride as his dwarves marched past. They left Sunhome in the care of the young and the old, while all the strong adults—males and females alike—joined the file toward war. All across the House of Tezca, he knew, the other villages of desert dwarves mustered as well.

He counted barely a hundred souls among the warriors, and he did not know how much they could accomplish against the apparently numberless horde of monsters spreading southward across the desert. But the vision of chaos had been so clear, so threatening, that they all knew they had to try.

Most of his dwarves were armed with weapons of *pluma*stone, but his village was still unique in the desert. The others had only begun to acquire the secrets of the superhardened obsidian and were for the most part bearing crude weapons more typical of Maztica.

Work progressed steadily, following the council at Sunhome, as each village had sent an expedition to the ridges around the City of the Gods. They had since returned to their homes, laden with the shiny black rock with which the dwarves now labored to create the tough, deadly weapons.

A few desert dwarves wielded metal axes or swords that predated the Rockfire, but these artifacts were reserved for chieftains and other venerable warriors. Luskag himself had borne such a battle-axe, but he had bestowed the weapon upon his eldest son, Bann. The chief himself carried a heavy axe of *pluma*stone.

Regardless of their armament, all of the villages had sent companies of doughty warriors, albeit warriors who had never known war. Yet the tradition of courage and combat lay deep within the dwarven race, and Luskag knew that they would fight well. So, too, he reflected sadly, would they die.

Luskag trotted to the head of the column, and the desert dwarves started across the sun-scorched realm of their home. They would gather at the City of the Gods, and there they would make their stand.

\* \* \* \* \*

Gultec nodded to Halloran, then bowed deeply before Erixitl. The sun had not yet risen, yet the sky was clear and blue, already promising a day of extreme heat. Eastward over the trackless desert, Pashtli soared in tight circles, as if impatient with the humans so far below.

"Lady of the Plume," Gultec began, "I must leave now. My destiny calls."

She embraced the Jaguar Knight but did not try to dissuade him. "I know of destiny," she whispered softly. "May it be a load you can bear."

Gultec looked into her face, holding her shoulders. "It can be a blessing as well as a burden. Whatever its form, it is laid upon you. You must not fight it."

A frown creased her forehead, but Erixitl sighed slowly and relaxed. She sensed a deep kinship with the Jaguar Knight, and she knew that he spoke wisely. "I will try to remember," she promised.

"The acts of the gods are not easily understood. Once I fought wars for the cause of Zaltec, and even worked with priests to further the causes of that god of war—god of death, more rightly!"

"I remember," Erixitl said dryly. They both smiled now, though the memory was not pleasant. Gultec had bound Erix and led her to an intended sacrificial death on the shores of the Eastern Sea. Only the arrival of the white-winged "sea creatures," later proven to be the ships of the Golden Legion, had saved her.

"But my own destiny took me to Far Payit, and there I

learned the ways of this god you call Qotal. His wisdom is proven in that he has chosen you as his herald."

Once again Erix shook her head. "What does that prove? How am I aiding the cause of his arrival—his *promised* arrival?"

"That I do not know. But know this, Erixitl of the Nexala: When the knowledge comes, you will be the first to receive it."

Around the two, the vast camp of Mazticans came slowly awake. Dawn's pale blue light filtered across the desert, shining on the feathers of the eagle that still circled to the east. Already word of the problems facing them on this day had spread among the refugees.

All had heard of the massacre the previous day of the band of stragglers, a thousand lives snuffed out in one brutal attack. Though the news caused tension and fear, Erixitl noticed no sign of panic among her countrymen, and this made her proud.

The people had heard of the bountiful valley discovered by Gultec and reported by other scouts as well. The swiftest of the marchers could expect to be there by nightfall, while the rest of the band would reach it by the middle of the following day.

Yet what good was such a fertile place if it would merely be swept over by the surging wave of war? At best, it seemed to offer a temporary sanctuary—a respite of a day, perhaps two—in a journey that threatened to become a way of life.

And then there was the matter of the great eagle. Many had witnessed the miracle, as the tale of the bird's appearance as Poshtli was now called, and they had insured that the story spread throughout the camp. But now the eagle veered away from the promised route to food and water, and the path to safety was no longer clearly defined.

Abruptly Gultec turned away. Erixitl gasped as his shape shifted, his transformed appearance clear in the cool light. He moved quickly then, in a flash of bright green feathers, and disappeared. She saw a large parrot take to wing, and then the bird turned one bright eye toward her as it fluttered higher into the air. In a few moments, it was gone, winging strongly toward the east.

"There, to the east," she said softly as Halloran turned to her. "That is where Poshtli flies, now Gultec as well. It is where I must fly, too. I know Poshtli shows us the path— toward what I'm still not sure." She looked at her husband, and he nodded. He, too, had observed the eagle's change of course. While a sheltered valley, with food and water, lay a day's march to the southwest, Poshtli now soared over arid lands, a broken waste of jagged ridges and deep, barren gulches.

"I'm coming with you," he promised. "But everyone?"

She shook her head. "Let the people go to the valley. They can stop there to rest. I believe Poshtli shows the path for me—for you and me—alone."

Halloran looked to the narrow ridge that loomed to the east, knowing of the bleak desert that lay beyond. Silently he vowed to do his utmost to see Erixitl safely through that waste. It was all another part of their search for a home, he told himself. And someday they would find one.

As the Mazticans bestirred themselves, many already starting on the trail toward the southwest, Erixitl and Halloran found Cordell and Daggrande among the camp of the legionnaires.

"We need your help," Halloran began. Cordell's eyes flashed at the news, and his hand went instinctively to the hilt of his sword.

"Speak," he requested.

"We are leaving the trail, following Poshtli to the east. He flies over the bare desert." Then Halloran described the lush valley that lay to the southwest, knowing that Grimes and some of the other riders had already found it as well. "Go with the people and keep an eye out for attack. If you can make a defensible position there, set up a long-term camp."

"Why do you think he's taking you that way?" Cordell had known Poshtli as an adversary, and a courageous one. Too, he had witnessed the man's appearance in the guise of the bird. But he wasn't willing to let Halloran and Erix go without some plan.

"Qotal." Erixitl replied simply. "Somehow I am tied in to his return. He is the only force that can counterbalance Zaltec and his creatures. I must do what I can to bring him back to the True World."

Halloran knew the resentment his wife felt for her enforced role in this game of the gods, yet he heard none of it in her voice. She spoke as a true believer, and Cordell accepted her faith without question.

"Good luck to you, then," he agreed. "I'll get the company together. The Kultakans will stand bravely, and so will these Nexalan warriors. I'm sure we can hold the bastards at bay!"

Cordell's voice carried renewed enthusiasm at the prospect of battle and action, as Hal had known it would. He understood as well as anyone the heavy toll that the long retreat had exacted from the aggressive general. Still, to Halloran the commander's optimistic assessment of his chances seemed almost reckless.

"I'm coming with you," Daggrande declared, facing Hal and Erix. He coughed awkwardly. "That is, if you think you could use some help."

Halloran looked at his old companion with deep affection. "I know we could use your help, my friend"

"Don't get mushy on me," huffed the dwarf, his own voice gruff with emotion. "Just let me get my whetstone—my damned axe keeps going dull, what with all the dust and all!"

Daggrande marched away, and Hal watched him with affection. A "dull blade" by the old dwarf's estimate was still as sharp as a barber's razor, he knew. The sturdy veteran's presence would greatly enhance their chances of survival.

Several Mazticans approached. Hal recognized the priest Xatli and the Eagle Knight Chical. Erixitl explained their plans and accepted their good wishes for their journey. The cleric of Qotal looked at her seriously.

"Out there in the desert, sister, I sense that your destiny awaits. I would offer to accompany you, to offer whatever feeble aid I can, but I know this: You will have the aid of someone far greater than myself."

"Who do you mean?" she asked, surprised.

The cleric shook his head. "I do not know, but I sense it

about you. You will be carried to your final challenge on the wings of your friends."

"I hope you're right," Erix admitted with a shake of her long black hair. She pulled her cloak, growing brighter with each minute of increasing daylight, tightly around her shoulders.

\* \* \* \* \*

The great monolith looked like a living form as it moved. Two great legs, thicker than massive tree trunks, supported it and carried it cumbersomely forward. Two arms, human-like in shape but tipped with wicked talons of crooked stone, swung at its sides.

The form of Zaltec disdained the broken causeways that still connected the island to shore. Instead, the huge stone form waded into Lake Tezca, striding easily through the thick mud. The water came only to the monstrous form's knees.

Then it emerged onto the lake's south shore, its heavy footfalls crunching into the ground. It passed the smoldering remains of Mount Zatal without a sideways glance. Instead, the glowering eyes, gray orbs of granite in a stark, stone face, remained fixed upon the desert, in answer to some distant and unknown compulsion.

And Zaltec marched on, until a watcher on the rim of the valley could have seen only a huge, monolithic form, moving into the remote wastes of the desert, like a towering, sheer-sloped mountain.

A mountain that walked.

\* \* \* \* \*

"Forward, beasts of the crimson hand!"

Hoxitl urged his minions into a lumbering advance. Earlier, while darkness still shrouded the desert, the ogres had stalked through the camp, kicking and cursing their charges awake. Now the ranks of orcs stood armed and restless, ready to move.

The route lay plain before them: the wide, flat-bottomed valley that curved gently through the desert. To each side, ridges of windswept rock, red and brown in color, provided a jagged outline to the track of their quarry.

"Today we will find more humans, and there will be more killing!" promised the beastlord.

The assembled creatures snorted and stomped at the pledge, pounding spear-shafts against the ground or clashing *macas* and clubs together. The throbbing noise rolled across the desert, all the way to the camp of his hated enemies, Hoxitl hoped.

How he hated the humans! The anger that had spurred him from the ruins to lead his army on this great march seemed a pale flame compared to the fiery loathing that now consumed him. With each slain body, with each life claimed for Zaltec, his fury had grown.

With an explosion of howls and roars, the beasts lumbered after Hoxitl as the great monster started to advance. They spread into a vast wave, moving down the same valley the humans had followed the day before, advancing at a steady trot. For an hour, the horde rushed forward, covering distances it had taken the humans four times as long to march.

The first clue was an odor on the dry wind, the sweet scent of prey. Hoxitl howled, and the cry arose from the ranks behind him until a horrid shriek of bloodlust filled the air, reverberating across the desert like a killing gust from the north.

Hoxitl searched the dry valley floor before them, but no sign of movement caught his eye. The humans had probably moved on early in the day, but his nostrils told him that they had been here, and very recently.

Then he saw them.

Atop one of the low ridges that bordered this desert valley, Hoxitl saw a flash of color. Squinting, he picked out several shapes—human, no doubt, though one seemed somewhat short and stocky.

And then a hot, hissing spear of light lanced into his eyes. The *colors!* The *brightness!* Screaming in pain and rage,

Hoxitl tumbled backward. His clawed hands scratched at his eyes in agony.

Very slowly the pain faded away, and the beast, with a low growl, sneaked another look at the ridge. He blinked in confusion and fear, and red spots swam before his eyes, but no further blaze assaulted his vision. Yet he recognized it for what it was: *pluma*. Only the power of feathermagic could cause such pain to his powerful senses.

Dimly he realized that the attack had come from the ridgetop, from that point of color up there. And with this awareness, all of his hatred, all of his rage, focused against that distant, slowly moving spot of color.

Hoxitl's heavy eyelids drooped over his wicked, gleaming eyes as he pondered this mysterious development. The great mass of humans, he knew, continued to flee along the valley floor. Yet the one who now climbed the desolate ridge must be one of special significance. Certainly the power of the *pluma* he had just witnessed indicated this.

He could not ignore the mass of victims awaiting his army. No, the taste of blood on the previous day had been too sweet, too tempting. Yet neither could he ignore the spoor leading to the east, into the desert.

He gestured to his trolls, long-limbed creatures who were very fleet of foot. "Pursue those who slip away to the east," Hoxitl ordered.

The green-skinned creatures lumbered away, in groups of three and four, from the rest of Hoxitl's army. Finally several hundred of the monsters—all of the trolls—broke away, heading for the sheer ridge. They lumbered forward in the rolling gait typical of the long-limbed creatures. The beastlord knew that they would move quickly and inexorably after the pathetic humans.

Hoxitl turned back to the rest of his beasts, the crowded mass of orcs and ogres. These he led toward the south, in the direction taken by the warm bodies that would make food for his hungry god.

* * * * *

Jhatli sat beside the trail, watching the long columns of his countrymen march past. They followed the unobstructed route of the valley, toward the water and food that they knew lay before them. The sight of yet another sullen youth, apparently without friend or family, was no longer enough to stir their hearts, so the Nexalans passed Jhatli with neither a look nor a word.

Running . . . fleeing! Jhatli looked at his countrymen in scorn. Was that all they could do? Why didn't they stand and fight? This was no life for a warrior . . . or one who would be a warrior.

Still, it was the life led by the Nexala now. The youth shook his head angrily, looking to the north, imagining the lumbering horde over the distant horizon. How long until they reached these people, until they forced them into a battle for which they were not prepared?

Finally Jhatli cast a look back over his shoulder. The first thing he noticed was the great eagle, soaring high in the sky to the east. Looking down, he spotted the trio: Erixitl, the Lady of the Plume; and the two soldiers, Halloran and Daggrande.

He didn't know where they went, but he suspected that it involved the hideous beasts that pursued them all. His own promise for revenge still burned in Jhatli's heart, and so he watched them carefully.

He had heard the story that the eagle was in fact Lord Poshtli. Jhatli well remembered that noble warrior, proud and aloof in his feathered cloak and his great, beaked helmet. Such a warrior, in the guise of this bird, would be a powerful ally and a wise leader.

Now Erixitl and her companions had broken away from the great bulk of the people to follow that eagle. It was only natural that Jhatli resolved to follow the eagle, too.

He waited until the three had begun to climb the rugged ridge that bordered the valley. Then he turned away from the column and trotted toward the same ridge, but some distance to the left of where Erix and her companions climbed it. Again the people took no notice—another youth trotting off to a fruitless hunt in the desert. Too bad his parents didn't keep him under control. Didn't they know that danger lurked out there?

Jhatli held his pace easily, quickly scrambling into a narrow, boulder-strewn ravine that seemed to lead up the ridge. For long minutes he climbed, sweat pouring from his wiry brown body. His footsteps fell sure, though, and his strong hands and arms pulled him through several narrow spots.

Finally he reached a small gap in the ravine that allowed him to step out onto a small shoulder of the ridge. He had climbed most of the way to the top, he saw. Perhaps half a mile away, he saw the flaming colors of Erixitl's cloak, already at the crest.

Suddenly Jhatli felt very dizzy. He looked at the cloak again, and the colors began to spin, weaving an incredibly beautiful pattern, images of birds and flowers and butterflies of every hue, before his eyes. Shaking his head in confusion, Jhatli sat down and looked away.

It was then that he saw the massive horde of monsters gathered on the valley floor, stretching to the far limits of his vision until they vanished into the rising cloud of dust made by their march. Unconsciously the youth recoiled against the rock, appalled at the extent of the horde.

Then he noticed movement closer to where he crouched. He saw a small group of creatures—huge, gangly beasts with green skin and gaping, fang-studded jaws—moving steadily away from the mass. They came forward in long strides, toward the ridge he watched from. In fact, they came toward the very ravine he had followed in his climb.

They came toward *him!*

\* \* \* \* \*

The colors faded as Halloran and Daggrande looked at Erixitl in astonishment. For a second, the pair had stood in the warm wash of light, very bright yet somehow vaguely cooling in the dry desert air.

"How—how did you do that?" Hal asked softly.

"It is the power of *pluma*," she answered, suddenly uncomfortable. "*I* didn't do anything. But look, it seems to have captured their attention!"

Indeed, they saw the horde in the valley surge toward them. Even at this distance, they heard the shrieks and howls, felt the pounding of weapons and feet upon the ground.

"Let's go!" Hal urged, and they swiftly started down the opposite side of the slope. Though they could no longer see the beasts of the Viperhand, the presence of the monsters lurked like a heavy cloud just beyond the ridge. They knew that soon it would wash up and over.

They saw with dismay that they descended toward a torturous landscape of jagged gullies, sharp outcrops of rock, and broad stretches of cracked and broken ground. Far away, blue with haze even through the clear air, stood another ridgeline.

Above them, the eagle still floated effortlessly through the sky. The great bird circled slowly, always leading them eastward. If they followed him, they would have to traverse the bleak and tortured ground before them.

"How are we going to cross *that?*" groaned Halloran.

"There! Follow Poshtli!" Erix pointed as the great eagle dove toward the ground. It appeared to follow the course of a twisting, broken chasm. From where they stood, they couldn't see the bottom.

Half-sliding, half-scrambling, they plunged down the steep slope. Their route took them right to the lip of the gully, and they saw a fairly clear floor of dirt. It took but another minute to find a negotiable route down into the gulch.

They looked upward between a pair of steep, rocky cliffs and saw only a narrow strip of sky above. On the bottom, they felt a little more secure, since only something airborne or standing at the very lip of the little canyon would be able to see them. Puffing with exertion, they started along the level ground, relieved to see that the eagle followed each twist and turn of the canyon above them.

For several hours, they pressed forward, not speaking, dripping with sweat, pausing only long enough to take a few drops of refreshment from their still-bulging waterskins.

Fortunately the canyon floor followed a generally eastward course, with many small twists leading slightly to the north or south.

It was at their third brief rest, as each rationed a few tiny drops from the skins, that Hal stiffened. Immediately the other two came alert. Daggrande's eyebrows raised questioningly.

"I heard something," Halloran mouthed silently. He drew Helmstooth, his keen longsword, and began to creep along the canyon floor. A few feet before them, the gully curved to the right, concealing the next stretch of its course.

Crouching, Hal raised the sword before him as he approached the turn. Then he sprang forward, turning to the side and stabbing the weapon viciously.

He almost fell as he suddenly twisted away, desperately pulling back before his thrust struck home. His initial astonishment grew into full-blown shock.

"What are *you* doing here?" he demanded.

Daggrande and Erix watched in amazement as Jhatli crept from behind the concealing rock.

"I—I came to warn you," the youth whispered. The urgency in his voice assured their attention.

"Of what? Why did you leave the others?" Halloran's anger filled his voice.

"The others!" Jhatli's indignation came through as scorn. "This is where I should be! I told you, I will be a warrior, not one who spends his life fleeing enemies like the rest of my people."

"Warn us?" interjected Erixitl quietly. "Warn us against what?"

"There's an ambush up ahead. Monsters—big, green ones! They watched you enter this canyon, and now they wait at the rim to kill you!"

Halloran squinted at Jhatli, but he believed the lad immediately. "Trolls. That was courageous of you. How far away are they?"

"I will show you, but first let us get out of this low place!"

They scrambled up a shallow draw in the slope. Once again on the slopes above the deep floor, they felt vulnerable. But they moved carefully, and could see no sign of the trolls as they emerged from the canyon.

They crept forward no more than a hundred paces, however, when Jhatli pointed. They saw three of the green humanoids crouched at the rim of the canyon, peering expectantly downward.

"There are more—six or eight—on the other side," Jhatli explained. "But I saw only these three over here."

"Let's try to slip away while they're still expecting us down below," Erixitl urged. The plan made sense, so they worked away from the canyon, slowly moving from one sheltering mound to another. Fortunately the rough ground made concealment easy.

It was almost good enough.

"Let's pick up the pace a bit," suggested Hal after they had left the trolls some distance behind. Accompanied by Jhatli now, they started toward the distant ridge, scrambling over, around, and through the many jagged obstacles in their path.

The roar from beside them was their first warning of attack. A pair of massive trolls reared up on a boulder, howling and barking, obviously calling to others of their kind.

Daggrande reacted instantaneously. He raised his heavy crossbow and let fly a thick steel bolt. The missile tore into the chest of the nearest troll, exploding from its back in a shower of gore. Bellowing, the creature toppled backward, out of sight.

The second troll leaped toward them, but Hal's reaction was nearly as quick as his old companion's. He felt the tingling of *pluma* around his wrists, the tiny cuffs of feathers adding to his strength. Helmstooth carved a silver arc in the air and sliced right through the troll's midsection. Soundlessly the two halves fell to the ground, wriggling in a growing pool of black blood.

But Hal's gullet rose in horror as the two halves of the troll didn't cease their movement. With horrifying determination, the torso began to crawl forward, using its taloned hands to pull itself along. The trail of black blood spurting from the wound slowed to a trickle and finally ceased altogether. Even as Halloran moved away, a tiny pair of legs sprouted from the wound, growing slowly, but with visible and inexorable progression. Hal stumbled backward, gagging in horror.

The legs, meanwhile, kicked randomly. That portion, too, quickly ceased bleeding. Though the regeneration proceeded more slowly, a small lump of flesh formed at the wound and began to sprout upward.

"Look out!" Erixitl screamed, and Halloran saw movement beyond the boulder. Horrified, he saw the troll that had been shot by Daggrande slowly claw its way back onto the rock. Then he saw more green heads—a whole file of trolls—moving up to attack.

"Run!" he shouted, swinging the deadly blade until his companions started to move away. He heard the *chunk* of Daggrande's weapon, and a second quarrel transfixed the troll's forehead.

But now six, eight, even more of the beasts swarmed toward them. Halloran spun and raced after his companions, his heart chilling at the thought of Erixitl's peril. Once again he stopped and turned, driving the first troll back and lopping a hand off another, a hand that continued to crawl, horribly, after its escaping quarry.

They dashed along a dusty path that slowly twisted upward along a narrow ridge. Halloran turned frequently to hack at the nearest trolls. Apparently the beasts felt pain, for they cowered back from his crushing blows, though they quickly leaped back to the pursuit as soon as the man turned away.

Daggrande paused to load and launch another missile. The force of the bolt knocked a troll from the narrow ridge, sending the beast tumbling in a cloud of dust to the gully below. Halloran knocked another into space with a clobbering blow from Helmstooth, but he faced the grim realization that all he could do was slow down their advance. He could not kill them.

Jhatli threw rocks, revealing a surprising strength in his youthful body as he lifted good-sized boulders over his head and pitched them at the green-skinned monstrosities. In the

lead, Erixitl tried to pick the safest route along the crest of
the eroded sandstone ridge. It narrowed perilously until
they worked their way along a trail only a foot or two wide,
with steeply sloping drops to either side of them.

Halloran stumbled, almost rolling off the ridge. He caught
himself with his free hand but then looked up in horror. A
troll lunged for him. Still off-balance, he knew he could not
counter the creature's attack.

Then a black and white shape soared across his vision as,
with a shrill cry of defiance, the great eagle darted past
them. The bird's powerful talons seized the monster's
coarse black hair and pulled it roughly to the side. With a
harsh bark of anger, the troll tumbled from the narrow
crest, the eagle releasing its hold to pull powerfully upward
again. Screeching and howling, the creature slid and
bounced down the jagged slope, until it finally stopped, broken and motionless, against an outcrop of rock. Even from
this height, they could see the twisted limbs and gashed,
bleeding skin slowly start to heal.

Halloran sprang to his feet, recovering his guard in time
to meet the next troll. The beast, drool spattering from its
black, fang-studded maw, growled savagely but stayed just
beyond reach of the deadly steel. Hal lunged and stabbed
and slashed, but always the gangly creature, towering high
over the human's head, stepped nimbly out of the way.
Loose rocks rolled from beneath the man's feet, bouncing
and tumbling into space on either side of the ridge.

Halloran briefly considered casting a spell—one of the
few he had learned as an apprentice magic-user. He quickly
discarded the thought, knowing a magic missile or enlarge
spell would be of little use.

"C'mon! Keep moving!" Daggrande snapped in frustration
from behind Hal. The dwarf itched for a chance to bring his
keen axe to bear, but the ridge was too narrow, and in any
event, he knew that the swordsman, with his enchanted
sword and the power of *pluma* in his arms, could do far
more damage to their enemies. Instead, the dwarf loaded
another of his dwindling supply of quarrels into his crossbow, remaining alert for a chance to shoot.

Halloran backed along the ridge, barely holding the lead troll at bay. Then his boot snagged on an outcrop of rock and he fell heavily. In that same instant, the troll sprang.

But Daggrande was there. He released his missile, and the heavy bolt tore into the troll's chest, right through the brand of the Viperhand. With a gurgling howl, the beast tumbled away, and by the time the next of the monsters lunged forward, Halloran had regained his feet. He met the charge with the bloody edge of Helmstooth, and again he managed to hold the rear for his retreating party.

The companions followed the serpentine landform for a half mile, staying just ahead of the trolls. Several of the beasts followed their progress at the foot of the ridge, and each of the humans knew that any misstep would send him rolling straight into deadly talons and fangs.

Suddenly their progress halted. Hal risked a quick glance at Erixitl and saw that she stood at the brink of a sheer drop. There was no way down, and still the trolls pressed at the rear. Below, several of the beasts had started to scramble up the steep sides of the ridge.

"A neat trap, this," grunted Daggrande. He fired another bolt at a climbing troll, sending the creature tumbling back to the bottom. "Two left," he said ominously as he reloaded.

With a chorus of growls and snaps, the trolls rushed forward to the attack.

\*   \*   \*   \*   \*

From the chronicles of Coton:

*Amid oceans of disaster, a small island of plumage holds us afloat.*

*Lotil, the featherworker, and I greet the passing of the monsters from Palul like the birth of a new day. The village lies in ruins below us, the inhabitants slain or fled. Only a few buildings, such as Lotil's house, still stand, passed by the horde in random whimsy.*

*In this mercy, I sense the destiny of this old blind man and the necessity of my aid to him. We are bound together now,* not just by the danger we have endured, but also by the road that beckons before us.

The horse of the strangers stands ready to carry us, and on this new day we prepare to embark. Both of us have dreamed vividly of the great pyramid in the desert, with its vibrant colors and the secret wonders, concealed beneath the surrounding sand.

The vision of pluma tells us where we must go.

And Qotal! The Plumed One will soon be here, and we understand that the great pyramid will be the place of his arrival. The horse, when we have mounted, carries us toward the south, toward the altar of the Feathered God's advent.

Both of us sense the rightness of the horse's course.

# ❧ 7 ❧

# THE CITY OF THE GODS

The nearest troll lunged upward, and Halloran slashed it away in a shower of black blood. Daggrande fired the last of his quarrels, then grimly unslung his axe, ready to fight to the last. The two fighters stood before the rest of the companions as dizzying cliffs plummeted into sheer gorges beside and behind them.

Halloran growled inarticulately, slashing at a troll, but then a strange dizziness whirled in his mind. Stumbling, he stepped backward and planted his feet firmly.

A cocoon of color swirled around them. Startled, Halloran looked at Erixitl and saw that she was equally amazed. Her cloak puffed outward and began to spin in a brilliant kaloidescope of color. Slowly the brilliance reached out to encircle the desperate party on the ridge.

The trolls gaped dumbly. The companions saw the desert through the filter of *pluma*, everything painted in bright greens, deep blues, and vibrant reds. The colors grew to blazing brightness, and the monsters cowered involuntarily backward.

"What's happening?" gasped Jhatli, gazing wide-eyed at the rainbow dervish.

Then, with a sudden blink, the world around the companions shifted. The ground fell away, and everything became a blurry maze of motion. In another second, they stood together, still, but in a different place. The ridgetop below their feet was wider, firmer. Most importantly, there was no sign of the trolls.

Below them lay the same bleak chasms and barren rocks that had blocked their passage this day. Yet now that landscape lay to the west, *behind* them!

"Here, where we stand! This is the ridge we saw this morning," Erix said. She pointed to the west. "We were over there!"

"How—what happened?" demanded Jhatli, sitting heavily on the rocks.

"Teleportation," Daggrande said gruffly. "And a mighty timely bit of it, too. We moved somehow across all that stuff down there." The dwarf gestured at the chaotic land. "It would have taken us days to walk this far!"

Slowly Halloran adjusted to the shock of the teleportation. He and Daggrande gazed westward, relieved that all sign of the trolls had now disappeared in the distance. Jhatli sat on the ground, an expression of blank astonishment on his face.

"Poshtli's coming!" Erixitl pointed to the sky. The eagle winged toward them in a shallow dive, accelerating out of the western sky. It soared forward, then flashed over their heads, continuing its dive into the valley to the east.

"And look," Erix said softly as her eyes followed the eagle's flight to the land beyond the high ridge on which they stood. "This is the place where he leads us."

"What in Helm's name is *that?*" gasped Halloran. Jhatli and the dwarf, equally surprised, could only stare in astonishment.

The valley to the east was surrounded by steep ridges, its floor an expanse of dry, sandy flats broken by massive clumps of jagged boulders. It was a place of wilderness, uninhabitable and uninhabited.

Yet that was the most astonishing thing about it, for in the center of the valley rose a structure so magnificent, so immaculate in its crisp lines, so fresh-looking in its brightly painted colors, that it could have been completed yesterday.

It was a pyramid, certainly. Yet it was a pyramid three times or more the height of the great pyramid in Nexal. It rose like a mountain into the sky, a series of tiers encircling it at regular intervals. The walls above these tiers were painted in bright colors, depicting abstract images of parrots, jaguars, and snakes in an eternal chase around the pyramid. A steep stairway ascended the side facing them.

Erixitl recognized the place, for her knowledge of the True World was the most complete of the four. More to the point, the place triggered a deep sense of reverence in her soul, and she felt that the object of their quest lay before them.

"This is Tewahca," she said. "The City of the Gods."

*     *     *     *     *

Zaltec lumbered southward. The monstrous stone figure covered twenty human paces with each step. Yet some profound sense of urgency caused the god to increase his pace until the earth thundered under each crushing footstep.

The god of war marched inexorably across the desert, taking no note of the parched land, the complete lack of life. The mountainous form stood out like some jagged, natural bluff, worn by wind and water into the crude resemblance of monstrous features. Yet in its motion, it belied the explanation, for it became a menacing, monstrous object of impossible scale.

Zaltec moved in a straight line, not veering for mountain or canyon. His eyes always remained fixed before him, as if he searched for a place he remembered from a long time ago.

A place where, finally, his destiny compelled him to return.

*     *     *     *     *

The companions approached the pyramid of Tewahca with an unconquerable sense of awe. Though it had seemed to loom, huge and near, from the ridgetop, its very size made that proximity an illusion. Each step they took toward it made it grow even larger, until they could only believe that the thing had been made by the gods themselves.

It had been midday as they recovered from the shock of the teleportation. Yet the sun had neared the crest of the western ridge by the time they had descended and crossed the valley floor before the pyramid. The structure stood in pristine beauty, shining over the wasteland of the valley.

On top of the mountainous edifice stood a tall stone temple. Unlike the sides of the pyramid, which were decorated in detailed mosaics and murals etched in vivid color, the temple walls were barren of symbology. Its door, huge and open, gaped like a black mouth awaiting nourishment.

As the companions walked, they noticed other shapes around them. Here was a square framework of stone, visible at the base of a dune. There stood a series of stone arches, surrounded by waste now, but once they must have supported a grand structure. A much smaller pyramid, now broken and eroded, with sand dunes drifting around its base, squatted off to the side. Gradually they realized that they walked among the skeletal remains of a once massive city.

"Tewahca," Erixitl breathed softly so that her voice did not break the thrall of awe that bound them. "Built by humans as a battleground for the gods."

Always the great edifice loomed above them, but now they identified a second, smaller pyramid off to the side. As they neared the base of the huge structure, they saw that they walked down what had once been a wide avenue, leading directly to the pyramid.

What had first appeared to be shapeless mounds of sand now assumed regular, evenly spaced forms—the remains of old buildings. Palaces, perhaps, or great temples.

"Look at this one," Daggrande indicated as they passed a wide, flat plaza, like the porch of some great structure. Square, blocky columns stood in long rows, like silent sentinels guarding a ghostly abode. Behind the columns, dark doorways, framed by partially collapsed stone mantels, gaped like dead, silent eyes.

Shadows lengthened among the many stone columns, and the companions shuddered, sensing the lingering presence of ancient lives.

"This place must be centuries old," Halloran whispered, as if he worried that the gods could hear.

"*Many* centuries," Erixitl agreed. "I can feel the age in the dust under my feet. It's been more than a thousand years since these buildings were abandoned. And how long before that were they built?"

"And all ruined," said Daggrande. "All except that one!" He gestured toward the great pyramid.

"It might have been painted yesterday," Jhatli whispered. "The colors are so bright, the pattern so vivid."

They reached the foot of the massive structure. The shadows lengthened around them as the fading sunlight slowly climbed the western face of the pyramid.

The steep stone stairway extended up the side of the pyramid before them, though from directly below, it was visible only as far as the first terrace.

"Look!" Halloran, gasping in surprise, looked at the dirt around the pyramid's base. He indicated a clear outline of hoofprints—the prints of an iron-shod horse!

"Could one of Cordell's scouts have found this place?" Daggrande asked.

"Not likely. He'd have to cross the same ground we teleported over. Can't see any horseman coming across that if he didn't have to." Halloran followed the prints along the base of the pyramid.

"They're fresh," Jhatli explained, looking at the dust swirling into the faint depressions. "Less than an hour old."

Further questions died on their lips as they rounded the corner of the pyramid. Two men stood there, before a black mare that nickered tentatively as Halloran came into sight.

"Storm!" he cried, astounded but absolutely certain that this was his faithful war-horse. He had given the steed up for lost, since Storm had been in the very heart of Nexal on the Night of Wailing.

Then he turned to the men, aware that Erix had already rushed into the arms of . . . her father! The blind featherworker was here, in the desert! Halloran identified the other man by his garb as a priest of Qotal, more wrinkled and stooped than others he had seen.

"My daughter! My son!" Lotil embraced Erixitl and reached out a hand to clasp Halloran. The old man displayed joy but not a great deal of surprise, Hal noted with interest. "This is Coton, patriarch of Qotal," added Lotil, indicating the priest. "Now we must hurry."

Erixitl looked at her father in surprise. "Hurry? For what? Why are you here? What should we do?"

"Why, to welcome the Plumed One, of course! Why do you think that we are here?"

\* \* \* \* \*

Harak blinked his deep-sunk, bloodshot eyes as he scanned the horizon for signs of the quarry. The huge troll was grateful that the brightness of the midday sun had begun to fade, yet he was irritated that he seemed unable to find the trail of the humans and the dwarf.

He led a portion of his creatures across the broken ground between the two ridges. The trolls, fearing for their lives should Hoxitl learn of their failure, had hastened to the east, propelled in that direction by some instinctive awareness that their quarry fled somewhere before them.

As dusk settled around him, Harak quickened his pace, at last leading the band of trolls up the steep ridge that followed their rough crossing. His heart pounded, and he felt as though he approached a place of great power. It awakened some dim, primordial feeling within him, a feeling that mixed loathing and terror with the most joyous exultation.

Before the Night of Wailing had showered its godsent change upon Harak, he—like most of the other trolls—had been a priest of Zaltec. The transformation had left his mind shriveled and weak, yet some of his learnings remained with him.

The former priest remained devout, for was not the power of Zaltec manifest in Harak himself? In his long arms and legs, the green and wart-covered skin a thin disguise for the strands of ropelike sinew beneath? In his hooked talons, or his long, curving fangs?

These thoughts propelled the great troll forward. The others of his kind, three hundred strong, lumbered after their leader. They had pressed through the barren wasteland in a long, straggling file, scrambling up steep slopes of dusty red rock or picking their way through chaotic, boulder-strewn expanses. Now finally they all quickened their pace. The sense of anticipation permeated the band until a frantic eagerness marked their scramble up the last, steepest portion of the ridge.

At last the beasts crested the summit and stood there, outlined by the last rays of the dying sun, staring in dumbfounded awe into the valley before them. The massive pyramid dominated the scene, but the ruins stood out clearly before the trolls, framed by lengthening shadows. The specks of the companions were invisible in the distance, for they had reached the base of the pyramid. Yet Harak knew that they were there—especially the woman who wore the *pluma*.

He thought again of this woman. In the dim memory of his brain, he knew she was called the Chosen Daughter of Qotal. He knew that she carried the blessing of the Plumed Serpent. Yet why would she come here?

And why would she draw him after her?

Then he felt another presence, an imminent sense of great power and great menace. He sensed its nearness and knew of its impending arrival. From the north it came, a growing and dominant power that shrank every other feeling into nothingness. Finally Hanak trembled in the glory and awe of his bloodthirsty god.

And at last he understood.

\* \* \* \* \*

"The warriors are ready, my chieftain," reported Tokol. The leader of the Kultakans was the first to report to Cordell, but this fact did not surprise the commander. Despite the disaster in Nexal and the long flight with his Nexalan enemies, Tokol had remained fiercely loyal to the general who had conquered his nation.

Cordell tried to shake off a grim feeling of unease as darkness settled over the vast camp. The Nexalans had reached the valley Gultec had discovered, and in truth it offered a lush bounty—not only water, grain, and berries, but an abundance of fish and fowl as well.

Also to its credit, the valley had a high, steep rim separating it from the natural pathway by which they had entered. Knowing that the beasts still pursued them, Cordell and the chiefs had deployed their fighting men along this crest.

At least, that was the plan. Tokol's warriors, some five thousand strong, promised a good hold on the right flank. Cordell's legionnaires would stand in the center. The left flank, which was the longest, had been entrusted to the Nexalans, who could muster some twenty thousand warriors. But now Cordell waited to hear back from Chical or any of the other war chiefs responsible for positioning that line.

He stiffened as he heard a sentry cry a challenge, but then the clatter of hoofbeats told him that one of his own men approached. Cordell turned to face Grimes as the rider dismounted and raised his hand in casual salute.

"They're out there, but still a couple miles back," he reported. "A big camp of 'em. They seem to be settling in for the night."

"Did any follow the decoys?" Cordell asked.

"You mean Daggrande, with Halloran and his woman?" asked the captain.

"Yes, dammit! Did they draw any of the beasts away?"

"One of my men saw a large company of big ones—trolls, the whole lot—heading for the east ridge. It seems likely that's who they were after."

"Well, that's something, anyway." Cordell turned as another shape emerged from the darkness. He recognized the tall, haughty figure of Chical, captain of the Eagle Knights.

"My warriors are emplaced upon the ridge. If they come, we will meet them. With the favor of the gods, we will throw them back." Chical reported to the captain-general, but he did not bow.

"Good," Cordell replied. The line of defenders was ready, straddling the route between the monsters and the Nexalans in the valley. At night they were most vulnerable, and this was when he most feared an attack. They could only wait for an attack, or dawn, whichever came first.

"With the favor of the gods . . ." he repeated after Chical

and Grimes had left. Could they ask for that much anymore?

*  *  *  *  *

The eagle perched on the platform atop the pyramid. His bright eyes glittered as he looked at the humans and the dwarf who climbed to meet him. The companions gasped for air under the strain of the long climb, while the drop to the highest terrace of the pyramid fell dizzyingly below. Each flight of stairs was successively steeper than the last until here, near the summit, they placed their hands on steps that seemed mere inches from their faces as they carefully scaled the last stone stairway.

"We have come, Lord Poshtli," said Erix quietly as they finally reached the summit. "You have called us and we have come."

The eagle cocked its head to the side, and it seemed to Halloran as if the bird understood her words perfectly. He remembered the noble warrior who had been his friend, and he wondered how this bird could be that man. Yet he never questioned the fact that this was Poshtli.

The top of the pyramid formed a broad square plaza, perhaps fifty paces on a side. The temple building itself occupied most of the square, though a wide shelf passed around the building on all four sides. Though the wall had appeared featureless from the distance, now they could see that intricate carvings of snakes, birds, and jaguars covered the sides of the temple building. The creatures, carved in detailed relief, had been left unpainted.

The huge door yawned before them, larger now even than it had seemed from the ground below. It loomed a good thirty feet high and nearly that wide.

But their sense of proportion vanished entirely as they stepped through the door. They entered a monstrously huge chamber, with floor and walls of stone and a roof of thatch supported by the longest tree trunks they had ever seen. A dim glow lighted the temple interior, though no source of light was visible.

It took only an instant to realize that the building, on the *inside*, was a far larger structure than it was on the *outside*.

"This is truly a place of the gods!" whispered Jhatli, staring around in openmouthed awe. The cleric Coton stepped lightly past them and turned to the companions. His face bore an impish, almost childlike smile.

The carvings on the outer walls continued within, extending across the high walls. A pattern of inlaid stones, depicting butterflies, fish, and hummingbirds in square relief covered the entire floor.

The eagle stepped through the door behind them and then, with a beat of powerful wings, took flight. Poshtli soared into the air and then coasted in gentle circles, high above the floor.

At the center of the vast chamber stood a clean white block of stone. No one had to tell Halloran that this was an altar dedicated to Maztican gods, though he felt a sense of relief at its pristine cleanliness. It was unmarred by the sinister, rust-colored stains that so often designated these sacred altars as the feeding plates of the bloodthirsty deities.

"What do we do now?" asked Hal, with a look at his wife.

"I know," she said. "I don't know how, but I *know.*"

Erixitl, with Hal at her side, advanced slowly toward the center of the huge chamber, reaching it after a hundred steps. There she removed her cloak and placed it on the altar. Then the pair hurried back to join the others just inside the door.

"What was that all about?" Daggrande wondered aloud, but he lapsed into silence when Erix ignored him. Instead, he, like the others, focused on the center of the room.

The shade of sunset spread across the entire valley floor around them, but the top of the pyramid towered high enough to linger in the last rays of daylight. Straight to the west now, the sun's illumination spilled directly through the western door, spreading across the temple floor and flickering across the Cloak-of-One-Plume.

For a few seconds, nothing happened. Then the cloak, laid carefully across the altar, started to shimmer. Its colors whirled and shifted, spreading like a rainbow across the room—many rainbows, actually, spreading outward from the altar of the gods.

Slowly, majestically, a dim outline took shape there. They saw its huge size first, then the serpentine shape of a sinuous body. Next they saw dimly a pair of monstrously massive wings, beating slowly but not stirring the air.

Coton and Lotil threw themselves facefirst on the floor. After a second, Jhatli did the same. Halloran and Daggrande stared, awestruck, while Erixitl slowly stepped forward. After a second, Halloran stumbled to her side, taking her arm. He could feel her trembling, but her advance did not slow.

Gradually, over a period of many minutes, a massive shape appeared, squatting above the Cloak-of-One-Plume. The serpentine image was clear yet insubstantial, as if a stone thrown at it would pass right through. A mane of bright feathers encircled its neck, brighter than a hundred rainbows. Deep, glistening eyes, golden and wise, looked down upon them. Its legs curved beneath it, tipped by swordlike talons. Even through the faintness of the image, the brilliant hues of the creature's feathered coat shone with unearthly brilliance.

Halloran had no doubt that they stood now in the presence of the Plumed One, the god Qotal himself. Yet it was a presence that was not fully there.

When the Feathered Dragon spoke, his voice was surprisingly gentle, yet it possessed a deep resonance that belied his vaporous appearance.

"You have done well, Daughter of the Plume," he said.

"I have done what I had no choice but to do," Erixitl replied simply.

"Yours is a faith that is all the stronger for its doubts. It is proper that you were chosen. And even now, I know, you have questions. You wonder why I come now, after disaster has swept the land? Why have I delayed so long?"

Erixitl, mute, nodded. She stood facing the huge image, her body tense but her courage unwavering. Hal remained at her side, trying to overcome his own sense of awe.

"Centuries ago I turned my back on my people in anger as they took up the cult of blood and killing." The dragon's voice was soothing and laced with sadness. His body remained insubstantial, yet it seemed to grow more solid with each minute. The rays of the setting sun shone full upon the cloak now, and it created a dazzling nest of colors below the great serpent.

"As years passed—decades and centuries of years—my anger faded, and I saw the foolishness with which I had acted. I resolved to return to Maztica, to right the wrongs that now scarred my land.

"But when I tried to enter the True World, I found that the cult of killing held me at bay. My brother Zaltec had grown so powerful, and his followers sated his gory appetite so well, that I lacked the power to overcome him.

"Then came this event you humans call the Night of Wailing. This cataclysm smote the followers of Zaltec as well as my own. In that chaos, his own power was weakened—weakened just enough that, with the aid of a human of strong faith, I might be able to return to the world that is my true home.

"You opened that passage for me by your act of faith, when you placed the Cloak-of-One-Plume in this sacred place—a place so holy it is one of but two such in all Maztica. Now I am coming."

Qotal's voice grew strong, a ringing challenge. "And when I am here, I will face the evil one and again I will smite him atop my pyramid."

"He comes here?" Erixitl asked in shock. "Zaltec comes here?"

As she completed the words, a great shadow fell across the doorway, blocking out the sunset. They turned in shock to see two massive pillars of stone, where before had been open sky. The great monoliths moved, then bent to reveal the torso of a looming giant of stone. It stepped quickly through the huge door. Once inside the temple, it stood upright again. Its rock-hard eyes fixed the Feathered Dragon with their impassive glance, even as the giant's legs cast the Cloak-of-One-Plume into shadow. The thing's face was a grotesque caricature of humanity, corrupted by an insatiable hunger for blood, for living hearts.

Halloran heard Erixitl moan in fear beside him. Jhatli dropped his bow in shock, while even the stalwart Daggrande gasped. Only Coton and Lotil remained apparently unaffected, the old men standing impassively while the shade from the giant's body darkened the entire vast temple.

And in that shadow, the image of Qotal began to fade.

\* \* \* \* \*

From the chronicles of Coton:

*Struck down and raised again in the face of war between the gods.*

*Qotal and Zaltec clash in the vast arena of the temple, a twilit battle that the Feathered Dragon cannot possibly win. The stone monstrosity of Zaltec looms over us, the power of its hate blazing like ruby pupils from its gray, granite eyes. And the vaporous form of Qotal, interrupted in its arrival, grows faint, slowly disappearing from our view.*

*We humans cower in the corner of the room, terrified by the anger of the gods. They take no note of us, intent instead upon their wrath. It is an eerie, silent battle—a clash of wills and might without violence, yet with an outcome that creates massive danger for the loser and for the True World.*

*Zaltec raises his arms slowly. His stone fingers, each larger than a man, unfold and spread from his hands, and a nightmare wind springs up, summoned by his supernatural command.*

*Qotal bellows his anger as he fades, and the wind howls loudly. It spirals about, raising the fine grit of stone and hurtling it through the air with stinging power.*

*And then the dust surrounds us and we see nothing more, though still we hear the violence and the fury of the gods.*

# ❧ 8 ❧

# THE SPIRIT WARDENS

The wind rose to a screaming crescendo, until it seemed that the rock walls of the temple itself must splinter around the companions. Shards of dust stung their skin. The howling noise of the whirlwind drowned any attempts at communication, even shouts.

Halloran caught a glimpse of white feathers high above them. He saw the eagle, Poshtli, diving through the dust toward the great stone statue. The massive shape of Qotal seemed to lurch forward, though it was difficult to see.

The magnificent bird disappeared into the cloud with an angry shriek, and the former legionnaire groaned inwardly at the courageous but futile act. He knew that Poshtli could be smashed by a casual, even accidental blow from one of Zaltec's fingers.

Erixitl moaned as the Cloak-of-One-Plume floated into the air, borne across the temple by the chaotic gusts of battle. The wind tore at the colorful garment with a maddened intensity, tearing brilliant plumage away, rendering it into minute tufts of rubbish. In a moment of awful violence, the cloak disappeared, and at the same time it grew darker still in the huge temple.

They heard a sharp squawk, and once again the eagle came into sight, wheeling high in the air. Tucking his wings, talons extended, Poshtli dove toward the mountainous block that was Zaltec's head.

The little party huddled together in a corner of the temple, paralyzed by fear and awe. Shaking his head and wiping the dust from his eyes, Halloran tried to peer through the dust. It was then he realized that others had entered the temple.

Dimly, through the haze in the air, he saw a lumbering figure move through the door. Others followed, and the brilliance of the setting sun outlined their forms clearly—trolls, the minions of Zaltec. More and more of the grotesque creatures crowded through, filling the space behind the stone monolith's feet.

Halloran groaned inwardly. Still, it seemed to him that he and his companions, crouched in the shadows and concealed by the raging dustcloud, had not yet been seen. But how much longer could they remain concealed?

Slapping Daggrande's arm to get his attention, Halloran indicated the monsters as still more of the beasts pressed into the temple to watch their master's battle—their master's victory.

For indeed it seemed that Qotal had faded from sight in the face of Zaltec's relentless might. Poshtli, too, had vanished. The huge stone figure began to lower its arms, and slowly the wind began to fade.

Halloran remembered the other door, in the east wall. "Come on!" he shouted, prodding the others ahead of him. With gestures, he urged them toward the door.

They crept along the base of the wall, desperately hoping to avoid the notice of the monsters. Halloran stayed in the rear, his hand near Helmstooth's hilt. He didn't want to draw the weapon prematurely, for its gleaming blade would certainly draw the attention of the trolls still stumbling into the temple. Daggrande, he noticed, carried his axe, the now useless crossbow slung across his shoulder beside his empty quiver.

Finally they reached the towering opening, as big as the one on the west, where they had entered. Behind them, Qotal shrieked in fading frustration. The contest obviously was nearly over.

"Run!" Halloran shouted. "Get down while there's still time!"

The little party burst from the temple, starting toward the steep stairway that lay only a few steps away. They had crossed half the distance when bellows of rage sounded on either side of them.

A pair of monstrous trolls, drool spraying from their curving fangs, sprang at them from beside the doorway. With startling quickness, Jhatli raised his bow and sent a stone-tipped shaft driving into the troll's belly.

Helmstooth seemed to leap into Hal's hand of the sword's own will. He lunged forward with liquid smoothness, driving the steel tip deep into the other troll's gullet. The *pluma* strength of his hand backed the blow, and then tore the blade free with a gory rip to the side. Daggrande, meanwhile, hacked at the beast that had been wounded by Jhatli. Fury and fear tightened his muscles, and the keen axe blade bit deeply into the troll's thigh.

Both beasts, painfully wounded, bellowed their agony as they fell. The surface of the pyramid shook to the heavy steps of their brethren, charging around the temple. In moments, more of the monsters burst into sight, charging from both sides.

The companions stood trapped on the strip between the temple and the edge of the pyramid. The stairway dropped steeply away, far too sheer a drop to allow for a fighting withdrawal. Any blow from an attacker above would send one tumbling down the stone steps hundreds of feet to the ground below.

"Your token, Daughter! Use it now!" Lotil spoke urgently. The blind man sensed, as clearly as any of them, their mortal danger.

"Use it? How?" demanded Erixitl. At her throat, the green-plumed jadestone medallion seemed to float in the air, but she was unaware of what power it possessed to stop the rampaging attackers.

"No time now. Take my hand. All of you, link hands!" Lotil barked the words like a warrior, startling Erixitl, Coton, and Jhatli into compliance.

But Hal and Daggrande stood to either side of the party, facing the onrushing monsters. The dwarf chopped savagely, knocking another troll off the side of the pyramid, while Halloran held his sword ready to meet the first crush, mere seconds away.

"My hand! Take it!" Erixitl shouted, sensing her father's intentions. Desperately Halloran reached behind him, feeling her firm clasp on his left hand. With his right he stabbed at the leading troll.

Daggrande, busily recovering his balance, focused on the charging horde. The dwarf didn't see Coton's hand extended toward him.

"Jump!" cried Lotil, urging them off the edge. Halloran heard, stumbling to the side as Erixitl pulled him. He hesitated at the lip of the steep drop, and then felt a tug as his wife hurled herself out into space. Groaning, he leaped after her.

Coton, patriarch of Qotal, looked up as he followed Lotil and Jhatli. With a sudden twist, he reached out and seized Daggrande's elbow. The dwarf cursed as his swing passed wide of its mark.

But then he, too, followed the others off the precipice. The dwarf clenched his eyes shut, preparing to die.

A soft swirl of wind arose underneath them, pressing upward like a cushion of down. They struggled awkwardly, twisting under a feeling of weightlessness. Erixitl's feathered token floated out from her neck, as if raised by the gentle breeze. And slowly, easily, like a leaf that falls from a tree, the companions drifted toward the earth below.

Howling madly, several trolls hurled themselves into the air, trying to reach the slowly settling party. Their leaps fell short and the creatures plummeted earthward, striking the stairway about halfway down and tumbling to the bottom, shapeless jumbles of shattered bone and torn skin.

The wind gusted, and the cushion drifted away from the pyramid, circling northward and then curving toward the west, still drifting earthward. In their haste to pursue, the beasts of the Viperhand raced down the steep stairs, several more of them stumbling and falling to their deaths. And always the steady wind carried the companions farther and farther away.

Too terrified to speak, they clutched each other's hands and prayed the spell supporting them would not break. Nothing visible or tangible supported them, and they couldn't escape a horrifying sense of falling.

"Don't look down," Halloran gasped, suddenly queasy when he made that mistake.

Settling slowly, drifting with the faintest breezes, the cushion of *pluma* supported them safely. They saw that it carried them toward the ruined avenue they had first walked along when they approached the pyramid.

Finally, with a parting swirl, the wind set them gently on the earth and gusted away. Half a mile away, the monsters howled with glee and charged, while the temple atop the pyramid had grown suddenly, ominously quiet. Nearby gaped the black doorways of the ruined building they had passed on their approach to the pyramid. The many columns on its porch still stood, so many mute sentries barring passage to an unimagined interior.

"Storm!" cried Halloran as he saw movement around the corner of the ruin. The black mare galloped toward him. She had fled at the approach of the monsters, but now she kicked up her heels in delight.

Coton silently raised his hand and pointed toward the black doorways. They all sensed his suggestion: They should take refuge there.

"That could be a dead-end trap!" growled Daggrande.

"We can't outrun them," grunted Hal. "We might as well fight them where we can put our backs to the wall."

Without further hesitation, they started through the forest of stone columns toward the black doors. Even in the darkening twilight, Hal could see that each column was carved elaborately into the standing shape of an Eagle or Jaguar Knight, with the customary helmet, beaked or fanged, capping the structure at perhaps ten feet tall.

Then they reached the first of the doorways, a ruined aperture with a capstone atop an almost fully arched entry. Beyond, a smell of must and decay, odd for its dampness in this harsh clime, wafted forth.

Coton led the way, with Daggrande and Jhatli close behind. Erixitl took her father's arm and followed, while Halloran, with Storm beside him, brought up the rear. He held Helmstooth high, ready for the pursuit he knew must eventually follow. Around them, he saw walls and dim, rubble-strewn chambers. They turned a corner and the doorway disappeared from sight.

Very quickly full darkness closed over them, broken only by the pale light from Helmstooth. A damp and oppressive sense of age seemed to linger here, along with a dim presence that Halloran could not identify. It was not his sense of smell or hearing—or any sense, really—that alarmed him, but the swordsman felt a vague menace that raised the hackles at the base of his neck.

Coton, however, seemed to see a path before them, for he led them deeper into the structure, turning his way through a maze of twisting corridors with uncanny accuracy.

"Wait," said Daggrande, suddenly bringing them to a halt.

"Do you see them?" asked Erixitl.

Around them, dark shadows pressed, and Hal raised the sword. Puzzled, he saw that the light did not penetrate these shadows.

Then his blood chilled. He saw that the shadows themselves came closer.

\* \* \* \* \*

Poshtli shuddered under the impact of a blow of incredible violence. For a moment, he felt certain that he had been killed, but slowly his senses returned. His talons clung tightly to something, some long trailing thing that he vaguely identified as the feathered mane of the Plumed Dragon.

Rage coursed through the eagle's proud body, fury directed at the bestial god who tried to drive Qotal from the True World. He shrieked his anger and tried to break free, to once again dive at that despised foe.

But the plumage of the dragon's body seemed to take on a life of its own, seizing and grasping the eagle's claws, holding it fast. Poshtli beat his wings in frustration, wondering why the god refused his aid, but he couldn't break free.

The battle passed its climax, and he could sense the Feathered Dragon's might failing. Knowing his mortal blows could help but little, Poshtli nonetheless craved the chance to flail against the hated figure of Zaltec.

Still he could not break free. Finally, vaguely, he became aware that the battle had faded to silence around him.

\* \* \* \* \*

The monsters of the Viperhand attacked the Nexalan refugees before dawn, hurling themselves in a vast wave up the shallow ridge that separated them from the humans and their lush valley. Atop the ridge stood a thin line of Kultakan and Nexalan warriors and legionnaires.

The Mazticans showered the attacking horde with arrows. Cordell's soldiers, those with crossbows, waited until the squinting, pig-eyed forms materialized from the darkness. Then the weapons chunked loudly, delivering a devastating volley into the attacking ranks.

In another moment, the two forces clashed with sudden, brutal violence. Spears set to meet the charge, the native warriors stood firm, driving their stone-tipped weapons home. But the bulk of the attackers pressed on heavily, and many of the spearshafts snapped and splintered from the force of the collision.

Obsidian-edged *macas* in the hands of both sides chopped and hacked furiously. The line twisted and bent, collapsing in places only to reform as the human warriors counterattacked and drove the monstrous foes back. The Mazticans fought with an unaccustomed fury, striking to kill instead of to capture.

And the monsters knew only to kill, for each death on the field was a sacrifice rendered directly to Zaltec.

The few horsemen remaining to Cordell charged into the line of orcs, and the humanoids proved as helpless as had the Maztican warriors to resist the plunging lancers.

"The ogres! Slay the ogres first!" The captain-general howled the command, and his riders turned their lances toward the hulking brutes, few in number, that loomed among the orcs.

A small band of orcs burst through the line. Howling, they

turned upon the flank of the defenders. Cordell's only reserve, several companies of Kultakan archers, fired volley after volley against the breakthrough, cutting down most of the orcs before the line could collapse. Finally the remainder of the orcs turned back toward the breach, only to find that it had closed behind them. The reserve company moved forward, cutting down the last of them with *macas* and daggers.

On the right, Tokol roared and shouted among his warriors, leaping into each breach with a shrill howl of combat lust, laying about with the bloody blade of his sword, single-handedly driving the orcs before his blows. The Kultakan leader fought like a wild man, driving his men to equal heights of frenzy. As his father, Takamal, had done for seven decades, Tokol elicited the greatest levels of courage and dedication from his warriors.

To the left, Chical, Captain of Eagles, stabbed with his lance, standing firm and, by example, holding the long line of Nexalan warriors. The tip of his weapon, formed from a sharp steel knife, drove into the bellies of the largest ogres, and the mighty strength of the Eagle Knight drove the weapon home, killing the beasts whenever they lumbered toward him. His example, like Tokol's, steadied and inspired his warriors to emulate him.

In the middle, Cordell himself fought like a maniac from the saddle of his prancing stallion, driving home his own lance until the weapon snapped in two. Then the shaft of his sword grew bloody at the cost of the orcan horde, while his steed bucked and kicked, crushing skulls and breaking limbs among the howling attackers.

In the end, these three men would carry the burden of victory or defeat.

Hoxitl watched the battle from the rear of his army, at first exulting in the momentum of the charge. But as the fight stabilized along the defenders' line, he sensed that the monstrous forces, without the trolls to form a spearhead, lacked the iron-fisted punch necessary to shatter the humans' line.

The beastlord knew that he had to act, and with a great

howl, he lumbered forward, cuffing his way through the ranks of his troops toward the hated enemy. The soft light of dawn fell incongruously on the harsh spectacle of pain and death, and the humans stared in horror at the monstrous apparition that now materialized in the dim light.

"There!" cried Cordell, sensing the faltering courage of the men at the appearance of the looming monster. Indeed, Hoxitl towered more than twice as high as a man on horseback.

Nevertheless the captain-general spurred his stallion forward, and the steed raced past the beastlord. Cordell's sword cut a deep wound in Hoxitl's thigh, and then the horse danced away, just beyond the monster's near-deadly return blow.

Tokol and Chical, too, saw the menace of the monster's attack and rushed forward to the aid of their ally. The Eagle Knight hurled his lance, and the weapon drove deep into Hoxitl's flank. With a howl, the monster tore the weapon free and hurled it to the ground, but at the same time Tokol stabbed him in the back of his knee. Before he could face this new threat, Cordell's stallion sprang forward, and the captain-general's sword struck a new gash across the beast's belly.

Howling madly, beset by painful wounds, the cleric's nature took over the monster's body. Fighting was a thing left to men of war, not their religious leaders. Still shrieking, Hoxitl stumbled away, driven by the painful blows of the human leaders.

Without the savage exhortations of Hoxitl, the orcs lost heart as more and more of their number fell before the arrows, swords, and horses of the humans.

"Charge them!" urged Cordell. "Attack!"

His words were heard only along a short portion of the line, but here the legionnaires and Kultakans surged forward. The sudden shock of the advance broke the stalemate of the battle, and sent several hundred orcs streaming away from the fight in panic. The orcs' retreat, sensed along the line, provided the weight to break the fighting morale of the rest of the monsters, at least temporarily.

Finally the wave fell back to the protection of the battle line, battered and eroded but still firm. Yet the beasts did not rout in terror, but rather withdrew in surly admission of their temporary failure.

Even as they slowly backed away, into the dusty vale where they had made their previous camp, the humans on the ridge sensed that their enemies would return.

\* \* \* \* \*

Black shapes pressed forward, darker shadows among the impenetrable black of the ruin. They seethed and danced among the rubble, pressing like smoke against the circle of light formed by the companions.

"It's a tomb," hissed Daggrande. "These are the ghosts!" The dwarf's voice carried an uncharacteristic tremor.

"They are indeed the spirits of the dead," said Lotil. The blind man seemed to sniff the air, as aware of the presence as any of them. "But they are not ghosts—not in the way that you think."

The shades did indeed appear vaguely manlike, for they raised shadowy arms and extended black, smoking fingers toward the companions. Jhatli shivered, backing away from an apparation that reared up beside him, while Daggrande whirled this way and that, his axe held ready—for what, he didn't know.

Halloran swallowed hard. He couldn't fathom the raging horror evoked within him by these shapeless denizens. He only knew that they twisted his stomach with fear and almost compelled his steps to turn back toward the monsters that pursued them.

He saw a black, sacklike form rise up before him, and he lifted Helmstooth high. Something held his hand from striking—perhaps the fear that his steel could not affect anything so intangible—but in the face of the gleaming blade, the shade did not waver.

"Flee! They come to us!" Jhatli's panic rang shrill in the cry of his voice as the youth turned and sprinted, piling into Erixitl and nearly knocking her off her feet. Beside Hal,

Storm reared back, neighing, her eyes rolled high into their sockets.

"Wait!" said the woman quickly, steadying Jhatli with a hand on his arm. "See? They do not attack."

Indeed the shades seemed to linger at the very fringe of their vision, dancing in a somber cadence as they slowly circled the companions. They could have been human in shape, Hal thought, or nearly anything else about the size of a man.

They closed in then, waving and swirling. Halloran saw tendrils of darkness reaching out toward them, and he felt cold terror grip his soul. Beside him, Jhatli whimpered, and he felt that the youth would have fled if not for the presence of his companions. Hal, too, considered flight as a serious alternative.

But some deeper calling bade him stay. He knew that the creatures outside this temple offered nothing but cold, sudden death. He had to trust the instincts of those who had led him here.

Coton started forward toward the ring of encircling darkness. Dimly Halloran saw something dark and intangible rise before the priest, and then Coton stopped, restrained by an invisible barrier. Hal's flesh crawled at the sight of dim fingers of darkness plucking at the cleric's robe, tugging him back toward the other humans.

If the cleric felt the same revulsion, he didn't display it. Instead, he slowly yielded to the insistent force, stepping back until he again stood among his companions.

"Ah, these are the spirit wardens," said Lotil softly, as if announcing a pleasant revelation. "They stand astride the paths of the gods, barring the paths to all."

Before the blind featherworker, Coton nodded gently, as if agreeing with Lotil's assessment.

"To all?" Halloran, his fear rapidly fading, growled in frustration.

"So it is said," Lotil replied with a shrug. "Though gods are fickle. Perhaps the right sacrifice may open the path."

Coton turned to regard Erixitl. The priest's eyes were soft and understanding. Behind them, they heard heavy footfalls and growling, snapping commands as the beasts of the Viperhand followed them into the ruin. Several guttural barks sounded close, and it seemed that the monsters followed the same path into the tangled ruin as the companions had.

Erix hesitated for a moment. She cast a pain-filled look at her father, and though the blind man could not see her, Lotil nodded slightly. Raising her hands to her shoulders, Erix lifted the leather thong suspending her amulet over her head. Holding it gently, allowing its dazzling presence to swing lightly in her hands for the last time, she stepped past the priest and laid it on the ground, at the very feet of the dancing shades.

Then the way lay open before them, though they couldn't see the darkness recede. Instead, it was a sense of lightness that propelled them forward, and they sensed no barrier to their flight.

The pale light of Hal's sword lit their path as he stepped into the lead. Coton led the horse, while the keen-eyed Daggrande brought up the rear. They followed a winding corridor, sensing its descent under their feet.

Behind them, the howls of their pursuers echoed from the stone walls, a cacophony of chaos hastening them along. Then the snarls turned to yelps of terror, and soon the sounds of pursuit turned to flight as the monsters fled the nightmare wardens of the tomb.

*     *     *     *     *

From the chronicles of Coton:

*In the long darkness of escape, we strive to reach the dawn.*

*Through the night we flee, following the roads of the gods beneath the City of Tewahca. Halloran calls on his power of sorcery, a power I have never seen, and brings a bright glow to the tip of his sword. This lights our way through the deepest of the maze.*

*And here we pass tombs of great kings and the graves of*

brave warriors. Rich chiefs, too, lie here amid great treasures—heaps of gold that sometimes rise higher than the burial mounds themselves or floating images of pluma that waft temptingly overhead.

From these hallowed niches, dark figures move toward us, some wrapped in their burial shrouds, others bare skeletons, animated by some dim and forgotten power. They stumble and shuffle in a ghastly facade of attack, and our courage is tested by each new nightmare.

But always the blessing of the spirit wardens looms over us, and it gives us passage where others would surely die. Finally we move from the deep tombs, working our way again toward the surface. The long night march leaves my companions and me exhausted, but there is no talk of pause nor of rest. Indeed, as we press forward and the hours pass, our urgency grows greater. Our steps fall quickly as haste compels us through the winding paths of darkness and death.

And then, as we climb a great stairway that seems to raise us from the bowels of the earth, a breath of wind touches our faces. Then we see the cave mouth, with the rich blue of dawn beckoning beyond.

# ❦ 9 ❦

# IN HOPELESS FLIGHT

The green parrot winged steadily across the desert lands, above the vast wasteland of sand and rock and brush. Nowhere along Gultec's eastward course did he see water; it seemed as though only the narrow strip of land followed by the Nexalans had received the blessing of the gods. The rest of the House of Tezca remained very much the same barren waste it had always been.

Finally the bird reached a long shore, where a smooth beach, outlined in foaming breakers, marked the end of the desert and the beginning of the coral blue Sea of Azul. This crystalline water filled the gap between the mainland of Maztica and the jungled penninsula of Far Payit.

Gultec felt the strain of the long flight in his wings, but the summons of his master, Zochimaloc, urged him onward. Now, however, the parrot dove, breaking its descent to race just above the glittering surface of the sea.

Then, in the blink of an eye, the bird did a strange thing: It dipped and dove into the crest of wave, tucking its wings close against its body and disappearing into the water.

The parrot vanished in a shower of spray. Two dozen feet farther along the bird's path of flight, a blue dolphin broke the surface, wriggling in the air for a second before diving back into the water. Sleek and powerful, the mammal dove and splashed its way steadily eastward, bursting from the sea in a rainbow of spray before nosing gracefully back into the cool, blue-green depths.

The dolphin that was Gultec dove after a school of small fish, feasting for several minutes before he again broke the surface to breathe. Gultec felt a wonderful sense of exhilaration, broken only by the knowledge that his master's summons indicated serious trouble ahead.

After a night and a day of swimming, the great sea mammal drew close to another shore. Where the eastern boundary had been backed by countless miles of dry desert, however, this beach appeared as a tiny strip of sand bordered by a verdant growth of jungle foliage.

Here again Gultec took to wing, shifting in midleap from the dolphin's body back to that of the bright parrot. Like a green missile, he shot into the sky, quickly gaining height. He soared over the tops of the highest trees, still climbing. He knew that Tulom-Itzi lay near.

Then an irregularity in the tropical growth caught the parrot's keen eye. Concerned, Gultec veered to the north, diving slightly to gain speed and a closer view. An inexplicable sense of urgency—an urgency that approached terror—compelled him forward.

The stench of rot reached him first—not a sweet, lingering odor such as always characterizes the jungle, but a thick, cloying wave of nausea that signified a horrifying extent of destruction and decay.

Soon he soared along a wide swath of death, a wasteland as devastated as the barren reaches of the House of Tezca. This waste shocked him, however, for very recently it had been lush. Like the body of a repugnant serpent, the pathway twisted through the jungles of Far Payit. Brown, naked tree trunks lay on the ground in a twisted jumble. Pools of muddy water lay spattered across the dead earth, breeding grounds only for the flies that feasted upon death.

Shock, anger, and finally rage propelled the bird's flight as Gultec tried to absorb the spectacle below him. He couldn't guess as to its nature, but he knew that he saw below him the reason for Zochilmaloc's summons.

The swath twisted inland, away from Tulom-Itzi, and so Gultec dove to the south. For the first time, he wondered if he might be too late. His heart lightened only slightly as he saw that the forests leading to that hidden city seemed unscathed.

Finally he saw the great stone dome rising before him and the bright, squared pyramids of the city's heart. His relief choked him as he tucked his wings and entered a long dive, feeling at last as though he had come back to his true home.

\* \* \* \* \*

The great stone figure of Zaltec stood motionless in the center of the massive temple. The dust had settled in a film across the floor. Nothing moved within the cavernous chamber.

If emotions could have played across the vast, stony surface of the war god's face, cruel triumph would have glared there, an ultimate explosion of hatefulness. But, instead, the granite visage remained impassive, as cold as ever.

Now Zaltec turned to face each of the four directions. Toward each, he knew, lay his domains. He had vanquished the only one who could challenge him. Now let the ultimate reign of Zaltec begin!

But where should the center of his power be? This the bloody god pondered long and hard while the sun passed beneath the world and rose again into the morning sky.

Tewahca sprawled around him, and his immortal memory recalled the place in all its splendor, with water and food and humans who worshiped him. But now, in its barren vistas, it was an old place, fit to be abandoned by men. How, then, should a god expect to make a home here?

Instead, Zaltec gradually turned back to the north, where lay the moist valley of Nexal, surmounted by its looming volcanoes. Nexal, where the beasts of the Viperhand dwelled; the ruined city, still guardian of buried riches, the seat of an empire that may yet rise again.

When full day blazed around him, Zaltec stepped from the temple and the pyramid, dropping easily to the dusty ground. When his footsteps again shook the earth, they resounded in the north, along the path to Nexal.

\* \* \* \* \*

Halloran and Jhatli emerged from the mouth of the cave first, while the others waited for their report. The youth veered to the right, readying an arrow and watching his companion while Halloran moved carefully forward.

After taking a few steps, Jhatli turned to look back at Halloran, a scowl on the youth's face. "Why is it we always run away?" he asked, his voice challenging. "Why do we never stop to fight?"

"You'll get your chance to fight, I'm sure," Hal retorted, looking around them at steeply sloping rock walls that rose on either side. The floor of a ravine created a narrow, twisting pathway immediately below them. "Believe it or not, there'll be a time when you won't look forward so eagerly to your next fight."

"Never!" boasted Jhatli, but Halloran ignored him.

"It's a dry ravine," the man called into the cave after completing his inspection. "It must be in the base of one of the ridges that surround Tewahca."

Slowly the others came forth, while Jhatli climbed the slope to see if he could get their bearings. The underground passage had led them to a stone archway in the side of a steep slope. Directly across from their exit, another slope climbed upward. To the left and right, the narrow bottom of a ravine snaked away, slowly climbing to the right and descending to the left.

Coton and Lotil sat upon a rock and breathed the sweet air of the desert dawn, while Daggrande led the black mare to some nearby flat ground at the base of the ravine. The blind featherworker breathed the fresh air with obvious relish. From somewhere beneath his cloak, he pulled out a sheet of fine cotton mesh and a small bag. Removing a bright blue tuft of plumage from the sack, he began to work it into the mesh.

Erixitl emerged last, with a lingering look into the darkened passage. She went to her husband, and he took her in his arms. For long minutes, they all remained still, resting quietly and remembering the sights of the long and terrifying night.

"Your quiver!" exclaimed Halloran suddenly, looking at Daggrande.

"By Helm! Where did these come from?" The dwarf

looked in amazement at several dozen straight quarrels, sturdy missiles tipped with heads of dark black stone. All of them remembered their despair when, the previous day, he had expended his last bolt at the pursuing trolls.

"During our walk through the paths of the dead," said Erixitl, softly, "the spirits have bestowed gifts upon us."

"In exchange for your token," said Halloran quietly.

"And the trolls didn't come after us." Daggrande added this important point.

They heard a clatter of stones, and Halloran instinctively reached for his sword, but soon Jhatli slid into view, rapidly descending the steep slope of the gully.

"I saw Tewahca!" he cried. "That way, to the south! And look! I've got a fresh supply of arrows!" Jhatli pulled forth a slender shaft, narrower than Daggrande's, with a thin sliver of a head. His own quiver held several dozen of the weapons. The keen tips, like the dwarf's, were formed from shiny black stone, thinner and sharper than obsidian.

For several moments, they absorbed the news, none of them venturing a suggestion to move. Finally Halloran felt the need to take some action, at least to plan.

"Where do we go from here?" he asked. "Back to the Nexalans?"

Erixitl gently pulled away from him and walked a few feet along the floor of the ravine. She turned to face the group and sighed slowly before speaking.

"Zaltec has barred Qotal's entry here. My cloak, which opened the path, is lost. There is no hope of Qotal returning to the True World through this portal."

"Indeed," agreed Lotil as Coton nodded silently.

"We cannot give up!" Jhatli barked. He brandished his bow, one of the new arrows nocked. "If not here, then somewhere else!"

"Precisely!" Erix agreed. "When the god spoke to us, he said that this was one of but two places in the world where he could seek to return."

"Great. He didn't tell us where the other one is, as I recall," interjected Daggrande.

"He didn't have to. I know where it is," Erixitl replied. Only

Coton's face brightened at her words, though none of the others noticed the cleric's delight

"Where would he come, if not to the city of the gods?" asked Jhatli.

"To the place that was built in anticipation of his return, the place from which he left Maztica so many lifetimes ago!"

"Twin Visages!" exclaimed Halloran, suddenly understanding. He well remembered the two huge faces carved in the coastal cliffs of Payit. It had been the first landfall of the Golden Legion along the shores of Maztica, and even at the time, it had seemed a place of great sacred tradition.

"Yes, of course," Lotil agreed. "Many of the stories predicted that Qotal would one day return there. But how can he, since he lacks the power to overcome Zaltec?"

"We can help him!" Erix said firmly. "We can hold Zaltec at bay long enough for Qotal to enter Maztica and reach his full strength. Then he can defeat the god of war and regain his former station."

"Let us go!" Jhatli cried. "We will fight our way there if we have to! I will fight at your side, sister!"

She smiled gently. "I know you will, my friend, and I am grateful to you. I know that all of you will, but it will not be easy."

"How far is it to Twin Visages?" asked Daggrande. He had seen the place—all the legionnaires had—when they had made landfall there. But he had marched and fought and fled very far since then.

"I don't know," Erixitl replied bluntly. "It will take us a month, perhaps more, just to cross the desert. Then we will reach the lands of Far Payit. Only when we have crossed those thick jungles will we reach the Payit country and finally Twin Visages."

Erixitl looked at her father, at all of her companions, frankly. "I was too hasty to condemn Qotal for a thing he could not control. I didn't understand that a god, like a mortal, can be constrained by factors beyond his power." She lowered her eyes, then looked up again before continuing.

"And perhaps I have been forced to admit that we need gods—or a god, in any event. We have all seen the threat presented by Zaltec. Qotal, it seems, is the best hope we have."

Coton rose stiffly from the boulder. He crossed to the woman and took her hands in his, looking steadily into her eyes. Erixitl met the silent cleric's gaze for a moment, then collapsed, sobbing, into his arms.

At the same time, Storm raised her head, ears cocked forward, alert. Daggrande and Halloran followed the mare's gaze down the ravine toward the open valley beyond.

"I think we've got company," grunted the dwarf.

Instantly the others turned to look, their hearts chilling at the apprehension in Daggrande's voice. The narrow ravine floor twisted slowly downward, the first bend some hundred yards away.

The first creature to come into sight was a hulking troll, its arms nearly dragging on the ground. Its black, expressionless eyes fastened upon the companions, and it threw back its head to utter a sharp, harsh bark.

Hal saw others, then—vacant-faced trolls with outstretched, clawlike hands, emerging from around the bend in the gully. The first troll leaped forward, covering the distance between them with prodigious bounds.

"Come on! Up the ravine . . . go!" barked Halloran. He took Erixitl's arm and bodily lifted her onto the back of the prancing Storm.

"Take her and her father! We'll try to hold them back!" he barked at Coton. With surprising quickness, the cleric took the horse's reins and started up the narrow draw. Lotil touched the mare's shoulder and started to follow, stumbling, but then Erix and the priest quickly boosted the blind man into the saddle.

Daggrande fired a bolt and Jhatli launched a steady stream of arrows into the approaching horde. The missiles cut deep wounds in their flesh, forcing howls of pain from the beasts. But even the trolls that fell continued to advance, slowly squirming forward in the wake of their charging comrades.

Halloran, with Helmstooth ready for blood, stood between and slightly ahead of the two archers. The trio blocked the narrow ravine floor. Several dozen of the beasts rushed toward them now, with more coming into sight every moment. Their snarls and barks filled the air, prelude to a slaughter.

The only victory he and his companions could hope to gain, Halloran knew, was time for the others to escape.

\* \* \* \* \*

The tribe from Sunhome linked up with Traj's warriors after only two days' march. Luskag saw with pleasure that those doughty fighters had progressed well with the *pluma*stone weaponry. Nearly all of Traj's dwarves carried blades of the shiny black stone.

Other bands of desert dwarves joined them steadily as they moved toward the City of the Gods, until nearly a thousand stocky fighters—called, by Mazticans, the "Hairy Men of the Desert"—marched across the House of Tezca in a long, apparently tireless column. More than half carried weapons of enchanted stone that seemed every bit the equal of steel.

The last of the tribes to reach them was Pullog's, since they had had the longest march. But finally the entire nation had massed, and with Pullog and Luskag in the lead, they began to march toward the dry valley near the center of the desert.

The night before their arrival, they camped in a low, dusty bowl a dozen miles from the City of the Gods. But even from this far away they could hear the thunderous conflict raging through the desert night.

"We are too late," muttered Traj dejectedly. "We hear the world torn to pieces before us!"

"Nonsense!" barked Pullog, surprising and pleasing Luskag with his encouragement. "We hear the sounds of battle joined, but we will arrive before a decision is reached." The southern chief patted the hefty stone axe at his side, a *pluma*stone blade given to him by Luskag.

"Aye," grunted Luskag, who had emerged as their overall leader, since it had been his initiative that had gotten the tribes together in the first place. "Though I sense that we must make haste."

So urgent was this sense that the dwarves broke camp without sleeping and trudged through the long night. At dawn, they arrived on the ridgeline surrounding the city of the gods.

And they saw their enemy below.

*　*　*　*　*

"Watch your back!"

Daggrande's shout pulled Halloran's attention around. The bloody tip of Helmstooth followed a split second later, plunging into the heart of the troll that had somehow slipped around him. Fortunately—and it was the only good fortune they had right now—the steep sides of the ravine kept most of their hulking attackers in front of them.

Hal turned back to the pressing numbers there. Daggrande, his crossbow slung over his back, now hacked with the keen blade of his battle-axe. Jhatli, following the orders of the two soldiers, had fallen back, and now sent his arrows arcing over their heads into the monsters that crowded the bottom of the narrow ravine.

Halloran didn't have time to see if Erixitl and the two old men had disappeared from view. A heavy club descended toward his skull and he skipped to the side, striking off the arm that bore it. A green-taloned troll lunged for him, and he sent the beast crawling, legless, back to its compatriots.

Daggrande hacked into the leg of another troll, crippling it. The stocky dwarf ducked nimbly away from yet another of the creatures, springing up beside Halloran to drive a third monster back with sharp chops of his own dripping blade.

"Can't . . . hold out . . . much longer," he gasped.

The bands of *pluma* around Hal's wrists sustained him, driving his blows with tremendous force. The magic couldn't overcome his own rapidly growing fatigue, however, but he roughly forced it away from his awareness. Hammering his weapon with brutal, mindless strength, he bashed and hacked and crushed the attackers in the apparently endless horde.

"Go," he panted. "Take the kid . . . see that others get to safety! I'll hold them off . . . as long as I can!"

With the fury of desperation, Halloran suddenly attacked, driving the whole pack of beasts away from him with a whirlwind series of blows. One troll, too slow to retreat, howled in agony as Helmstooth sliced open his gut. Daggrande, following, silenced the brute with one chop of his axe.

"Can't leave you now," growled Daggrande. "Not when we just got back together again!"

"We've had some good fights, eh?" Halloran fell back slightly, catching his breath while the monsters recouped their courage. His throat tightened at the evidence of the dwarf's loyalty.

"None better than this one." The dwarf, too, gasped for air, then raised his axe in the face of renewed attack.

A trio of massive trolls forced their way to the front of the monsters packing the ravine floor. Each held an obsidian-studded *maca*, and they loomed high over Halloran even as they crouched and advanced.

A sudden shower filled the air over the ravine as shapes darted through the air like locusts, or driving rain . . . or arrows! Soundlessly, a volley of sharp missiles dropped from the high ground into the close-packed ranks of the trolls. The unseen archers launched another volley, and the attention of the monsters immediately shifted to this new threat.

"Where are those coming from?" demanded Daggrande, astonished.

"From our friends, whoever they are," Hal answered, equally dumbfounded.

The beasts howled in pain and chaos, turning their faces skyward in time to receive another volley of dark, stone-tipped missiles. As the trolls plucked the arrows free and the bleeding wounds slowly closed, yet another shower sent stone tips digging painfully into monstrous flesh. The arrows came from the shoulder above the ravine floor, but still the archers remained unseen.

Then the narrow gulley resounded with fresh, hearty whoops of combat. Growling and cowering, the trolls raised their weapons and gaped upward, confused and frightened.

"Look! Here they come!" Halloran pointed upward as the fringe of the ravine suddenly shifted into movement. Their rescuers, they saw, had lain in plain sight on the slope above but were so effectively camouflaged that they had been virtually invisible.

They saw a swarm of small figures pouring into the ravine from the rim of the gulley to their left. Howling with instinctive fury, the new attackers descended upon the creatures before Hal and Daggrande, striking them with sharp, brutal strokes of their stone axes.

"I can't believe it," Daggrande declared, lowering his axe and watching the fight, too astonished and too exhausted to attack.

"They're *dwarves!*"

\* \* \* \* \*

From the chronicles of Coton:

*In the light of day, we tremble now, as the bloody hand of Zaltec is nigh.*

*We wait for the future, our fate determined by the strong arms and keen weapons of a soldier, a dwarf, and a youth; and though the enemy numbers many, our faith is great, for the one true god of goodness watches over us.*

*We three, two old men—one blind, the other sworn to silence—and a young woman who grows more round with child every passing day, can do naught for the battle. Yet our fate is tied irreversibly to those who strike blows in the name of Qotal.*

*And so we pause in the heights of the twisting ravine. The horse can climb no farther by this path, and even could we proceed, we have no future if our friends fall in this fight.*

*But again the blessings of Qotal are manifest.*

*Now we find proof of goodness and also the truth of leg-*

end: *We learn that the Hairy Men of the Desert do in fact exist. Indeed, they have saved us, for the beasts of the Viperhand flee back to their master, bleeding and defeated. We greet our saviors with curiosity, and so do they regard us—but we are allies in a great cause, and in our first contest together we have prevailed.*

*And now only the desert extends around us, and our goal beckons to the east.*

# ☙ 10 ❧

# STALKERS IN THE JUNGLE

Halloran thought that it must be the strangest victory celebration ever. The companions sat beneath the desert sky, its immaculate dome of stars arcing from horizon to horizon, among a throng of a thousand dwarves. No fire blazed, even though the night was chill, and their newfound allies spoke in subdued, almost awestruck, tones.

From somewhere, Luskag, the chief of the desert dwarves, had produced a number of jars of a bitter draft, more powerfully intoxicating than anything Hal had yet sampled in Maztica. Now they sat in groups, gathered along a wide, flat bluff, drinking the liquor and basking in the glow of victory.

Jhatli amused the dwarves by whooping and dancing about, describing to anyone who would listen the deadly rain of arrows with which he had showered the trolls. The youth spun wildly and leaped into the air, and the gruff dwarves chuckled at the spectacle.

Daggrande and Luskag, meanwhile, talked earnestly in the dwarven tongue that linked them. They passed one of the gourds of drink between them, and Hal wondered blearily whether the two of them would be able to finish the thing. After all, he himself had had only a few swigs, yet already he found a strange nonchalance flowing gently through his limbs.

"Sure," he said to the grinning desert dwarf who squatted beside him. "I'll have another taste." The stuff coated his tongue like pungent ink and cut a swath of fire down his throat, but then in his belly it became a flame of gentle warmth.

Daggrande clumped over to him, walking with a steady

gait. Yet when Hal looked at his friend's face, he saw that the dwarf's eyes blazed and his cheeks were flushed with a ruddy glow.

"This was their first battle ever!" exclaimed the dwarf, collapsing beside Hal.

The man shook his head in amazement. "Din't do too bad, did they?"

Daggrande smiled, his eyes glowing brighter. "That's dwarves for ya. You can take the dwarves out of the fight, but you can't take the dwarves out of the fight. . . no, that's out of the war . . . something like that." He shook his head, suddenly morose at the lapse in his memory.

"I know what you mean," Hal chuckled.

Suddenly the dwarf looked up. "Where's yer wife?" he asked.

"Isn't she right over . . ." Hal's head whirled around. "I dunno," he admitted. He climbed awkwardly to his feet, surprised when the ground seemed to shift under him. Odd the way the stars whirled around, too. . . . "I better go find her," he mumbled.

A cool wind blew across the desert, cresting the bluff of their camp briskly, with freshening force. The air seemed to clear his head slightly, but Hal still found it difficult to maintain his footing. Not knowing why he did it, he headed toward the edge of the crest, away from the dwarves and his companions.

In a few minutes, he saw, or imagined, a brightness ahead of him. He was not surprised when he found Erixitl sitting quietly and looking upward at the stars.

He sat—fell, actually—beside her, and she laughed gently. When he tried to explain, she placed a hand to his lips to silence him.

For a long time, they sat together, watching the stars wheel gracefully across the heavens. A feeling of well-being encircled them in hope and promise, and they did nothing to break the spell.

"Our lives have changed these last few days," Erixitl said softly. "We start on a new path—a long journey across the face of the True World."

Halloran held her tightly. He wanted to remind her that they had new allies now, and new prospects for success. They were together, they would have a child. . . . A million thoughts raced through his mind.

For now, he remained silent, sensing that she knew these things and shared his contentment. Challenges and hardships awaited them, they both knew, and the success of their mission was far from guaranteed.

But for now, for tonight at least, all would be well with the world.

*     *     *     *     *

Hoxitl groaned in weariness, a bleak sense of exhaustion he had never before suffered. The fight against the humans had been savage, so close to victory! But ultimately so futile.

How he had missed the trolls! If only he had kept those savage creatures alongside him, instead of sending them after the woman! The monsters had returned to his camp now, with their own tale of failure, and a great lethargy settled over all the beasts of the Viperhand.

Somehow, although the flush of victory fed him and his creatures with energy, the frustrations of defeat sapped their strength in equal measure.

He considered the effort needed to make another attack against the position defended by legionnaires, Kultakans, and Nexalans. He could plainly see the breastworks on the ridge above him, and once again weariness coursed through his body.

Instead, Hoxitl squatted on the ground and tried to focus on a plan. His army remained strong, still savage and bloodthirsty.

Then, deep within Hoxitl's awareness, Zaltec called to him again. The god of war had but one true enemy, and that enemy had been deflected but not destroyed. The Plumed One could not return to Tewahca. The altar had been destroyed, and this was the scene of his defeat.

But where else could he go? Nexal? That ruined metropolis, heartland of Zaltec's power, certainly could not beckon one such as the Feathered Dragon! Yet, still, Nexal had hosted temples to Qotal and the other gods as well as to Zaltec. A great fear began to grow in Hoxitl, a fear that even as he stood here, wasting his time in battle with these humans, his true enemy could be taking shape behind him, sneaking his way into Nexal itself.

Zaltec's summons finally stirred Hoxitl's beast body, and the cleric felt the threat foreseen by his god. Roughly the monster rose to his full height, still stiff and battered from his epic struggle. Zaltec, he knew, would gather his strength for the battle with Qotal that was still to come. Hoxitl, meanwhile, mustered his force. They would turn from the humans before them.

Instead, they would return to Nexal, and there they would await the command of Zaltec.

\* \* \* \* \*

"My master! I come in answer to your summons!" Gultec bowed deeply before Zochimaloc, relieved to let the peace and serenity of Tulom-Itzi once again wash over him.

"Ah, my brave warrior," said the teacher affectionately. "I wish it were not so, but now we have need of your skill. You must lead our people in war."

"With the scourge that mars the jungle?" Gultec asked. "I have seen its spoor, but I do not understand its nature."

"Yes, this is the enemy, arisen from the bowels of the earth and now spreading its stain across all the lands of Far Payit."

As always, Zochimaloc was a mountain of solidity in the world. Gultec felt a peculiar joy in his heart just to be with the old teacher again. His words, the warrior thought, offered the wisdom of the ages.

The pair spoke in one of the gardens of Tulom-Itzi, beside a fountain that sent shimmering rainbows of light dancing in the sun. Yet that beauty fell away, forgotten in the horrors that the teacher described to his student. Zochimaloc told Gultec of the ants he had seen in his vision, of the villages that had been reduced to decaying compost, and of the inexorable march of the great insect army.

"You saw its path, swinging to the east," he concluded. "But now our people hear that the army has turned back. No longer does its path wind like a snake across the land. Now the ants march true, cutting a straight swath toward their target."

"They come here, do they not?" Gultec already knew the answer, though Zochimaloc nodded his assent. "How far away are they now? And how fast do they march?"

"It seems that they will reach Tulom-Itzi in four or five days, unless we stop them first. Gultec, can we stop them?"

The warrior growled, oddly discomfited at being asked a question by one he had always assumed knew everything. "We can only try," he admitted.

For the next three days, he gathered together the men of Tulom-Itzi. Though the people had no tradition of warriorhood, they were skilled hunters, and during his studies under Zochimaloc, Gultec had trained them to put these skills to battle use. Now the women made arrows while he sent parties of men into the jungle to observe the approaching army and to learn how to harass its seemingly inexorable approach.

These parties came back with tales, not only of the monstrous ants that seemed almost impervious to arrows and spears, but also of the horrible creatures that led the insects toward war. These dark, bloated figures, scuttling upon insect bodies with the heads and torsos of men, seemed to Gultec an even greater and more unnatural menace than the ants themselves.

He listened to a tale of a large village, well prepared for the attack and even surrounded by a thorny wall of wood, that had lain in the path of destruction. The ants had swarmed over the wall, tearing it down in the process, then scurried through the huts and buildings, even crawling over the village pyramid. Wherever warriors had tried to stand against them, they had perished to the last man. Only a few ants had died in the entire battle.

He tried to plan a firetrap to ensnare the insects in a forest blaze before they reached Tulom-Itzi. But here the rain god, Azul, schemed against them, for daily showers drenched the jungle, and the foliage remained constantly wet and steaming. Despite their most vigorous efforts with oil and tinder, it could not be made to burn.

Finally he went to his teacher again, knowing that the ants would reach the city on the following day. His heart broke as he looked into Zochimaloc's eyes, so wise and now so sad in the twilight of his life.

"My teacher," Gultec said haltingly, "it grieves me to speak thus to you, to give you this message that tears the heart from my body. But I fear I have no other choice."

"Speak, my son, and fear not," counseled Zochimaloc.

"We cannot stand against these ants," Gultec said finally. "As a Jaguar Knight, I am not afraid of a hopeless fight. Indeed, a year ago I should have rejoiced at the thought of giving my life in such a worthy battle, though the outcome be preordained."

Gultec paused, and Zochimaloc waited, sensing the warrior's deep resistance to his own conclusion. "Yet in the time I have studied with you, I have learned some things—things which have made me question the basic principles I have held throughout my adult life." Gultec spoke more quickly now, growing sure of himself.

"You have made me question the glory of war, and even to see the hurt it can cause. You have shown me a people of courage and grace and learning—people who do not practice war and have not known it during their lives.

"If people such as this can be happy and prosperous, I must doubt that war is a necessity—at least, war for the sake of warfare. Warfare has its place, for there are threats that must be countered. This too, you have taught me, and you have shown me as much by bringing me here to teach your people how to fight.

"But a battle here, before Tulom-Itzi, would merely be a fight for the sake of pride and courage. It would not be war for victory. We cannot hope to win a victory over this army, at least not now. I know, teacher, that you will not question my courage when I offer you this counsel:

"Our only hope of survival is to abandon Tulom-Itzi and seek shelter in the jungle."

"It shall be as you command," said the master, with a deep bow.

\* \* \* \* \*

Poshtli clung to the feathered mane with both hands, desperately trying to retain his hold. He didn't know where he was or what he was doing, but he sensed that to let go was to die. So he held tight to the plumage and ignored the pitching and bucking that threatened to tear him free.

It was not until later—much later—that he understood the transformation that had come over him. Finally, though, he realized that he was holding on with *hands*—human hands, with fingers and thumbs! Making a sensory inspection of his body, he realized that the eagle's shape no longer cloaked him.

Once again he was human.

But where was he? All around him, he sensed movement, though no wind whipped at him. Bright, soft feathers cushioned and surrounded him, and he realized that he held on to a huge living form.

Qotal! The Feathered Dragon carried him in flight, away from the scene of the terrible fight. But why, then, was there no wind?

Hesitantly Poshtli turned his head away from the great neck. He saw only gray nothingness, a thick, swirling vapor that surrounded them both and masked any sense of up or down. He stared away from the dragon, in the direction he guessed must be up, but he could see no sign of the sun through the mist.

Slowly, carefully, the Maztican changed his grip on the flowing plumage of the huge serpent's mane. He crept upward, until his head emerged from the plumage. Now he looked over Qotal's head and saw that more of the gray emptiness yawned before them.

He could see that the serpent's massive wings beat strongly to either side of its great body. The bright plumage on those wings seemed even more colorful now, in contrast to . . . well, to nothing. Try as he might, he could discern no color or shape, no irregular feature within the encloaking fog.

Qotal's wings still beat steadily as the Feathered Dragon carried him swiftly toward an unknown destination. Poshtli could only thank the mercy of the god for saving his life and be grateful that he now rode in relative security, wherever it was that they went.

But still, he wondered, why was there no wind?

*  *  *  *  *

The great eagle soared slowly to earth, settling to the ridgetop where the line of warriors still stood watch against the threat offered by the horde of the Viperhand. The earthworks, abandoned for the most part, still stood like proud, steep sentinels along the heights overlooking the dusty wasteland to the north.

In the valley to the south, around the lake the Nexalans had named Tukan, a small community slowly grew. Many grass huts lined the shores, while a few dugout canoes probed the deeper waters, where great schools of fish swam. Already stones had been gathered and a low pyramid built—a pyramid dedicated to Qotal, sanctified with offerings of flowers and a multitude of butterflies.

The eagle dropped to the ridge, and then his form shifted, shimmering briefly in the bright sun. The shimmer faded and revealed Chical, Lord of the Eagle Knights. He approached Cordell, and as he did, the Maztican warrior's face broke into a faint, reluctant smile.

"Good news, man?" asked the captain-general. He spoke a rough mixture of Nexalan and commonspeech, understood by the Eagle Knight.

"It would seem so," Chical responded in the same bastardized tongue. "The beasts march northward, back toward Nexal!"

"Hah!" Cordell exclaimed his joy, throwing his hands skyward at the news. He restrained an impulse to embrace his ally, knowing such an approach would offend the proud, aloof warrior.

But even Chical's face split into a grin then, as did Tokol's when the chief of the Kultakans arrived and heard the news.

"So we have turned them back?" he asked incredulously. "They will not attack again?"

"For now, anyway," Cordell conceded.

"But why?" Tokol seemed reluctant to accept their good fortune.

"My former enemy is right to question," added Chical, with a respectful look at the Kultakan. "What could have drawn the enemy away from us? We certainly did not rout them from the field!"

"True," Cordell admitted. "The best guess is that they have some other pressing concern, perhaps another war to wage. They know we are no threat to them here. Perhaps they feel they can come back and deal with us later."

"That is a great waste of marching, when they stood at the brink of our position but one day ago," said Chical skeptically. "Still, we need not question our good fortune too heavily."

"Indeed," Cordell agreed, clapping both warriors on their shoulders. "And we have time now—time to make sure that when and if they do return, we will be more than ready to meet them!"

The three allies, feeling a sense of great relief, turned from the north and started toward the slowly growing community below.

*　*　*　*　*

The people of Tulom-Itzi left their city swiftly and silently, disappearing into the jungle from which, legend had it, they had once emerged. They took only those possessions they could carry, and the strong men aided the young and the old alike.

They could not help but weep, knowing that they were abandoning the city that had been theirs for more generations than any living person could hope to count. Now they gave it over to a horde of ravenous insects, and even then they had no guarantee that their escape from the ants would be successful.

Many there were who muttered that they should stand and die in Tulom-Itzi rather than run like rabbits into the jungle. But the people worshiped Zochimaloc as the divine descendant of the gods themselves, and so they could only obey his command.

The wizened master and teacher remained in his observatory as his people left. He watched Gultec commanding great companies of archers as they went forth to observe the approach of their enemy and try to harass the ants as much as possible. Such tactics were costly, for the ants moved swiftly through the brush, and many an archer fell to a horrible fate between grinding mandibles or to the black arrows of the half-men, half-insect creatures.

But they sent volleys of well-aimed missiles at the ants before melting back into the jungle. They had tried shooting at the human-torsoed beasts that commanded the ants but had found their black metal armor impervious to the shark's-tooth arrows. Through costly experimentation, they learned that an arrow that struck an ant in the eye confused and disoriented it. An ant struck in both eyes was quickly dispatched and devoured by its follows

The harrassment claimed the lives of many brave archers, for always the ants rushed ahead to try to overtake the humans. One stumble in the dense underbrush was enough to cost a man his life, as the giant insects gave him no time to regain his feet. A side effect of the tactic, unnoticed at the time, was that the man-bugs accompanying the ants took to following toward the rear of their column. Though none had been slain by the missile fire, they valued their lives enough to take such precautionary measures.

Finally the archers fell back to Tulom-Itzi itself. They rapidly crossed the gardens and avenues, passing the pools and the fountains, the great pyramids and palaces, to melt into the jungle beyond.

Only when the last of his people, accompanied by Gultec himself, passed through the city did Zochimaloc leave his domed place of solitude. It was with a feeling of heartbreaking sorrow that he joined his pupil in flight, turning to the jungle as the ants claimed Tulom-Itzi.

\* \* \* \* \*

"Where are the humans?" demanded Darien, spitting venomously in the height of her rage.

"Fled," replied the faithful drider, Hittok. That creature had scuttled among the great edifices while the ants had ransacked the wooden houses and thatch huts. They had found much to eat, but nothing to kill.

"Filthy cowards! How can they leave us this treasure, offering it up without a fight?"

"Perhaps they fear us too much," suggested the male.

"Indeed," mused the white drider, her rage gradually matched by her curiosity.

Darien strode among the pyramids and great stone palaces, looking in wonder at this city in the jungle. Her eight legs carried her smoothly up the steep stairways, until at last she stood upon the platform of a high pyramid. She saw that the forest pressed close around this great open plaza of stone buildings. The wooden structures stood within the forest, and these were currently and systematically destroyed by her army.

The ants spread like a scourge from the city center, tearing the leaves from trees, trampling and devouring the mayz in the fields, and tearing the lush gardens into rubbish and rot. The stone buildings the ants plundered for food, but they left the structures intact.

"That domed place—what is it?" Darien wondered, pointing to the observatory on the low hill in the center of the city.

"It was empty," replied Hittok. "It has gaps in the roof—holes to let light in, I think, though they are oddly placed."

"And the humans? You say that they have fled into the jungle?"

"Yes, mistress."

For the first time since entering Tulom-Itzi, Darien smiled. She nodded her slender, milky-white head. "Very well.

When we have finished with their city, we shall pursue them. They cannot hope to long avoid my army."

"Indeed. We shall quickly overtake them."

"And then—" Darien concluded, her thin smile growing tight and menacing, "then we shall kill them all."

\* \* \* \* \*

"The faces, Captain! The faces on the cliff!"

Don Vaez emerged from his cabin, trying to conceal his excitement from the crewmen who clamored for his attention. The leader of the expedition, always conscious of appearances, was determined to display no untoward sign of agitation.

Yet internally his heart pounded with the news. They had almost reached their goal! Pryat Devane had given him a good account of Cordell's route, and he knew that this massive edifice had been his rival's first landfall on the shores of Maztica itself.

Despite these preliminary reports, however, Don Vaez was not prepared for the awesome impact of the scene before him.

The cliff at the headlands of the Payit country loomed some five hundred feet in the air. The clear blue waters of a sheltered lagoon lay placid, protected by a coral reef encircling the shore. Beyond the water, a slim belt of white sand fringed the base of the cliff, backed by a strip of jungled greenery.

But over all, the two faces—Twin Visages, he had heard them called—stared ominously eastward. A male and a female, the faces were similar in aspect: oval-shaped, with thick lips, broad noses, and keen eyes that belied their sculpted origins as they seemed to stare into Don Vaez's soul itself.

He shook his head, trying to break the thrall. "Pilot! Fetch me the charts!"

"Here they are, Captain." Rodolfo, the grizzled navigator who had plotted their course across the Trackless Sea, offered several rolled sheets of parchment to Don Vaez.

The captain took them without a word but looked up as he unrolled them. He would need the navigator's help in deciphering the rough charts, since map-reading had never been one of his strengths. And besides, these crude guides had only been prepared through distant and brief communication with the late Bishou Domincus. They were altogether lacking in crucial detail.

"Cordell sailed along this coastline," offered Rodolfo, indicating the course with a blunt finger. "Until he discovered this city—the natives called it 'Ulatos.' "

"And that's where he erected his fort?"

"Yes . . . at the anchorage near the city. It's likely just an earthen redoubt, but the harbor there is supposed to be well protected. He called it 'Helmsport.' "

"Helmsport." Don Vaez let the name roll off his tongue. "I like that. The name will stay. The fort, however," he added with a grim chuckle, "is about to gain a new master."

Barely pausing before the huge carvings in the cliff, the twenty-five carracks of Don Vaez's fleet set a new course due westward along the coast. All lookouts kept their eyes peeled for the first sign of Helmsport.

\* \* \* \* \*

From the chronicles of Coton:

*Emerging from the grasp of the desert, we finally reach the sea.*

*For weeks, the desert dwarves lead us eastward across the House of Tezca. The perils of the passage are many, but the numbers of our escort hold the creatures of the deep desert—even the fire lizards—at bay. All of us become inured to the sun, browned by his rays and toughened by his heat.*

*Our only water comes from the sand mother, the plump cactus that these desert dwarves use so well. As to food, Qotal sustains us through the limited powers he has granted me, his faithful priest. We grow thin and lean, for the sustenance must feed many mouths.*

*Erixitl grows in the fullness of her motherhood, as if her vitality increases in challenge to the bleakness that surrounds her. Halloran and Daggrande march like the soldiers that they are, while Jhatli struggles to emulate them. Lotil rides, and as he rides, his fingers work their pluma, his mesh showing a steadily growing splash of color.*

*And then one glorious morning we crest a low, rocky ridge and see the strip of blue beckoning us on the horizon. The Sea of Azul!*

*By nightfall of that day, we reach the shore. The desert dwarves shun the water, staying well back from the soft breakers. We humans, however, and the horse, and even the dwarf Daggrande enter the brine, soaking and splashing and playing like children. We relish the cool wash of the waves, though we take care not to drink.*

*But this is a splendid landmark. We have our bearings, and we know that the desert will soon fall behind us. Now our path will turn north, to follow the shore, and soon we will enter the lush realm of Far Payit. Payit, and our goal of Twin Visages, lies beyond.*

# ❧ 11 ❧

# ROADS TO PAYIT

The rider left a dusty plume across the brown valley bottom, a floating cloud of dry silt that was visible for many miles. The captain-general remained atop the high breastwork, watching the growing dust cloud, hoping for good news.

As the horseman drew near to the fortified ridgetop, Cordell stepped down from the earthwork where he had been supervising additional entrenchments. He recognized Grimes and met him at the base of the redoubt.

"What did you find?" asked the commander, even before the horseman had dismounted.

"The eagles are right," said the scout, sliding from the saddle and stretching muscles stiff from a long ride. "They're gone. Seems like they've pulled back to the north."

"Excellent!" Cordell clapped the man on the back. "I don't know how we beat them, but we did!" He turned back toward the earthwork, only to hear Grimes clear his throat.

"Uh, General?"

"Yes?" Cordell turned back to his captain of horse.

"Some of the men . . . that is, uh, I've been wondering. Now that we don't have a pack of orcs on our trail, do you have any plans to head for home? It's been more than a year, and some of the fellows have families back in Amn. And with the gold lost, it doesn't seem like there's much more for us to do here. . . ."

Cordell thought for a moment, unsurprised by the question. "Pass the word," he offered. "As soon as our work here is done, we'll be moving on. I am not prepared to accept the loss of all our profits, but we have to start thinking about a return. It won't be long."

Grimes nodded gruffly. "Thank you, sir," he added before leading his horse toward the lake below. Turning to watch him, Cordell saw Chical approaching. The Eagle Knight wore his black-and-white-feathered mantle and the wooden, hooked helmet that shaded his face. He had a pensive expression on his smooth, coppery face.

"Captain-General, I have some information you will be interested in," said Chical as he reached Cordell. The Eagle Knight seemed oddly guarded in his manner.

"Yes? What is it?" Cordell grew steadily more fluent in the Nexalan tongue, and now he used it to converse with his fellow warriors.

"As you know, eagles have been soaring across the True World, observing the horde of the Viperhand and also scouting other dominions to see how far the catastrophe has spread."

"I know. Have they found something important?" Cordell studied Chical, wondering about the Maztican warrior's hesitancy.

"Yes. Carac, one of my strongest and most reliable warriors, has just returned from a very long flight. He journeyed to Payit, where he saw the city of Ulatos and the fort you built nearby."

"Helmsport? Does it still stand? Do my men live?" He had left a garrison of several dozen men behind in the fort, not nearly enough to hold it in the event of an attack. He had hoped that the crushing victory his legion had inflicted upon the Payits would prove enough of a deterrent to aggression.

Now, of course, all those assumptions had fallen by the wayside. That remnant of his legion represented little threat to the Payit people should they choose to revolt against their conquerors. The thought of danger to his garrison at Helmsport brought Cordell's blood to a boil, but he forced himself to listen to Chical's information.

"Your men? This I do not know. But Carac reports that many more of your countrymen have arrived—a fleet of those great canoes such as you sailed. They have landed at Helmsport."

"More of my people? Soldiers?" The news fell upon Cordell like a bolt from the sky. He had almost forgotten that a world existed beyond Maztica, a world of magic and steel and power that seemed like a distant dream to him now. "How many of them? What did Carac see?"

"He counted five and twenty great canoes. In the field before Helmsport, some one hundred horses stood. And many of the silver-shirted soldiers debarked from the vessels. There may be more, but that is what he saw."

"A new force—here, in Maztica?" Cordell couldn't keep the amazement out of his voice. An army larger—perhaps twice the size, or even more—than the legion I brought to Maztica a year ago!

"Have you summoned them here?" Chical's voice was heavy with suspicion now.

"No!" Cordell didn't even think to lie. At the same time, his mind reeled with questions and possibilities. Who could these men be? How had they located Helmsport? Who was their commander? And perhaps most important, were they his allies or his foes?

"I don't know who they are. I have not summoned them, but perhaps they have been sent to aid me by those who funded my own expedition." He turned decisively toward the growing site of Tukan, in the valley below. Chical stepped beside him.

"Whatever the case," Cordell explained, thinking as he walked, "I must go to them as quickly as possible."

I must insure that they aid me, that they do not take what spoils I have earned and still keep. His mind whirled with suspicions and half-formed plans. And yet, with a new army, with fresh troops, perhaps my mission need not end in failure!

Chical remained with Cordell, still suspicious, as the commander summoned his legionnaires and the chief of the Kultakans, Tokol. They started to gather around him in a great meadow that would someday be the city square of Tukan.

Before the assemblage was complete, Chical pulled Cordell to the side and spoke to him seriously.

"We have fought together, you and I—and also we have fought against each other." The Eagle Knight's voice was steady, and his black eyes faced squarely into Cordell's own. "Know this, my new ally: If this is a new army, brought here to make war on my land, we will fight it every step of the way. And this time, our warfare will not be held in check by the whims of Naltecona!"

"I speak the truth when I tell you that I do not know who these men are or why they come. But I will make you this promise: If I can reach them and bring them to follow me, I will use them as your allies."

Chical still stared, with a concentration that disquieted the captain-general. "I pray that you speak the truth," he said finally.

"Let us make a plan. I ask your help now." Cordell's tone remained level. "You and your eagles have flown over most of this country. Can you sketch me a rough map of the coast-line near hear?"

Chical took the tip of his dagger and inscribed an outline in the dust on the ground. "This is the land of Payit, and be-low here the jungles of Far Payit, sticking like a thumb into the sea. Where the waters come around it, between the des-ert and the jungle, it is called the Sea of Azul."

"Good!" Cordell exclaimed. He saw that the coastline curved inward, bordering the great desert for much of its extent.

"I will take all the men I can mount, and we will ride to Helmsport," he told the captain of eagles. "If you and your eagles will fly with us, we can reach these men quickly. Then we shall see what their purpose is and how we can make that purpose fit our own."

Chical thought for several moments. "I cannot bring all the eagles from our valley. The danger is still too great. But some of us will accompany you, and we will see if it is as you say."

"Very well. I cannot ask for more." Cordell turned away, startled to see that the assessor of Amn, Kardann, had come up quietly behind him. The pudgy accountant's face be-trayed a look of passionate hope.

"Rescue!" he whispered loudly. "They have come for us! We're saved!"

"They've come for *something*," Cordell allowed. "But I'm not so certain it's to save us."

"What else could it be? Surely you will go to them, place us all under their protection?"

The captain-general looked at the little man with distaste. Kardann had been the one member of the original expedition assigned him by the merchant princes who had funded him. Cordell had never liked him, and nothing during the defeat-stained retreat from Nexal had changed this opinion.

"We will go there, to be sure—but we go cautiously, a small number of us, to investigate. If they are here to help, that is very well, but if they are here to obstruct us, we shall learn this first."

"But—" Kardann's objection died on his lips. He nodded quickly, hiding a crafty smile that played across his lips, before looking up at the captain-general. "That, of course, is only sensible. I ask you, please—allow me to accompany you when you return to Helmsport."

Cordell frowned. Little did he relish the thought of the little man's constant presence. But he realized that, as an official of Amn, Kardann could prove useful in negotiations with any relief expedition. And whatever other considerations he had faded to the background in the face of one truth that had become totally clear to him: These newcomers to Maztica must join him and accept him as their leader. He would not subordinate his force, small and beleaguered though it was, to another. And to this end, Kardann might prove useful. As he thought, plans began to crystallize in his mind. He grew anxious, pacing absently as he prepared to take action.

Finally the legionnaires and the Kultakan chiefs had gathered, so Cordell turned to speak to them all. Briefly he explained the news brought by Carac. The legionnaires raised a hearty cheer when they heard that more of their countrymen had landed in the True World. If any were as puzzled or concerned as Cordell about the origins of this new expedition, they kept their misgivings to themselves. Then, referring to the map of Maztica provided by Chical, he began to give specific orders.

"Horsemen, you will prepare your mounts for a long ride—across the continent, back to Helmsport. We will reach the anchorage, where the ships now await us." He studied the faces of his men, his voice ringing confidently. They looked back, filled with hope and enthusiasm for the plan, *any* plan, that would bring them closer to a return to the Sword Coast.

"I want the footmen and Tokol, with your Kultakans, to march southeastward from here. You will reach the coast of a tropical sea. Your force will be some five thousand strong."

His men shouted hurrahs. None raised any questions or objections, and indeed Cordell would have been very surprised if they had.

"It is my intention to send the fleet at Helmsport—twenty-five ships in all, according to the count of our good eagle—around the Payit peninsula. They will meet you at the coast, and there you will embark for the return to Helmsport. Once we have gathered there, fully reinforced, we will be ready to stand against the Viperhand." Or any other threat that I identify, his mind added silently. Cordell admitted to himself that his purposes, in his own mind, had not yet fully crystallized. He only knew that he saw potential before him that he would not have imagined a few days earlier.

"The warriors of Nexal will remain here," he continued. "The threat to the north has receded, but not disappeared entirely. However, with the breastworks on the ridge and steady vigilance, Tukan will remain safe.

"Then, when all of our forces have gathered, we will be ready to claim Maztica together for humankind!"

Once again his men raised a cheer, and this time the Mazticans joined in.

\*   \*   \*   \*   \*

"I don't even care that it's salty," Halloran admitted, with an expansive gesture across the rich blue Sea of Azul. "It's wet, and a lot cooler than the air."

"It's better than that accursed desert, I'll grant you that," Daggrande agreed. He gestured toward the long file of desert dwarves marching before them. "How they can live in that hellhole is beyond me."

"How did they come to be there?" Jhatli asked. "Often I have heard of the Hairy Men of the Desert, but no human had ever seen them before, or so it is said."

The trio brought up the rear of their group as they marched along the sandy shore. A short distance ahead, Erixitl rode Storm, while Coton and Lotil followed behind the horse.

The barren terrain of the desert stretched to the limits of the horizon to the left, yet the companions were considerably refreshed during this portion of their march. The blue waters of the Sea of Azul, to their right, provided an often used cooling agent. In addition, the smooth, sandy beach made for much easier traveling than had the rough ground of the desert.

The latter fact was of particular importance to Halloran, who had grown increasingly worried about Erixitl and the child who now rounded her belly to a rich fullness. Across the desert, during the many weeks of the trek to the sea, she had walked steadily. But the rugged journey had taken its toll, and though she tried to conceal her moments of weakness, the caring eyes of her husband were not deceived.

She had protested only feebly when he insisted that she ride the horse, and now she spent most of each day in the saddle. Lotil had ridden through the roughest of the desert, but now, on the smooth sand of the beach, the blind man found the walking easier. He proved apparently tireless over the long days of march, as long as he had a hand on a horse or companion to show him the way.

Halloran knew that the long trek had been very hard on Erixitl, though she bore the strain with little complaining. She had never spoken of the terrible loss she must have felt after giving up her feathered token, though Hal knew she had carried the object since girlhood. Not only was it a cherished memento of her father, but it was also a token with magical powers that had saved their lives more than once.

He knew, in fact, that it had saved their lives one last time when she used it to secure passage through the Halls of the Dead.

Lotil still carried the *pluma* bundle with him, and when they stopped each evening, he carefully worked a few more feathers into the cotton mesh. The design there had not yet begun to take shape, yet Halloran saw bright colors and a magical sense of beauty in the small portion of the *pluma* fabric already completed.

Hal turned back to his companions, realizing that Daggrande was answering Jhatli's question about the desert dwarves.

"Luskag told me the story, at least as much as they know of it." The grizzled legionnaire had found that, despite the vast differences in their backgrounds, the desert dwarves and he basically spoke the same dwarven tongue, with minor variations. He spent much time talking with the chieftains, exchanging stories and experiences with his unusual cousins.

"It happened after a war with the drow—one of the wars that dwarves have always fought with the drow. Something they call the Rockfire destroyed the caverns and tunnels that connected them to the rest of dwarvenhood. It must have been some underground volcano, or an earthquake, maybe.

"Anyhow, they thought that all the drow had been killed, and they thought that being cut off from their kin was a small price to pay to get rid of their worst enemies. It seems that this is the first warfare they've known since that time."

"They're certainly good at it, for folks who are out of practice," Halloran said. The memory, nearly two months old, of the desert dwarves' timely arrival in the battle with the trolls lived fresh in his mind. They all knew that they had faced certain and imminent death.

Now they marched with the dwarves in friendship, enjoying the gruff curiosity and solid competence of the Hairy Men of the Desert. The friendship had grown quickly to respect as together they had borne the rigors of the desert trail. Days of blazing sun had followed one after the other, broken only by short, clear nights of startling chill. Their only water had come from the plump, precious cactus that the desert dwarves seemed to be able to smell from miles away, or from the blessed magic of Coton's clerical power. They had shared the food he created among all of them, and somehow they had stayed alive.

And when the pair of fire lizards had attacked the companions and the desert dwarves, their respect had become an unbreakable bond, for they proved in battle that each possessed courage and skill worthy of the other. Two dwarves had paid with their lives in the first brunt of the attack as the giant, dragonlike creatures had charged from their dry caves.

But the keen missiles from Daggrande and Jhatli had distracted one, while Luskag had led his dwarves in a circular attack against the second. Halloran, with Helmstooth carving a deadly swath through the desert air, had felled the first with a blow to its neck, while the *pluma*stone weapons of the desert dwarves had disemboweled the second.

The fight had also provided the one night of epic feasting along the barren trail when they seared the tough meat on hot fires of brush and pretended they were devouring the tenderest of delicacies.

"And now the Hairy Men march with us to Twin Visages?" Jhatli was still trying to get a picture of this vast land called Maztica. Though he had lived here all of his life, until four months earlier he had never been beyond the valley of Nexal.

"The story goes that they had some kind of collective vision—at a place they call the Sunstone," Daggrande explained. "I'd like to see it sometime—a lake, high inside a mountain, that seems to be made of silver!" The dwarf shook his head in wonder. "There they saw an image of darkness, and a flower of light within it. As soon as they saw Erixitl, according to Luskag, they recognized her as that flower. So now they've pledged to help her drive back the darkness."

They moved steadily northward, following the long file of the desert dwarves. Always the memory of Twin Visages lay before them, with the hope that Erixitl's guess was right. Qotal would await them there, they told themselves over and over again, and they would stand fast to open the god's passage into the True World.

What happened after that would be left in the hands of the gods.

\*　\*　\*　\*　\*

The verdant foliage surrounded Gultec, masking his position from the advancing enemy. The Jaguar Knight drew back his longbow, sighting on the first of the approaching ants, and then he let the arrow fly.

The missile struck true, in the left eye of the monstrous insect. The creature reared back, antennae flailing wildly. Other ants rushed forward, scrambling over their wounded cohort. The creature struck by Gultec's arrow spun in confusion, finally rushing into the brush off to the side of the army's path.

Six of the giant ants rushed straight toward Gultec, only to draw a flurry of arrows. A dozen bowmen of Tulom-Itzi stood behind their leader, and several of their missiles struck the insects' vulnerable eyes. Three more of the ants, wounded and disoriented, began to circle in agitation.

Quickly the humans melted back into the woods, following the winding trail that allowed them to make rapid progress. Gultec, who went last, retreated away just ahead of the leading ant, before turning to launch another missile. This arrow caromed off the creature's tough-skinned head, however, and the Jaguar Knight sprinted for his life.

Ten minutes later, the men paused in a grassy glade to catch their breath. The ants would reach them soon, but experience had taught them that they had a few minutes to regroup. When vines and underbrush restricted the path, an ant could press forward as fast as a man or even faster, but with a trail to follow, a running man could swiftly outdistance one of the giant insects.

"Good shooting," Gultec announced. "We hurt them that time."

"But there are so many!" protested Keesha, one of the finest archers among the Itza. "How long can we keep harassing them thus? Every time we take our lives in our hands—and we cannot stop them!"

They all knew that several dozen men had already lost their lives in these dangerous delaying tactics. And despite their losses, the ant army marched implacably onward, pursuing the fleeing Itza toward the north.

"By tomorrow we will reach the mountains," explained Gultec. "There it is my hope that we can create an ambush and trap many of the beasts at once." He looked at Keesha and the others sympathetically.

"We also may succeed in drawing one of their leaders toward the front again," he added. "If we can attack these man-bugs, then we may begin to stop the army."

In the face of the frequent attacks from the forest, the driders commanding the ant army had taken to following in the path of their insect horde. While this protected them from the attacks, it also considerably lessened the drive and direction of the army. The column of ants tended to veer toward whichever threat presented itself, giving a party of archers nearby a chance to strike its flank and distract it from its original target.

A scream—a very human cry of nightmarish pain—tore through the jungle, and the warriors stiffened reflexively. They were but one of several bands of archers harassing the ants. One of the other groups, they knew, had just paid the price for their tactics.

"Let's go!" Gultec growled, leading his men in the direction of the scream. Though they had no trail to follow now, the chance to make a diversionary attack in the flank of the column was one they could not ignore.

They soon heard the crunching and rustling of the army before them, and they pressed cautiously through the brush. Soon they saw the giant red bodies, the segments glistening in the patches of sunlight that broke through the overhanging canopy of leaves. The ants advanced past them from left to right. A flash of feathers indicated their fellow Itza archers, quickly disappearing into the jungle.

A harsh cry arose from nearby, and the ants surged forward. Gultec saw one of the man-bugs jerkily scuttling forward. The creature held a long black bow, from which it fired a slim shaft in the direction of the retreating archers. Then it barked again in its strange tongue, obviously commanding the ants to pursue.

The Jaguar Knight's pulse raced. Here was the chance he had been waiting for! "Hold your fire until Keesha gives the command," he told his warriors. "I'm going after that one."

Gultec sprang upward, grasping a tree limb and pulling himself into the foliage of the jungle's heavy canopy. His shape shifted as he crept forward, hands and feet sprouting claws, becoming soft, padded paws that conformed easily to the rough surface of the limb. His Jaguar Knight's helm shrunk over his head, and then, from between fanged feline jaws, a deep growl rumbled. The jaguar's spotted hide blended perfectly with the verdure as Gultec squatted down to wait.

"Now!" He heard Keesha's command, and a dozen arrows burst from the brush to land among the ants. Several of these struck the man-bug but bounced harmlessly off its black metal shirt. Once Gultec would have thought that was the creature's skin, but his experiences with the foreigners had shown him the powers of metal armor. He knew now that the black shell was such a material.

With the new attack, the ants twisted in confusion until the man-thing commanded them to turn and race toward the new threat. The bug's path, Gultec saw with grim anticipation, took it very near the jaguar's tree.

Ignoring the ants jerking and twisting around him, the great cat's yellow eyes fixed upon the humanlike torso pitching and lurching among the insects. The drider passed the tree, still barking in its harsh, foreign tongue, and the ants pressed into the brush after Gultec's band of archers. Keesha had already commanded them to fall back, the jaguar saw with satisfaction.

Then came the moment, as the man-bug moved away, its attention fixed steadily on the jungle before it. Silently the jaguar's muscles flexed, hurling the heavy body into a great leap.

Gultec soared through the air and crashed heavily to the back of the drider. The weight of the cat bore the thing to the ground, and the human torso twisted frantically as the black-skinned face turned toward its attacker.

The drider screamed once, very quickly, as it saw the gaping jaws studded with curved, gleaming fangs. Gultec's claws scraped for a hold on the hard carapace as his jaws clamped around the slender neck. He bit hard and felt bones snap beneath his jaws.

Instantly the creature went limp beneath him. Ants twitched in confusion, many turning toward him while others circled in aimless agitation. Manidibles snapped at the great cat, but before any could reach the creature's spotted hide, Gultec flexed his muscles again.

With a powerful kick of his hind legs, he sprang straight up into the air. His forepaws seized an overhanging branch, quickly pulling the rest of his body behind them.

Then he leaped to another tree, darting away from the army, and in another second, he was gone.

*　*　*　*　*

The companions and their escort of desert dwarves had followed the smooth, barren coastline north for nearly a week when they began to encounter signs of increasing vegetation. First a fringe of hardy brown grass appeared, covering the dunes and spreading inland. Next, clumps of brittle brush—dry and weatherbeaten, but very common—began to dot the land.

Hills rolled along the shore, though the beach itself remained smooth and sandy. Finally they noticed trees nestled in the valleys between the hills.

At last, near noon of a typically hot and cloudless day, they reached an irrefutable sign that they had left the desert behind.

"A stream! Running water!" Jhatli, who had been scouting ahead of the procession, came racing back across the sand with the news. He looked older now, though his face still brightened with a childlike eagerness for good news. His body, however, had been toughened over the trek, even as he had grown an inch or more. Now wiry muscle rippled beneath his dark skin and tiny creases of concentration showed around his eyes.

Storm's ears pricked upward at the scent of fresh water, and with Halloran jogging beside her, the mare carried Erixitl forward at an eager trot.

They reached a shallow grotto, where the stream flowed into the sea, and wasted no time in drinking and bathing. By the time Coton, Lotil, and the dwarves caught up, the three humans had drunk their fill and were basking peacefully beside the placid brook.

"The edge of the forest country," remarked Luskag, staring in suspicion at the clear stream. He gestured to the wooded hills beyond. "The mountains of Far Payit lay there, to the northeast. We will skirt them as we continue to move north."

For several more days, they journeyed along the coast, but now it was a forested shore, with realms of flat savannah or rolling, wooded hills fringing their trail. The beach itself often disappeared, replaced by rocky crags and small, sheltered coves.

But game was plentiful, and so was water. The companions made good time now and didn't complain when Luskag told them that their path must veer northward, away from the Sea of Azul.

They made their way through grassy valleys, lush with blossoms, berries, and wild mayz, and followed a multitude of streams and lakes. The desert dwarves spread out in tentative exploration of this new environment, soon overcoming their discomfort in the face of a multitude of food and water sources.

Erixitl slowly regained her strength. Her skin, darkly tanned and dried from the desert, grew smooth and fresh again. Every day, it seemed, the baby within her grew larger. Halloran rejoiced to the sensations of its kicks against her abdomen. For long hours, the journey became a pastoral adventure for them as they forgot about their mission, forgot about the dangers that lay before them. But then thoughts of the looming confrontation with the gods returned, and it would be as if a heavy cloud had moved across the sun.

Several days after leaving the sea behind, they called an early halt so that the dwarves and Jhatli could hunt. While Coton and Lotil rested in the camp, Hal and Erix went for a quiet walk on their own. It was their first opportunity to be alone together in a very long time.

"These are good lands here," observed Halloran. "Beautiful and fertile. I wonder why there are no settlements of humans."

"I don't know. We have not yet reached the lands of Far Payit. Yet I had always thought nothing but desert lay beyond. Perhaps this place has not been discovered by humans yet."

The thought was an intriguing and pleasant one. For a while, it seemed as if they were on an exploration. However, the long trek had been marking their days, and it seemed wrong somehow to stroll aimlessly for a few hours, as if they had nowhere important to go.

"It seems that life has become nothing but a series of long marches," Erixitl sighed wistfully. "I look forward to the time when we can make a home again and live there in peace."

"It will be soon," Halloran promised. "When this child is born, he—or she—will not have to run from enemies or chase after gods! And neither will we."

"How much longer will *that* be?" she wondered lightly. "I'm afraid I've lost track. I think I have about two more months," They both knew that their estimation was rough at best.

For a while, they walked through a shady vale, past meadows of brilliant flowers. They approached a rocky niche where, earlier, they had observed the top of a waterfall. Now they pressed through mossy underbrush, hearing the growing noise of a cascade that told them they were getting closer.

Finally they broke from the brush to stand on the smooth, sandy shore of a small pool. Before them, tumbling from high above into the other side of the pool, flowed the object of their exploration.

"Isn't it beautiful?" she asked him. He could only stare in wonder at the falls, a narrow plume of white far above that grew from a whispering ribbon of water into a foaming cloud on its plummet into the clear pool.

"A place made just for us," he said softly. He took her hands in his, and for a moment, the despair wracking Maztica was forgotten, an unwanted intrusion into this splendid grotto and its quiet solitude.

A slight movement off to the side of the grotto drew Halloran's attention, and he turned with shock to stare into the face of a feathered warrior. The man was naked, with black and red paint in alternating stripes covering his face.

More significantly, he carried a short, sturdy bow, with a wooden arrow. The tip of the missile pointed unwaveringly at Halloran's face. He saw a gummy liquid, brown and thick, smeared on the tip of the arrow.

*Poison!*

Only then did he notice that the man stood barely three feet tall.

\* \* \* \* \*

From the chronicles of Coton:

### THE MAKING OF THE LITTLE PEOPLE

*When the great gods created humankind, according to the wishes of Qotal and Zaltec and their children, they made man tall and strapping, fitted for war and for hunting. Soon, they knew, he would become master of his world.*

*But other gods—Kiltzi and her younger sisters—stole the mold used to make man. They found their brothers' tastes too warlike and saw that man was too big. They desired a toy, a little person that could become part of the forest world without becoming its master.*

*So the sisters began to work on their own mold. They copied everything that they could from the shapes created by their brothers, but they made their humans smaller, that they might more easily serve as toys.*

*And when the little people had been made, the sister gods set them free in the deepest forests, where they might forever escape the notice of their larger brethren. They bade them to hunt and fish and populate the forest, but not to become its masters.*

*The Little People promised to obey, and they did.*

# ❧ 12 ❧

# CAPTIVITY AND FLIGHT

"Who was it?" Darien inquired, her voice icy cool yet taut with seething rage. Hittok had found her in a grassy clearing, and now they squatted among the tall blades, only their elven torsos showing above the vegetation.

"Dackto. The cat bit him right through the neck and broke his spine." Hittok explained the death of the drider dispassionately, yet the news had struck them all a shocking blow. For the first time since Lolth had corrupted their drow forms, one of their number had perished.

"The cat was a human, no doubt—probably a Jaguar Knight," guessed the albino. "No animal would be so brave or so foolish."

"One of those we pursue, whose city we took?" Hittok ventured.

"Certainly. And when we catch these humans, they—all of them—shall pay for this affront. How fares the chase?"

"The humans flee quickly through the forest, remaining just ahead of the leaders," Hittok explained. "Yet the ants are tireless, and the people will eventually begin to fatigue. Then we shall encircle them and take them all."

"Very well. We must maintain the pace at all costs. Have you plotted their course?"

"Yes, mistress. It seems that they head for a pass through the mountains we have observed before us. Perhaps there they will be foolish enough to stand and fight so that we may overwhelm them."

Hittok gestured to the purpled massif that lay to the northwest. For days, they had been approaching it, and now they could discern individual peaks and ridges, softly outlined by verdant, jungled slopes. In another day of pursuit, if the people of Tulom-Itzi held to their present course, they would enter the foothills of the range.

"Press forward with redoubled haste!" Darien barked the command, raising her own swollen abdomen from the ground to stand on her eight spidery legs. "Let us insure that the humans are fatigued when they reach the mountains." She gestured to the others of her tribe, the nineteen remaining driders, who pressed forward in the wake of the marching column of ants.

"There we will finish the matter, for once and for all."

\* \* \* \* \*

"Don't move. Don't startle him," Halloran said quietly. Slowly and carefully he stepped between Erixitl and the short man with the lethal-looking arrow.

"Look. There's more of them," Erix whispered.

He risked a glance around and saw that suddenly they were surrounded by the diminutive warriors. Each bore the shocking stripes of red and black war paint, and several wore feathers in their earlobes or tied to their elbows and knees.

Each native also carried a short bow and arrow, with a black daub at the head.

Desperately Halloran's mind whirled through the few spells he knew: enlargement, light, magic missile . . . a few others. None offered any hope of extricating them from this crisis. Indeed, a sudden use of magic might be enough to provoke an attack. That was the last thing he wanted to do. The gummy substance tipping the arrows of the short warriors seemed a clear indication of fatal results.

Erixitl placed a hand, involuntarily he thought, to her throat. He knew she remembered the token she had given up to purchase their passage past the dead of Tewahca. He doubted that the thing would have helped them in this predicament, but the gesture made him feel their terrible vulnerability more acutely than before.

The first bowman gestured sharply with his weapon. Several others pressed forward, although they stayed out of sword range—not that Halloran could have risked a fight here. A terrifying picture flashed in his mind: He saw his wife's pregnant body, unprotected by armor, punctured by those obviously venomous darts.

The little man stepped up to him, demanding something in an imperious tone. He made a gesture toward the sword at Hal's side. Slowly, grimly, Halloran ungirded the weapon and held out the blade and its belt and scabbard toward the warrior.

Jabbering something else in a rapid-fire, chattering tongue, the little man commanded one of his fellow warriors to step forward and carry the weapon. The bowman kept his weapon trained on Halloran. When the sword had been moved out of reach, he stepped forward, holding the bow and arrow in one hand. With the other, he reached up and tapped the steel breastplate. His dark eyes squinted at the hard metal.

Then he spun on his feet and stalked away, turning to stare impatiently at his captives.

"I think he wants us to go that way," Hal said in common.

"Then we'd better do it," Erix replied in the same language.

The first of the small warriors, who seemed to be the leader, preceded them around the shore of the pool, while the others fell into file behind them. He pushed beneath some overhanging vines, forcing Hal and Erix to crouch low to follow.

A narrow trail, surrounded by dense verdure, lay beyond the screening vines. To their left, the moss-covered rock wall of the grotto climbed away. The warrior broke into a trot, and the natives to the rear moved up, raising their bows menacingly.

They picked up the pace, Halloran keeping a protective hand on Erixitl's elbow. In her condition she couldn't run, and the warrior in front of them turned and gestured impatiently.

"Wait!" snapped Hal in Nexalan.

For a second, he regretted his harsh tone and thought he would pay for it with his life as the chieftain raised his bow.

"I . . . can't go . . . any faster," Erixitl told him breathlessly, speaking the Payit tongue. The warrior scowled as though he understood and disapproved. But when he turned to resume the march, he went a little more slowly. A short time later, he removed the arrow from his bow and slung the weapon across his back. The warriors behind them, Hal noticed with a quick look, still kept their weapons ready to shoot.

They followed a deep cut in the rock wall of the grotto, and soon granite cliffs towered on each side of them. In places, the rocks were wet and slippery, and it seemed to them that the sun must never reach to the bottom of this crack in the bedrock. The warrior never hesitated, leading them forward as the niche grew more and more narrow.

Finally they reached a steep progression of stairs—whether natural or hewn from the rock, Hal could not tell—and proceeded to climb. The cool, mossy rock pressed close to either side, and only a thin strip of blue sky, visible straight above them, gave proof they had not entered a cavern.

After a very long climb, at least two hundred steps, they emerged at the top of the cliff. Here the path led through a deep forest glen, winding along damp dirt. Halloran saw Erix begin to stagger, tired from the long climb.

"Stop!" he ordered in his firmest martial tone.

The chieftain whirled around in surprise. Hal blinked, stunned at the quickness with which he had snatched his bow from his shoulder and renocked an arrow. "Can't you see she's tired? She needs to rest!" The two stared at each other for long moments.

Erix leaned against a tree, breathing hard. Gently Halloran took her arm and lowered her to sit upon the mossy ground. The warrior jabbered something, raising his weapon, but Hal continued to meet his gaze.

He studied the little man, curiosity not banishing his fear but beginning to rival it. For the first time, he noticed the man's feet. Like the rest of his body, they were barren of clothing. The tops were covered with tufts of coarse black hair.

In all other respects, proportionally and facially, he looked like a human. His features, behind the garish paint, bespoke a person of pride and confidence. The look in his face, even when confronting a man twice his size, displayed courage. He had a strong chin, a smooth, straight nose, and dark, intelligent eyes. Whether his skin color was the darkened copper of Maztican humans or simply bronzed by a lifetime in the sun, Halloran could not tell.

In any event, the man apparently decided to let Erixitl rest, for he lowered his weapon and squatted on the ground. For a few minutes, he and his fellow warriors waited, immobile.

"I'm all right now," Erixitl said to her husband, awkwardly rising to her feet.

"Do you think they speak Payit?" Halloran asked her as they started to move again.

"Can you understand my words?" she asked in the tongue of the Payit. Halloran did not know that language, but he watched the little man with interest.

"Speak not with Big People," the little warrior answered awkwardly. "They kill us, many always times."

"Why have you taken us prisoner?" she inquired. "We offer you no harm."

"All Big People bad," he grunted, turning away to lead them along the trail.

"Where do you take us?" she prodded.

"To village—to feast," he explained. With these ominous words, he ceased to answer her questions, and they could only follow his tense, naked form through the seemingly interminable forest.

\* \* \* \* \*

"They press too closely," gasped the Itza warrior. "The children, the old people can no longer keep ahead of them." The man leaned weakly against a tree, bleeding from multiple wounds. His eyes focused only vaguely on Gultec, and the Jaguar Knight could see that they were dull with shock.

Gultec growled in frustration. Around him tumbled the

steep hills at the foot of the Verdant Mountains. The fleeing Itza formed a long file in the valley bottom, pressing forward toward a pass high up along the crest of the range. But the ants had accelerated the pace of their pursuit, and the Jaguar Knight began to wonder if he had led these people into a colossal trap.

"The only one left . . . me. The others . . . all killed, burned!"

Gultec noticed as the man talked that the hair on one side of his head had been burned away. His arm on the same side had blackened, as if he had held the limb in the coals of a hot fire.

"My company . . . good men, all of them. Why me? Why?" The warrior looked at Gultec helplessly.

"Be calm," ordered Gultec, and the man's breathing slowed. "Now, what happened?"

"They did not come after us as they used to," he explained, breathing more easily. "Instead, they continued past, ignoring our arrows. So we pressed closer, knowing the importance of our task."

"Then did they turn?" asked Gultec.

"No. They continued on. We finally tried to advance, to get in front of the column again. Then we saw this *thing*—like those man-bugs, only this one was white all over, pale like a slug. It had the face of a woman." The warrior's voice choked with horror as he remembered the scene.

"She raised her hand and called out a word. We saw a tiny bubble of flame, no bigger than a pebble, float toward us from her finger. And then the world became hell, with fire exploding everywhere, scorching the trees, killing the men. By the grace of the gods, the fire only singed me, but I alone escaped. All of the others were consumed, left as blackened corpses when the flames receded."

"The white one did this, you say?" Gultec had heard the tales of the pale bug-thing that lurked among the ants. He remembered another white creature, the albino wizard of the Golden Legion, who had incinerated a hundred brave Eagle Knights with similar magic. That attack, plus the sudden arrival of the horsemen, had doomed the defense of Ulatos and secured the legion's conquest of the Payit.

Once again the Jaguar Knight growled. He looked at the column of Itza marching past, the old men and women helping the children, all of them casting anxious looks to the rear. It would be many hours before they could even reach the next valley in the range, and many more such valleys in their path before they reached the pass.

"We face the risk of disaster if we do nothing," he finally concluded. "Gather all the warriors together. We will meet at the tail of the column." His voice was a deep growl, grim with reluctance and foreboding. Gultec's plan, born of desperation bordering on despair, seemed reckless and mad even as he prepared to enact it. He knew that the Itza had no training, no tradition of melee warfare.

Yet it filled him with pride, and guilt, to see how willingly they followed his command. But he could see no other alternative.

"Then, when the creatures move up, we shall attack."

*     *     *     *     *

Poshtli sensed no hunger, no thirst. It never grew dark, nor did the gray mist show any signs of thinning or dissipating. Yet he knew that many days must have passed since he and Qotal had escaped from the Temple of Tewahca.

For all that time, he had ridden on the great dragon's shoulders. Nestled among the bright, flowing plumage, he felt no danger, knew no desires. He had not spoken, nor had the Plumed Serpent made any communication with him. A sense of timeless peace possessed Poshtli, and it seemed to him that it didn't matter where they were or where they went. His human body seemed like an old friend.

Finally, though, he knew that this sense of stasis must begin to fade. He felt something that was not boredom, but instead a slow, restless stirring that compelled him to speak or to act.

"Where are we?" he asked finally, his voice low but level.

*We soar through the ether, away from the plane of men.* The answer came into his mind clearly, and he could almost imagine it spoken in low, articulate tones. Yet there had been no sound after his own question.

"Why am I here with you?" Poshtli inquired.

*I admired your bravery. You were willing to die for me in the battle. We lost that fight, but there will be another.*

"When? How?"

*The woman, the Daughter of the Plume, is very wise. She will know where the battle must be fought, and she will go there. We wait for that moment, and then I shall challenge Zaltec again.*

*And I will triumph.*

Poshtli wanted to ask more questions, to talk about the details of their entry into the world. He wondered briefly how long their wait might be, or how much time had passed since they had entered this stuff that Qotal called "ether." But something in the dragon's mental tone discouraged any further questions, so he settled back into the lush plumage.

There would be time enough, he suspected, for all these answers and more.

\* \* \* \* \*

A flight of two dozen eagles soared overhead, following the dusty spoor across the rolling desert terrain. On the ground, Cordell and fourteen other riders held their steeds to a walk in order to conserve their strength. The journey to Helmsport would be a long and tiring one, but no part would be as difficult as this first leg, the crossing of the House of Tezca.

For the first week they had moved northward, retracing the route of their flight and following the path of the horde, which now apparently returned to Nexal. Water had been plentiful along this route, and they carried sufficient food for the passage, at least until they again entered settled lands.

But now they cut to the northeast, both to avoid the tail end of the monstrous army, which moved much more slowly than the riders, and to trace a more direct path toward the Payit lands. Chical and the other eagles soared

ahead and above, informing them that the fertile lands of
Pezelac lay another week's journey in this direction.

Loading the horses with as much water as they could
carry, the men carefully rationed the precious liquid and
embarked upon this scorching trek. Cordell, accompanied
by Captain Grimes, the assessor Kardann, and twelve stalwart lancers, rode toward Helmsport. The rest of his legion
and its Kultakan allies marched toward the sea.

Only the gods, or fate itself, would decide whether they
would again be reunited.

*　*　*　*　*

"Gultec, I must speak with you now." Zochimaloc said with
uncharacteristic force. Despite the mounting pressures of
the attack that he was about to launch, the Jaguar Knight
turned to heed his teacher. Around him, the warriors of
Tulom-Itzi crouched among the underbrush, awaiting his
command.

"I understand the importance of this attack, and I know
that Itza warriors, perhaps many of them, will die as they
make it," continued the old man.

Gultec nodded, uncomfortable under Zochimaloc's patient gaze.

"But take care of one thing, my student and my friend," he
said. Gultec flushed with pleasure. Never had his teacher
called him "friend" before. "Take care that you survive the
battle."

"Why do you tell me this?" Gultec scowled. "I cannot lead
the warriors into battle, all the while taking care to pre-
serve my own life!"

"You are important to us, to all Maztica. Perhaps more important than you know. If you were to perish now, all that
you have won for us would be lost. The future would become despair."

"What have I won for you?" the Jaguar Knight challenged.
"Thus far, your city has been sacked, your people have fled
into the jungle, and now they stand at the brink of disaster.
You know that the ants must be diverted, or at least slowed

here. Otherwise we will never make it to the pass in the mountains. There will *be* no future for the Itza!"

"Please do not ask me to explain," continued the teacher. "But promise me that you will take care. Keep my words in your mind."

Once again Gultec felt very strongly his teacher's deep and patient power. What this strength personified, other than intelligence and wisdom, the warrior did not know. But he sensed it as a majestic might that could only be obeyed.

"This I will do," the warrior promised. "Now the attack must begin."

"Fare well in the fight, my son."

"I will do the best that I can, Grandfather," Gultec said with a bow.

He turned back to the warriors. Already the hulking black forms of the ants were visible among the underbrush. With a heavy heart, his teacher's words ringing through his mind, Gultec ordered his warriors forward.

*     *     *     *     *

The shrill howl of a thousand war cries split the jungle stillness, heralding the attack against the head of Darien's inexorable column. The monstrous ants, marching eight or ten abreast, didn't hesistate, nor indeed take any notice of the assault.

Instead, the first rank trekked forward into the chopping daggers and axes of the Itza. These ants fell, quickly overwhelmed by the onrushing warriors.

The next rank, too, advanced to its doom, and the third followed. Still the insect legs drove the segmented bodies forward, while cold eyes sought enemies for the killing. The humans, too, pressed forward, a savage wave spreading to both sides of the massive insects, disrupting the march and forcing the column to dissipate and turn to its flanks.

But soon the creatures began to exact the price of battle in human blood, which quickly soaked into the damp earth of the forest. The ants reacted with mechanical precision, chopping and mangling targets as they presented themselves, marching forward as long as no obstacle stood before them. But as brave men fell to the rock-hard mandibles, others swept around them, still pressing the attack.

In moments, the column of ants disrupted into complete confusion. The creatures turned upon themselves, seizing the torn bodies of their fellow insects and instinctively carrying the corpses to the rear. Others turned to the sides, striking and advancing to the right or the left, and the impact of the narrow column diffused into the tangled forest. The file spread, and the insectoid advance lost all sense of direction.

Warriors threw themselves at the monstrous foes, striking for eyes, trying to hack the glistening black bodies apart where the bulbous segments joined. A wild melee spread beneath the jungle canopy as men and insects both perished in mortal clash.

"What is the humans' intent?" Darien demanded from her position with the other driders near the center rear of the column. The attack had caught her by surprise, but she felt curiosity, not dismay. She believed implicitly that human warriors could not hope to stand in battle against her mighty, unfeeling host.

The drider's intuitive command, sensing the opportunity in the clash, reached her mindless creatures.

*Kill, my soldiers! Kill!*

The ant army surged forward, spreading into a broad front, facing the attacking warriors who now spread to the right and left of the column as well as to its front. Insects crawled over the bodies of their fallen kin, seeking human flesh.

"Hittok! Go now! Strike them with missile fire! Take the archers—now!" She barked the command at her drider lieutenant, and the grotesque creature sprang through the tangled column, his eight legs propelling him quickly past the steadily marching ants. The other driders followed, launching their black shafts into the faces of the attacking warriors.

Darien herself muttered a quiet command, instantly disappearing from view with the casting of an invisibility spell. She followed this with another chant, a teleportation spell that carried her to the flank of the human advance.

Here she crouched, unseen, among the underbrush. She saw ant and human alike fall to the assaults of the foe. Raising her invisible hand, she sighted an imaginary line along the Itza attack.

"*Kreendiash!*" she snapped, unleashing the power of her magic as explosive energy.

A yellow bolt of lightning crackled from her hand, searing through the fleshen ranks of the humans. Men screamed in shock and pain, horribly wounded, while others fell dead, instantly slain by the hot magic. The bolt seared a black swath through the forest, killing vegetation, ant, and human alike.

Again she shouted, and another bolt blazed its path of blood and pain. Now the arrows of the driders began to take their toll, piercing human skin and muscle with driving power. A flush of ecstasy thrilled Darien. She saw horrible devastation wrought among the humans and knew a joy she had not known since her days as a drow.

*Advance! Slay them all!*

The ants surged forward now, a wave of inevitable death, tearing into the suddenly faltering Itza attack. Men cried out in pain as they fell to horrible maiming and death beneath the tearing jowls of the inhuman foe.

She saw a warrior, clad in the skin of a jaguar, and sensed instinctively that this was the one who had slain Dackto. She raised her hand, and a bolt of magical energy, like a sizzling arrow of light, hissed forward. It struck the warrior in his left shoulder, spinning him around and dropping him to the ground.

She pointed once more. There was a crackling hiss, and another magic missile exploded from her fingertip. Before the second bolt struck, however, a surge of warriors swirled around the fallen knight. The blast seared the back of one of the warriors, slaying him instantly, but she shrieked her hatred and frustration as her original target vanished behind the protective shield of his fellows.

Again and again her magic crackled through the air, but now the humans fell back toward the sheltering jungle. The cohesion of her insectoid column broken, the creatures scattered after individual targets, often dragging a fleeing man to earth, where others of the ant army set upon him and tore him to pieces.

Many of the warriors escaped, but many did not. Darien counted, with grim satisfaction, the remains of several hundred among the bodies of her own slain ants. Now the insects swarmed about the gory corpses, spreading into a vast feeding horde as the remaining warriors vanished into the forest.

Hittok and the other driders came toward her, with the scuttling, crablike gait of her kind that she still found so revolting. Counting quickly, she saw that none of the driders had been slain.

"They escape!" cried Hittok, with a gesture toward the now motionless forest fringe. "We must pursue!"

Darien raised a restraining hand, her face creased with an ice-cold smile. "Let them go," she countered. "There will be time for more killing tomorrow."

\* \* \* \* \*

From the chronicles of Coton:

*In mystification over the acts of the gods.*

*Lotil continues the steady working of his pluma. His tapestry takes shape slowly before us, though I still cannot tell whether he creates a blossom, a bright bird, or perchance an elegant butterfly. Perhaps he blends all three into a design, a piece of artwork as alive as its subjects.*

*It is a wonder and a glory to see the skills of this man, to observe him in the creation of something that is such evidence of the sublime glory of the gods—of Qotal, who gave us pluma.*

*At the same time, I sense a great stirring of evil as Zaltec emerges from his slumber. He has recovered from his battle with his brother and has begun to think again, to plan and to move.*

*As he schemes, he knows that Qotal can have but one more opportunity, and then he concludes where that chance must come.*

*And so I feel evil move toward Payit, where it prepares for the final confrontation with the Feathered Dragon.*

# ❧ 13 ❧

# RITES OF CAPTURE

"I don't like it. It's not like Halloran to be gone so long." Daggrande huffed in annoyance, but he couldn't conceal his concern. Anxiously he paced about the small campsite while Luskag and Jhatli looked at him sympathetically. Lotil listened impassively, his short, blunt fingers dextrously working a tuft of plumage into the cotton mesh he held upon his lap.

The camp of the desert dwarves filled a broad clearing in the forest, with several dozen small fires lighting the area. They had feasted on the forest's bounty, for several deer had fallen to their bows that afternoon. And still Halloran and Erixitl had not returned.

"He's always been a good lad—reliable, responsible. A true companion, the kind of fellow you'd like to have at your back in a fight."

Jhatli looked at Daggrande in surprise. Obviously the characterization of the brawny fighter as a "lad" struck him as somewhat unusual. Still, he hadn't previously appreciated how far back the paths of the two legionnaires were linked. There was something paternal in the way the gruff dwarf spoke of his human companion.

"'Course, I never told him that," continued Daggrande, his tone angry. "The big lunk wouldn't have understood!" Daggrande looked at the group around the fire, as if he expected someone to challenge him.

"What're you starin' it?" he growled at Coton as the cleric eyed him curiously. The priest made no answer, and Daggrande sat down with a sigh. "I don't know what's got into me! Surely they're all right somewhere. They've got to be!" He couldn't allow himself to think of any other alternative.

"Maybe they just wanted some time by themselves," guessed the youth. Still, a look at the darkening jungle around them dispelled this suggestion even as he made it. The forest at night did not create a very romantic environment.

"Should we search for them?" asked the chieftain of the desert dwarves.

"Yes—but not now," came Daggrande's response. "We'll only get more of us lost in the jungle, and we can't hope to find anything until morning."

"They could be back before then, in any event," Lotil offered, though the blind man's tone suggested that he shared the dwarven captain's concern.

"At first light, then," said Luskag. "If they haven't returned, we shall commence the search."

*     *     *     *     *

Hoxitl stirred in his stench-filled lair, which had once been the grand temple of Zaltec in Nexal. Now ruined stone walls leaned and tilted around him. Where once a proud archway had created the entrance, now a slimy tunnel cut through the piles of rubble.

Beyond the lair, the monsters of the Viperhand prowled restlessly through the ruins of the city. Gangs of orcs snarled and fought with each other, only to scatter, howling, at the approach of looming ogres. After the long march across the desert, the creatures had returned to their city with crude pleasure. Yet now, after many weeks of enforced idleness in the brackish ruins, the pleasure turned to boredom. The beasts, Hoxitl knew, needed activity.

He himself had succumbed to a lethargic passivity that had verged on the comatose. For a time, he lay unknowing, his mind vacant, awaiting the command and the vitality of his god. The towering statue of Zaltec, near his lair, stood impassive and unmoving as the weeks became months. Finally, not knowing why, the monster Hoxitl raised himself from lethargy into stiff, unpleasant movement.

Gradually a command took shape in the cleric-beast's

mind, an image of a destination and a growing compulsion to again put his beastly force into motion. At the end of this march, he sensed, there would be killing, and hearts to feed the god, and final, ultimate victory over the humankind of Maztica.

Hoxitl emerged from his cavelike lair and raised his voice in a high, ululating howl. The sound echoed from the great mountains around the valley, rolling across the muddy, swamplike stretches that had once been lakes. Among the ruined streets and cesspools, the orcs looked up from their bickering. The cry called forth other orcs and ogres and trolls from slumber or feeding. All took up their weapons and responded.

Slowly, by ones and twos, then by dozens and scores and hundreds, the beasts of the Viperhand moved to their master's call. They gathered across the sprawling chaos of the great plaza, perching on ruined temples, clustering in the few flat expanses of the stonework, all of them turning their beastly faces toward the great stone monolith that was their power and their glory.

"Creatures! My children!" Hoxitl bellowed in his grotesque language, and the creatures listened attentively.

"Zaltec calls us, and we must obey! Again we shall march so that all Maztica will know the terror of our presence!"

His creatures responded with dull roars of anticipation. The long days of inactivity weighed heavily upon them, and now they stood, once again ready for war.

\* \* \* \* \*

"Chief Tabub, we bring two of the Big People as prisoners," explained the little man, who was called Kashta, after placing his bow and arrows—the tips of the deadly missiles wiped clean of their *kurari* poison—beside the door to the chief's low hut. Kashta carried Halloran's sword with him into the hut. The weapon was as long as the warrior himself.

"It is as I dreamed, as the Lord of the Jaguars told me in my sleep," said Tabub in a low monotone. The chief sat cross-legged, flanked by two of his wives. "A man and a woman . . . she carries a child?"

"Indeed," whispered Kashta, awed.

"They must go to the pit tonight," pronounced the potbellied chief. Like Kashta, his face was painted red and black, though in vertical stripes while all the other warriors bore their marks in horizontal lines.

"But this man, he is like no other I have seen, no other man in the world," the warrior objected tentatively. "His face is covered with hair, like a bearded monkey's, and he wears a shirt of hard silver. He bore this great knife, also of silver."

"Let me see," said Tabub. He drew the weapon from its scabbard, and his wives shrank back as the glow from the enchanted blade filled the tiny hut. Tabub reached out with one short finger and traced it along the keen edge. "Ah," he grunted, without any display of pain, as blood ran from a gash in his skin. "This is a potent weapon indeed."

"The stranger speaks gibberish, also like a monkey, but the woman understands him. She can talk, too, in the normal language of the Big People."

Tabub's visage grew stern. "You know the commands! You may not speak with the Big People! They must be placed in the pit, and there they die!"

"But always we kill the Big People! We place them in the pit, and the Cat-God devours them! For how many years must it go on this way?"

The chief's scowl didn't waver. "You know of the words of the god, as told me by my father, and his father before him, and on through the history of our people!"

Tabub's eyes closed, and his words came forth rhythmically, reciting the prophecy that had long been lain on his folk.

"The Big People are our enemies, and they will kill us unless we kill them first. They go to their deaths to appease the gods, and the gods are pleased, and the Little People will live on."

"But the killing must end sometime, to that same tale," argued Kashta. He, too, spoke the rote of long-taught prophecy: " 'There will come a man, a giant even among the Big

People, who will turn night into day and lead us into the peace of a new age.'"

"Is this man a giant?" demanded Tabub.

"He is tall, even for a Big Person. Yet truly I could not call him a giant," Kashta admitted.

"Then he will be fed to the Cat-God." Tabub, his pronouncement final, turned with studied arrogance to inspect his newest wife. Kashta knew that the interview was over.

\* \* \* \* \*

The small garrison of Helmsport, some thirty men, rushed to the shore, shouting hurrahs, at the appearance of Don Vaez's fleet of carracks. Their delight swiftly turned to chagrin when, after landing his troops, the commander of the relief expedition ordered them thrown into irons and imprisoned in the very fort they had guarded for so many long, lonely months.

Helmsport was in fact little more than a huge, rectangular earthwork. It stood upon a low hill, commanding the sheltered waters of Ulatos Lagoon, where first Cordell and now Don Vaez had anchored their fleets.

The wall itself enclosed a rectangular compound, although a low gate had been built, a notch in the earthen wall where horses, men, and even carts could pass through. The rest of the rampart loomed some thirty feet above the surrounding ground and supported a wide walkway at the top. Any defending force occupying the top of that wall would have a commanding advantage over an attacker forced to scramble up the steep outer slopes.

The base of the wall within the fort was lined with wood and grass huts, with roofs of thatch. Several wooden barns had been erected plus one framed structure, much like a house, that had been intended to serve as Cordell's headquarters. Several smaller, but solid, wooden buildings served as storage sheds. It was to one of these that the captain ordered the garrison members, still chained, to be confined.

"What's the meaning of this?" howled Sergeant Major

Tranph, the burly veteran Cordell had left in command, when Don Vaez confronted them in their rude dirt cells. "What manner of enemy are you?"

"Cautious," explained the blond-haired captain, unruffled by his prisoner's outburst. "You are suspected of treason, of betraying the charter of Amn. Rest assured that you will have ample opportunity to defend yourselves. It may be that you were duped by the real villain in the affair."

"Cordell?" Tranph gaped at Don Vaez, understanding his meaning but disbelieving just the same. "Surely you jest! What has he done to arouse the ire of the merchant princes? Why, his profits after conquering Ulatos alone would pay for the expedition tenfold!"

"Those profits have not been delivered into the proper hands. Indeed, we have evidence that he is concealing them from the just owners. Where is the eminently loyal captain-general? Why does he not appear to defend himself?"

"Profits delivered? To Amn? By Helm, man, we haven't had contact with the Sword Coast since our landing a year ago!" Tranph sputtered, indignation wrestling with outrage.

"And that, in itself, may be at the root of the treason." Don Vaez suppressed a yawn. "But come now, my good sergeant. Where is your general? Surely he is the one who must provide the ultimate answers."

"I tell you, he has marched on the capital of this land—a city reported to hold more gold than you can possibly imagine! Our last message from him told us that he had entered the city and was engaged in negotiation with their ruler. We have heard nothing else from him for these last four, maybe five months."

"Nor will he hear aught from you," promised Don Vaez with a tight smile. "When he returns, we shall have a quiet reception—call it a trial, if you will—and he will have ample opportunity to answer the charges against him. Perhaps if his mission is a success, he will return with enough gold to convince us of his noble intentions.

"Then he will accompany us—in chains, of course—on a return to Amn." And then my own triumph shall be complete! he added silently.

Don Vaez, in a flurry of blond curls, turned on his heel and marched from the cell. A burly guard slammed the door shut behind him, while a company of trusted watchmen stood as sentries about the small building.

Rodolfo, the veteran navigator, stepped over to Don Vaez as he left the shed. "Beggin' your pardon, sir," he began, "but I wonder if we're bein' a bit hard on these lads here."

Don Vaez's eyes flashed, and he fixed the man with all the glare his clear blue eyes could muster. "You're not being paid to wonder but to follow orders! If I were you, I'd have a care to remember that!" he barked.

Rodolfo met the gaze in those blue eyes for several seconds, but Don Vaez couldn't read the look he saw there. He held his own gaze firm, and the navigator finally nodded slightly.

"As you wish, Captain," he replied softly. Rodolfo turned and disappeared into the darkness collecting in the fortress. Don Vaez watched him go, pleased with the result of the confrontation. He knew that he had gone far to secure his position as unquestioned leader of the expedition. The only question now was what to do next.

Still, it was a fine start to the mission! Don Vaez congratulated himself as he crossed the compound within Helmsport, toward the large wooden building—the only permanent structure here—which he had claimed as his headquarters. Within that house, he knew, Pryat Devane worked his auguries, trying to determine with the aid of Helm what would be the appropriate course of action. That was useful, thought the commander, but not essential. He had time now, and could afford to wait.

He took no notice of the eagle soaring in serene circles high overhead.

*　*　*　*　*

"We have folk like this where I come from," Halloran explained. "They're called halflings."

"Do they lack clothing and take your people prisoner?" Erix wondered.

Hal chuckled grimly. "No—they're more of a nuisance than a threat. Most of them live among humans, in the same cities and towns and villages. Sometimes they're brave, sometimes cowardly. They're just like other men, except a little smaller."

He and his wife sat on the ground within a small cage fashioned from sturdy wooden bars lashed together with toughened strands of hemp. Around them, the Little People settled down to their evening's cooking. The village was a collection of straw huts, with overhanging roofs of heavy thatch and low, rounded doorways. Racks in the center of the structures held a variety of meats over low coals.

Night settled across the surrounding jungle, a night filled with the heavy drone of insects, punctuated by the shrill howls of monkeys and birds. Every once in a while they heard the rumbling cry of a jaguar, and for a few moments afterward, the forest fell still.

Several children advanced cautiously toward the cage, watching them with wide eyes. Erixitl smiled at them, and they quickly scampered back to the shelter of their parents' cookfires.

If Erix was frightened, Halloran thought, she didn't show it. He tried to hide his own fear, even though he didn't fear for himself. But what kind of hope was there? What were their prospects of flight, even if they could get away, with Erix carrying the burden of their child within her.

"What do you think they'll do with us?" she asked.

Halloran could only shrug. "At least I don't see a pyramid or an altar. But who knows what their plans are? Have you heard of these folk before?"

"In the same sense as the 'Hairy Men,' the desert dwarves," she admitted. "The Little People are told of in ancient legends, and some claimed that they dwelled in the deepest jungles of Far Payit. But like the desert dwarves, no one seemed to take the stories seriously. I have never heard of anyone who has seen them before."

"We *are* the lucky ones," Hal remarked dryly.

For a time, they lapsed into an uncomfortable silence. Finally Erixitl shook her head and offered her husband a wan smile. "Still, I believe things will be all right," she said. "I don't know why, but I do."

"Me, too," Hal agreed, though neither of them believed him. He had to do something, he knew—but what?

"Big People, you come with me now." The remark drew their attention, and they saw the same warrior who had been the first to accost them at the waterfall approaching.

"Where are you taking us?" asked Erixitl as the little man opened the cage door. Several other warriors stood well back from the pair, carrying the short bows with deadly-looking arrows, ready to shoot.

The native didn't reply, instead commanding them with a peremptory gesture to follow him. They walked among the small grass huts of the village to a clearing on the far side. A dozen warriors, each bearing a blazing torch, stood in a ring at the center of the area.

Halloran's chest tightened in fear, again for Erixitl and the unborn child. Instinctively he understood that the prisoners would be at the center of the evening's activities. He wondered what rite these diminutive warriors had prepared for them.

"Go here," commanded the warrior who led them.

As the ring opened to allow them to pass, Halloran saw a circular pit, perhaps twenty feet across, in the center of the circle. He couldn't see the bottom until he and Erix were prodded to its edge. Then he saw that it was about twelve feet deep.

Opposite their position, at the base of the pit, he saw a door made of heavy wooden bars. Something dark and shadowy moved beyond those bars, and his fear grew to sick horror.

"Go in now," ordered the warrior. His voice carried a trace of reluctance, but he displayed no hesitation as he raised his weapon menacingly.

No ladder or other means of descent presented itself. Halloran knew that a twelve-foot leap might very well prove deadly to Erixitl or the baby.

"Wait!" he objected. "Leave her out—let her alone! I'll go in there by myself!"

The warrior looked at him, and Hal thought he saw sympathy through the garishly painted lines on his face. But then another of the Little People came up, with a peremptory air that made Halloran suspect that he was some sort of chief. This one had the same war paint as the others, though his was drawn in vertical lines and he had long feathers tied to his ears and his wrists.

The stocky leader raised a hand and gestured toward the pit. A group of archers behind him raised their weapons, and Halloran looked at the bristling row of arrowheads.

Suddenly the chief pushed Erixitl in the small of her back. With a startled scream, she tumbled forward off the edge of the pit as she twisted to face Halloran. His heart froze at the look of terror on her face.

But his body remained mobile.

"My hand!" Hal shouted. Erix spun in the air as he tumbled to the side, seizing one of her hands in both of his. He fell prone at the lip of the pit as she dropped and grunted in pain. But he held firm, arresting her fall halfway down.

"I'm okay," she gasped. "Let me down."

Halloran gasped as another warrior kicked him in the ribs, pushing him toward the edge. He felt Erix slip from his grasp and drop the rest of the way to the floor of the pit. Then he rolled off the edge, twisting in the air to land on his feet beside her.

Erix threw her arms around him, trying to choke back her terrified sobs. "Are you hurt?" he asked her, and she shook her head, sniffling.

Then they heard, from the darkness across the pit, a deep and very menacing growl.

*     *     *     *     *

The surviving Itza warriors pressed through the dense tangle of the valley bottom, pushing their way toward the heights above. Gultec, at the rear of his army, saw that the ants did not pursue after the bloody skirmish.

That, at least, was something. He hadn't had time to count their losses, but he knew that more than a hundred of the

Itza warriors had fallen in the short, violent engagement. But they had accomplished their objective. The man-bugs had apparently paused to regroup. If the rest of the people had the opportunity to gain the pass because of the sacrifice of some, the warriors had not died in vain.

He remembered, with a cold chill, the pale white monster who had lashed out with magic against them. Once again he thought of the battle against the foreigners at Ulatos and how the magic of the albino sorcerer had broken his army.

Could there be a connection between the two powerful spell-casters? He didn't see how, and yet the distinction of their whiteness seemed too obvious for coincidence. One had been a humanlike elf, the other was a grotesque and unnatural beast. Yet something about the beast's face seemed similar, in its alluring femininity, to the elf.

He pushed his speculation aside, focusing instead on the rigors of the climb. The warriors straggled across a swampy valley bottom, a flat depression that marked another barrier in their long march up the pass.

From here he could look before him into the black dome of the star-speckled sky and faintly see the outline of the narrow pass above. It looked impossibly remote and distant, yet somewhat closer than the last time he had seen it. Most of the Itza people should be passing through it even now.

"You have made us a good plan," said Zochimaloc, appearing out of the darkness to walk softly beside Gultec. "The high route must be the safest."

The Jaguar Knight sighed. "I wish it were true. But I fear no place is safe from the kind of enemy that pursues us."

"You must know that your attack was successful," countered the old man, stepping nimbly over a low vine. "They have fallen behind us now, and this gives us time to escape."

"Time? Can it be *enough* time?" Gultec wondered. "Is there enough time in the world?"

Zochimaloc chuckled, a patronizing, grandfatherly sound that somehow made Gultec feel more confident. "There is time, now, for the old people, the children, and the mothers to go through the pass and over the mountains. Perhaps there is time, too, to have faith."

The warrior looked up at the pass, still outlined against the stars. Perhaps Zochimaloc was right. Indeed, many of the Itza must have already reached the far side of the mountains. By morning, the warriors would reach the summit of the pass. Once there, they would have to turn and face the inevitably pursuing enemy. There they would make their stand.

*  *  *  *  *

From the chronicles of Coton:

*In wonder at the mysterious ways of the One True God.*

*Around me the dwarves pace and grunt in agitation over our missing companions. Lotil, too, fears for his daughter. He tries to work, but his fingers cannot perform their pluma-weaving. Instead, they tremble in a way I have never seen before.*

*And in truth, the disappearance of Halloran and Erixitl is sudden and mysterious.*

*Yet I find it difficult to express fear for them. There is too much of destiny about the woman for her to suffer a random mishap in the jungles, this short of our goal. She may not triumph, I know, but her ultimate resolution will be encountered at Twin Visages. Of this, I am certain.*

*Wherever she has gone, it is good to know that she has Halloran's strength with her. Whatever her lot on this dark and impenetrable night, I feel certain that it has a purpose in the pursuit of our goal.*

*The dwarves will seek them in the morning, and I will wish them well. Perhaps my optimism is but the senile dodderings of an old man. My companions may be correct in their assessment of danger.*

*In any event, we must wait for the morning to know.*

# ❧ 14 ❧

# NIGHT OF THE CAT-GOD

Halloran placed one arm around Erixitl's shoulders and moved himself between her and the source of the rumbling growl. He felt very conscious of the baby within her and terribly vulnerable in his own unarmed state. He was determined to die before allowing harm to reach Erix.

The couple stared across the darkened pit, and slowly their eyes adjusted to the dim light. The stoutly barred door remained closed, but again they saw shadowy movement beyond it.

Then that resonant growl rolled through the pit again.

"It's opening!" Erix gasped. They saw the barred door rise slowly, and then the black shape beyond it crept forward with an oily smooth motion. It crept toward them, slowly moving away from the shadows around the wall of the pit. As it reached the center of the enclosure, they saw its sleek black pelt, its ears laid back along a broad, flat skull.

"A black jaguar!" Hal hissed, shocked at the horribly menacing visage of the great cat. Its yellow eyes burned through the darkness like glowing spots of hellfire, while its jaws gaped open just enough to reveal long, wickedly curved fangs. The animal's shoulders equalled Hal's waist in height, even as the creature crouched. It stared unblinking, the dark tail flicking back and forth in excitement.

"It's too huge. It can't be a jaguar!" Erix objected, though she couldn't imagine what else menaced them in this nightmare pit.

"There are other great cats in the world—tigers, lions, even more horrible things like displacer beasts," Hal whispered, desperately seeking a plan of action. "Maybe it's something like that."

"I am the Lord of the Jaguars."

For a moment, the voice shocked them into stillness. It flowed with oily smoothness, yet it contained traces of the deep growl that had already raised their hackles in fear. The great cat blinked, and Halloran swore those jaws twisted upward into a horrible caricature of a smile.

"I am the Lord of the Jaguars, and you are mine."

"It *talks!*" Hal hissed. He tried to shield Erixitl, staring into that monstrous, leering face.

"I talk. I talk before I kill."

"Who—*what* are you?" Erixitl demanded. "Why do the Little People keep you here?"

"I stay because I choose to stay," rumbled the black beast. "They do not *keep* me. No one *keeps* me!"

"Why do you choose to threaten us, then?" Halloran asked. "We offer you no harm."

"No one offers me harm," sneered the cat. "I desire your blood and your flesh. It pleases me that you shall die to feed me."

Halloran's mind raced. Stunned by the bizarre communication with an animal that belonged among the beasts of the forest, he sought a way to argue or reason with the creature.

"Are you old and feeble, so that you cannot hunt for yourself?" he asked.

"Silence!" The jaguar lord's voice shook the air around them, a roar of command.

"I will not be silent!" Hal barked back. "Why do you depend on them for food? Why do you live in a cage? That's no life for a lord!"

The force of the creature's roar slammed into his face like a physical blow, hurling him back against Erixitl. Quickly he stepped forward, his jaw jutting belligerently. He stared in challenge at the monster, aggressively raising his clenched hands.

Then his attention faded and his eyes grew heavy. Halloran felt an almost overpowering urge to sleep.

"What—what's happening?" asked Erix softly from behind him. "I . . . feel so . . . tired."   Her voice faded to a soft whisper. He felt her slump against the wall of the pit and sink slowly toward the ground.

Before them, the Lord of the Jaguars grinned his evil grin. Hal stared at those yellow eyes and thought for a moment that they no longer seemed so threatening. Indeed, they were gentle now, their look caressing him like the kiss of sunlight on a warm summer day.

"Sleep, insolent human," hissed the great cat. "Stare into my eyes and rest."

Halloran shook his head angrily, realizing that something was very wrong. But what? Now he had a hard time forcing his mind to work, as if a thick and cloying fog permeated his skull. He didn't dare sleep, with this savage beast ready to attack! Or was it savage, after all? Now it seemed benign to him, like an old friend.

The Lord of the Jaguars took a step closer.

In the darkness of the pit, all Hal could see now were those two gleaming eyes. Erixitl groaned softly as she sprawled on the ground behind him. He couldn't break his eyes away to look at her.

"See how the woman sleeps? She knows peace now." The creature's voice remained silky smooth, gentle and friendly. "You must rest, too."

"No!" Halloran marshaled all of his will, suddenly twisting his gaze away from that deadly stare. He had to do something! Think, man!

All around him pressed that grim darkness. The bright eyes remained the only source of illumination, tugging at his will, compelling him to look back into their light. Suddenly the night seemed as much an enemy as the great cat. He had to drive that enemy away. The yellow eyes of the jaguar called to his memory, wide and staring, penetrating the darkness with their large, dilated pupils.

The memory of a spell came to him, and he acted without thought.

"*Kirisha!*" he shouted, turning back to the leering, monstrous face. He pointed as he cast, and a magical ball of light appeared in the air. Instantly it expanded to a white brightness, and it hung directly before the creature's eyes. Above, the illumination blossomed out of the pit, and he heard the gasps of the Little People around them.

With a shrill cry of rage and terror, the jaguar sprang back. Its howls rent the night, silencing the jungle around the village. The pit stood outlined in the clear illumination of the light spell, brighter than a dozen torches.

"Demon!" spat the beast. "What manner of man are you? You shall pay for this outrage!"

Halloran saw that the jaguar blinked and shook its head, all the while growling and snarling. But now there was an element in those cries that had not been there before—an element of fear.

Above him, he heard the excited jabbering of the Little People. None of them ventured forward to look into the pit, but he plainly heard their cries of alarm and confusion.

"Good!" he hissed to himself. "Maybe that'll shake up their confidence a bit."

Erixitl moaned again, still on the ground behind him. Keeping a wary eye on the cat, Halloran crouched down and helped her to lean against the wall of the pit.

Then the cat growled, and once again the creature's voice throbbed with anger and power. Its fear had become tension, and it crouched and stared, its black tail swishing back and forth in agitation. Hal sensed it working up the nerve to attack.

"You seek to defeat me with simple tricks?" The Lord of the Jaguars shrilled his rage, a snarl of bestial fury. "For this you will die slowly. You will watch me devour your woman before you perish!"

"You're an old hornless goat, not fit to be lord of anything!" Hal snarled back. "You're not fit to be a servant of toads! Too weak to hunt for your own food! You seek to defeat us with magic because you are the one who is afraid! Your fangs rot! Flee back to your hole, craven one!"

For a moment, he wondered if he might be right. Indeed, the monstrous feline still crouched, staring. He saw long, wickedly curved claws extend from its forefeet. Desperately he wished for a weapon. His mind raced through the few other spells he knew. None of them, he realized, had any hope of halting a creature of this size and power. Still, in his desperation, he sought any tactic, any thing that might help him against the nightmarish beast.

Then the monster pounced.

\* \* \* \* \*

"They have moved into Helmsport. Your men, the ones you left there, have been imprisoned in one of the huts." Chical explained the results of his reconnaissance to Cordell as the two men rested beside a quiet pool. Around them, the horses eagerly lapped at the water while the legionnaires and other eagles prepared for an evening's rest.

"What about the commander? Did you see their leader?" Cordell asked, angry and perplexed by the news.

Chical shrugged. "I do not know how to tell your leaders. You do not wear the feathers of rank such as does a general of the True World."

Beside them, Kardann looked up anxiously. "They come from Amn, I tell you!" he warned. "Because we sent no messages back—no tribute! If you had listened to me—"

"Be silent!" Cordell barked, and the pudgy assessor quickly obeyed. "I need to think!"

"It would seem that they do not come to aid you," observed the Eagle Warrior, with no trace of irony in his tone.

"At least, their captain does not. I am certain that there is someone behind this behavior. It is not typical of soldiers from my country to thus turn on those who offer them no harm and no threat.

"There is more," noted Chical, and the captain-general sighed.

"What?" Cordell asked, fearing the answer.

"The beasts of the Viperhand have mustered in Nexal. They begin to march from the city. Now they are led by a monstrous colossus of stone. It is a figure that walks like a man but towers as high as once did the Great Pyramid."

Cordell cursed. "Can you tell where they're going?"

"They march eastward, toward Kultaka—back along the route you yourself took when you marched to Nexal."

"They could be going all the way to Payit, then—to Ulatos and Helmsport?"

"Yes, naturally," replied the Eagle Knight.

"One more question," said the captain-general. "If we maintain our present pace, will we get there before them?"

Chical thought for a moment. "Yes, by several days at the very least—perhaps a week or more. We are already closer than they are, and I believe we move faster."

Cordell looked frankly at the warrior who had once fought so savagely against him. "Your information is very valuable to me—more valuable than I can explain. To have the freedom of the skies, the ability to cross the continent in a few days time and observe our enemies, is a power that any commander from my country would give very much for. I begin to think that it is one of the few advantages remaining to me—to us."

Chical nodded. "It is a thing that an eagle does, but truly it is our greatest power."

"Thank you for accompanying me and my men," Cordell added. "You give me some small hope, at least, of success."

Chical shrugged. "Maztica is changing. You yourself have done much to see that the True World will never be the same place that it once was. But you are a brave man, and for now, anyway, we fight for the same cause."

The Eagle Knight studied Cordell for a moment, and the general squirmed slightly under the scrutiny of those piercing black eyes. "But remember my warning. If you should again use your forces to march against the humans of the True World, you will find us united against you."

"My friend," said the captain-general with a sigh, "I find it much more comforting to have you on my side."

"Then I pray that we shall remain on those terms," said Chical. The warrior stretched and rose to his feet. "Now," he added, "I will get some sleep. I must fly far in the morning."

*　*　*　*　*

"They await us in the mountain heights," reported Hittok. The drider had skulked forward, dangerously close to the rear of the fleeing Itza column, to gain his information. Fortunately the night was dark, and the drider's vision was far more acute than any human's under these conditions.

"They flee no longer?" Darien heard the words of her comrade, and already her mind wondered at the reasons behind the news.

The long column of ants had slowed to a crawl, as even the nearly indefatigable creatures felt the strain of the long climb and the days of ceaseless marching. The white drider allowed them to pause in this mountain valley, not so much to rest as to allow the rear of the long column to catch up. Then when she pressed ahead in the morning, she would be able to bring her entire force to bear.

"So far as I could tell." Hittok continued to detail his findings. "I saw many warriors positioned along a rocky crest that rolls across the valley. Beyond them, I did not go. It could be that, as before, the men sacrifice themselves that their women and children can escape." Hittok's voice showed his scorn for the tactic.

"They cannot do so for many more battles," noted Darien grimly. "We killed more than a hundred of them the last time, when they took us by surprise. Now if they wait for us, we shall be prepared."

"Indeed," agreed the black drider. "The valley bottom is open before them. The ants can spread into a wave and quickly sweep up and over them."

"But they must have some plan," countered Darien. Her alabaster features twisted into a frown. "Humans do not sacrifice themselves for no purpose."

"Perhaps," Hittok said with a shrug, "they only desire to die like men."

"Perhaps," said Darien quietly. Still, the thoughtful expression on her face as she examined the mountain height before them showed that she remained unconvinced.

\* \* \* \* \*

"*Gigantius!*" shouted Halloran at the instant the Lord of Jaguars sprang. The spell of enlargement, one of the last he had learned from Darien's spellbook, was the only enchantment that leaped into his mind. Once he had employed a potion to expand his size; now he tried to emulate that effect with a memorized enchantment.

He saw a nightmare visage of feline hatred, jaws widespread, streak toward his face. The light spell still illuminated the pit, but by now the great cat's eyes had adjusted, and his aim was true.

Halloran met the creature's leap with a charge of his own. His hands wrapped around the beast's neck as all the strength in his arms and shoulders combined to hold the deadly fangs away from him.

Razor-sharp claws raked across his breastplate. The cat shrieked in rage, its powerful muscles driving its jaws slowly toward Hal's face. He twisted, thinking only that he needed to keep the creature away from Erixitl, and the two of them rolled across the ground in the pit.

The monstrous jaguar squirmed, the claws of its hind feet scoring deep gashes in Halloran's legs. Only the *pluma* cuffs at the man's wrists saved his life, pumping strength into his grip and slowly forcing the drooling fangs back from his face.

The great cat twisted again, and Hal pushed it away, the force of his act shoving him back against the wall of the pit. The cat crouched, snarling, but suddenly it seemed smaller than it had before. Halloran loomed over the beast, staring down into those blazing, hate-filled eyes.

Then he realized what was happening. The spell had taken effect. Vaguely he sensed the Little People shrieking in horror and fleeing back from the edges of the pit. Erixitl, lying against the wall at the base of the enclosure, held her hands protectively over her belly as she gaped up at him. For the first time, he saw fear in the Lord of the Jaguars' blazing yellow eyes.

The spell increased his size, although it did not enhance his strength. Still, the *pluma* around his wrists and the fear and anger burning in his own heart gave him strength that he would not otherwise have possessed.

He lunged at the monstrous cat as the creature tried to

spring toward Erixitl. It twisted in midair, dragging its sharp talons across Hal's forearm and leaving cuts that quickly welled with blood. But the man stood now nearly fifteen feet tall, and he seized the monster by the scruff of its neck.

The cat howled in terror as he lifted it from the base of the pit, raising it over his head and shaking it. The *pluma* and his rage possessed him, made him a man mad with battle lust. With a grunt of effort, he hurled the shrieking, spitting beast from the pit, full into the faces of a pair of gaping villagers.

The little folk screamed in terror, bolting away from the horrifying apparition of the flying jaguar. The cat, itself fully terrified, landed on its feet, crouched, and sprang toward the shelter of the surrounding forest. In another instant, the black shape disappeared into the equally dark confines of the enshrouding jungle.

"Come on!" he urged, reaching down and lifting Erixitl up to the edge of the pit. His mind whirled with images of poisoned arrows, and he knew that it would be mere moments before the warriors recovered their senses enough to shoot. His size, he realized, would be no protection against the strike of one of those venomous missiles.

He sprang upward after Erixitl and then crouched beside her, trying to shield her from the natives. Where could they go? How could they get away?

Even as he groped for answers, he saw that it was too late. The area around the pit was crowded with warriors, all of them armed with the deadly darts. Bellowing in rage, he stood up and lunged forward, determined to smash a few of the archers before he died.

Then he slowed his charge, halting after a few steps to look around in puzzlement. The light spilled from the pit, clearly illuminating the painted halflings. One by one, they laid down their weapons and fell on their faces, pressing themselves to the ground in obeisance.

The one who had seemed to be the chief crawled forward. He looked up at Halloran, his face twisted by fear and grief. He moaned something, then hastily pressed his face back to the ground.

"What's going on?" Hal wondered aloud, looking back to Erixitl. The chief, speaking to her, repeated his words in the language of Palul.

"He calls you Master," she said, her voice full of wonder, "and begs your apology. He says that he didn't know who you were."

"And who does he think I am?"

"He says that you are the king, destined to lead them from the jungle—just as it was foretold in the prophecy."

\* \* \* \* \*

"Here—footprints beside this pool!" Luskag gestured to the ground, and Daggrande trotted over to the desert dwarf. They had traced Halloran and Erixitl's path from the day before to this sheltered pool, where the towering waterfall spilled from the heights above.

"And here!" called Jhatli from the underbrush nearby. "There are many prints, as if a group of warriors waited in ambush."

Daggrande's heart tripped in fear. He turned to the young man as Jhatli looked up at him in puzzlement. "What is it, lad?"

The crossbow-wielding legionnaire, together with Jhatli and a score of desert dwarves, had followed the trail. The rest of the dwarves scoured the surrounding country, except for a few who remained guarding the camp with Lotil and Coton.

"The warriors must have been children," he explained. "Their feet were very small."

In moments, the young hunter had found the path beneath the encloaking vines, and in another minute, the stairway through the rocky niche stood revealed.

"They must have gone this way, whoever they were," Jhatli guessed. "And they probably took Halloran and Erixitl with them!" For once, the youth did not loudly proclaim his intent to attack and kill whatever enemies stood in their path. Indeed, Jhatli's face was creased by a frown of deep, undeniable concern.

"Should we get the rest of the dwarves?" asked Luskag, with a look to Daggrande.

"Let's go," grunted Daggrande, hefting his shining axe. "Once we find out what we're up against, we send for help—if we need it." His tone, combined with the steely glint in the veteran legionnaire's eye, gave his impression of the prospects for the latter circumstance.

Luskag and several dozen desert dwarves quickly fell into file behind them as they started up the cool, mossy passage. None of them spoke, as each focused on his own apprehensions. Daggrande silently vowed vengeance against whoever had captured his old friend, while Luskag wrestled with a deep curiosity about the diminutive footprints.

Jhatli led the way, always the alert hunter, his own bow and arrow ready for instant use. The youth wanted to bound up the stairway but forced himself to slow his pace so that the slower dwarves could keep up.

Soon they emerged into the damp glen. The well-beaten path lay before them, and though it showed no specific footprints, Jhatli ascertained with a quick inspection that their quarry had kept to the trail.

They set off at a trot, twenty-two grim warriors in search of an unknown enemy. All of them were cautious, but none were afraid.

"Hsst!" Jhatli paused with a whispered warning, raising his hand and shrinking into the underbrush beside the trail. Instantly the desert dwarves followed suit. "Someone comes," the young hunter told Daggrande.

They stared at the trail before them, and soon the sound of steady footfalls—many of them—reached their ears. They heard, too, the hum of animated conversation.

"They're not trying to sneak through the woods, whoever they are," Daggrande hissed. He checked his weapon and raised the heavy crossbow to draw a bead on the trail before them. A second later, he lowered it in surprise and relief.

"Hal!" he shouted, springing to his feet. The desert dwarves and Jhatli quickly followed suit. Halloran, accompanied by Erixitl, looked up in surprise. The pair had been walking easily down the jungle trail, in apparent unconcern of danger. The crossbowman saw movement behind his friend, but he couldn't see who was there.

"Daggrande, you old griffon's tail! What are you doing out here?" The man raced forward to embrace his companion.

"Looking for you!" sputtered the dwarf. "What do you *think* I'm doing! And who are *they?*"

He gestured toward the file of small warriors, still painted in black and red, who followed Halloran and Erixitl down the trail. The man turned with a flourish, indicating the leading warrior.

"Captain Daggrande, meet Chief Tabub of the Little People."

Erixitl repeated the introduction in Payit, while Daggrande looked back at Halloran with raised eyebrows.

"They are my warriors," said Hal, with just a hint of a smile, "and our newest marching partners on the road to Twin Visages."

\* \* \* \* \*

From the chronicles of Coton:

*As our numbers grow and our march proceeds towards its rendezvous with the god.*

*We make a colorful file now as we advance along dark forest trails. A thousand desert dwarves, new to the jungle and intrigued and mystified by its sights, smells, and sounds, lead the file. With them, speaking with their chiefs and marveling at their ways, walks the legionnaire dwarf Daggrande.*

*In the center, we have five humans—six, to count the one carried by Erixitl. With us walks the great war-horse, Storm. The creature is a wonder to all of us Mazticans, for most of us have never seen an animal so large, and none of us have known one so useful.*

*And now our column is trailed by more warriors, hundreds of tiny bowmen who have sworn allegiance to Halloran because he answers the call of their prophecy. They* call it a miracle, and though I know it was his magic that "turned night into day" and caused him to be "a giant, even among the Big People," I am not inclined to dispute the miraculous explanation.

Now we pass through the rolling country to the west of high, forested mountains. Though more adventures doubtless lay in our path, I cannot help but feel that our march to Payit gains unstoppable momentum.

# ❧ 15 ❧

# A MOUNTAIN RAMPART

The summit of the narrow pass loomed as a tight bottleneck in the rugged ridgeline known to the Itza as the Verdant Crest, the range that formed the border of the Far Payit country. Here Gultec stood with the men of Tulom-Itzi, prepared to make a final stand against the army of ants that had ravaged their city and their lands. Those who could not fight had already proceeded down the western slopes of the range, there to await the resolution of their future.

Climbing the east side of the range, following the tracks of the Itza warriors toward the high pass on the crest, came the steadily advancing swarm of giant ants. Devouring, destroying, and always marching inexorably forward, the monstrous insects swept upward like some malevolent tide.

In places, Gultec and his warriors had crossed slopes and valleys of dry brush. These they torched now, in the face of the ants. But the living wave simply swept to the sides of such obstacles, and the few ants who perished in the flames were left unmourned in the wake of the steady advance.

Through the narrowest valleys they pressed, and up the steepest slopes. The humans outdistanced them, taking temporary refuge in the sheer heights of the range's central divide. Yet the monsters below and their masters, the driders, had only to look up and they would see their ultimate objective looming before them.

Darien welcomed the chance to battle the humans who had fled before her horde for so long. The fact that the warriors had chosen good ground to defend meant little to her and to her army. What problem were vertical cliffs and sheer heights to creatures that could scale the smoothest shelves of overhanging granite?

The rocky crest stood barren of trees and bushes. Composed mostly of crumbling granite covered with mosses and lichens, the snakelike summit of the ridge towered above the rest of the range. All around, lower ridges, covered with lush foliage, dropped away to the distant, jungled flatlands. The trail from the lower reaches crossed back and forth across the sheer face of this highest ridge until it finally crested the long, rolling peak.

For the last thousand feet of this ascent, the trail broke free of its verdant surroundings, winding in the sunlight and open air through this region of broken, rocky ground.

Gultec looked back across the trail below. The slopes to the east dropped steeply away into a flat, dishlike valley. Water and silt had collected in the bottom of this valley, forming a wide, tangled swamp. Hours before, the last of the Itza warriors had pressed through that swamp and made their way up the tortuous trail to this crest.

Gultec knew that the fetid waters of that dank marsh swarmed with snakes and crocodiles, yet he didn't delude himself into thinking these would provide any obstacle to the ant army. If anything, the tangled vegetation and finger-length thorns sprouting from many a bush would delay the beasts only momentarily. The respite would delay the inevitable attack by a mere few minutes.

Beyond the muck and mire of the marsh, the jungle commenced again, cloaking the lower slopes of the range in green velvet as far as the eye could see. Somewhere within that carpet, Gultec knew, advanced the insect army of his unnatural and terrifying foe.

For a moment, he paused in reflection. He wondered what had corrupted these beasts into their monstrous forms, what had brought them under the command of these other creatures, the man-bugs with their sleek black skin? And what was the secret of that white one, with her bizarre appearance and her shocking powers? Why did all these foul presences work to destroy Tulom-Itzi?

But in the next moment, he shook his head with an angry, self-conscious growl. Why, indeed, did he worry about such things? He was a warrior, and now he had an enemy in war.

It was a cold and implacable enemy, to be sure, all the more frightening for its complete lack of humanity. But nevertheless it was a problem of war and demanded a warlike solution.

His mind resting once again on firm, familiar ground, Gultec looked around at his warriors. They stood ready all along the crest, though still no sign of their enemy appeared below. They will be here soon enough, Gultec thought grimly.

"Are the others, the women and children, safely away?" Gultec turned to an Itza warrior, a man who had supervised the further retreat of those who would not be able to fight in this battle.

"They are nearly dead from fatigue, but they are safely off the heights. They have made camp at the western foot of the range."

Now only the warriors stood along the crest. Proud and alert, the line of men provided the last barrier between the mandibles of the pursuing horde and the people of Tulom-Itzi. Brown bodies lean and muscular after weeks of warfare and marching, the men of Tulom-Itzi didn't show their weariness. Their bodies remained taut, their black eyes dark and intent, staring into the murky forest below.

They wore their long black hair pulled back, away from their faces. Unlike other armies of Maztica, no feathered banners fluttered overhead. Aside from Gultec, no man wore the spotted garb of the Jaguar Knight, and there were no Eagle Knights among the Itza at all.

But these men who had been born and lived in peace now proved ready to make a last stand in war. They stood in ranks of ten or twenty. Each rank had gathered a large pile of rocks and boulders nearby. Each man carried a bow and several dozen arrows, all of the precious missiles that the women of the tribe had been able to make.

The warrior beside Gultec cleared his throat nervously. "All the old ones and the children are safely down the slope, that is, except Zochimaloc. He insisted that he would see the battle, though I tried my best to persuade him otherwise."

Gultec cursed. "Where is he? I will speak to him myself!"

The warrior pointed to the old chief. Zochimaloc sat upon a high knob of the ridge, his legs crossed comfortably before him, looking as if he desired nothing more than a few moments of quiet meditation.

Gultec cast another look into the valley below. The file of ants had not yet emerged from the forest, so he judged that he had several hours before the battle would begin. Trotting along the ridgetop, he headed toward his teacher.

"Master," he said, with a peremptory bow, "you must not remain here! You can add nothing to our defense, and your life must be spared! What will the people do if you perish?"

Zochimaloc smiled, an irritating, patronizing look that nearly brought Gultec's blood to a boil. "Patience, my son," said the old man. "You must not talk to your old master this way!"

Gultec flushed. "Forgive me, but I speak strongly to reflect the depth of my concern! What do you hope to gain by remaining here?"

"Remember," Zochimaloc chided him gently, "that although you have learned many things, you do not know everything. Perhaps there is a surprise or two in this old gray head.

"Or perhaps I simply wish to have a look at what war is like," the old man concluded with that same smile. "I have never seen it, you know."

"It is not worth seeing," replied Gultec. "I thought you knew that."

Zochimaloc chuckled quietly. "There was a time when you would have argued long and hard with yourself over that very point. It is true that your time in Tulom-Itzi has changed you."

"But you are still the same stubborn old man I first met," the Jaguar Knight retorted. His deep affection for Zochimaloc would not allow him to speak more directly, but he dearly wished that his teacher would depart from the mountaintop.

"If the ants press through," Gultec continued, trying a different tack, "we will have to flee quickly. Even young warriors, fleet of foot, may not survive. How do you expect to outdistance such monstrous creatures?"

His teacher smiled a trifle sadly. "I know enough of war to understand that this mountain is the only place you have a chance of stopping them. If they press through here, what will there be to flee to?

"Now, see," added Zochimaloc, drawing Gultec's attention with a pointing finger. "Here they come. Do not worry yourself about me, but instead tend to your warriors and your battle. I shall take care of myself."

The warrior turned to stare into the valley bottom a thousand feet below. He saw a red rank of crawling insects advance from the jungle fringe and press forward into the swamp. More of the segmented bodies surged behind, then still more, and soon it seemed that the earth itself was a crawling mass of festering destruction, creeping toward the base of the cliff.

The ants looked oddly proper from this height, like the tiny insects that they were supposed to be. The Jaguar Knight suppressed a shudder as he tried to imagine the dark and corrupt power that had perverted the creatures into the monstrous horde below him.

Gultec growled in frustration with Zochimaloc's stubbornness and in genuine shock at the extent of the insect army. Always before he had seen it as a long, snakelike column stretching into the distance, but to a distance that he could not see.

Now the creatures had massed into a broad front, and still they came forth from the forest. There were many thousands of them, and still they came! How could his line of mere humans hope to stand against such an assault?

At the same time, he knew that they had no choice. He trotted back to the center of the line, pausing to pat a warrior on the shoulder here or to speak encouraging words to a young man there. The men of Tulom-Itzi stood ready to fight—and to die.

They watched, tense and fearful but still determined to hold their ground, as the huge creatures forced their way through the entangled brush of the swampy valley bottom. Caught in the tangles, some of the ants hesitated, and these were buried by the press of others behind them. Soon the bodies of the slowest sank into the mud, forming a ghastly bridge for the following ranks.

The ants pressed forward, faster and faster as their footing became more secure. Soon they reached the base of the steep slope. They scrambled ahead and upward without pause, and finally the last of the creatures emerged from the forest. Gultec tried to spot the man-bugs among them, but among the sea of insects, he could see no sign of the larger black bodies—or the white one.

"Archers, stand ready!" he cried.

A thousand bows tensed, slim arrows tipped with sharks' teeth, nocked, and pointed downward. The Itza warriors awaited Gultec's command. Though the ants were still far away, a great portion of that distance dropped away from them, so the Jaguar Knight judged that they were within range.

"Now! Shoot!" he called, and the missiles soared into the air. "Keep shooting! Aim for their eyes!"

The insects crept up the mountainside while the shower of arrows rained down. The ants took no note of the steepness of the terrain, clutching the clifflike shoulders of the rock as if they were low obstacles on level ground. Many of the arrows clattered harmlessly from the stony surface of the rock, while others bounced from the tough, shell-like carapaces of the monsters.

But still others found the vulnerable eyes, or, aided by the momentum from their long descent, struck the upraised heads of the ants and punctured the hard shells. One ant, then another, then many of them altogether slipped backward and tumbled from the rock face, falling among the moving mass of their fellows below.

The archers fired volley after volley, sending the sharp and deadly heads of their missiles into the steadily advancing faces of their foes. But finally, when most of the arrows had been exhausted, the firing tapered off.

Still the ants crawled and crept upward, twitching and grasping as their six-legged forms gripped the nearly vertical surfaces with apparent ease. They crawled over the knobs and shoulders of the slope's higher places, gathering in thick red streams to cluster upward in the shallow ravines.

Closer and closer they came, advance seemingly unaffected by the cessation of arrow fire. They climbed at the same methodical, unhurried, yet inevitable pace as they had before.

Only now they were close enough for the Itza warriors to see the flat, transluscent surfaces of their many-faceted eyes, close enough to hear the clicking jaws of the creatures' mandibles, opening and closing hungrily. They climbed steadily and came closer still.

Now Gultec stood ready to unleash the second, and most potent, line of his defense.

"The rocks! Let them go! Push them back to the mud where they belong!"

Instantly the Itza warriors dropped their missile weapons, seizing the great boulders that they had carefully stacked along the ridge. Two or three men combined to move the larger stones, while others hefted good-sized rocks by themselves. As the ants pressed upward, one warrior raised a heavy stone over his head, staggering under the weight, and then pitched the rock with both hands toward the swarming mass below.

A trio of warriors nearby pushed a boulder toward the slope. The missile teetered backward for a moment, but then they heaved mightily. Slowly it toppled forward, and then it rolled over. The rock quickly gathered momentum, plunging and bouncing down the steep-sided ridge.

The stone plummeted some fifty feet and then crashed into one of the highest of the climbing ants. It smashed past the creature, leaving the ant flailing with the three legs on its right side. Its left legs had all been crushed by the boulder, and slowly the monster slipped to the side. In another second, it fell free, toppling unnoticed past the ants that climbed behind it.

The boulder, at the same time, continued its destructive plunge. It crushed the head of another ant, much lower than the first, and then tore through the joint between the segments of a third. It continued to crash downward, smashing and crunching into anything that lay in its path through the heart of the ant army.

Another boulder tumbled free, followed by a handful of fist-sized stones and large rocks that a single man would raise over his head, pitching it into the insect horde. Beginning as a small clatter, punctuated by a dull roar, the deluge of stones started toward the unnatural enemy below.

All along the line, the men threw and rolled their missiles, until the air resounded with the cracks and crashes of smashing rock. A hail of stones tumbled downward into the faces of the advancing ants. The rocks bounced and crushed their way in sharp descent, careening along the slope of the mountain, some of them cracking and splintering into clouds of debris, while others ricocheted far out into the air, tumbling away from the climbing horde.

But many of the boulders rolled true, striking straight into the center of the ant army. They continued downward to crush more heads and snap more legs, cracking the shell-like carapaces and even, occasionally, tearing through an ant and breaking it in two.

The men raised a spontaneous cheer as they saw the attack start to take effect. For the first time, the inexorable advance of the ants seemed to waver. The entire front rank of the ants tumbled away, carried downward by the momentum of the stone storm.

More and more of the boulders crashed downward. Some of these broke away parts of the cliff face itself, and great masses of rock, a few as big as small houses, plunged into the face of the insect horde. More and more of the creatures fell, crushed by the weight of the granite assault.

"See! They fall away!"

"We drive them back!"

"Tulom-Itzi is avenged!"

The normally unwarlike Itza erupted in howls of triumph and cries of savage glee as they saw the bodies of the hated invaders twist and break and fall. A heap of dead and crippled ants formed at the base of the cliff, and still more of the rocks tumbled downward.

Broken ant bodies, too, continued to fall. Many of these twitched and writhed pathetically at the bottom, only to slowly vanish beneath a steadily increasing pile of debris. Other ants attempted to crawl free of the danger area, finally perishing of the grievous injuries they had already suffered.

Then a whole section of cliff wall broke away, raising a massive cloud of dust as it tumbled downward. A sound like thunder shook the high mountain valley, and the earth itself trembled underfoot. Whoops of glee continued as more and more rocks contributed to the deadly rain.

The dust billowed below them like the smoke of a great fire, obscuring the ants, covering the whole valley wall with a dense cloud. Still the noise and the shaking continued, and more and more rocks were added to the chaotic scene below.

Finally the boulders gathered along the ridgetop had all been dropped. Everywhere the air was thick with dust, and crashes from below continued to echo through the valley as occasional rocks toppled free and tumbled farther. At last even this postlude slowly faded.

For a moment, the high pass, with its shroud of dust and bodies, was silent. Even the wind died, as if to let the men of Tulom-Itzi savor their accomplishments. Weary, exhausted, yet hopeful, the warriors peered into the murk below. It seemed impossible to believe that anything could have lived through that deluge of crushing granite.

Then dark shadows appeared through the dust—shadows that moved with a familiar, mechanical precision that was all too terrifying in its recognizability. The cliff wall itself seemed to ripple with movement.

But it was not moving earth. The shapes that emerged from the dust, still climbing, still hungry, were those of the giant ants.

*  *  *  *  *

"There are many humans up ahead," reported Luskag. A small group of dwarves and halflings had preceded the main column, and now they had returned with the news.

"A community?" Halloran wondered. "Men of what type, what nation? Could you find out?"

"No city," replied the desert dwarf with a shake of his head. "Not even a hut or two. Just a big camp in the forest. From the looks of it, I'd say it hadn't been there for very long."

"Where could they come from?" Halloran asked. "Do they live in these lands?"

"Tabub says no," replied the desert dwarf. "The jungles west of the Verdant Range are inhabited by no one. Only an occasional human comes here to hunt."

"An army, then? Who else could they be?"

Again the dwarven chieftain shook his head. "There are no warriors among them—only women and children and old folk."

Erixitl, astride a slowly walking Storm, and her father Lotil came up to them. The rest of the dwarves and halflings paused while their leaders conferred.

"Let's go talk to them," Erixitl suggested. "There must be a reason they're here, and if they're not warriors, they don't represent a threat to us."

An hour later, accompanied by Jhatli, Daggrande, Luskag, and several of the halfling bowmen, the couple approached the clearing that contained the huge, and obviously temporary, camp in the forest. They saw no shelters of any kind, save for a few crude lean-tos. The lush grasses in the meadow had been trampled flat but were still green, solid evidence that these people had not been here long.

But the people! In many ways, it was like a journey back to the House of Tezca, for they recognized instantly that these were displaced folk. They had few possessions with them, and they looked undernourished and frightened.

They saw people in cotton tunics and mantles, bedraggled and dirty. Many of them looked emaciated, and they all looked up in fright when the foursome emerged from the edge of the forest. Children ran screaming to their mothers. The complete absence of young men among the throng was conspicuous.

Several older males, white-haired and frail yet carrying sharpened sticks as if they were spears, advanced suspiciously, brandishing their makeshift weapons.

"Who are you? What do you want?" they demanded in the language of the Payit.

"We are travelers, seeking to pass through this country. We journey to Ulatos, and then on to Twin Visages," Erix answered. "But who are you, a people that we find here without houses or crops?"

The first of the men looked at her suspiciously, and then sighed. "We are the folk of Tulom-Itzi. We have been driven from our city by the horror that comes out of the earth."

"Tulom-Itzi! But—but that's where Gultec was called to!" she exclaimed to Halloran. At the knight's name, the men started.

"Do you know Gultec, Knight of the Jaguar?" the first speaker asked.

"He is our friend and companion," she replied. "He left us to journey back to Tulom-Itzi after he was called by his master . . ." She tried to remember the name Gultec had told her. "Zochimaloc?"

"Yes, our great and wise chief."

"Is he here? Is he alive?"

"He is not here. He was alive this morning, but who knows now? All of our men, led by Gultec, stand at a pass high in the mountains." The man gestured to the ridgeline, looming high and remote to the east. "There they stand against the horror."

He went on to explain the nature of the attacking army, their flight from the city, and the skirmishes that had preceded the warriors' stand at the pass. "Now we have fled until we can flee no more. If the pass is held, we shall remain here. If our warriors are killed, we shall perish soon afterward."

"We have warriors with us," Erixitl exclaimed. "Perhaps we can help. How far is the pass you speak of?"

The man gestured again, brightening for a moment but then sighing and shaking his head. "I thank you. The battle may be won or lost by now. We left the warriors hours ago, and the ants were not far behind."

Erixitl explained the situation for the others, and Halloran studied the rolling, jungled mountains.

"Monstrous ants!" exclaimed Jhatli. "I am not afraid! I have faced other monsters before. Now let me face these! I will slay them all!"

Luskag turned his eyes to Erixitl, his face an expressionless mask. The revelation of the Sunstone had sent him and his people to her; now, it was clear, he would follow her decision in the matter before them.

Tabub and his diminutive warriors, in the meantime, looked to Halloran. He alone would make the choice that would send them into battle or not.

Erixitl sighed and went to her husband, taking his hand in both of hers and holding it. They didn't speak for several moments as he looked down at his wife, suddenly afraid. She was full and round with child, and a freshness had returned to her face now that they had left the dry country behind. Halloran thought of their peaceful march and the quiet moments they had enjoyed in the forest along the way.

But always there was the thought of the obstacles before them, and now they came upon the people of their friend, in need of help. There was no choice to be made, really; instead, they simply needed a few moments to grasp the one course of action they could take.

"Gultec crossed half of Maztica to come to us after the Night of Wailing. He led us to the fertile desert," Hal said softly as Erixitl nodded. Still, the images of horror in his mind caused by the insect army described by the Itza affected him deeply.

"You must stay here," he continued firmly. "I'll take the desert dwarves and the Little People. We'll head up toward the pass and see if we can get there in time."

"You have to go, I know," said Erixitl quietly, but with equal firmness. "So you can understand that so, too, do I."

His objection died on his lips, for she was right. He really did understand.

\* \* \* \* \*

Don Vaez entered Ulatos, with full martial pomp, at the head of a marching column of more than fifteen hundred men. Nearly a hundred of these rode prancing chargers, and they led the way. The citizens of the city, the greatest metropolis in the lands of the Payit, turned out to stare at the spectacle.

Ulatos stood out proudly from a flat, coastal savannah. The wide grassland supported many fields of mayz, as well as small villages near the fringes of the city. But the city itself was the dominant feature of the land.

Tall, colorful pyramids rose throughout. Wide streets, some even paved with stone, separated its buildings. Many of the buildings themselves were made of stone, and even the adobe structures were meticulously whitewashed. Green gardens filled the gaps between many of the structures, and the city was lined with cool bathing pools. Flowers burst in chaotic abundance from bushes that grew at every street corner.

Now all the people from this mighty city gathered along the widest street, an avenue that led directly to the central plaza, where stood the tallest pyramids and the biggest houses. They stood in silence and awe, standing well back from the path of the approaching marchers.

Never had they seen such an awe-inspiring sight! Cordell, at full strength, had brought a mere forty horses and five hundred men.

Now they saw that many crossbowmen alone, followed by several hundred harquebusiers. The latter demonstrated their weapons in the center of the city square, stopping sharply and wheeling left at their captain's command.

They raised the heavy weapons, each loaded with a full charge of powder—though no shot—and fired a thunderous volley. The report fell like a crash of thunder across the crowd, and the accompanying clouds of smoke instantly concealed the soldiers from view. They smartly faced right and resumed their march, emerging from the cloud with their weapons again braced over their right shoulders.

Many of the Payits fell back in terror from the explosion, more impressive than anything Cordell had shown them.

Then they slowly crept back to watch the grand spectacle.

Don Vaez himself, in a blaze of silken color and long, silver-blond curls, rode a white stallion. The creature reared and trotted, lunging this way and that, as the proud rider led his army through the city's grand square.

Beside him rode Pryat Devane, and the cleric's mode of transport impressed the Payits even more than did his commander's. The cleric of Helm sat cross-legged upon a thin, floating piece of cloth, like a litter of *pluma*, only much smaller. As the flying carpet darted about, the Mazticans saw that the flight of this foreigner was far faster and more controlled than any gentle floating of feathermagic.

The priest of Helm looked disdainfully at the savages around him, for he had inherited his mentor's revulsion toward things Maztican. Indeed, the hatred Bishou Domincus had held for these barbarians and their bloodthirsty gods was one of the primary drives in Devane's determination to follow in the Bishou's footsteps. Now he enjoyed the sensation of his own superiority, and he darted the carpet back and forth to terrify and awe the onlooking Mazticans.

All around them were the pyramids, clean structures, many brightly painted, that had once been dedicated to the glory of Maztican gods. Since the city's fall to Cordell, worship of those gods had been banned from public ceremony, though many citizens doubtlessly continued to worship them in private. Instead of the old temples, statues, and altars that once had honored their heights, the banner displaying the All-Seeing Eye of Helm fluttered from each pyramid.

Caxal, once proud Revered Counselor of Ulatos, had been reduced to a spokesman for the conquered after the battle with the Golden Legion. Now he stepped hesitantly forward to meet this new general, wondering if the nightmare his life had become now grew even darker.

"Greetings, Silver One," he said in commonspeech. He used the term that the Mazticans had created for Don Vaez after they had seen the care he took with his shining locks.

"And who are you?" asked the commander.

"Your humble servant, Caxal, spokesman for these folk of

Ulatos. Have you come to aid our conqueror, the captain-general?"

Don Vaez evaded the question. "Where is the captain-general now? Do you know?"

"He journeyed to Nexal, Silver One, many months ago. There he intended to confront the great Naltecona. There he shall win his greatest victory!"

"Splendid!" replied the rider, with a tight smile. "And when he returns here, I shall be waiting to . . . 'reward' him."

\* \* \* \* \*

The houses of Kultaka City stood empty as the streets resounded to the steady cadence of the vast, brutal army. Hoxitl's column marched into the abandoned community, but well aware of the monstrous advance, the Kultakans had fled into the surrounding hills some days earlier.

Had their army been here, the courageous people might have stood against the onslaught. But the Kultakan force had accompanied Cordell to Nexal and had now been driven far to the south, beyond even knowledge—not to mention rescue—of their homeland.

The great colossus of Zaltec now led the army, and the humans fled from his image in terror whenever it loomed imminent. Hoxitl walked just behind the towering monolith, though his twenty-foot height was dwarfed by the size of Zaltec. The slavering beasts of the Viperhand followed in the tracks of both monstrous forms.

Ogres and orcs smashed through the doors of houses, seeking whatever foodstuffs had been left behind. Objects of gold and silver, plus the few weapons left in the city's armory, fell into the hands of the brutal invaders.

The trolls scrambled up the stairs of the city's pyramids, plundering the temples for their objects of value. All of the creatures sought human victims, but there were none to be found.

For the first time, as they pillaged the abandoned city, the creatures of the Viperhand began to work in the units that

Hoxitl had begun to designate. They divided the city into sections, and each area became the property of a great regiment of orcs, accompanied by its masters, the ogres. The beasts took a savage joy in working in such brutal teams, and Hoxitl began to instill in them the discipline to remain together in their regiments on the march and in battle.

Finally, after only a few hours of rampaging, Hoxitl summoned the creatures before him once again.

"Creatures of the Viperhand!" The cleric-beast's voice rolled through the great square, a deep and rumbling command. "We shall not tarry here. Our true target lies on the coast. Only there we will confront our destiny!"

The beasts formed into ranks for their long march, exhorted by their master's commands. Their brutish faces turned once again to the east, and they started on the long leg of the march that would take them to Payit and Twin Visages.

Before them, as always, lumbered the montrous monolith of Zaltec. The great stone image had come to represent a mountain of strength to these creatures, and behind an image so mighty, so obviously unstoppable, it's no wonder that they felt a savage sense of invulnerability. Each of their leader's footsteps caused the earth to tremble, and the numbers of his army swelled and pressed forward, ready to kill for their master's pleasure.

*   *   *   *   *

Poshtli sensed a change in the Feathered Dragon's flight as Qotal veered to the side, or coursed downward—or somehow altered his direction. Always that accursed ether surrounded them, and the warrior had no sense of direction or bearing.

"What is it?" he asked.

*A summons—a plea*, rumbled the great dragon. *Someone calls me.*

"Who?"

*It is one of great power, great wisdom, else I should not be able to hear.*

"Can you tell where he is?" Poshtli tried to see through the gray haze, but as always there was nothing there.

*In the True World. I cannot go to him, but I can let him feel my power.* The dragon's thoughts contained determination and regret.

"To help him? How, if you cannot go back there?"

*He channels my power through himself.*

"Is this a way for you to return? Can Erixitl, perhaps, bring you back this way?"

*It is not a return, but a projection of power, and it entails dangers of its own. The Daughter of the Plume could perhaps reach me thus, but I would not ask it.*

"Why not?"

*Because such a transfer is not without cost—indeed, the cost is tremendously high.*

"What is the cost?" asked Poshtli, though he began to suspect.

*It is nothing short of the life of the caller.* The dragon began to dive.

*     *     *     *     *

Gultec stared in dismay at the climbing insects. A thousand or more of the giant ants lay at the cliff base, killed or broken beyond further menace. But those that still lived far outnumbered the slain, and the Itza warriors' weaponry had been all but exhausted.

Now they picked up their *macas*, their spears, their clubs, and their knives. They had no more missiles to cast or to roll, so they could only stand to meet the onslaught with their courage and their strength.

Slowly, distracted by thoughts of his own failure, the Jaguar Knight passed his eyes over the brave warriors who stood with him here at the pass. They knew now that there was no hope, yet none wavered or fled.

"Men of Tulom-Itzi, you make me proud," he whispered.

*Gultec . . . hear me well, my son.*

The voice came into his mind, though no sound had been carried on the wind. Instinctively he looked to Zochimaloc, still seated upon the high rock outcrop in the center of the pass. The old man was a great distance away, perhaps two hundred paces, and dust from the rockslide still drifted thickly through the air.

Yet Zochimaloc's eyes hovered before Gultec's face, so clear that the warrior felt he should have been able to touch his mentor's face.

"What is it, Grandfather?" he asked quietly, understanding without question that his teacher could hear.

*Take the warriors now. Fall back down the valley, toward the rest of the people.*

"But that is folly! Here is the only place to fight them—here, at the crest of the pass. Perhaps we cannot win, but here we can make them pay for our deaths!"

*Hear me and obey,* ordered Zochimaloc, his voice thrumming with uncharacteristic strength. *This is my command, and it shall be the last I ever give to you.*

"What do you mean?" Suddenly Gultec feared for the wise man, his teacher and mentor. Why did he give such a rash order? What could he hope to gain by resuming flight? Surely he understood that the folk of Tulom-Itzi could not flee forever!

*Go.*

The final word, sent with such a quiet air of confidence, and a hint of sadness as well, removed from Gultec any further desire to argue. The Jaguar Knight raised his hand in a single, sharp gesture, the signal to retreat. He was surprised to note that all the warriors along the ridgetop seemed to be watching him, as if they had sensed his internal debate with their chief.

But unhesitatingly they turned to obey Gultec's order. Swiftly, silently, the men of Tulom-Itzi fell back from the pass and left Zochimaloc there alone.

The Jaguar Knight was the last to go. As the ants crept steadily up the sloping wall of the high pass, he cast an imploring look at the old man who meant so much to him. But Zochimaloc paid him no more attention.

Slowly Gultec stumbled away, nearly sick with grief. Why did his teacher have to remain? He, Gultec, was the warrior—he was the one who should die before the onslaught of their enemies.

Then the Jaguar Knight felt a strange stirring in the ground below his feet. Zochimaloc remained immobile, sitting cross-legged atop his promontory of rock.

The chief of the Itza raised both of his hands over his head. He uttered a strange, ululating cry.

Then Gultec felt the power in the air, and it was the power of Zochimaloc. But it was also the power of the Feathered Dragon.

\* \* \* \* \*

From the chronicles of Coton:

*Encounters in the wilds, and our future course remains beneath a shroud.*

*They have gone, now, to the aid of Gultec and the Itza warriors.*

*Halloran and Erixitl, fearing for their friend, Gultec . . . Jhatli, once again thrilling to the promise of battle . . . Daggrande, Luskag, and the dwarves, because there is another job to do . . . and even the Little People, because their Lord Halloran goes.*

*Lotil and I remain here, with the Itza, and we learn of their trials and terrors. It is a tale that seems all too familiar, for in a sense it is the tale of the Nexala, of all Maztica. We humans see our land taken from us, given over to the rampaging of evil. Everywhere we are driven from our homes, pursued and slaughtered.*

*But suddenly now, like a flash of pure lightning through a dark, cloudy night, I sense him. Qotal is near! His power is a bolt of hope penetrating the True World.*

*And it strikes very close.*

# ❧ 16 ❧

# VICTORY AND VENGEANCE

"They gain the summit!" cried Hittok. Along with the other driders, he stood with Darien in the valley bottom, looking upward at the ants creeping steadily toward the rounded, rocky crest. The creatures of Lolth had witnessed the attack of their army, had seen it weather the heaviest defenses the humans could muster.

Impassively they had watched their soldiers slain by the hundreds. They had seen the march up the mountainside slowed by the deluge of arrows and rocks. Imperturbably they had observed the dust cloud that cloaked the slope, obscuring the ants from their sight. Then they had seen the dust fall away, and were not surprised when the ants appeared, still numerous and still steadily ascending.

True, a great number of ants had fallen during the attack, especially to the destructive power of the man-made rockslide. Yet more than half the ants survived, and they represented more than enough power to overwhelm the last mortal line of resistance.

The driders remained behind, at the fringe of jungle before the swamp. They watched the army advance and anticipated its inevitable triumph. They didn't shout or cheer, yet each drider's eyes blazed with a frightening intensity, like the wicked gleam of a cat before it crushes the life from the hapless mouse.

"Indeed, they have done as I expected," Darien said quietly. Hittok looked at his pale-skinned companion. Why did she not share his triumphant joy?

"Do you feel that?" Darien asked, her voice a harsh whisper. The white drider settled her great body to the ground, cowering as if in fear.

"What? What do you mean?" the black drider asked.

She didn't reply. Instead, she kept her eyes fixed upon the summit of the pass. The six-legged insects continued to work their way up the wall, the first rank already disappearing from sight.

"The human warriors—they have gone," she said, still in that soft, thoughtful tone.

"They flee—not that it will do them any good!" Hittok replied with a sneer. "They will live a few moments longer. That is all."

"No, wait." Darien stared at the pass. "Look. One remains, the man sitting at the very top."

Hittok squinted. The sky was overcast, but the brightness still caused him discomfort. "Where?"

"He is very dangerous. I can *feel* it," replied the female.

"I see him! Wait . . . no, I don't. Where is he?" Hittok squinted at the sky, cursing the shimmering that seemed to trail along the top of the ridge.

"He was there, moments ago. Now I cannot see him, but worse, I *feel* him, down deep. I feel a great menace in the air."

Then they heard, or felt, a rumbling within the earth itself. The ground below them heaved and buckled, staggering the driders. Gaping upward in terror and awe, the creatures saw waves ripple across the land. Several shelves of rock broke away from the slope, slowly tumbling downward, carrying a few of the ants with it.

The ground heaved again, and even the eight-legged beasts of Lolth had to squat low to keep their feet. Energy surged through the earth. The crashing of the rock shook the very foundations of the mountains.

An explosion wracked the valley then, like an unspeakably monstrous crash of thunder. The man at the top of the pass vanished in a cloud of dust and smoke. More rumbles emanated from the ridgeline, and the horizon shimmered and shifted under a wave of convulsive pressure.

Great cracks, each with the explosive volume of a thunderclap, shot along the rock face of the high ridge. More convulsions twisted the ground, sending huge rocks soaring into the air. Many of the ants tumbled from the sheer wall, shaken free by the force of the upheaval to crash among the bodies at its base.

Suddenly the whole mountain collapsed in a deluge of rock and earth. Sheets of cliff broke away, and the ridge itself collapsed. Thunderous explosions rocked the driders, and they watched the heart of the ant army swept away by rockslide and avalanche. Darien and her companions remained safe, beyond the destruction, but they watched the instruments of their power obliterated before them.

Massive sheets of gray rock broke free, tumbling and pounding into shards on the stone shelves below. The ridge collapsed, swept away by a force the driders could not see but with effects that wracked the broad vista before them.

The roar reached a crescendo as clouds of dust and debris sailed into the air. The entire crest of the ridge dropped, as if it had been lowered gently to the ground. But then lower support fell away completely, and the summit twisted and collapsed, vanishing quickly into the massive cloud.

A few of the ants crept around the fringes of the landslide, still heading implacably upward, as if unaware of the disaster visited upon their fellows. The great majority, however, perished in the crushing assault of rock.

A rolling dust cloud, far greater than that raised by the human rockfall, billowed outward, swelling across the swamp toward the watching driders. A smell like bleak decay filled the air as rocks and debris crashed into the stagnant waters. Finally the cloud swept around them, and the image before them vanished from view.

Most of the ant army vanished with it, their tough bodies crushed under a thunderous deluge. To the right and left of the wide gap, small bands of the giant insects struggled to retain their footing, though more and more of these tumbled from the sheer cliffs as the mountain trembled beneath them, falling into the rumbling maelstrom below, crushed by millions of tons of mauling stone.

\* \* \* \* \*

Gultec gaped in shock, staring at the place where the top of the mountainous ridge had stood. It was *gone!* And with it, he knew, had died the army that had so terrified and relentlessly pursued his people for the last weeks.

He and the Itza warriors had been making their way down the western slope of the pass. The route here was not so steep as that on the east, following as it did a wide and relatively shallow valley. The valley floor was lined with dried brush, and the Jaguar Knight had been eyeing its potential as a firetrap, preparing for the inevitable pursuit he had expected from the ant army.

Now he stared, horrified by the might that had claimed Zochimaloc. Then slowly he forced himself to understand that which seemed to defy explanation. Yet he knew that it had to be the truth:

Somehow his teacher had *summoned* the power to tear the mountain apart. The damage had been total in the area of the summit, yet the destruction had stopped short of Gultec and his retreating warriors. The army of ants, however, had been caught in the full brunt of the earthquake.

The warrior shook his head. What kind of power was it that could cause such damage to the very world itself? Without thinking about it, he knew that it had to be the power of a god, and he said a silent prayer of thanks.

Still dazed by the event, he looked around, and then his shock deepened to a consternation that made him wonder if he was losing his mind.

He saw another army approaching! And this one came from the west, opposite the ants! A vast band of men advanced hurriedly along the valley bottom, coming toward them, apparently from the flatlands below. They marched in files and carried axes and short bows and arrows.

Even more unreal, however, was the appearance of these men. Most of them were only half as high as a normal human! Some of them were broad-shouldered, with bristling beards sprouting from their faces. They looked like the dwarves who had come with the Golden Legion, except that they were dressed as crudely as any desert-dwelling savage.

Who were these newcomers? Would the Itza have to fight

again so soon after the climactic battle with the ants?

A shout from one of his men pulled his attention back again to that original threat. Here came more of the ants now, finally emerging from the chaos around the fringes of the destruction. They were but a pitiful remnant of the army, to be sure—the former thousands numbered but a few hundred—but still they came implacably onward. Desperately Gultec swung around to study the army approaching from below.

The Itza warriors raised their weapons against this new threat, and the approaching force slowed. The small warriors did not lift their axes and their bows; indeed, they did not look as if they intended to attack.

Then the final, stunning event told him his mind was certainly gone. There, in the lead of these newcomers, was Halloran! And there, upon the horse that trailed them, was Erixitl!

In the next moment, the group separated, the diminutive humans breaking to the right and the dwarves to the left. Immediately Gultec's warriors perceived that these were allies, here to combat the remaining ants.

"My friends! You have found us!" Gultec shouted at Halloran as the soldier approached, and the two men took a brief moment to clasp hands. "Thank you," the warrior said quietly.

Behind Hal and his warriors, Erix followed, riding Storm at an easy walk. The surviving ants crept toward them, but now the defenders far outnumbered their monstrous foes.

"Let's finish this thing," said the Jaguar Knight. Halloran merely nodded as the halflings and dwarves rushed past, weapons ready. With whoops, shouts, and whistles, the Itza warriors turned and joined the attack.

Out of the dust of the shattered mountain, giant red ants straggled forward, to be met by the *pluma*stone weapons of the desert dwarves or paralyzed by the *kurari*-tipped arrows of the Little People. And when the men of Tulom-Itzi swarmed around the shapes of their enemy, hated and feared for so long but now finally vanquished, not a one of the monsters was left alive.

* * * * *

Darien watched the slaughter from the high vantage to which she had teleported, trying to see what could be salvaged from the disaster.

Nothing. Not today, in any event. The ant army was gone, wiped out by the cataclysm, the few survivors falling to the humans and their fortuitous reinforcements.

The drider considered, for a moment, a vengeful idea. She can teleport herself into the midst of the humans and launch spells of great destruction—fireballs, lightning bolts, even clouds of poison gas. She wouldn't be able to slay them all, but she could make them know her wrath.

Something held her lips as she began to mouth the spell. A spot of color appeared among the onrushing army—behind them, actually. A brightness struck the drider's eyes with painful intensity.

It was a familiar pain.

Suddenly Darien hissed her rage, for she *knew* that brightness. It was the woman who had thwarted her in the Highcave, the one who was responsible for the disaster!

For the first time, the drider backed from her crest, crouching to make certain she avoided detection. Now her rage was tinged with another emotion, a stranger to the vicious drider.

Darien was afraid. She remembered the power borne by that woman.

In the face of that fear, she paused. There would be no vengeance today. This was no longer an attack against an anonymous human population, motivated by only the fundamental need to slake her hatred with blood.

Now she had an enemy with a face and a name. A potent enemy—one who could be overcome only with a careful and meticulous plan, but indeed a foe who *would* be overcome.

Darien shook herself angrily, her torso flexing like a dog's when it dries its soaking fur. The power of Lolth had twisted her shape, corrupted her soul, and given her an army. But now that army was gone, and the enemy of her life was a woman of *pluma*, feathermagic. Hatred and rage seethed within her, and since she was a creature of Maztica, these emotions fused into her own power, into might that could challenge the feathermagic of the woman Erixitl.

The opposite force would be needed, Darien understood, and her arcane knowledge and skill, fed by her hatred, fused toward the magic of *hishna*, the magic of talon and claw.

*Hishna* was the power that would allow her to overcome the Chosen Daughter of Qotal.

* * * * *

Cordell and his picked group of legionnaires pressed through the forests of Payit, as often as not dismounting to hack their way through encloaking brush, leading the horses at a painstaking crawl. Overhead, Chical and the eagles soared, marking the progress of Zaltec, Hoxitl, and the beasts of the Viperhand.

Of all of these, the massive and animated statue of Zaltec seemed most menacing to Cordell and his men. Though they couldn't know that they saw the form of a deity among them, the fact of its awesome power and apparently irresistible strength were obvious simply from its size.

Cordell still hadn't told Kardann about the giant figure that marched with the monster army. Indeed, the captain-general had often come to wonder about the wisdom of bringing the whining assessor along on this arduous journey. Such thoughts, then, brought him back to the questions at the very root of their march:

Who were these adventurers who had landed at Helmsport? Why had they made captives of Cordell's garrison? And what would be their reception for Cordell himself, once he arrived?

Unfortunately the fate of the men he had left behind offered no encouragement for him. Now Cordell began to wonder about plans and schemes—about ways to reach these potentially lifesaving men and bend them to his will. But now he would have to use his wits, for the force of strength certainly belonged to the other side.

And even then, supposing he could gain mastery of these newcomers, using them as the reinforcements he so desparately needed, how could they stand against a hundred-foot-tall giant? Perhaps the newcomers had brought mages and their power would give them hope.

Still, it seemed an impossible task, with several other impossible tasks to accomplish before it could even be attempted.

\* \* \* \* \*

"What will it be, Father?" asked Erixitl quietly as she watched her father weave tufts of red feathers into his work of *pluma*. The marchers rested comfortably, scattered among many soft glades in the forest. Tomorrow, with the Itza warriors joining them, they would embark on the final leg of their journey to the Payit country and the sacred site of Twin Visages. Many weeks of travel remained, but the roads were known and the land ahead was fertile.

Lotil smiled, not slowing in the deft workings of his fingers. "I do not know," he said, with a hint of secrecy in his voice.

"Certainly you must have something in mind," she prodded. "At times it looks like a great blanket, with an image of an eagle, and I think you are making a cloak for a warrior. Or else it looks like a lake, with forested hills all around, and I think you are making us a home."

The *pluma*worker chuckled. "It is all these things and more, my daughter.

"Sometime, perhaps, it will be a feathered shield for our young warrior here, to protect him from the blows that one so brave is certain to attract."

Jhatli looked up sheepishly at hearing the words. Though the youth had been silent, Lotil had somehow known where he sat, for the old man gestured to the youngster as he spoke.

The tale of his fight with the ants had spread rapidly through the group. Jhatli had sprung on the back of one of the creatures and sawed it in half with his *maca* as it squirmed and twisted beneath him. It was a feat that had earned him the instant respect of the Itza warriors.

"Or perhaps I weave a birthing blanket for you, my daughter. Your time draws near, I know, and we have little chance of knowing where we shall be then. You will need a proper mat upon which to give birth to such a child, the first to be born of both Maztica and the world beyond."

Erixitl nodded, resting her hands over her round abdomen. She felt a kick and looked at Halloran, surprised to see tears in the corners of his eyes.

"Or, again, maybe I shall create a royal robe for your husband. Who better to wear the mantle of a king, eh?"

"No!" Hal sat upright, his voice taut. "I want no part of kings or armies when we are done with this. I want a place to live with my wife, to raise our child. That is all."

Lotil lapsed into silence then, his sightless eyes passing around the group in the glade. His fingers, tireless and unerring, continued to work their *pluma*.

\* \* \* \* \*

From the chronicles of Coton:

*On the joyful journey toward a meeting with the One True God.*

*Our numbers grow steadily, it seems, and I sense the hand of the god in our strength. We are joined now by the warriors of Tulom-Itzi and the brave Gultec. The Itza grieve for their lost chieftain, but we hear the tale of his passing with many songs. Zochimaloc has died a hero of legend, and in his passing, he has destroyed those who would destroy his people.*

*He was a man of pluma, this Zochimaloc, and he had the power to reach the Plumed One himself. It was this power that purchased victory for his people, and it is this same power that gives me the hope and the proof that Qotal is indeed near. He awaits, I'm certain, only the successful conclusion of our quest toward Twin Visages.*

*And now the Jaguar Knight brings his warriors, a thousand stalwart bowmen, into league with us. While the rest of his people return to their great city, this legion of warriors falls into file with our desert dwarves and the Little Men.*

*Now we form a great host. Halloran is our commander, and Erixitl is our leader. Even I, peaceful old cleric that I am, feel the martial splendor of our might.*

*I believe that nothing can stand in our path.*

# ❧ 17 ❧

# CONFRONTATION AT HELMSPORT

Cordell scrutinized the banner fluttering from the pole above Helmsport before turning to Chical with a muttered curse. The two men lay in the low concealment of a patch of brush on a flat, low rise in the wide savannah. "That's the symbol of Don Vaez," the captain-general informed his Maztican ally.

"You know this captain, then?" inquired the Eagle Knight.

"An old rival," Cordell explained. "We fought as allies in the Pirate Wars, but he was never one I would have turned my back on. He's always been jealous of the successes of others. I'm sure he leaped at the opportunity to come after me, though how he won the appointment is beyond me. There are many other, far worthier, mercenary captains along the Sword Coast."

"His presence here . . . does it aggravate our problems?"

"I'm certain he's not here to help—not to help me, in any event. This will require some careful planning. On the other hand, he's not the best-loved officer ever to lead his men to war, and this fact may work to our advantage."

The fifteen riders and twenty eagles had completed the long journey from the desert site of Tukan to the Payit city of Ulatos after weeks of hard riding—or flying, in the case of the Maztican warriors. Now the rest of the band of travelers remained behind, hidden in the jungle some distance back from the savannah, while Cordell and Chical had wormed their way forward to study both the city and the earthen fortress on the coast.

The dark walls of the rampart enclosed a large courtyard, protecting it against approach from three sides, while the fourth, to the north, abutted against the shore. The walls sloped steeply upward to a platform around the top, but not so steeply that they could not have been climbed.

Beyond Helmsport, Cordell saw the masts of the ships, twenty-five in number, that had carried the new expedition to the shores of Maztica. A sizable herd of horses grazed on the flat, grassy savannah between the fort and the city. Sunlight glinted from the steel armor of many sentries who walked the ramparts of the fortress.

"Carracks . . . a good fleet," the captain-general muttered absently. "Mostly bigger ships than the carracks and smaller caravels that brought my legion over here."

"Enough to bring your legionnaires and the Kultakans here?" Chical inquired. Those troops should have reached the coast by now and made semipermanent camp there. The next step in their utilization could only occur after Cordell gained control of that fleet.

"I think so. The problem, of course, is getting them to sail down there and get them. I know Don Vaez will never do it simply because I ask him. We're going to have to be very persuasive indeed."

The Eagle Warrior smiled grimly. He suspected that his companion didn't speak of the kind of persuasion performed with words.

"Still, we are too few to carry the fort by storm," Chical pointed out.

Cordell turned away from the sight, his bearded face creased in a heavy scowl. In silence, he crawled back through the low brush, followed by Chical. They worked their way back into the jungle for some distance before standing. Then, certain they had remained unobserved, they hurried back to the rest of their companions. Quickly they briefed them on the situation at Helmsport as they had been able to observe it.

"There's got to be *some* way! Who are his men? Where did Don Vaez get an army like that?" Cordell asked the questions aloud as his mind whirled.

"The Golden Legion?" guessed Grimes. "The fellows we couldn't take along with us? There aren't a lot of mercenaries to be raised in Amn, save the ones you left behind."

"Good possibility," Cordell admitted. His legion had numbered more than a thousand men on several occasions. Many loyal soldiers had been left in Amn when the expedition departed, limited by the capacity of Cordell's ships.

"The bulk of them have to be mercenaries—men hired for coin, loyal only to profit," continued the horseman. "They'd probably be as willing to serve you to as to serve Don Vaez."

Indeed, that captain's reputation as a womanizer and dandy had earned him scorn from more than one honest fighting man, a fact known to any mercenary who had ever worked on the Sword Coast. Cordell, on the contrary, was widely known to be a fair-minded, well-paying officer. Too, there was the fact that his missions had been almost universally successful.

Until now, he reminded himself, disturbed by the sudden memory of the Night of Wailing.

"Still, he'll have his loyal crew of officers," Cordell said. "We'd have to work fast and take them all out of circulation. Then it would be up to the men."

As he thought further, plans and possibilities began to form in Cordell's mind. Grimes and Chical helped him to shape those opportunities into a course of action.

None of them took note of Kardann sitting nearby, his eyes narrowed to thin slits as if he dozed. But, in fact, the assessor of Amn was very much awake.

\* \* \* \* \*

A mysterious compulsion drove the driders as they left the mountain valley where their army had perished. Darien, cursing and abusing the others, pushed the band forward. They scuttled northward, along the jungled mountains, pressing their bloated bodies through the tangles, using their black-bladed swords to chop the underbrush from their path. Their fur-covered spider legs propelled them swiftly, and only the terrain held them from a full gallop.

Darien didn't understand why she drove herself and the others so relentlessly. Her army gone, obliterated beneath the collapsing tonnage of the mountains themselves, she had nothing left but her hatred. Now she could at last revile her fiendish goddess Lolth and curse and—ultimately—ignore her. With the destruction of the ant army, she sensed that her old powers had deserted her. Now she had only instinct and rage to direct her on a course of vengeance.

But that rage had focus, in the person of the woman of *pluma*, the wife of Halloran. Darien's mind seethed with images of her earlier encounters with Erixitl—of the Maztican woman's feathermagic protecting her from the elf's sorcery during the massacre at Palul; of the encounter in Nexal, on the Night of Wailing, when the woman had pursued Darien and her drow allies throughout the palace complex, thwarting their every plan of attack.

This hatred drove her now even more relentlessly than before. The driders pushed through the jungle, slaying the few humans they met, killing and eating as they needed, sleeping for a few hours each day whenever exhaustion claimed them.

It was during a period of brief, fitful sleep that Darien's hatred began to reform into vengeance.

She twisted and groaned, spitting and clawing reflexively, at a picture that formed in her mind. Dim memories awakened within her, memories from another life, another body. She recalled images of the Golden Legion, of its first landing on the shores of Maztica . . . of two great faces, carved in stone, which stared out to sea as if they awaited her arrival.

She saw the image of a place by the coast where a great battle would rage, with hatred and killing aplenty.

She saw the image of Erixitl, her beauty a taunt, a spiteful affront to the bloated form of the drider. And as she thought, as her mind created vivid pictures, the black essence of foulness crept through her being. Power collected in her bloated abdomen, and the might of her malevolence began to take form in the world.

Around the vivid picture of the human woman, Darien saw a dancing, swaying framework of images that melted indistinctly together. Then slowly this framework took on a more solid definition.

Now she recognized the bobbing, swaying head of a snake, its mouth gaping slightly to reveal curved, venomous fangs. She saw the sinuous form of a crocodile twisting around the other images, and then she sensed long, hooked talons reaching toward the picture of the woman Erixitl.

Darien could not know it, but a new god was working his power within the female form of the drider. The power of that warlike deity rose and spread through the corrupted body. More and more images bombarded her, images of *hishna*, the magic of talon and fang and venom. Soon this power would explode. The precise time she could not know.

But of the place, she could be certain: the low pyramid, high on the coastal bluff; the great faces carved into the face of that bluff; even the sheltered lagoon within its encircling wreath of coral. She knew, and they would go there.

Darien would lead her driders to Twin Visages.

They pressed ahead with renewed determination and drive, pausing to rest even less than before. Darien thrilled to the quarry before her, often throwing back her head to laugh out loud, a shrill screech of horrible triumph that put the jungle birds to flight and sent monkeys whooping away through the trees.

She stopped occasionally, when the images assaulted her mind, and slowly the power of *hishna* grew within her. Then she would scramble through the brush, seeking, and after a few moments of search, she would emerge with a snake, or a lizard, or, once, even a jaguar cub. With relish, she put the creatures to death, and each of them nourished her growing power of talonmagic.

Ever northward they went, toward the headlands of the Payit country, east of the city of Ulatos. Darien moved straight toward the great sculpted cliff, not out of any sense of immortal destiny but simply because this was where her hunger directed her. And all the while, black and murky, the power of *hishna* swelled within her. Fertilized by the fuel of her hatred, the seed of talonmagic coalesced, gathered from the talismans she collected in the forest. Slowly, gradually, the power became a driving source of energy, a self-sustaining explosion that could not be contained.

When the driders paused, near collapse from exhaustion, Darien sat in a meditative trance. She took no sleep, instead picturing the fire of light before her. Her mind reeled with enchantments, fragments of forgotten spells, supplications to dark deities.

Sweat poured from her pale face, across her breasts and stomach to trickle onto the hard shell of her spider body. Her eyes tightly closed, she imagined the light she saw. Powers coalesced within her.

Finally the seed of hatred bore fruit. A black fog of festering evil gathered in Darien's soul, clamoring for release. *Hishna* seethed upward and away, breaking free of the bonds of her body. Slowly, inexorably, the power grew within her and began to escape.

As she started to move again, the effluence of her might drifted ahead of her through the jungle, like an invisible toxin carried by the wind itself. Swirling about with the eddies of the breeze, it crept through the forest as if it were a living creature that sought a destination.

\* \* \* \* \*

"First we meet the desert dwarves and the Little People. Now Gultec rejoins us with a force of warriors. It has to be a plan, part of some great design!" Halloran felt a tingling anticipation of success as they moved steadily northward. They neared their goal, finally, after a transcontinental march of some five months' duration.

Erixitl rode beside him as he walked. Her time of childbirth loomed near, and the last weeks—now perhaps the interval could be measured in days—of the journey to Payit wore heavily upon her.

"A thing concerns me, though," she admitted. "If this is destiny, why are we provided with an army? Does this mean we'll have to fight when we reach Twin Visages?"

"We're ready if we have to," declared Jhatli, brandishing his bow and arrows. "I will be a great warrior when I have the chance!"

Halloran chuckled, feeling like an older brother listening to the enthusiastic ravings of his younger sibling. "Jhatli, you are already a warrior of such stature as to make your people proud. I don't think you have to worry about that anymore."

The young man looked at him, pleased with the compliment and somewhat smug in his acceptance of it. "And you told me I would grow tired of battles and war! Little did you know—each fight is grander than the last!"

"That's because we've won them, for one thing," the former legionnaire said wryly.

Jhatli grinned at his companion. "And we will win the next fight as well!" he boasted.

Erixitl sighed, and Jhatli looked at the woman with a trace of guilt on his dark brown features. "I'm sorry, sister. I know how you feel about such talk of war. It is a topic best left to men!"

The youth looked toward the dwarves, up at the front of the column. Daggrande and Luskag engaged in earnest discussion of tactics and weaponry, as they had done for the past months of the journey. "Like the dwarves, I shall be a fighter of legend, a crusader against the evils that threaten our land!"

"Do not be too hasty to wish for that chance," said Lotil quietly. The *pluma*worker followed beside Storm, his hand on the horse's flank, his feet plodding steadily beside the trail. The blanket of *pluma*, more than half done, was wrapped in a bundle tied to his back.

"Aye," agreed Gultec, coming up to join them. "I have spent my life preparing for war, and yet I would be happy never to have to see it again."

"How much farther is it to Ulatos?" the youth asked.

"Word from the last village is that we might get there in three days," replied Halloran. And beyond the city, a short distance along the coast, lay their true destination of Twin Visages.

Coton followed them all, and Halloran turned to look at the priest as they walked. As always, restricted by his vow, the cleric said nothing. Yet his face bore a dreamy expression, as if his thoughts were very far away.

Erixitl swayed in the saddle suddenly, and Halloran looked at her in sudden alarm. Her face twitched, as if from the memory of a horrifying dream.

"What is it? Are you all right?" Hal reached up to take her hand.

In the next instant, her eyelids dropped shut. Suddenly limp, she collapsed from the saddle as if the life had been drained from her body.

\* \* \* \* \*

Heavy clouds swept in from the great Eastern Ocean, soon blocking out even the faint rays from the crescent of moon that rose over the Payit jungles. A night of inky darkness fell across the city of Ulatos and the earthen bulk of Helmsport.

Within the city, torches blossomed here and there, and hearthfires burned in the homes. The compound of the fort stood outlined in the white light of lanterns as the soldiers of Don Vaez went about their routine duties of maintenance, shoeing horses, cleaning and sharpening weapons, oiling leather boots and saddles.

Then gradually the lanterns winked out. One by one the torches and fires faded into coals, and then even the coals settled into gray ash. The city and the fort fell into the silent slumber of a long, dark jungle night.

A score of lonely sentries stood duty from midnight to dawn, marching listlessly around the top of the earthen ramparts. Each carried a crossbow and a short sword, but their attention to duty was not so rigorous as it had been weeks earlier, when they had first landed in Maztica.

At that time, this had been a land of mystery, filled with unknown dangers and rumors of great treasure. The unexplained disappearance of Cordell's expedition was a fact known to all of them, adding to the potential terrors of the strange new continent.

Now they looked over a placid and unthreatening land, a place that had become the site of another boring campaign.

Don Veaz showed no inclination to move from this base of operations, and no threat to the force had materialized, or even been rumored, anywhere across this foreign world.

Those sentries who attended to their duties more diligently looked outward, down the sloping walls of the fort. Within the enclosure itself slept more than a thousand men—all of them Don Vaez's troops, except for the few of Cordell's original garrison who now languished in prison. Clearly there was no threat there.

It is doubtful that any of the guards even thought to look skyward.

Yet from the clouds came the attackers, two dozen in number, settling silently to the rampart on the wings of eagles. Chical led the way, his keen vision penetrating the night enough to locate the metal-shirted figures, dully pacing the walls.

The eagle floated to earth behind one of these men, shifting to his human body a moment before landing. The guard turned with a start, sensing the presence behind him, but Chical's heavy club fell once, sharply, across the man's temple. In another second, the guard dropped, still without making a sound, to the hard surface of the rampart.

All around the circumference of the rampart, the eagles descended, attacking simultaneously in silent, sudden precision. Within moments, the entire sentry patrol had been immobilized without alerting the rest of the garrison.

Chical slipped to the edge of the earthwork, out of sight of the interior of the fort but exposed to the south, across the savannah. He touched a flint to the steel dagger Cordell had given him, quickly igniting a small straw torch. He fanned the glowing object before him three times before snuffing it beneath his heel. Then he turned back to the courtyard, peering from the wall top into the crowded space below.

A half-mile away, Cordell, Grimes, Kardann, and the other legionnaires saw the Eagle Knight's signal. They trotted forward on foot, having tethered the horses within the shelter of the nearby forest. As soundlessly as possible, they approached Helmsport, scrambling up the sloping wall of the earthwork to join Chical.

"There," the warrior said, pointing to the large wooden building in the center of the compound. "That is where this Don Vaez makes his headquarters."

"Let's hope he sleeps there, too," grunted Grimes softly.

"He will," whispered Cordell confidently. "It's the biggest and most comfortable place in there. The rest are storage sheds, armories, and barns."

Momentary bitterness gripped him as he looked at the familiar surroundings. He had ordered this fortress built as his own base! Daggrande had supervised the actual construction and excavation, but the site and the layout had been Cordell's. Even the spot in the walls where the gold of Ulatos was buried, he remembered. Now to have this interloping pretender claim it . . .

One by one the other eagles joined them. When the entire group had assembled, Cordell and Chical led them down the inner slope of the breastwork. Somewhere within the compound a dog, one of the shaggy warhounds of the legion, barked, but a gruff curse followed and the animal fell silent.

The rest of the soldiers slumbered around them in tents or in the buildings Cordell had indicated earlier. Creeping carefully through the shadows, the intruders moved past a large frame building that smelled like a horse barn. Next they passed a long rack of weapons—spears and arrows—beneath an open-sided shed.

Finally they approached the large headquarters building, a wooden frame house with oilskin windows, where several candles glowed in still-lighted rooms. Before the front door stood a pair of spearmen, weapons upraised and backs placed squarely to the wall.

"I'd bet all the gold in Nexal that Don Vaez is in the bedroom upstairs," whispered Cordell. Indeed, as they watched, a shadow passed before the oilskin, a profile wherein the long, curling locks of hair were plainly visible.

Cordell turned to Chical, and the Eagle Knight nodded. Melting into the shadows with three of his men, he suddenly shifted and dropped. In another moment, his powerful wings carried him upward, followed by his comrades.

The four eagles soared swiftly and silently to the peak of

the roof over Don Vaez's building. The men on the ground saw them as alternating shades of black and pale gray as they shifted back to human form.

Creeping to the edge of the roof, they sprang suddenly to the earth. With swift, silent blows, they immobilized the two startled sentries.

"Let's go!" whispered Cordell, starting toward the door.

A harsh clatter, like someone spilling a cartload of firewood, suddenly crashed through the compound. Cries of alarm arose from many of the tents, as sleepy men-at-arms struggled free of their bedrolls.

Furiously Cordell whirled to see Kardann, standing beside the heap of weapons that had moments earlier rested neatly in their racks. The assessor looked at the captain-general, a terrified expression upon his pudgy face. With a muffled curse, Cordell started toward him, but he instantly realized that recriminations would have to wait.

"Hurry!" he commanded, sprinting through the darkness toward the house. A dozen legionnaires and an equal number of Eagle Knights, led by Grimes, raced after him, weapons drawn and ready. Kardann remained behind, shrinking into the darkest shadows, unnoticed by the charging band.

The front door of the building swung open as Cordell approached, revealing several men in breastplates carrying drawn swords. Chical and the other warriors pressed back in the shadows to either side of the door.

"Who's there?" one of the men demanded.

Dogs barked throughout the fortress as more and more men stumbled from tents or barns.

"You there! What's happening?" The man at the door barked the question at Cordell, then gaped in astonishment as the captain-general dove toward the door.

"Sound the alarm!" cried the guard, trying to slam the portal shut. Shouts and challenges echoed throughout the fortress as rudely awakened men suspiciously accosted their neighbors. In several places, the clash of steel rang out briefly.

Cordell crashed into the door with the full force of his charge and felt it spring inward. He bowled over the guard just beyond and trampled past another who tried to stand against him in the hallway.

The stairway led upward before him, and Cordell charged up the steps. He crashed through the door to the sleeping chamber just in time to see a silken-gowned figure spring through the window.

Cordell raced across the room, looking below in frustration as Don Vaez sprinted away from the house. By now the entire garrison was alarmed, and a hundred men gathered around their commander.

Chical entered the room, where Cordell still stared out the window, bitter defeat burning in his gut.

"We are all in the house," reported the Eagle Knight, "but it would appear that they have us trapped."

"Surrender, Cordell!" cried Don Vaez. Triumph filled his voice. "Give yourself up and things may go easier with you!"

"I will not deliver my sword to a scoundrel!" Cordell shouted back, placing all the strength of his will into his voice. "A scoundrel and pirate! Why do you hold my men, the garrison of this fort, in chains? Surely they offered you no threat."

"*You* are the renegade!" taunted Don Vaez. "You planned to keep the riches of Maztica for yourself!"

"You're mad!"

"Give up, and you shall have ample opportunity to testify at your trial. Defy me, and you shall certainly die!"

Cordell leaned backward with a groan. He looked at Chical, sensing rather than seeing the ranks of crossbows and harquebuses leveled at the house from the outside.

"You'd better think about escape," he said grimly. "No sense in your warriors getting caught in the snare that's wrapping around me."

Chical looked at the encircling forces. He knew that he and his eagles could take wing and escape Don Vaez's trap. Yet what would they do then? The Beasts of the Viperhand marched steadily closer, and their options for resistance steadily shrank.

Abruptly they saw a form fly toward their window. A metal-helmed figure sat upon a small flying carpet, and as he approached, they saw that he wore the silver gauntlets that displayed the all-seeing eye of Helm. The cleric hovered on his carpet out of arrow range, yet able to see in the high window. He needed only the command of Don Vaez to soar inside and cast a spell against the intruders.

"Cordell is in there!" Kardann shouted, his voice rising several tones in his excitement.

Cordell heard Kardann's unmistakable squeal. He saw the little man burst from the shelter of his hiding place, pointing wildly up toward the window. The assessor ran over to Don Vaez and, panting, blurted out his explanation.

"I tried to stop them. I raised the alarm so that you'd see them! Now you have him, and *he's* the one who knows where the gold of Ulatos is hidden!"

The last phrase got Don Vaez's attention. Meanwhile, the cleric hovered outside the window, speaking firmly. "You will surrender now or my captain will have the house torched. Surely you do not wish to perish thus, in the flames?"

Cordell whirled to pace rapidly back and forth in the small room. Finally he cursed, then nodded. "I have no choice," he said to Chical. "But please, get your warriors and prepare to fly."

He turned back to the window. "Very well," the captain-general called down. "We're coming out."

Leading his men down the stairs, he waited as Chical gathered his warriors at the house's upper windows. When he judged that they must be ready, he opened the door and stepped outside.

A smirking Don Vaez advanced to greet him. "Your sword, sir!" demanded the pompous adventurer, extending his hand expectantly.

Barely suppressing his rage, Cordell ungirded his blade. He handed the weapon, hilt first, to his rival.

"What's that?" demanded one of the men-at-arms, pointing skyward.

"Treachery!" snarled Don Vaez, cuffing the unarmed Cordell with the hilt of his own sword. "What is the meaning of this?" He gestured at the sky.

Great birds lunged from the windows of the house, winging upward and swiftly disappearing into the night sky. "Shoot them! Stop them!" cried the captain.

Archers launched their missiles into the air. Several harquebusiers raised their weapons as the birds vanished into darkness. A sound like the explosion of thunder crashed through the fortress as the loud, smoky weapons hurled their iron balls after the fleeing eagles.

One of the creatures squawked loudly and suddenly came back into view. It fluttered desperately on one wing, but it couldn't fly. In another moment, it crashed to the ground before Don Vaez.

\* \* \* \* \*

From the chronicles of Coton:

*Amid the suddenly darkened paths, we make our way toward a destiny that has grown terribly obscure.*

*Erixitl's affliction is no natural malady, of this I am certain. All of the blessings of pluma worked by her father and all of the clerical arts worked by me prove to be of no avail.*

*The source of the darkness, I know, is hishna, though in a strange and unfamiliar form. I sense the power of talonmagic assailing her, yet it is a more potent attack than any I have previously encountered. A great and black power has seized her, and so she resists all of our attempts to draw her back to the world of the living.*

*Instead, she slumbers as one who is dead, and if she dies, our hopes perish with her.*

# ❧ 18 ❧

## CAPTIVE ARMIES

Gloom descended like a heavy cloud over the entire vast expedition of halflings, desert dwarves, and Itza as soon as word of Erixitl's strange affliction spread through the ranks. It was as if the bright hope that had brought them together and led them so steadily toward Twin Visages had suddenly and universally been extinguished.

Now the woman rode in a wide litter, lined with leaves and blossoms. The front of the framework swung from Storm's saddle, and the rear dragged along the ground when the path was clear. All too often, however, the way was obstructed, and at these times Halloran lifted the rear of the litter, carrying it over every obstacle.

Halloran would allow no one but himself to perform this task. Erixitl's breathing remained steady, but she did not regain consciousness. Even the most potent of Coton's priestly ministrations could do nothing to return her to awareness or even cause her to flicker her eyelids or make the faintest of sounds.

For two days, they continued onward, pressing northward through the jungle. Luskag, Daggrande, Jhatli—even Lotil—all tried to aid Halloran as he strained over the rough ground. But he clenched his teeth and ignored them, even as salt sweat stung his eyes and the miles rolled endlessly on.

They stopped only after it was fully dark, and at one of these camps, Halloran made some decisions.

"I think we should take her to Ulatos instead of going directly to Twin Visages," he announced as they finished a meal of venison and fruit around a low fire.

"Why?" asked Luskag. The desert dwarf had become convinced of Erixitl's vision and knew that she believed Qotal would return at the faces on the cliffside.

"It seems more and more like some kind of spell that has her in its grasp. In the city, at least, we will find more clerics, perhaps an apothecary—a chance to help her."

Coton, the priest of Qotal, nodded silently. Lotil voiced his own opinion. "We can take my daughter to the temple of Qotal in the city. Perhaps there we can find aid for her. This is a good plan."

One by one the others agreed. They didn't know how far ahead of them lay the coastline, and hence Ulatos and Twin Visages, though Gultec estimated that they were only a few days away. A native of Ulatos, he recognized that they had long since left the deep jungles of Far Payit behind.

After they had reached a decision, Halloran rose from the fire and went to see Erixitl. She lay motionless on the soft mattress they had made for her. Her chest rose and fell with the rhythm of her breathing, and the roundness of her belly seemed so unmistakably alive that Hal almost convinced himself that she merely slept. He placed his hand upon her abdomen, where so often he had felt the kicking and squirming of their child. Now he felt no movement at all.

\* \* \* \* \*

"Summon your cleric, man! We need him now, or Katl will die!" Cordell stormed about the tiny makeshift cell, slamming his fist into the door repeatedly. Beside him, the Eagle Knight moaned in pain and delirium, his smashed right arm bound crudely by Cordell and Grimes.

The wounded eagle, Katl, had been placed in the cell with Cordell and his legionnaires. Slowly, in his unconsciousness and delirium, his body had shifted back to its human form. As they ministered to him, they had seen that his arm bone had been crushed by the force of the ball. It seemed unlikely that he would ever use it for anything useful again.

Outside the door, a trio of armed men stood, trying to ignore the prisoner's outburst. They guarded the captain-general and the legionnaires who had accompanied him into the fort in a boarded-up stall within a small wooden barn. Hired by—and loyal to—Don Vaez, the men-at-arms were nonetheless nervous about imprisoning a personage of Cordell's high reputation.

Finally one of the guards left, but when he returned it was not with a man of healing. Instead, he came back with Don Vaez himself.

"I understand you're creating a disturbance," chided the blond-haired captain.

"I've tried to tell them this man needs a cleric. The fever has taken him, and without aid, he doesn't stand a chance!"

"Why should you care?" inquired Don Vaez with a disdainful look at the Maztican warrior. Katl lay on the floor in the cell, surrounded by the fifteen legionnaires who had been captured with Cordell.

"He's a good man and my friend," replied Cordell, his voice cold steel. "Why should you want him dead?"

"I don't really care one way or the other," chuckled Don Vaez. "Perhaps if you were to cooperate, you would find that I can be . . . accommodating."

"What do you mean?" The captain-general scowled, studying his rival.

"We have learned that you claimed much gold from your conquest of Ulatos. Yet we have not been able to find it—your man, Tranph, has insisted he does not know, even after we applied some vigorously, ah, *persuasive* techniques."

*You animal!* thought Cordell, but he tried to keep his anger from his face. He took a deep breath. "He told the truth. Tranph didn't know where the gold is buried. None of the men I left behind knew."

Don Vaez nodded; it was a precaution that he could understand. "Nevertheless, the good assessor has told us that it's buried somewhere within the walls of this fort. Unfortunately, he doesn't know exactly where."

"The little bastard!" Cordell blurted, though the tale merely confirmed his understanding of Kardann's treachery.

"You, however, *do* know," observed Don Vaez. He cast another look at Katl and clucked his tongue in false sympathy.

"Perhaps, before it is too late, you will decide to tell me."

With a sly smile and a twirl of silver-blond curls, the adventurer turned on his heel and stepped lightly from the building.

*     *     *     *     *

A massive block of stone fell among the trees, splintering the trunks and crushing the wood to pulp. Another, identical block fell beside it. Then the two massive bludgeons repeated the process.

Thus Zaltec entered the forested lands of Payit. The jungle trails vanished beneath the verdant canopy of the treetops, but the huge form had no use for such amenities as paths in any event. Instead, the monolith of stone made its own path, clearing a wide swath at the head of its army simply by the force of its passage.

Behind the huge, lumbering statue that was Zaltec trailed the beastlord Hoxitl, and then the teeming thousands of his army, the beasts of the Viperhand.

During the long month of their march, they had become more than the ragged horde that had left Nexal in search of blood and treasure. Now they marched in ranks, the ogres controlling the orcs, and the trolls maintaining their own tight, fast-moving companies.

Hoxitl strutted at their head, full of devotion for his hungry god. He knew that soon they would meet an enemy. Which one, he did not know, caring only that it was composed of warm bodies, bodies with hearts that could be given over to Zaltec's greater glory.

*     *     *     *     *

"I've got to tell him where the gold is," Cordell admitted to Grimes shortly after Don Vaez had left the prisoners. Katl groaned and tossed, his fever seemingly intensifying every minute. It was obvious that the Eagle Knight was very near to death.

Beyond the cell, the trio of guards paid them no attention,

instead focusing on some game of wagering that they played on the dirt floor of the barn. Cordell was about to tell the guards to summon their captain when the door to the barn opened and a man entered.

The newcomer passed the guards, who looked up from their game and obviously recognized him, for they made no objection to his presence. The man approached the door of the cell.

"Rodolfo?" asked Cordell in surprise. "Can that be you?"

"It is, I'm ashamed to admit," said the navigator, with a look to insure that the guards were out of earshot.

"I thought you gave up the sea when you married," said the captain-general quietly. "Otherwise I surely would have had you at the helm of my flagship a year ago!"

The grizzled navigator shook his head sadly. "I was a land-lubber for five years, but then the plague swept through my village. It claimed my wife and my two young sons."

"I'm sorry, old friend," Cordell reached out a hand to clap Rodolfo on the shoulder. He waited quietly, sensing this was not the reason Don Vaez's navigator had come to see him.

"We've heard what you said about the army on its way here . . . led by a giant made of stone! A lot of the men, I don't mind telling you, aren't at all certain how Don Vaez will fare against such a threat."

"He doesn't even believe it exists," said Cordell in disgust. "He assumes the tale is some sort of ruse I'm using to gain my freedom."

"Your freedom . . ." Rodolfo cast another look at the three guards, who were still engaged in their vigorous game of knucklebones. None of the trio looked up from the scattered coins and bones on the ground. "There are those besides me who would like to see you gain that freedom. Don Vaez is feared, but not greatly admired, by these men."

Cordell smiled grimly. "Your words give me great hope and encouragement. Now we need a plan."

Katl groaned behind him, and the captain-general turned toward the wounded man. Then he looked back to Rodolfo. "I'll still have to tell Don Vaez where the gold is hidden. That's the only way he'll send the cleric to help Katl. But perhaps, with your help, we'll find a way to keep it out of his hands in the end."

\* \* \* \* \*

Tabub came rushing back to Halloran, gesturing wildly at the sky and the jungle before them.

"Eagle!" panted the chief of the Little People. "Him land! Now he Big Person! Come quick!"

Hal's first thought was Poshtli, but by the time he had laid Erix's litter down and followed the halfling warrior forward, he had dismissed the idea of seeing his old friend here as wishful thinking.

But the sight of Chical, standing beside Daggrande and Coton, was nevertheless a welcome one. As far as Hal had known, the warrior was somewhere deep in the House of Tezca helping his people erect the city of Tukan.

The Eagle Warrior dispensed with the greetings quickly and told them of the mission that had brought the eagles and the horsemen to Helmsport and the fate that had befallen Cordell there. "He has been taken prisoner by this one he calls 'Don Vaez,' " continued Chical. "They have kept him inside one of the buildings, so I'm not even certain that he lives.

"This morning, one of my eagles flew a short way southward over the Payit forests and discovered you. He did not know who you were, so I flew here to investigate." Chical looked around at the odd mixture of dwarves, halflings, and human warriors.

"A short way?" Hal repeated. "How close to Ulatos are we now?"

"No more than two days' walk. You could make it in a single long march."

"Don Vaez." Daggrande spoke the name, accompanying it with a curse. He spat in disgust. "That little weasel doesn't have the guts to do anything on his own, but he's always chased after the Golden Legion's glory. I'm not a bit surprised that he tossed Cordell in irons."

"We must free him if we can," said Chical quietly. Halloran

looked at the warrior in surprise, sensing that a bond had formed between the Eagle Knight and the foreign soldier—a bond that was all the more surprising in light of the opposing roles the two men had played in the battle for Nexal. Chical had commanded the Maztican warriors surrounding the Golden Legion, while Cordell had desperately strived to gain escape for himself and his men.

"Why?" asked Gultec directly. "Why should it matter to us which of the bearded men commands their troops?"

Chical nodded, understanding the Jaguar Knight's question. He told them of Zaltec and the monstrous army marching on Helmsport and Ulatos, and of Cordell's orders to his own legionnaires and the Kultakans he had left in the desert. "He planned to send those ships for them on the shore of the Sea of Azul. If they had returned in time, they would have greatly increased our numbers!"

"Do we still have time?" asked Daggrande. "Those men must be hundreds of miles south of here."

"I don't know," Chical admitted. "The beasts will be here within a week, a tenday at the most. It depends on how fast the ships could sail—but they will only sail if Cordell gives the order."

"Twin Visages!" said Halloran, suddenly understanding. "Zaltec doesn't march against *Ulatos*. He goes to Twin Visages!"

The giant god would have to march past the Payit city, of course, but Hal suspected that his eventual goal would be the scene of his brother's attempted return. Suddenly the workings of fate, in providing them with the army that now marched with him, began to make sense.

"You're right," he said, turning back to Chical. "We've got to get those ships sailing. How can we free Cordell, though? It wouldn't make sense to attack Don Vaez's force. They're not the real enemy."

"Still, your presence here can only be described as fortuitous," replied Chical. "And it has given me an idea. . . ."

As the warrior explained his plan, they saw it for the desperate scheme that it was. Still, none of them could think of any alternative. They asked questions and finalized details of timing. Finally, when Chical again took to the air, they knew what they had to do.

They rested only briefly, through the darkest part of the night, and by moonrise, which occurred several hours before dawn, the entire force had resumed the march toward Ulatos. They pressed forward through a long, hot day. Halloran again bore the burden of his wife's unconscious form.

At sunset, none of them showed any inclination to rest. Spurred on by the knowledge that the city was nearby, Halloran desperately wanted to get Erixitl to the sanctuary of the temple. In addition, their plan with Chical required them to reach the open fields around Ulatos during the dark of the night.

It was nearly midnight when Halloran and Gultec, in the lead, broke from the fringe of the jungle and saw the torches of the Payit city glowing across the fields.

Accompanied by the Jaguar Knight and the priest of Qotal, Halloran left the bowmen of Tulom-itzi, the dwarves, and the Little Men in the savannah beyond Ulatos. They knew their part in the plan and immediately started gathering dry wood, collecting it in hundreds of different locations.

Meanwhile, the trio took Erixitl into the city to seek the temple of Qotal. As the marching column made camp under a moonless night sky, the three companions hurried through the city streets toward the pyramid. Though the torches they had seen earlier flickered around them, they saw no one awake or active at this hour.

Finally Coton led them to a whitewashed adobe building beside the dark, vine-covered pyramid.

"Wake up! Wake up in there!" Halloran cried, pounding on the temple door.

After several moments, they heard footsteps shuffling inside. "What is it? What in the name of the Feathered Dragon brings you here at this hour?"

The door flew open, revealing a plump, clean-faced priest in a white gown. "Yes? What do you want?"

"My wife needs care, and she needs a comfortable place to rest. We've traveled far, and our mission is extremely important—important to the Feathered Dragon himself!" Halloran pushed through the door, Erixitl in his arms, as the priest stammered his objections.

"Why do you bother *me?*" he asked indignantly. "Who *are*—"

Just then the priest caught sight of Coton lingering behind the others. "F-Forgive me, Patriarch! I did not know— By all means, bring the lady in! Follow me!"

Halloran dogged the footsteps of the suddenly obsequious priest, with a grateful look back at the enigmatically smiling Coton. The young cleric led him to a warm chamber, small but with a thick mattress of straw.

"Here—she can rest here," he explained. Halloran pushed past him and laid his wife on the mattress. Her chest rose and fell slowly from the movement of her breathing, but this was the only way he knew that she lived.

Her face had a dreadful pallor, and her eyes—those impossibly beautiful eyes, so deep and rich and dark—remained closed.

He wondered if he would ever see those eyes again.

\* \* \* \* \*

The door to the shed opened, and a wash of yellow lamplight illuminated the dreary cell. Cordell blinked, waking quickly, and saw Rodolfo enter, followed by several brawny swordsmen. The time was some numberless hour past midnight.

"Hey! No one's allowed in here after dark!" objected one of the guards, climbing sleepily to his feet and standing in the navigator's path.

The guard said nothing further as the metal gauntlet of one of Rodolfo's companions crunched firmly into his jaw. The man collapsed while his two companions stumbled backward, stammering in surprise. The other intruders pressed the tips of their swords to the throats of the remaining two guards, effectively convincing them of the merits of silence.

"Don Vaez is sending most of the fleet back to Amn with

the gold," the navigator hissed. "We've got to act now. He's given orders to sail with this evening's tide."

"The repulsive dog!" Cordell hissed quietly. "I made an agreement with him. I told him where the gold was buried, in exchange for his promise to send the cleric to tend my man."

Rodolfo looked at the pallid, groaning warrior and knew immediately that Don Vaez hadn't kept his side of the bargain.

"Quick—the keys!" Cordell said, pointing to one of the guards. Rodolfo's brawny companion pressed his sword slightly, and the guard gulped, quickly withdrawing a clinking ring of keys.

"It's th-this one," he stammered, identifying the proper key.

In the next instant, Rodolfo threw open the door, and Cordell and his men stumbled from the cell. They stood together in the barn, blinking in the bright lamplight.

"Tie them up. Gag them, too," ordered Cordell.

"Beg the gen'ral's pardon," said one of the guards, slowly backing away from the sword at his throat. Cordell saw that the man looked vaguely familiar.

"Name's Millston, sir. I served with you against Akbet-Khrul and his pirates. I'd like to come with . . . that is . . . I'm on your side, sir. I've heard about the giant and the trolls and them others. Sir, the only way we have a chance is if you're in charge. That prissy courtier'll get us all killed."

Cordell studied the man and then made his decision. If he was to be successful, he needed a lot of Don Vaez's men to come to the same conclusion as Millston.

"Glad to have you," he said, nodding to Rodolfo's accomplice. "Give him back his sword."

The conspirators extinguished the lamp. They brought the feverish Katl from the cell and made him as comfortable as possible on a bed of straw. The other two guards, bound and gagged, were locked in the cell for good measure.

Cautiously they opened the door to the barn. The headquarters house stood across the compound, and men were moving about everywhere. A series of bright lanterns illuminated the top of the rampart to the south, on the side facing the grassy savannah.

Cordell realized that Don Vaez had organized a work crew that now labored to excavate the gold hidden in the rampart wall. The fort was being destroyed, just when its greatest threat marched toward them in the shape of Zaltec and his monstrous army!

"What's that?" Urgency hissed through Grimes's voice as the officer whirled, raising his sword. "Chical!" he added with relief.

Cordell saw the Eagle Knight advance from the shadows beside the shed. He clapped his friend on the arm, his throat tightening with emotion.

"I came to set you free, but I see others have done the task before me."

"I'm glad you came," replied Cordell quietly.

"I bring news," whispered the Maztican, quickly explaining about his meeting with Halloran and the plan they had formed. At the same time, they heard a commotion arise among the men on the work crew. From their vantage point, they looked over the field toward Ulatos and clamored in excitement and alarm.

"That must be them!" said the knight.

"Let's go!" cried Cordell, leading his small party at a trot toward the high walls of the fortress. "Follow me!" he shouted to the rows of tents sheltering Don Vaez's men. The workers and guards turned in surprise to see Cordell climb the sloping earthen surface of the wall, turning to face the courtyard.

"Listen to me, men of the Sword Coast! I warn you of a great danger. A monstrous force approaches, one that will require all your valor to face." The captain-general's voice rang throughout the fortress. The men of Don Vaez gathered below, listening carefully.

"We can face it, but we need allies. I ask you now—look into the field before you."

The men on the wall top, working to excavate the gold, had already seen the savannah. Now they shared their knowledge with their companions in the fort below.

"An army camped on the field!"

"I see a thousand campfires, all come to life at once!"

"There are twenty thousand men there!"

What they actually saw were the campfires, some six hundred in number, made by the desert dwarves, the Little People, and the Itza warriors out on the savannah. But the dark night made exaggeration easy. In a few moments, the overly observant lookouts had spotted a hundred thousand men, with elephants and chariots and huge catapults, all gathered before the fortress of Helmsport.

"Seize him! Stop him!" Don Vaez's command urged his men toward the charismatic captain-general. Panic made the man's voice shrill.

Beside the silver-haired adventurer, Cordell saw the cringing figure of Kardann in the lamplight. It figured, he thought, that the assessor would be on hand when the effort to dig up the gold was made. Now, in the midst of the confusion, Kardann groaned in fear. He took a long look at Cordell and then spun wildly, racing down the outer slope of the rampart to disappear into the darkness of the savannah.

Good riddance thought Cordell with dark satisfaction. It would suit him if he never saw the little maggot again.

One man decided to take action in the face of chaos. Pryat Devane leaped onto his flying carpet, darting into the air. He began to mouth the words to a potent clerical spell, a casting that could have masked Cordell from all who tried to see and hear him.

But another form lurked in the sky. As the cleric raised his hand, his carpet soaring toward the captain-general, a great eagle swooped toward him from above. The priest screamed as talons ripped across his face, and his carpet twisted beneath him.

The eagle dove away but the cleric had already lost control. As his carpet careened toward the rampart where Cordell stood, the pryat desperately struggled to maintain his balance. He could not.

With a terrified cry, the priest slipped from his carpet and fell heavily to the ground, perhaps twenty feet below. He groaned and thrashed his arms, one of his legs twisted unnaturally beneath him.

"Men of the Sword Coast, hear me! These are my allies camped on the field beyond the fort!" cried Cordell, his voice pounding through the vast courtyard. "Join with me, with us, and we will stand against the foe and claim the victory and the treasure that we all deserve!"

The men working at the excavation scowled at Don Vaez, then looked again at the many fires twinkling across the field. They looked, to the imaginative watchers, like a sky full of stars.

Immediately several of the workers grabbed their erstwhile captain and dragged him forward. Don Vaez protested loudly, until one of the men cuffed him soundly.

"Cordell!" A shout rose from the men among the tents.

"Hail, Cordell!" It was echoed by the workers on the rampart above.

In the meantime, the captain-general descended from the rampart and crossed to the injured cleric. The groaning Pryat Devane struggled to straighten his leg out so that he could cast a spell of healing upon it.

"Wait," ordered Cordell, standing above the terrified priest. "There's somebody else I want you to heal first. Pick him up," he ordered several of his loyal legionnaires.

With the sputtering Don Vaez in tow, they started toward the cell where the injured Eagle Knight, Katl, still lay.

\* \* \* \* \*

From the chronicles of Coton:

*In thankfulness to the god who has seen so much of our journey completed.*

*We arrive in the plain before Ulatos late at night, exhausted from the last stage of our march. We make camp on the savannah, building our cookfires, though the hour is past midnight.*

*Later we learn that these fires, seen by the men in Helmsport, gave them fear of Cordell's army. The joke is a good* one, on all save the hapless Don Vaez. Cordell is indeed a charmed soldier, it would seem, for now he takes a fort of fifteen hundred men with the help of twelve legionnaires and two dozen Eagle Knights.

Already, at first light, the twenty-five ships of the newcomers are sent to the south under the command of a veteran navigator. They intend to sail around the jungles of Payit to the Sea of Azul. There they will gather the remainder of Cordell's men and the warriors of Kultaka as well.

. And as to us, we shall rest here in Ulatos. Erixitl still slumbers, and not until we can restore her awareness will we make the final leg of our journey. But ultimately, I am confident, we will trek to Twin Visages, and there we will seek the coming of the Plumed God.

# ☙ 19 ❧

# A GATHERING OF POWERS

Halloran approached the brown bulk of Helmsport, Storm cantering easily across the fields. Concern for his wife formed a cold knot in his chest, but that didn't completely vanquish his alertness and caution.

Word had spread through Ulatos with the coming of dawn: The conqueror, Captain-General Cordell himself, once again commanded the great fortress! By now the streets were filled with the news, mostly spoken by Mazticans with a mixture of trepidation and awe.

To Hal, however, the news had carried the prospect of hope, which now led him to seek out Cordell. Erixitl remained unconscious, guarded by Gultec and Jhatli, while Daggrande had started over to the fortress on foot. Halloran had not wanted to wait.

Still, how would Cordell receive him? Now that the captain-general had regained an army and once again held a position of command, would he cooperate with the request of a former fugitive?

Pulling in the reins as he neared the entrance to the fortress, he nodded to the two halberdiers flanking the wide notch in the earthwork. Their polished breastplates and clean, unpatched leggings looked odd to Halloran, whose own equipment and clothes wore the marks of more than a year's campaign.

They regarded him with suspicious frowns until he spoke.

"I'm here to see the captain-general," he barked. "Where will I find him?"

Blinking in surprise, the guard quickly pointed to the large headquarters building. "He's in there now."

Halloran wasted no time, spurring Storm into a speedy trot across the huge courtyard of the fortress. Around him, he saw companies of horsemen drilling, while other troops did laundry or polished armor. The harquebusiers worked at cleaning their cumbersome muskets.

Before the headquarters building, he reined in and dismounted quickly. Two guards barred the door, but the portal suddenly opened to reveal the captain-general himself. Cordell wore a shining breastplate. His black hair and beard were neatly trimmed, and a long green plume danced from his gleaming helmet.

"Halloran! Good work, man. What a surprise to see you here!"

"And a surprise for me as well," Hal replied, taking the hand that his old commander offered. "How fared the Nexalans at Tukan?"

Briefly Cordell recounted the tale of the horde's withdrawal, coupled with the discovery of Don Vaez's arrival. "And this is where the eagle brings you now?" Cordell finished with an inquiry.

"I haven't time to explain. I come for a different purpose." Quickly Halloran described their experience at the City of the Gods and the mission that now sent them to Twin Visages. He told of the mysterious affliction that struck Erixitl. "I need a cleric, the best one you have, to see if he can bring her out of it! As long as she remains unconscious, we don't have a chance!"

"This might explain the giant the eagles observed with the Beasts of the Viperhand," said Cordell, describing the image of the looming stone monolith as told to him by Chical.

"Yes—that's Zaltec himself. We must get to Twin Visages before him to allow Qotal to return to Maztica. He's the only one who can battle his brother! And only Erixitl can open the path for him!"

Cordell looked thoughtful, a hand stroking his beard. "It's true that there are several clerics among these men. They could offer some aid, I'm certain. One of them, in fact, just healed himself after an unfortunate . . . accident. He is a pryat in the service of Helm."

"Please—send him to the temple!" Hal blurted.

But Cordell's eyes narrowed. "But tell me now, why should I? After all, you have renounced service in my legion. You made that very clear."

Halloran's face flushed. His anger nearly compelled his fingers toward Cordell's throat, but he forced himself to hold still. "It's *important* that she recover—not just for me, but for all of us!"

Cordell acted as though he hadn't heard. "Of course, I'm sure we could work something out." He smiled, as if a pleasant idea slowly took shape in his mind.

"You know, I'm short of good horse captains! It's no secret that you were one of the best, *Captain* Halloran. Now, if you were to join with me quickly—now—I would have no cause for denying you the services of these faithful men of god."

Halloran looked at Cordell in disbelief. Unconsciously his hands clenched into fists, yet he forced his voice to remain calm as he replied.

"You know that I can't do that. I am a man of Maztica now. Whatever the purpose of this new army of yours, I can make no pledge to support it—or even to stand aside when you march."

Cordell sighed. Halloran waited, wondering what the captain-general would do next. The door to the building opened again, and Hal looked up to see a fully cloaked Eagle Warrior emerge.

"Chical," Halloran said, with a bow.

"It is good to see you, my friend," replied the knight. Then Chical turned to Cordell. "You must give him the help he seeks. He is right when he says that his wife's task is important to all of us."

Cordell looked at the Eagle Knight sharply, annoyance creasing his brow. Clearly he didn't like the interference of another in what he considered to be his own prerogatives of command. Then he looked back at Halloran.

"I shall send them immediately—as I was about to do. My ploy was just that, an attempt to get you back. I meant what I said, Hal—you *were* the best."

Halloran studied Cordell, trying to figure out if he was

telling the truth or merely attempting to save face. Finally Hal held his hands up. "I'll take the help you send, and gratefully."

\* \* \* \* \*

Kardann groped his way through the tangled forest, propelled only by fear—fear of what lay behind him. All of his nightmares, all the terrors that Maztica had aroused in him in the past, seemingly endless months were as nothing compared to the dread in which he now held Cordell.

Didn't he *see?* Couldn't the captain-general *understand?* Kardann was loyal to the merchant princes of Amn. They had *hired* him, he had *responsibilities!* Now, Don Vaez was clearly the duly appointed representative of those worthy nobles. Kardann's loyalty belonged to him, not Cordell!

Yet truly Kardann realized that Cordell would never understand. Just when it had seemed his nightmare was about to end, when the actual prospect of sailing home again loomed before him, catastrophe had to strike.

Indeed, Don Vaez had promised to send the assessor home on the first ship, with the shipment of gold they had been about to unearth. Then somehow the treacherous Cordell had escaped, and Kardann's future became a ruined shambles. Don Vaez's men had turned to the new commander with no thought toward legalities or even common decency!

What was the matter with those men, anyway? How could they renounce an oath of loyalty and accept a new commander in the middle of a campaign? But such they had done.

Immediately Kardann had understood that the new organization would have no place for him, or if it did, that place might well be found at the end of a rope. Without thinking, he had fled from the fortress, from the eager hands of fickle soldiery suddenly so anxious to do Cordell's bidding.

So now he found himself in this infernal, eternal jungle. He pressed forward, cursing as thorns pricked his hands but not slowing his pace as his robes were slowly torn away. All he could think of, all that drove him now, was the thought of getting as far as possible from the madman who now commanded Helmsport.

*     *     *     *     *

Ether had assumed the dimensions of infinity to Poshtli. For a timeless era—an entire lifetime of a man, for all he knew—he had ridden the shoulders of the god Qotal. Bright plumage surrounded him, softly cushioning and comfortably warm. His body craved neither food nor drink.

Yet still the god remained little more to him than a great transport, carrying him across the worlds, yet conveying little of his mission or his might.

Indeed, Poshtli had begun to sense that the god needed little from humans, save that they open the passage for him again to return to the world. Once he reached Maztica, however, Qotal would feel no compulsion to heed the pleas of his worshipers. They were puny mortals to him, and as such, beneath his cosmic concerns.

But now Poshtli sensed a nearness again, a form of substance somewhere, not too distant, but still invisible within the ethereal fog. For just once, briefly, that mist parted.

He saw revealed before him a shore of verdant green surrounding a small, lichen-encrusted pyramid. Below the pyramid, on a high, seaward bluff, two faces gazed impassively outward. And then Poshtli understood.

They looked seaward, and they searched for the return of the god.

*     *     *     *     *

The week following Cordell's usurpation of command passed quickly. Erixitl remained comatose, and nothing that anyone among the Mazticans or the foreigners could do seemed capable of provoking any kind of response.

Chical and the eagles maintained a steady vigil over the approaching monsters and the huge stone god that led them. The miles passed quickly beneath their footsteps, and all in Helmsport and Ulatos felt growing fear as word of the inevitably approaching mass reached the city.

It was early in the morning, seven days after Cordell's victory, that Chical once again glided to the earth within Helmsport and quickly shifted back to his human form. The captain-general already stood before him, summoned by guards who had seen Chical approaching and who knew how eagerly Cordell awaited this important report.

"They are very close now," Chical reported. "They no longer march as an untamed horde. They have been trained into an army."

"When will they get here?" Cordell asked.

Chical looked at the sun, just rising above the eastern horizon. "I would guess sometime today, perhaps as early as noon if they press on as vigorously as they have been."

"No need to lighten their pace now," growled the commander. "Not when they're this close. Is there any word from the city about Erixitl?" he inquired.

"No change," reported the eagle, who had stopped at Ulatos before coming to the fort.

Cordell grimaced. He didn't know why he placed so much hope in the recovery of this young woman. There certainly seemed to be no rational reason for it. Yet after these long months in Maztica, coming so close to ultimate victory only to have it changed, by the caprice of the gods, to complete catastrophe, Cordell had begun to think differently about the world.

He knew that Pryat Devane had worked his best magic upon Erix, yet the man had returned to Helmsport in failure. He hadn't understood the affliction that assailed her, though he had predicted that it would wear off in time. But too he had sensed a greatness, a power in the young woman, that had clearly awed him.

While Erixitl remained unconscious, there seemed little that they could do except plan to make war on the horde of monsters that marched inexorably closer. This Cordell and his new army had spent the last week doing.

His new soldiers accepted his command enthusiastically, and quickly began preparations for the battle that Don Vaez hadn't believed was possible. That captain now languished in the same cell that had held Cordell. Though the captain-general fully intended to free his rival when they both returned to Amn, he had no intention of doing so prematurely. Fortunately even Don Vaez's most loyal officers had proved remarkably willing to accept Cordell's leadership. Now they toiled in the service of their new commander with more diligence and military bearing than ever they had given the old.

Cordell had reviewed the men, finding that he commanded a well-balanced force, though several of the companies had had little experience in actual battle. Others, however, consisted of mercenaries who had served him before—men such as the guard, Millston—and these men he knew he could trust implicitly.

The harquebuses were weapons that Cordell had never before utilized. Still, when the men provided a demonstration of the loud, smoke-spewing weapons, he felt that they might prove useful in delaying or arresting an enemy charge. He was dismayed, however, with the long time required before the weapons could be readied for a second volley. In actual battle, it seemed that the harquebusiers would be likely to get off one shot, then would have to fall back or rely on their short swords to keep them alive.

Finally, the captain-general was pleased to discover that the merchants had sent a team of young magic-users to aid in Don Vaez's expedition. Two dozen in number, they would prove very useful, he felt certain. Though none of them even began to approach the power of his own onetime ally and lover, the elf-mage Darien, the power of even minor spells could sometimes prove decisive.

The twenty-five carracks, of course, remained at sea on their mission. Privately, now, Cordell had come to doubt whether they could reach the Sea of Azul, pick up the remaining legionnaires and the Kultakan warriors, and return in time to make a difference.

He would have to stand with the forces that he had. Even with the addition of Don Vaez's men and the archers of Far Payit, plus the desert dwarves and the halflings, he had fewer than four thousand men. He would gain perhaps an equal number of spearmen from the Payit city of Ulatos, but this still seemed like a small force when facing an army of thirty thousand savage orcs and their even more powerful masters.

Cordell looked back to the city, its pyramids standing out proudly above the savannah. He thought of the woman, nearly bursting with her child, who slumbered comatose there.

"Wake up, Erix," Cordell whispered softly. It was very close to a prayer.

\* \* \* \* \*

The Lord of the Jaguars roamed restlessly, his belly growling with the hunger that had been his constant companion for all the weeks since he had fled the village of the Little People. Curse that foul human and his sorcery! The cat snarled at the memory of that horrible night.

The growling predator remembered his life among the halflings with fondness. Food had not been plentiful, for it was only rarely that they caught one of the Big People, but they had thrown him wild game during times when there were no captives. Never had he had to work for his meals. Instead, he could sleep for days on end, which was truly the way the Lord of the Jaguars preferred to spend his time.

Of course, never would the ancient, once-powerful beast admit that the man had been right, that the Lord of the Jaguars was indeed too old, too slow to kill in the wilds. Yet, unfortunately, that had proven to be the case. Despite his shrewd intellect, equal or superior to a human's, and his great size and long, sharp teeth, the predator had been unable to kill anything for himself save an occasional rodent or snake.

Now he growled again, for never had be been so hungry. And he craved *real* food now, red meat, with the juices of the kill still flowing. Pacing the forest paths restlessly, he traveled far in search of a kill. Sometimes, seething with frustration, he spoke aloud in the human voice that had proven so hypnotically frightening to his victims.

The cat-lord's travels had taken him far to the north of his home among the Little People. Food had been scarce there, and he had hoped that this country—the land of the Payits, he knew—would prove more fruitful. Thus far he had been disappointed.

Yet still he kept prowling and searching. Sometime soon, he knew, he would *have* to make a kill.

\* \* \* \* \*

The quarry at the end of her quest now compelled Darien into a quivering eagerness. She sensed it even as the hunting cat senses the weakness of the crippled fawn, and it provoked a similar quickening in her hunger.

The driders followed her, now, in resigned deference to her commands. They dragged themselves through the forest, ignoring the demands of hunger and thirst. Several collapsed, perishing slowly and left by their stronger kin.

Still, fifteen of the monsters remained alive as, at last, their goal emerged from the forest before them.

The pyramid at Twin Visages stood in the center of a wide clearing. At one side of the open area, to the north, a sheer bluff dropped precipitously toward the shoreline and its coral lagoon below. Three sides of the clearing fronted on the jungle.

And from the jungle emerged the driders, waiting for the coming of twilight to creep forward. They spread out, cautiously encircling the structure, nervously sniffing and searching for any sign of a trap. Nothing unnatural disturbed the calm of the forest night.

Finally they surrounded the structure and then hesitantly climbed the fifty-two steps that led to its crowning platform.

No sound emerged from the forest as the stars slowly winked into sight above. The moon, half full, cast its dry light across the driders, leaving faint shadows.

"We are here," said Hittok, with a tired bow toward his mistress. "What do we do now?"

"Now—" said Darien, with a look toward the forest and

what lay beyond, "now we wait for our quarry to come to us."

As the drider settled into a crouch, she relaxed, her tension dissipating for the first time in weeks. And with her easing came the breaking of *hishna*. Through the air, over the short distance between Twin Visages and Ulatos, Darien sent the sundering of her spell.

Now she was prepared to meet her enemy.

\* \* \* \* \*

"What happened? Where am I?" Erixitl asked weakly as her eyes fluttered open and she saw Halloran seated beside her bed.

For a moment, he could not speak, so great was his joy and relief. "This is Ulatos," he said finally. "The temple of Qotal. By the gods, Erix, I was so afraid. . . ." His voice faded, choking.

"Shhh," she urged, sitting up slowly. "No harm could come to me as long as you were here to watch over me." She squinted in concentration, trying to think. "I remember a horrible darkness settling around me, dragging me down and holding me there. It's gone, now—finally."

Suddenly her eyes widened. "Finally! How long has it been?"

"It has been ten days since I have seen your eyes," he replied, his voice tight. He blinked several times and took her hand in his.

Fear flamed in Erix's eyes. "We've got to go—to get to Twin Visages!" She struggled to get up as he tried gently to ease her back onto her pillow.

"You need to rest!" he said. "The baby—"

She pushed him back with surprising vitality and sat facing him. "The baby will come with me. We must go *now!* Who knows how much time we have!"

"The army of the Viperhand will be here soon—probably today, according to Chical," Halloran went on. "The eagles have been observing it all along."

"And what will happen then?" Erix gasped. "There will be

battle, and the Little Men, the desert dwarves, Gultec's warriors, they'll all be killed!"

"There are fifteen hundred men-at-arms from Amn here, too," Hal pointed out. "And Cordell has sent the ships to collect the rest of his men and the Kultakans." Hal admitted privately that the latter forces had little chance of debarking before the issue would be resolved.

"But Zaltec is with them. And *he's* the one who can stop Qotal. We have to get to Twin Visages—now, *today!*"

Jhatli, summoned from a nearby room within the temple, quickly agreed. The youth went to get his proudest possession, a steel short sword given him by Cordell from the arsenal of weapons brought by Don Vaez's expedition.

Coton stepped forward, and there was no question but that the priest of Qotal should accompany them. Daggrande was with the legionnaires in the fortress, commanding a company of crossbow and harquebus and helping Cordell to integrate the Maztican troops into the tactics of the Sword Coast.

Then Lotil, his feather blanket nearing completion, emerged from his room. His blunt fingers, as always, worked traces of plumage into the fine mesh of cotton.

"I will come, too," he said.

Halloran started to open his mouth in objection, to plea with the blind man that such a gesture merely endangered Lotil's own life. But he stopped, feeling Erix's touch on his arm.

"Of course, Father," she said. "You shall accompany us."

\* \* \* \* \*

For more than a week after leaving Kultaka, Hoxitl had pushed his monstrous horde with maniacal frenzy. They marched along the coast, following the wide track laid down by the lumbering, monstrous form of Zaltec. The giant stone image appeared to take no note of the thousands of creatures following in its wake, but this, to Hoxitl, was as it should be.

Finally they pressed along the shore toward Ulatos, knowing that just beyond lay the culmination of the Payit lands, the point of Twin Visages.

The army of the Viperhand marched grimly now, a hardened edge marking troops that had pursued the Nexalans as a ragged, bloodthirsty mob.

The ogres had assumed complete control over the orcs, and the entire force was organized into companies comprising five to ten ogres commanding a hundred orcs. Hundreds of these companies formed the thirty great regiments, each regiment consisting of one thousand orcs and their ogre officers and two companies of ten bloodthirsty, regenerating trolls.

Hoxitl, towering over even the tallest of his trolls, ruled this army with an iron hand. The most savage of his troops cringed when the cleric-beast raised his hand. The most veteran and trail-worn of his companies puffed with pride when he praised their appearance or their acts.

And before them marched the great, imposing form of their god. Zaltec was capable of crushing a row of houses in one monstrous footstep. In a few hours, he could reduce a city to rubble. If any doubts assailed the cleric-beast, they concerned what use such a mighty deity would have for *any* army, however toughened and well organized.

The great force moved through the Payit country, driving the inhabitants in panic before them. Thus, when they approached the Payit city of Ulatos, word of their approach was sure to precede them.

Still, when they reached the savannah before that city, it gave Zaltec joy to see the enemy arrayed to meet him. The sun had long since risen and climbed high into the morning sky. The humans and their allies had advanced into the wide savannah, anchoring their position on a pair of small villages.

The beasts of the Viperhand saw them and prepared to attack.

\* \* \* \* \*

"By Helm, look at the size of that thing!" Cordell gasped in astonishment and dismay. He stood, with Daggrande and

Grimes, atop the rampart of Helmsport, looking over the forest to the west and watching the steady, unhurried approach of the monstrous statue.

"We'll never be able to stand against it," Grimes said matter-of-factly.

"Erixitl *must* get to that pyramid," Daggrande added. "It's the only hope we have. We might be able to hold out against the monsters, but you're right, Grimes—there's nothing we can do about the big fellow."

"When did they leave?" Cordell asked.

"An hour ago, no more," admitted the dwarf. "It'll take them most of the afternoon to get there." The giant form of the god, they knew, could cover the distance in a fraction of that time.

The great monolith marched to the edge of the forest, but then it paused. The trees of the jungle came only to its waist, and its gray, impassive eyes stared to the east, in apparent unconcern for the army that gathered on the savannah before it. The watchers could not see, but they sensed, the monstrous army gathering around the statue's feet, spreading along the edge of the forest, staying within the concealment of the verdant canopy.

The giant remained impassive, still staring. If it suffered any impatience, no clue was visible across the craggy, granite features of its face. It no doubt knew that the true goal of its quest lay just a short distance beyond the bothersome humans arrayed before it, humans who were beneath the notice of one so magnificent, so unstoppable.

But still it waited.

\* \* \* \* \*

Kardann collapsed into a sobbing, miserable heap. He had fled for days through this miserable forest, surviving on the few pieces of fruit he could find, cringing and fleeing at every sound. Finally he knew he had reached the end of his endurance.

For a full day, he lay still, certain at any moment that he was about to die. And, in fact, he began to wish for death as the only conceivable release from the death by starvation that now seemed his inescapable destiny.

Suddenly he heard a sound and sat instantly upright. Perhaps, he decided, he didn't really want to die—not yet, in any event.

But what was that? He heard another noise and pictured the approach of some horrid beast, certainly about to tear him limb from limb.

Then he sagged back, almost crying out with relief. It wasn't a horrid beast, for he heard a voice, an unmistakably *human* voice. He couldn't recognize words, or even a language, but the deep and resonant tones could be nothing other that a man engaging in deep and serious conversation.

"Here! Here! Help me," he cried, scrambling to his feet. "I'm over here!"

He would not have been disappointed to see Cordell himself coming toward him; at least the captain-general might reasonably be expected to provide him with a decent meal before hanging him!

"Please, come here!" he shouted again, climbing to his feet and pushing through the brush toward the source of the sound.

Then he stopped, dull horror creeping over his senses and freezing him in his place. He came to the source of the voice, but it was not a man in earnest conversation. Instead, he looked into a bestial face, with a mouth full of long, curving fangs. It was a mouth that, even as Kardann watched, slowly spread into a wide, horrifying grin.

"Hello," said the great cat, in its soft, well-modulated tones. "I am the Lord of the Jaguars, and you are mine."

\* \* \* \* \*

From the chronicles of Coton:

*In the certain approach of the Plumed Grandfather.*
*We leave Ulatos knowing that, shortly behind us, the horde of the Viperhand will reach the city of the Payit. A*

city of long-lasting peace, it will see its second war within the year. The faithful warriors who have accompanied us here will try to buy us the time to work a miracle.

But if anyone can do so, I suspect it will be this black-haired woman who bears the child of two peoples. She is truly the Chosen One of Qotal, and her goodness is manifest. She may yet open the gate to the Feathered Dragon's passage.

The menace looms behind us in the monsters of Zaltec. The unknown lurks ahead, an encloaking darkness that beckons and yet dissuades. I pray that we, that Erixitl, has the power to shed that darkness.

# ❧ 20 ❧

# THE SECOND BATTLE OF ULATOS

The beasts of the Viperhand, guided by the battle-hungry Hoxitl, waited for nightfall to launch their attack, allowing time for the entire monstrous army to gather at the edge of the savannah. The great regiments pushed forward along the coastal trail, and the column gradually expanded into a vast front within the protective jungle.

Cordell, conversely, had been forced to prepare for an assault as soon as the horde reached the fringe of the savannah surrounding Ulatos at noon. His men stood under the blazing Maztican sun throughout the day, ready for battle. But as the hours of afternoon passed into twilight, the battle did not come.

At least, the captain-general realized, they were spared the damage that could have been inflicted by the monstrous image of Zaltec. The stone colossus stood there throughout the waning afternoon, staring above and beyond the savannah and the armies that gathered around its feet. It was as if the humans were too pathetic, too unworthy even of his notice for Zaltec to take the trouble of wiping them out.

Finally, before dusk, the giant stepped onto the savannah, scattering the desert dwarves of Luskag's tribe, for those unfortunate warriors stood in the god's direct path. Fortunately the nimble dwarves all raced out of the way of the monstrous footsteps, and Zaltec continued marching steadily to the east.

Cordell, along with the rest of the army, watched him go and felt an unmistakable sense of relief. Still, some of them, including the captain-general, knew that the battle to be fought at Twin Visages was at least as important to their future as the one about to occur here.

The latter, however, was Cordell's only concern now. His troops were in position, though they seemed a pathetically frail line to stem the tide that they knew lurked in the nearby jungle. Desert dwarves, carrying their sharpened weapons of *pluma*stone; tough, veteran spearmen from Tulom-Itzi; halflings armed with shortbows, tipped with the paralytic poison, *kurari*; an assortment of mercenaries with crossbow, harquebus, sword and buckler, a hundred cavalry; it seemed an oddly diverse core to an army.

To these numerous formations, the city of Ulatos and the lands of the Payit had added seven thousand additional warriors, a total that had pleased and surprised the captain-general. A year ago, the bulk of the Payit army had accompanied Cordell on his disastrous march to Nexal. Though not so accomplished in war as other nations of the True World, the Payits were brave and loyal fighters. Thus, when the one who had conquered them had ordered them to join his ranks, they had done so willingly and without question.

The Payits had made the march with the Golden Legion, participating in Cordell's successful battle to subdue the Kultakans. That conquered state had then become the captain-general's ally as well, and a source of great reinforcements in his march on the great city of Nexal. The Payits, Kultakans, and legionnaires had all entered the city and taken up residence in its central plaza.

Unlike the Kultakans, however, the Payits hadn't been fortunate enough to fight their way free of the dying city on the Night of Wailing. They had perished there almost to a man. Now the city of Ulatos and the surrounding countryside had precious few warriors with which to defend themselves.

The defenders' position stood anchored on the sea, in the strong block of Helmsport. Here one of Don Vaez's former officers, newly sworn to the service of Cordell, commanded legionnaires—a hundred crossbow and a hundred sword. The fort would provide a refuge for much of the force if the line broke. Here also the commander had posted many of the young magic-users who had come with Don Vaez's force, the rest of the spell-casters being scattered along the length of the line.

Yet Cordell knew that simply holing up in the fortress and allowing the monsters to rampage freely outside the walls was a defeatist strategy; instead, he formed a long line of resistance stretched across the savannah, with the fort as only the far right end of that line.

The defenders' position stretched inland from the fortress, nearly a mile to the small village of Nayap. Here Cordell had posted a large block of swordsmen and archers, for the little cluster of houses formed a disruptive obstacle to any attack from the jungle.

Beyond the village, the line curved back to the left for another half a mile until it reached another small village, Actas. Neither of these settlements numbered more than four dozen buildings, and most of these were structures of thatch or adobe. Each contained a small pyramid, however. Though these ceremonial centers were barely twenty-five feet high, Cordell used them as platforms to mount his archers, while men with swords, halberds, and pikes gathered around their bases to protect them in melee.

The entire position, unfortunately, stretched only a third of the way to the city of Ulatos. Interspersed companies of legionnaire crossbowmen and harquebusiers, plus the archers of the Little Men and the Itza, stood along the front. Alternating with them were companies of legionnaire swordsmen and axe-wielding desert dwarves, as well as the companies of Payit spearmen.

Behind the line, Daggrande commanded the reserves, a company of legionnaire veterans armed with axes or shortswords. Beside him, Grimes rode with a hundred-odd horsemen. The chief task of the cavalry would be to prevent the monsters from sweeping around the left flank of the defense.

Throughout the hot afternoon, the defenders had stood ready while the attackers gathered their forces. After the colossal figure of Zaltec marched on to Twin Visages, they expected the attack momentarily. But slowly afternoon faded to dusk, then twilight.

Finally, after full darkness settled across the fields, the men sensed movement in the night. A soft rustling swept through the grass, and then the tread of many heavy feet thudded through the earth.

Suddenly, with shocking abruptness and crushing volume, a great roar arose from the masses of orcs and ogres. The beasts rushed from the fringe of the jungle, shaking the ground with the pounding cadence of their charge. Wooden whistles and conch-shell horns added to the din. The ranks hurled themselves into the open, ten great regiments sweeping toward the line on the savannah, rushing through the night toward their rendezvous with death.

Hoxitl remained in the jungle, staring from his treelike height with eyes that took no notice of the darkness. He saw the line of his enemies and the sweeping mass of his own charging troops.

The defenders stared in awe, trembling at the din and trying to steel themselves for the coming clash. It was good, for the sake of their confidence, in any event, that they didn't know the first awe-inspiring rush came from but a third of Hoxitl's entire force.

Moments after the attack commenced, light spells suddenly dispelled the night as the smattering of young mages among Don Vaez's expedition cast their weak magic, serving a vital function.

Instantly the archers of Tulom-Itzi launched the first volley of their missiles. The shark's-tooth heads penetrated bodies of orcs and ogres and trolls. Several of the lumbering creatures fell, and again and again volleys of deadly arrows flew.

Next came the heavy *clunk* of crossbow fire, and a volley of heavy quarrels darted like steel scythes into the face of the foremost regiment. Even huge ogres grunted or doubled over in pain, while the smaller orcs often fell dead, slain by a single bolt.

Then a sharp crash, like explosive thunder never heard in Maztican battle before, erupted from the harquebusiers. A cloud of gray smoke instantly blossomed among them, but not before lethal balls of lead shot thudded into the enemy.

The crude muskets dropped many an orc, but the wielders had to lower their weapons after the first volley. The charge came on too fast for them to reload.

Finally the Little People launched their darts. The tiny arrows were little more than pinpricks to the hulking beasts, but they could not so easily ignore the *kurari* venom smeared on the tips of the little arrows.

A spearhead of trolls led the attack, forty of the gangly beasts, claws outstretched, their ghastly faces split by grimaces of battle hatred. On each, the pulsing crimson brand of the Viperhand stood out from the scaly green skin on the creature's chest.

The bolts and arrows and lead balls that struck the trolls occasionally knocked the creatures down, but invariably the monsters crawled back to their feet, plucked the missiles from their bodies, and charged forward in the wake of their companions' attack.

The first trolls hit a company of mercenary swordsmen. Heavy green fists bashed shields out of the way, while cruel talons and fangs sought human flesh. The men stood for a brief moment, chopping and hacking, only to see the wounds they inflicted in the trolls' skin heal almost as soon as the dripping blades came free.

The fight raged with chaotic savagery as small bands of men fought for their lives against the much larger trolls. Shouts of warning and cries of rage split the night, as well as the shrieks and groans of the wounded. Weapons clashed against shields with ringing force, while the howls and bellows of the trolls rose above all, adding a monstrous and inhuman cast to an already nightmarish scene.

Swordsmen fell dead, ripped to pieces by the fangs and talons of the trolls, while some of the monsters limped and crawled back from the fight to allow deep wounds to regenerate. But the latter returned, while the former were lost forever, and this began to turn the tide of the melee.

Finally the company of swordsmen collapsed, just as the ten thousand orcs, heavy with the momentum of their charge, crashed into the rest of the line.

Howling and shrieking madly, each tusk-faced creature

inflamed by the burning of his own crimson brand, the orcs struck with brute force. Their *macas* and clubs hammered into the shields of the defenders as rear ranks instantly stepped forward to fill the multitude of gaps formed by their fallen comrades.

"There!" bellowed Daggrande. He saw the trolls burst through the line. The mass of green split into two groups, wheeling to the right and left, respectively.

The first group faced the flank of Tabub's diminutive archers. The Little Men turned and showered the trolls with arrows as Luskag and the desert dwarves extended their line to protect the front of the halflings against the charging orcs. The monsters cursed and howled in pain as the tiny arrows pricked them. Several of them, those that had been hit many times, suddenly stiffened with reflexive gasps and then collapsed to the ground, motionless and rigid.

The reserve company rushed forward, surging into contact with the second group of trolls. Daggrande chopped his axe into the back of one of the creatures, driving it to its knees. Savagely the dwarf attacked the troll, his blade delivering a hailstorm of blows. He left the troll a mangled mass on the grass, while the last rank of the reserve company stopped to shower the corpse with oil and touch a flame to it. In moments, a pyre of stinking black smoke marked the demise of the troll.

Around Daggrande, other veteran soldiers attacked with halberds or long, two-handed swords. The trolls fought back savagely, and many a brave warrior fell before their talons or drooling, wicked fangs. But the persistence of the dwarf's company, coupled with their skillful use of fire, finally began to drive the trolls back.

Daggrande knew the breach had been stemmed—for now.

Behind the dwarf, Grimes saw one of the monstrous regiments swing wide of the defenders' line, starting a great wheel around the entire flank.

"Charge!" Grimes cried, gesturing with his sword. The horsemen, in five companies of twenty, surged into a broad line. Lances lowered, they plunged into the regiment of orcs, scattering the creatures beneath their hooves, breaking them into panicked remnants.

The ogres stood firm, clubs upraised, before the rush. But the deadly lances found these, and many a hulking monster shrieked in mountainous pain before falling to the earth before a charging rider. Desperately the dying monsters struggled to hold their torn bodies together as the last remnant of their life fluid seeped over the ground.

The horses wheeled and rode back, wracking the regiment again, trampling the survivors beneath the crushing hooves. The surviving orcs broke and fled toward the shelter of the jungle. Grimes, minus a few of his riders, pulled the horsemen back behind the line.

Another regiment pressed forward, pushing around to the rear of the village of Nayap. Payit spearmen resisted them courageously, even felling several ogres with their long, obsidian-tipped weapons. But then a dozen trolls ripped into the center of the warriors' line, and in moments, the whole company fled in disorder.

Howling in triumph, the monstrous formation rushed to fill the gap and encircle the village. But then a small form darted across the sky, soaring over the onrushing beasts.

Pryat Devane rode his flying carpet at high speed, bringing the little platform to a sudden stop when he reached a position a hundred yards in front of the charging regiment.

"By the power of Helm, I call a plague upon you!" he shouted, raising his metal gauntlet and pointing to the first monstrous rank.

In the next moment, the buzzing, hissing, and clicking of millions of insects rose across the plain, competing with the din of battle in its intensity. Immediately the leading ogres howled in pain and surprise, slapping at their skin and twisting grotesquely in an effort to escape.

Wasps, bees, hornets, flies—all manner of stinging insects flew among the monsters, and instantly the momentum of the attack vanished. All the beasts could think about was escape, and the entire regiment dissipated as the creatures raced in every direction to escape the insect plague. Some of them tumbled through the ranks of a neighboring regiment, one that pressed against Nayap itself, and for a little while the weight of that savage attack eased.

For long, bloody minutes, the battle stood in terrible balance. Humans, orcs, dwarves, ogres, halflings, horses, and trolls, all bled into the dark earth, beneath the encloaking clouds that blacked out even the slightest glimpse of stars or moon.

Hundreds of lives expired. Companies of orcs or humans, decimated by battle, turned to flee. Others on each side expanded their fronts to cover gaps thus exposed. An exhausting, costly equilibrium held along the front.

Then another horrifying sequence of whistles and bellows erupted from the forest. The din of the battle faded to insignificance against the cacophony of fresh strength symbolized by that throaty, hungry roar.

More hulking shapes emerged from the forest, their shadows spreading across the savannah. Another powerful wave of destruction, they pressed toward the cringing shore as Hoxitl threw another ten regiments into the fight.

\* \* \* \* \*

Erixitl stumbled forward, helped by Coton and Halloran. They made their way slowly down the shore toward Twin Visages on foot, since the ground in places was too rough for safe travel by horseback. Jhatli led Lotil by the hand.

They followed the coast, since all the paths through the jungle from Ulatos to Twin Visages were obscure and difficult to follow. The shoreline route took longer but was far more certain.

"It's not much farther," Erix said finally, after hours of marching. The sun neared the western horizon, and now they strived to reach their goal by nightfall.

Halloran remembered the place called Twin Visages, the place where he and Erixitl had met. It had seemed even then to be a place of dire portent and deep, abiding power. Now it felt like the focus of his world, the place toward which all his roads had been leading.

"When we get there, do we climb the pyramid?" he asked. That structure, much smaller than the one in Tehwaca, seemed hardly large enough to support the massive dragon they had glimpsed, so briefly, in the City of the Gods.

"Yes."

"And the god will arrive there?" Halloran asked.

"I think so," Erix replied. She shook her head in frustration. "I don't *know!* I can only do what seems right!"

She gasped in sudden pain and bent double. "It's . . . all right," she said, pushing herself along.

The ground rose beneath them as they moved onto the bluff that formed the broad headland of the point. Silently they walked on, pushing along the fringe of brushy ground between the deep jungle and the sheer drop toward the wave-battered shore below.

Then Halloran stopped, raising a hand before him and soundlessly pointing. Erix looked and saw it, too, even though the moon had set an hour before. She would never forget that horrible place where she had come so close to death.

Before them stood the squared bulk of the pyramid and Twin Visages. Beyond, etched in streaks of sunset, stretched the lagoon and the endless ocean. They couldn't see the top of the pyramid, but the last rays of the sun brightened the side facing them.

Erixitl groaned again in sudden pain. With a gasp, she grabbed her belly and sank slowly to the ground.

\* \* \* \* \*

Flames exploded into the dark sky from one after another of the huts of Nayap. Metal-armored soldiers from Amn fought desperately for each square foot of ground, making the beasts pay for every forward step with one, two, a dozen lives. But the monstrous army could afford the price.

Finally the defenders gathered around the pyramid, attacked on three sides by a howling, slavering mass. Fire and ash and smoke drifted around the squat structure, though the din of battle drowned any sound of the blaze.

A great ogre bulled his way onto the steps of the pyramid, crushing the skull of a metal-helmed soldier with a blow of his heavy club. Laying about him to the right and left, the beast lumbered up several steps. A swordsman leaped at it from the side, driving a steel blade deep into the beast's thigh. With a howl, the ogre turned, seizing the courageous soldier as the monster tumbled down the steps, crushing the life out of the man during the brutal fall.

In the meantime, a thousand orcs—a full regiment of the beasts—pressed around behind the village. The insect plague cast by the cleric had dissipated by now, and the few warriors who stood in the regiment's path had been brushed easily aside.

Even as the defenders fought courageously to hold their key outpost to the last, the monstrous advance slowly cut them off from all retreat. In the smoke and the chaos of the night battle, this maneuver went undetected until it was too late. Abruptly the men on the pyramid realized that the village had been taken around them and that all connection with the rest of their army had been severed.

And now the breach in the pyramid's defense had been opened. More ogres, followed by orcs, rushed onto the side of the structure. The archers atop the pyramid poured a deadly fire into the creatures' faces, sending many of them tumbling back. But others—others without number, seemingly without fear—advanced from the darkness to take their places, and slowly the beasts pressed higher up the four sloping sides of the pyramid.

The arrows of the defenders couldn't last forever, and when the last missile was exhausted, the archers drew their short swords and prepared to die fighting. Now, with the village in flames around them, the pyramid cut off by the orcs behind it, they could think no longer of escape. They could only fight and die like the men they were. In another moment, the last of them fell, and a dozen orcs howled their triumph from the top of the structure.

"Back! Fall back!" Cordell shouted the command, and trumpets brayed in echo. Along his line, decimated by the first phase of the battle, the exhausted fighters pulled away from the equally exhausted monsters. The second rank of Zaltec's attack rushed across the muddied ground, still a mile from the withdrawing defenders.

Nayap, the foremost village in the defensive line, now spouted smoke and ash, a funeral pyre for the men who had died there. Indeed, the only men remaining in the village were those who were dead.

"Where to?" grunted Grimes, riding beside the captain-general.

"Hold Actas." The captain-general pointed to the village that formed the inland end of his line. "Hold it at all costs, but we've got to shorten the line! Keep your riders ready to watch our flank!" Cordell gestured to Daggrande, who trotted over to him.

"Divide your men into two companies," the commander ordered. "If all else fails, you'll have to cover our withdrawal into the fort."

"All right," grunted the dwarf, grimacing at the thought of splitting his already depleted company. He saw the line shortening as the companies of Mazticans and foreigners drew closer together, filling in the gaps left by their fallen comrades.

The second wave of the monstrous attack now rumbled through the line of the first battle, knocking their own battered comrades aside. The beasts lumbered through the smoldering ruins of Nayap, paying no attention to the bodies around them, uncaring even whether the fallen had been human or their own bestial kin.

Some of the survivors of the first attack, the most aggressive among the monsters, joined in the second wave, and a powerful force of orcs, ogres, and trolls rushed toward the narrowed band of defenders.

Once again the shower of arrows, the thunder of the harquebusiers, the speeding darts of crossbow and halfling, took their bloody toll of the attackers. But now there were fewer missiles and more monsters. The effect could only be lessened.

The first of the attacking regiments crashed into the thin rank of the desert dwarves under Luskag. But here the monsters, who towered over their dimuntive opponents, as well as outnumbered them, met a rude surprise.

The dwarves ducked low at the first impact of the charge, darting beneath the shields and raised weapons of the attackers. Their keen weapons, with the razorlike edges of *pluma*stone, struck upward, and hundreds of orcs reeled backward, screaming and wailing in agony. The wounded monsters fell and writhed and died, and the desert dwarves attacked their ogre masters, slicing and slashing with their murderous blades of shiny black stone.

Even the ogres fell as the nimble dwarves twisted around them, evading the heavy but clumsy blows of the monsters. In moments, the entire regiment fell back, the beastly faces of its troops distorted by fear of these small, ferocious slayers. The shrewd Luskag, however, allowed only a moment's pursuit before calling his warriors back into line.

Other regiments of Hoxitl's horde turned from their advance to press the desert dwarf force with renewed vigor. This could have proven a critical weakening of the cleric-beast's attack, except that nowhere else along the line were the defenders prepared to resist so sturdily as in that portion manned by the desert dwarves.

On this assault, two of Hoxitl's great regiments swung wide of the line, passing around the far village of Actas. The rest of the force lumbered into the thin line, and once again the defenders struggled to hold.

Cordell looked to his left as a series of torches waved through the field. A small band of Payit warriors, concealed in the grass before Actas, held up the suddenly blazing brands. In the yellow light, the commander saw the movement of the monsters that attempted to move past the village.

"Grimes! Slow them up!" shouted the captain-general, and his commander of horsemen immediately urged his steed forward.

The lancers once again swept around the end of the defenders' line in order to prevent a flanking movement such as they had earlier destroyed.

The cavalry thundered forward, ripping into the ranks of

the monstrous regiments. First one, then a second of the formations turned and scattered under the onrush. The horsemen wheeled, lances and swords lowered, and started toward the flank of a third regiment.

But here the monsters changed tactics. As Grimes led the riders forward, the orcs suddenly broke into three huge blocks. The beasts in each block pivoted on all four sides, so that everywhere they faced outward. The horsemen rode into the side of one of these crude squares, trampling many of the monsters.

The formation, however, did not break. Slowly, grimly, the beasts of the Viperhand fought the riders who now bucked and trampled in their midst. These creatures did not turn and expose their vulnerable backs; instead, they attacked, slashing viciously at the legs and flanks of the pitching horses.

Turning and plunging, the riders tried to work free. The steeds reared and trampled, while the horsemen hacked about with their bloody blades. Finally, with a lunge between two huge ogres, Grimes drove his stallion free of the melee, beheading one of the ogres as he raced past. The rest of the riders followed, quickly widening the gap made by their captain.

Elsewhere, the leading regiments smashed into the thin line of Cordell's defenders. Daggrande threw one, and then the second, of his reserve companies into the line, each time barely stopping a critical breakthrough.

Magic missiles crackled on the right flank, where the two dozen mages who had come with Don Vaez sniped at the enemy from the walls of Helmsport itself. The din of magic and fire, of death and destruction, crashed across the field, rising to a nightmarish crescendo.

Desperately the horsemen charged again, slashing and chopping their way into, and then free of, the monstrous ranks. Another regiment hurled itself at the riders, threatening to surround them again, and it took all of Grimes's leadership and courage to break his men free of the enemy. Even so, they left dozens of their number behind.

Every man, every dwarf and halfling, fought for his life in

this night without end. The cloud cover thickened, the light spells waned, and they fought on in nearly total darkness. Somehow the desperation to live gave them enough vision to combat the pressing horde.

Again and again the riders slashed at the fringe of the attacking mass, always springing away before the jaws of another trap could snap shut. Crossbows and steel swords drank deep of monstrous blood, while the boom of a harquebus occasionally cracked across the field.

The *kurari*-tipped arrows of the Little Men found the trolls, for they had learned that these weapons, when they struck with adequate numbers, could actually slay the hulking green beasts that simply regenerated after suffering other types of wounds. The *pluma*stone axes of the desert dwarves chopped and gouged, holding great presses of orcs at bay.

Then another great cry erupted from the forest, piercing the night with its promise of catastrophe. Whistles and horns and drums added to the din, and the legionnaires and the other defenders knew clearly that the noise sounded an end to their hopes.

And inflamed the desires of Hoxitl, for now the lord of the beasts threw his final ten regiments into the battle.

\* \* \* \* \*

"Hsst! There's something out there!" Darien could scarcely control the savage joy in her voice. The *light!* The treasure she had so long envisioned, the killing she had lusted for, at last drew near.

The other driders huddled on the platform atop the pyramid, thankful that the moon had already set. Like shadows of black thicker even than the forest, they clung to the edges of the structure and peered into the murky forest surrounding them.

"It comes from Ulatos, from the city," said Hittok after a moment. Darien, too, sensed that the menace lay to the west.

Gradually the driders' keen eyes detected the shapes moving from the jungle into the near pitch-blackness of the clearing. In Darien's sight, one of these glowed, so brightly that she could scarce dare to breath. Against that halo of hot, tempting light, she could not make out the identity of the treasure.

But already she began to savor the thought of its death.

"Shall we strike them down with arrows?" asked Hittok, his voice a bare breath of wind against Darien's perspiring cheek.

"No!" In her agitation, she spoke louder than she had intended. The driders held their breath as the humans below hesitated, but it was not Darien's remark that had alerted them.

Staring into that light, Darien saw that one of the humans moved slowly, as if in pain. Then she began to see . . . it was her, Halloran's woman! She was the burning force that tempted the drider's appetite.

"No," the white creature hissed, softly this time. "No arrows. We shall await them here, and when they start up the steps, we shall attack."

"Very well," said Hittok, slinging his bow over his shoulder and pulling forth his dark, black sword.

"And know this," Darien cautioned, tension again ringing in her voice. "All of you remember: When we attack, the woman is mine!"

\* \* \* \* \*

Erixitl collapsed with an inarticulate groan of pain. She curled up into a ball of misery, wincing from the pain of a sudden contraction.

"The *baby!*" she whispered. "*Now* is the time!"

Halloran's mind went blank. All during the march, through the months in the desert and jungle, during their entire epic journey to Ulatos, he had been telling himself, preparing for this event. But now that his wife lay here in agony, he couldn't think of a thing to do.

"The pyramid!" said Lotil quietly. "We must take her up the pyramid!"

Halloran looked at the blind man in astonishment. "That has to wait!" He turned back to his wife. "We'll get you back to the woods, to some mossy clearing. It's going to be all right!"

"No!" Erixitl's voice carried surprising strength. "Lotil is right. We must go up the pyramid!"

Halloran looked from daughter to father in astonishment. His eyes met Coton's, and the cleric looked at him with an expression of deep understanding—but also of steely-eyed will. Halloran knew that they had to ascend the steep stairway with Erixitl. The destiny that had driven them this far now compelled her presence atop the looming structure.

"The baby!" he protested. "We must get her to shelter and make her comfortable!"

"Listen!" Erix gasped, her teeth clenching. "*On the pyramid! Take me to the altar!*"

Halloran stared at her in disbelief. It was the same altar where she had so nearly met her own death! What if this was the cost of the god's return, a ghastly sacrifice of his wife or his child?

"No!" Hal couldn't allow it. He stood firmly against the men, but he couldn't ignore his wife's groan, and when he looked down at her and saw the pleading in her eyes, he was lost. "Very well," he said quietly, kneeling beside her again.

"The pain has passed for the moment," said Erix, slowly sitting up and climbing to her feet. "Let's go!"

Jhatli led them toward the base of the stairway. Around them, the deep black of the night closed in, past moonset, as a last shroud of darkness before the first traces of dawn. Feeling his way rather than seeing anything in particular, he started up the stairs.

He had taken no more than four steps when strong, sinewy arms grasped him. A hand clapped roughly across his mouth, and insistent arms pulled him against a body.

A body covered by a hard, bony shell.

\* \* \* \* \*

**DOUGLAS NILES**

From the chronicles of Coton:

The beasts of darkness sweep from the steps of the pyramid. Jhatli, taken first, struggles for a moment and then grows still.

I stare in consternation and cannot help but recoil, for these are beasts every bit as corrupted as the creatures of the Viperhand. They bear every mark of a god's punishment, in their misshapen bodies, their fur-covered, spider-like legs.

Now, among the creatures of night, I see one of pale whiteness, standing apart from the rest, looming over us all as we look upward from the ground. This one, clearly female, is full of might and danger.

And this one also is a creature of talonmagic. I sense the power of Zaltec within her, and I know that she is a menace that must be destroyed.

# ❧ 21 ❧

# A WINDSWEPT DAWN

Possessed by his full battle instincts, Halloran did not stop to think. Through the dark of the black night, he saw the horrible shapes descending the pyramid as the first one grabbed Jhatli and held the youth several steps up from the structure's base.

Instantly Helmstooth gleamed in his hand. In another moment, the sticky black blood of the leading drider dripped from the blade. The creature died as it stepped onto the ground, and the next one backed cautiously upward, away from Halloran.

With their eight legs, the driders had little difficulty supporting themselves on the steep stairway. Keen eyes, adapted to complete darkness, gave them an additional advantage in the Stygian night. Helmstooth's glow faded almost to insignificance against the opacity surrounding them.

"Help!" cried Jhatli, trying to twist away from the powerful black arms encircling him. He kicked reflexively, shocked by the suddenness of the attack and by the ghastly nature of his opponent. The driders moved around him, and he saw three of them advance on Halloran on the ground below.

Erixitl sank to the ground beside Hal, and the terrible knowledge of her vulnerability was like a physical tie binding him to her. The fight was inevitable; indeed, it had already begun, and he could not allow it to rage at his wife's side. Coton and Lotil went to the woman as the swordsman advanced to Jhatli's aid, stepping onto the first steps of the pyramid.

"Get it off me!" Jhatli squirmed in the drider's grasp as another of the creatures rushed at him, raising a keen black blade. Helmsooth came between them, deflecting the drider's blade as Hal climbed up another step. He lunged upward, driving the tip of his blade into the flank of the drider holding Jhatli, and the youth tumbled free. Halloran deflected two attacking driders, backing down the steps until once more he stood upon level ground.

Jhatli sprang to his feet beside him, drawing his own shortsword. The steel blade gleamed, reflecting Helmstooth's brightness almost as if it held a fire of its own.

Behind them, Erixitl moaned again, and more of the driders swept toward them. Both of their blades clashed with dark steel, and then another pair of driders tried to slip past them. Jhatli spun to the side, lashing outward, but his inexperience with the blade proved a costly handicap.

The drider met his thrust squarely and parried the blade downward and away, to Jhatli's right. For a brief moment, the youth's chest and stomach lay exposed to attack, and the drider was swift to capitalize. His black blade darted down, thrust powerfully forward, and Jhatli gasped in pain. Blood spurted from a deep wound, and he collapsed, motionless, in the dust.

Shouting a dark curse, Halloran whirled on the killer, driving Helmstooth with the power of his *pluma* and his rage. The drider's eyes widened in terror, and it raised its weapon, only to have the blade shatter like glass when it met Hal's blow. The gleaming scythe that was Helmstooth continued its driving force, slicing through the skull and the neck and half the chest of the creature.

But he had no time to tend to his friend nor grieve for him. He saw the white shape of a drider, a pale freak among the black creatures, and deep in his gullet, he recognized her. Then her creatures swarmed toward him, and he stood before his wife and the priest and the blind featherworker, raising his sword, the only barrier between the helpless trio and certain, horrifying death.

Halloran fought the fight of his life. He charged the driders, feeling the *pluma* cuffs at his wrists driving his blade forward with a power he had never imagined. He sprang to his right, leaped to his left, darted forward and back again as the driders closed in. Helmstooth struck an arm from a drow torso and a leg from an arachnoid body. The blade carved deep into a dark elf trunk and shattered another sword of black steel.

A quick drider scuttled sideways past Halloran, while two more lunged in frontal attacks. Helmstooth found the heart of one as Hal's entire being cried out from the threat of the flank attack—not for him, but for the suddenly silent Erixitl behind him.

Flexing every muscle in his body, he tore the blade from the first victim, slicing the head from the second drider in front of him without slowing the momentum of his spin. His momentum carried him through a sideways tumble, and as he rolled, he cut two of the drider's left feet out from under it.

The creature hissed its frustration, slipping backward and raising its sword. With a snarl of pure rage, Halloran sprang at the drider, driving it backward with two hammering blows. The second knocked the creature's sword from its hand, and without hesitation, Hal swept Helmstooth through a vicious arc, severing the upper portion of the drider from its monstrous, eight-legged body. Both halves twitched grotesquely as the drow hands seized the body, as if to pull itself together once more. It died while Halloran turned back to the threats before him.

Now more of the creatures rushed forward, and he realized his vengeance had cost him a second of time he could not afford. He deflected the first blow, losing his balance and stumbling. The second he avoided by twisting away as he fell. But then he was on the ground, and the driders were swarming around him, some of them straight *past* him!

"Erixitl!" He thought of her name but did not realize that he called it out loud.

He saw a black sword raised over him, and then he saw only darkness.

*　*　*　*　*

Her first plan had been to obliterate the man with a blast of magic, so that she could linger over the death of the woman beyond. But then Darien had remembered: Too often in the past she had wasted powerful magic at Halloran and his woman, only to have the spells thwarted by the woman's magical protection.

Instead, Darien had crept carefully down the steep steps of the pyramid, letting her driders fight the battle for her. She had only one goal: the sweet flower of light that beckoned her with irresistible temptation.

She saw the woman now, curled on the ground in the agonizing prelude to childbirth. She sneered at Erixitl, caught as she was in such a moment of weakness, a weakness that would prove fatal.

The white drider crept around the periphery of the fight, watching her creatures attack and die at the hands of Halloran. In a cold, aloof sense, she admired the human for the savagery of his battle. Indeed, she found the sight of his sweat- and blood-streaked form exciting in a way she had not known since the Night of Wailing.

Yet she had known that his fight would be futile, and she watched him fall with a vague sense of pity, as if a good horse had been wasted.

Now Darien advanced toward the woman on the ground. She saw two old men beside her and heard her cry out in pain. But Erixitl's dark brown eyes met Darien's and surprised the drider with their anger and their power of will.

\* \* \* \* \*

Erixitl groaned and threw back her head as convulsive pressure pushed against her womb. She saw the horrid, leering face of the white drider, and she knew that Halloran had fallen. She feared that she would lose her mind.

Lotil suddenly stood up beside her. The blind *pluma*-worker held in his hands a soft, rich blanket, a blanket of lush colors and deep, seductive shades.

Darien paused for a moment, feeling oddly confused. Around her, the others of her kind hesitated as well.

Lotil spun the blanket gently in his hands, and the colors whirled in a most alluring fashion, forming a swirling vortex that seemed to pull the white drider forward with compelling, deeply persuasive force.

The man shuffled away from his daughter, moving carefully so that he did not trip. The blanket he raised before him, spinning it faster and faster. He stopped walking, though he kept twirling the blanket as he reached the still form of Jhatli.

"Father—no!" Erixitl whispered.

But Lotil dropped the blanket. It settled like a shroud over the lifeless form, and then the blind man stepped to the side. His hands spun only the air before him; the *pluma* cloth lay on the ground. Yet somehow the colors lingered in the air, a spinning column that pulled the driders together, compelled them to follow.

Lotil moved on, the center of a whirlwind of *pluma* that grew into a column taller than his head, rotating faster and faster. He drew away from the pyramid, crossing the flat clearing, and his daughter watched him go. The light of his magic illuminated the entire clearing, and she saw the driders, the eight or ten that still lived, following her father in a dense pack. The white one, Darien, led the way.

The swirling colors around Lotil swelled up like a tornado, towering high into the sky. The area of the mist expanded, reaching out to clasp all of the driders in its brilliant embrace. The group moved slowly, steadily toward the precipice at the clearing's edge.

"No, please," Erixitl whispered, collapsing in the brief respite of the passing contraction. "Father . . ."

But her voice was weak, and Lotil undoubtedly would not have heeded her even if he could have heard.

*　*　*　*　*

Darien couldn't take her eyes off the seductive, powerful luminescence before her. The power of the spell of *pluma* enthralled her, captivated her and her companions as surely as could any physical snare.

They followed the man as he shuffled across the meadow. Sometimes he paused to twirl and bow, as if he performed some kind of ritual dance. Then quickly he started moving again, and the driders followed.

Somewhere within Darien's being, a nervous twinge of alarm began to pull at her. The objects of *hishna*, the talons and venom and snakeskin that she carried in her pouch, tugged against her side, their weight an oddly increasing burden. That dark power surged in her mind, trying to tear her eyes from the potent and hypnotic image before her.

But always that compelling brilliance lurked before her. She struggled to push forward as the other driders crowded past, but the weight of *hishna* held her back.

She did not see the cliff as it fell away behind Lotil. Indeed, none of the driders did. They all knew that it was there, but that knowledge lay in some distant, logical part of their minds, a part that was no longer functional. Instead, they knew only the maddening desire to seize this brilliance, to take it to themselves and consume it.

Then the driders lunged together, and Lotil stepped backward. The creatures grasped at him, their fingers snaring his robe, their legs propelling them after him.

Man and monsters tumbled over the side of the cliff, a whirling vortex of *pluma* that plunged in eerie silence toward the jagged rocks far below. The crash of their bodies against the stone was a sickening, final sound.

At the last moment, the dark powers within Darien held her back. She felt a compelling urge to leap; in fact, she stumbled forward and lost her footing at the lip of the precipice. But she slid a few feet and then grasped some curling roots of brush that grew along the face of the bluff.

Gasping for breath, she scrambled for footholds. She found purchase for enough of her legs to support her, then collapsed, suddenly exhausted. Shivering in a sudden chill, she wondered at the nearness of her escape. The rest of the driders, together with the blind human, had perished on the rocks far below.

She clutched the cliffside, unseen by those above. For a time, she needed to rest. Her anger and hatred seethed anew, directed at these humans who had so nearly defeated her. But she still lived, and her strength slowly returned.

Soon she would return.

\* \* \* \* \*

The final ten regiments of Hoxitl's army doomed the defense of Actas, the second village on Cordell's defensive line. The orcs rushed forward in force with untamed fury, sweeping around both sides of the village.

Grimes led charge after charge of the slowly shrinking company of horsemen, but he may as well have tried to hold back the ocean tide. Finally the riders fell back to regroup, realizing the futility of further attacks.

Rather than expend his army in Actas in a hopeless holding action or allow it to be annihilated, as had happened to the defenders of Nayap, Cordell ordered his trumpeters to sound the withdrawal.

The defenders broke away from the savage onslaught, struggling to hold their formation as they fell back toward Helmsport. The cavalry operated as four small companies, driving back the foremost spearheads of the pursuit.

Sharp volleys of harquebus and deadly showers of arrows dissuaded the attackers from vigorous pursuit. Didn't they have their foes in full withdrawal, in any event? Now that the battle was won, why press? No fighter, whether human, dwarf, or orc, wants to be the last to die in a victorious campaign.

The slow, pale light of dawn began to wash across the field, revealing that many a brave warrior lay behind on the once-grassy savannah that was now a sea of mud. Dwarves of the desert, the Little People of the jungle, warriors of Payit and Tulom-Itzi, mercenaries of the Sword Coast—all mingled their blood in the earth, no longer caring of the differences that had separated them or the alliance that had brought them together.

But many more of these fighters, the defenders of that alliance, remained alive. These were the ones who reached Helmsport's high, earthen ramparts. They fell back in good order, and were met at the walls by Cordell or Daggrande. These officers quickly directed the retreating companies into useful positions on the fortress ramparts.

As the last ranks of Hoxitl's regiments reached the battle, there was no fight to be found, for all the defenders had gone. Thus they swept on in victorious glee, a surging wave of chaos roaring toward the breakwater of the solid fortress.

That rampart served its function as the orcs and ogres and trolls roared up the steeply sloping outer wall. At the top, they met an array of defenders, tightly packed together and holding the high ground. The horde was too big to bring all of its strength to bear against this limited front, and Cordell took advantage of the fact. Now his men fought shoulder to shoulder, spurred on by the knowledge that there could be no further retreat.

In Helmsport, they would hold or they would die.

\* \* \* \* \*

The massive monolith that was Zaltec had neared the clearing at Twin Visages early that terribly dark night. The god of war had sensed the powers there, powers of both *pluma* and *hishna*. Also, it had sensed that its moment of confrontation with Qotal had not yet arrived.

So the mountainous figure of the war god had waited, standing impassively as Halloran fought for his life, as the driders threatened the woman, and as the *pluma* whirlwind carried the creatures of Lolth to their deaths.

Zaltec sensed the nearness of the childbirth, and this tiny spark of life, insignificant in scope when viewed by one who had overlooked armies, gleamed like a tempting morsel before the blood-hungry god.

And so Zaltec stood silently, watching and waiting. Soon the moment would come, and he would gain his greatest victory.

\* \* \* \* \*

Coton raised his hand from Halloran's forehead as the swordsman sat up with a groan. The cleric immediately went back to Erixitl, who gasped for breath in the throes of another volley of pain. Hal climbed to his feet, his head throbbing, and quickly went to kneel beside his wife. He noticed, with vague detachment, that the driders and Lotil were gone.

The woman moaned again and threw back her head. Her legs spread limply on the ground, and she clenched her teeth, striving to push her baby into the world.

The priest held a hand before her and gently shook his head. Grimly, as the pain slowly lessened, she nodded in understanding.

"I know," she whispered. "Up there."

Painfully, awkwardly, she rose to her feet. Halloran supported her, while Coton went to pick up the blanket of *pluma* that Lotil had dropped over Jhatli. The youth lay still and cold below it, and his blood had soaked into a portion of the feathered surface.

Slowly and agonizingly they made their way up the steps of the pyramid, stopping each time Erixitl was seized by another pain. It took them countless minutes of ever-increasing daylight to reach the top, and by the time they did, the sky was light blue and the moments between Erix's contractions had shortened dramatically.

Coton spread the cloak on the platform on top of the pyramid some distance away from the grim altar. Immediately Halloran lowered Erixitl, and once again she gasped.

Then she screamed and wept. She threw back her head and cried out loud. She hissed through her teeth and pushed with all of her strength. Again and again she strained.

Pain became her constant emotion, a way of life that seemed as if it could bring only death. But she fought against that pain with all of her strength, striving and pushing to overwhelm and defeat it. With a groaning curse, at last she felt herself collapse. The pain was still there, but now it was a fading sensation, unimportant any longer.

Halloran, in one stunning second, found himself looking

at, and then gathering up, his son. The baby squirmed and kicked on the blanket of *pluma*, wrinkling his face and then uttering a sharp, demanding cry.

"A boy," he said reverently. He handed the child to his wife and she clutched it to herself.

Coton surprised them by tugging insistently at the blanket of *pluma*. He pulled it free and Erix gasped in surprise. "The Cloak-of-One-Plume!"

Indeed, the cloak woven from countless tiny feathers by her father Lotil now looked exactly like the one she had worn, the one that had marked her as the chosen daughter of Qotal.

Slowly, devoutly, Coton rose to his feet in the pale blue of the dawn. He carried the billowing cloak in his arms, and then he gently spread it across the altar.

At that moment, the sun crested the eastern horizon, and the first rays of the day fell upon the altar. The cloak reflected these, sending up a dazzling rainbow of light.

\* \* \* \* \*

The feathered dragon twisted violently, plummeting into a steep dive. For the first time, Poshtli felt the tug of gravity below him, and then he saw the ocean, pale blue in the dawn and spreading to the far limits of his vision to each side.

But not before him. There, a thin green line of land emerged from the distance, quickly growing into the bluff at Twin Visages. Now he saw the two faces he had seen before, still staring out to sea, waiting . . . waiting for *him!*

Or more precisely, for Qotal.

"She has given a life that I may return!" the Feathered Dragon exulted aloud.

"A sacrifice?" Poshtli demanded.

"No—not yet," replied the god ominously. But now the Plumed Serpent had no time for mortals.

The great dragon soared toward the small pyramid, settling slowly to earth. He landed, bracing one massive foot on each of the four corners of the pyramid's top.

Poshtli slid from the wide, plumed neck for the first time in countless weeks. His feet landed solidly on the top of the pyramid, and at the same time, he heard a great splintering of wood. He looked up to see a colossal stone figure, vaguely manlike but with grotesquely etched facial features and massive, clawlike fingers, lumber toward them from the forest. The monstrous thing crushed trees beneath each powerful footfall.

"Poshtli!" The warrior heard his name and turned, startled.

"Halloran!" he cried in delight and surprise.

Then the dragon once again took wing.

* * * * *

The surging horde of monsters crashed against the summit of the rampart again and again, to be met by arrows and swords and the explosions of the harquebuses. With increasing fury, Hoxitl commanded his beasts to attack, to press up and over the embankment.

Dawn grew to full daylight, and yet each attack fell back, repulsed with bloody losses. Many defenders paid with their lives, but the sloping outer wall of the fort was littered with hundreds upon hundreds of bodies, each marked with the serpent's-head brand of the Viperhand. Finally, under the increasingly blue sky, the beasts fell back to rest. For the first time in many hours, silence blessed the field.

As the sun crested the horizon, it gleamed off the clear blue waters of the lagoon. The vast ocean stretched to the horizon, rich, blue, apparently endless. Pure light and pure clarity marked the view of the sweeping sea.

But not so the land. The slopes of the fortress and all the earth around it had been churned to a sticky brown mess by the passage of heavy feet. Smoke drifted across the savannah from the ashes of the two burned villages, and the volleys from the harquebusiers had sent a new cloud rolling down from the walls of the fort.

Now the Beasts of the Viperhand gathered in their great regiments, camping and resting across the savannah.

Though none of the formations had been obliterated, nine or ten had suffered catastrophic casualties and now numbered a mere fraction of their original thousand-orc complement.

Hoxitl knew, however, that the humans were trapped. The long night of battle had taken its toll on attackers and defenders alike. Now it served his purposes to allow his beasts to recover their strength in anticipation of the next attack.

And the next, and perhaps the one after that. However long it took, Hoxitl knew that his force would prevail.

\* \* \* \* \*

Darien had slowly, carefully pulled herself up the last portion of the bluff. Now that the sun had risen, she had to take care not to be seen by the humans, yet instinctively she knew that they would not be looking for her.

She had seen the great dragon soar overhead, and she understood implicitly that it was her enemy—more to the point, *the* enemy, even the very antithesis, of her *hishna*. But now its passage gave her the chance she needed.

She saw the creature, its broad, brilliantly colored wings flapping gently, perch upon the top of the small pyramid. It faced away from her, toward the looming colossus in the jungle.

Darien scuttled across the field to the base of the pyramid, certain that she had not been observed from above. Slowly, carefully, she climbed the steep stairway. She held her body low against the steps to avoid being spotted.

When she was partway up the stairs, the great dragon sprang into the air. The drider cowered against the pyramid as the serpent soared away. Awestruck, she watched it race toward the stony giant that was Zaltec.

The two deities collided, and the earth splintered around them. Great fissures opened in the ground, swallowing trees and earth, as the force of the onslaught caused the colossus to stagger backward. But then a massive, mountainous fist crashed into the neck of the Plumed One, and the dragon tumbled back. For a moment, one wing folded back against its side.

Qotal fell to the earth, crushing dozens of trees and sending more fissures tearing through the soil of Payit. The pyramid rocked upon its base, and Darien clung with her hands as well as her legs to keep from being shaken off the stairs.

The dragon reared back, a hissing cloud of flame and smoke erupting from its widespread jaws. The sizzling inferno surrounded the god of war, but Zaltec ignored it. Again he lunged at Qotal, and this time the dragon pounced away.

The gods waged their war, uncaring for the living things around them, be they trees or animals or humans. The destruction of their combat crushed miles of forest and spread earthquakes and chasms that threatened to consume all of Payit.

Darien sensed her opportunity. She crept up the last few steps of the pyramid and cautiously peered onto the crest. There, as she expected, all eyes were directed away from her, toward the battle between the gods.

Black *hishna* surged in Darien as the moment of her triumph lay before her. There was the wife, sitting up weakly, staring in awe at the war god. She held a bundle to her breast, and Darien's smile tightened savagely.

Very slowly, the drider climbed onto the platform atop the pyramid. The talonmagic within her caused all of her energy to focus on the target of *pluma* before her.

Then she attacked.

\* \* \* \* \*

"How many did we lose?" Cordell spoke to Grimes atop the rampart, where he could keep a careful eye on the beasts arrayed around the fort.

"Thirty horses—only twenty riders, though." The cavalry captain sighed in weariness and despair.

"You saved a hundred times that many," the captain-general told him. "Without you to screen us, we never would have made it back to the fort."

Grimes smiled faintly. "Still, don't know what good that does us," he said, with a gesture to the horde gathered beyond.

"More than you might guess. It buys us time. Time to rest. Time for Rodolfo to get here with the ships. Time for Erixitl to work a miracle. Time, and whatever that time can do for us." Cordell clapped the horseman on the shoulder. "Now, you get some rest. There'll be plenty of work later on, I'm sure."

The captain of horse nodded gratefully and turned to leave the rampart. As he did so, his eyes swept across the lagoon and the ocean to the north and east. Immediately he stiffened.

"What?" Cordell, seeing his reaction, spun to look out to sea.

The white sails were barely visible on the horizon but coming swiftly. At first indistinct, they quickly became identifiable—the fleet! The carracks he had sent to the Sea of Azul were returning! In a few moments, they could count them—all twenty-five vessels.

"Rodolfo!" Cordell shouted, and the cry resounded and echoed through the fort. The carracks swiftly pulled closer, and all of Helmsport shouted.

As the ships drew near, they could see their Kultakan allies lining the decks, as well as a few of the legionnaires who had remained behind in the desert—in all, more than five thousand fresh troops, eager to throw their strength into the battle.

\* \* \* \* \*

"*There* you are. What happened? The baby!" The voice pulled Hal's attention away from Poshtli in surprise. He looked into the equally surprised face of Jhatli as the youth ascended the last steps to the top of the pyramid. For a moment, the epic struggle between the gods was forgotten at his joy in seeing his companion.

"You're alive!" cried the swordsman. He seized his young companion and looked into his face. Jhatli's eyes were bright and curious. Hal saw, with a cautious look at his chest, that no wound showed there, even as a scar.

"The magic of *pluma*," said Erix, softly so as not to disturb her child. The baby suckled noisily, content with his world now that he was being held by his mother and fed.

Halloran turned back to Poshtli, clapping his companion on both shoulders. "And to see you again, my friend, is a wish I would not have dared make."

"I have been . . . fortunate," Poshli said dryly.

"But what— Look out!" Jhatli's eyes widened as he looked past Halloran.

Coton turned with sudden quickness, surprising Halloran into looking away from the spectacle before him. And in that instant, he saw Darien, hissing and spitting and racing toward his wife and child.

But even before the swordsman could react, the priest of Qotal seized the cloak—the brilliant plumage that lay over the altar, that had, after its miraculous transformation during Erix's childbirth, opened passage for Qotal into the world. The cleric whirled it at the drider.

Darien shrieked in hatred and revulsion. At the same moment, the cleric threw himself upon her. Coton moved with surprising quickness, and by the time Halloran had drawn his sword, the cleric and the drider were clasped together like a pair of grim lovers, the cloak of plumage bright between them.

Again the gods clashed, and the world shook. The dragon breathed another spout of fire, and whole sections of forest burned away to ashes. Zaltec pummeled the dragon with his great stone fists, and where the blows fell, great barren craters opened in the ground. The chasms in the earth widened, and it seemed as if the loser must take Maztica with him when he perished. Earthquakes wracked the point, and parts of the bluff fell away, crashing into the ocean below. The world seemed ready to fall apart around them.

Coton, too, sensed this imminent peril. A lifetime of service to his god had led him to this, to the end of all life. Once again the land rumbled, and the pyramid settled lower on its foundation. The drider and the cleric lashed around atop the pyramid, a mingling of *hishna* and *pluma*, of the respective magics of Zaltec and Qotal.

The battle continued to rage, and then the cleric of Qotal did a thing that surprised even his god. For more than two decades, he had remained silent, bound by a vow to this god who now threatened imminent destruction.

Coton threw back his head, and he cursed out loud.

"Damn your pretensions!" he shouted, and the gods paused in their strife. "Damn your greed and your cruelty—yes, both of you!"

For a moment, the gods held their blows, turning their great heads to this impudent mortal. Then Qotal bellowed in rage, lunging toward the cleric who had betrayed his vow and now cursed his god. Zaltec, too, lumbered toward him, ready to slay the one who dared interrupt the immortal tasks of the gods.

Coton twisted to look at Halloran. The cleric's face tightened with the agony of his struggle as he clasped Darien, still holding the blanket of *pluma* around her, enclosing her own power of *hishna*.

Then the priest spoke to Halloran. "They will destroy us! We must send them back—remove them from this world. They do not belong here!"

"But—but how?" demanded Halloran, his blood chilling as the monstrous figures loomed closer.

"You dare curse my name?" Qotal's voice was a rumbling bellow, nearly shattering their ears. "You, who have prayed for my return, pleaded for my presence?"

The two gods loomed overhead, one the source of *pluma*, the coalesence of all its power; the other, the dark font of *hishna* and the root of its dark might. They looked with cold detachment at the mortals. They saw a man of *pluma*, bearing a cloak of high feathermagic, wrapped about a foul creature of *hishna*. The essence of the two powers flowed through the blood of these tiny creatures and gave them the vitality to carry their fight across the world.

The priest whirled back to Halloran. "Kill me!" he hissed, his voice taut. "Kill us both—now! It's our only chance!"

The gods loomed closer, rearing above the pyramid, ready

to squash them all into nothingness. But Halloran couldn't force his hand.

"Now! There is *no time!*" Coton's voice was a desperate plea.

Halloran stood mute and helpless. He couldn't bring himself to strike this old companion who had silently and patiently accompanied them across the True World. He tried to force his hand to his blade, but it wouldn't move. Erixitl looked at him in terror, clutching the baby in her encircling arms.

But one man was free of those restraints. Poshtli suddenly grasped the sword from Halloran's hand. Whirling toward the combatants as the Feathered Dragon spread his jaws, ready to immolate them all, the warrior sprang.

And he thrust the keen blade home.

The bloodstained tip of Helmstooth cut easily through the cleric's body, tearing the cloak of *pluma* and driving into the drider's bowels. Darien shrieked in pain, staggering backward with a force that pulled the blade from Poshtli's hand.

But the cleric clung to her even as he died, and as the blood of *pluma* and *hishna* mingled and flowed onto the top of the pyramid, the power of the gods waned.

Qotal's jaws emitted a short gasp of smoke, but already the dragon had begun to fade from sight. The stone behemoth of Zaltec, meanwhile, staggered weakly backward. Then it teetered once and crashed to the ground with thunderous force, shattering into so many lifeless boulders.

By the time the dust had settled, Qotal could no longer be seen.

\* \* \* \* \*

Tokol joined Cordell and the defenders of Helmsport on the field before the fort. Together they watched the beasts of the Viperhand withdraw from the field, disappearing into the jungle.

"Did our arrival scare them away?" the Kultakan war chief wondered.

"Perhaps," replied the captain-general. "Or perhaps it was

something else. All of the urge to fight seemed to leave them."

"Let's hope the urge is gone for good," growled Daggrande, with a scowl at the retreating foe.

"Chical tells me there's no sign of the colossus, either," added Cordell.

A weary party approached along the shore, and they hurried over to greet Poshtli, Halloran, and Jhatli. Erixitl, carrying the baby, rode in a makeshift travois pulled by her husband.

"The gods are gone—back to their own immortal planes," Halloran told them quietly. "They have left the world to us."

"To make of it what we will," said Poshtli, with a meaningful look at Cordell.

"What's that?" wondered Daggrande, pointing to a scroll of painted symbols that Halloran carried.

"Coton's chronicles. He painted the tale of our adventures on these scrolls. They tell a good part of the history of the True World."

"A history that changes by the hour," Cordell added in a rare thoughtful moment. Then he shook his head quickly, as if forcing his mind back to the present. He looked at Halloran. "The first ships sail for Amn in a few days. You've earned passage, should you desire it."

The weary swordsman looked at his former commander and shook his head. "My home is here now, in Maztica. It may be that I'll return to the Sword Coast, sometime, for a visit. But for now, I—we—won't be going anywhere."

# Epilogue

A wind sweeps in from the Trackless Sea, blowing from the east and carrying with it an unstoppable force. It whips the waves and hurls breakers against the shore.

The wind sweeps up the bluff of Twin Visages, abandoned now, its surrounding jungle torn by fissures and chasms, the trees splintered and trampled. The pyramid still stands, and the two faces still stare outward from the bluff into the teeth of the wind, but the sea before them remains empty for now.

Next the wind swirls and soars on to Ulatos, which has burgeoned into a bustling trade city, combining with the harbor of Helmsport to become the main port of call along the entire coast of the True World. From Ulatos, treasures beyond gold—treasures such as rich cocoa and lush mayz—are carried to the east. And other cargoes—horses, steel, wagons, livestock, and more—arrive here from the Sword Coast and make their way across Maztica.

Westward with the wind, now, to Kultaka. The city has lost its traditional enemy, for Nexal is an empire no more. But instead, the Kultakans stand at the border of a hellish land, and so their warlike vigilance remains undying.

Then the wind swirls past the volcanoes of Zatal and Popol, touching only briefly the still smoldering valley of Nexal. It is as if the air here is an affront to this wind from the sea, and so it quickly soars upward and past the valley, leaving it as a stinking ruin, lair of many thousands of monstrous inhabitants. Somewhere, of course, beneath the muck and the ruin, an empire's ransom in gold lies buried. And so it shall remain, if it is up to the wind.

Now the wind whistles to the south, along freshly ripening fields of mayz, down fertile valleys where once barren desert had lain. The wind follows these valleys to the rapidly growing city of Tukan, where the ways of the True World remain, but not untouched by the arrival of the foreigners. The gods of sacrifice are gone, banished by men who claim the world for themselves.

Here, in this strong city, a man and a woman come to live, and between them bring the strongest things of each of their worlds. Their child—soon, their children—grows and flourishes, and their home knows love and peace.

And the wind, as if satisfied, turns gently back to the sea.

# Meetings Sextet

### Kindred Spirits
Mark Anthony and Ellen Porath

The reluctant paternal dwarven hero, Flint Fireforge, is invited to the elven kingdom of Qualinesti, where he meets a young, unhappy half-elf named Tanis. But when Laurana, the beauteous daughter of the elves' ruler, declares her love for Tanis, a deadly rival for her affections concocts a scenario fraught with risk and scandal for both the half-elf and his dwarven ally. On Sale April 1991.

---

### Wanderlust
Mary Kirchoff and Steve Winter

Tasslehoff Burrfoot accidentally pockets one of Flint's copper bracelets and Tanis good-naturedly defends the top-knotted newcomer to Solace—triggering a thoroughly unpredictable tale, which includes a sinister stranger who has evil on his mind for the three new friends. On Sale September 1991.

---

### Dark Heart
Tina Daniell

At long last, the story of the beautiful, dark-hearted Kitiara Uth Matar, from the birth of her twin brothers, the frail mage Raistlin and the warrior Caramon. Kitiara's increasing fascination with evil throws her into the company of a roguish stranger and an eerie mage whose fates are intermingled with her own. On Sale January 1992.

# ▪ THE HARPERS ▪

### A Force for Good in the Realms!

This open-ended series of stand-alone novels chronicles the Harpers' heroic battles against forces of evil, all for the peace of the Realms.

## The Parched Sea
### Troy Denning

The Zhentarim have sent an army to enslave the fierce nomads of the Great Desert. Only one woman, the outcast witch Ruha, sees the true danger—and only the Harpers can counter the evil plot. Available July 1991.

## Elfshadow
### Elaine Cunningham

Harpers are being murdered, and the trail leads to Arilyn Moonblade. Is she guilty or is she the next target? Arilyn must uncover the ancient secret of her sword's power in order to find and face the assassin.
Available October 1991.

## Red Magic
### Jean Rabe

One of the powerful and evil Red Wizards wants to control more than his share of Thay. While the mage builds a net of treachery, the Harpers put their own agents into action to foil his plans for conquest.
Available November 1991.

## THE INNER PLANETS TRILOGY

Book One:

# FIRST POWER PLAY
### John Miller

As the New Earth Organization rebuilds an Earth shattered by the Martian Wars, NEO sympathizer Kemal Gavilan receives a corpse and a cryptic message from the asteroids. The Mercurian prince sends master pirate Black Barney to find out what he can, but the answer is hot: they've uncovered a weapon that can focus the sun's energy for global annihilation! The Martian and Venusian powers insist they're innocent. Kemal is forced to rejoin the royal family he once rejected to learn the awful truth.

Book Two:

# PRIME SQUARED
### M. S. Murdock

Having discovered his own family's plans for a colossal laser device, Kemal prepares to head back to Earth to inform NEO. The prince learns, however, that Ardala Valmar has snared a prototype of the weapon. Kemal is compelled to stay and destroy the greater of two evils—his family's nearly completed full-scale model. The Mercurian prince maneuvers through one double-cross after another, trying to keep his uncle, the reigning Sun King, from uncovering his true allegiance.

Book Three:

# MATRIX CUBED
### Britton Bloom

Kemal unravels instability in the Sun King empire and finds himself thrust into daunting circumstances. His problems are compounded by the fact that others—including RAM— may have developed remarkably similar laser projects. Available in May 1991.